PALACE
OF
DESIRE

Naguib Mahfouz

PALACE OF DESIRE

The Cairo Trilogy II

Translated by

William Maynard Hutchins

Lorne M. Kenny

Olive E. Kenny

The American University in Cairo Press

With appreciation to David Morse
— The Editor

This edition published in Egypt in 2001 by
The American University in Cairo Press
113 Sharia Kasr el Aini
Cairo, Egypt
www.aucpress.com

Second printing 2002

English translation copyright © 1991 by
The American University in Cairo Press

Copyright © 1957 by Naguib Mahfouz

First published in Arabic in 1957 as *Qasr al-shawq*
Protected under the Berne Convention

Dar el Kutub No. 8945/01
ISBN 977 424 682 9

Printed in Egypt

PALACE
OF
DESIRE

1 🖋

Al-Sayyid Ahmad Abd al-Jawad closed the door behind him and crossed the courtyard of his house by the pale light of the stars. His step was lethargic, and his walking stick sank into the dusty earth whenever he leaned on it wearily. He felt on fire and craved cold water so he could wash his face, head, and neck and escape, if only briefly, from the July heat and from the inferno in his belly and head. Cheered by the thought of cool water, he smiled. When he entered the door leading to the stairway, he could see a faint light coming from above. It flowed along the wall, revealing the motion of the hand that held the lamp. He climbed the steps with one hand on the railing and the other on his stick. Its successive taps had long ago acquired a special rhythm, which identified him as easily as his features. Amina was visible at the head of the stairs with the lamp in her hand. On reaching her, he stopped to regain his breath, for his chest was heaving. Then he greeted her in his customary way: "Good evening."

Preceding him with the lamp, Amina murmured, "Good evening, sir."

Once inside his room he rushed to the sofa and collapsed. Letting go of his stick and taking off his fez, he threw his head back and stretched out his legs. The sides of his cloak fell open, and the caftan underneath rode up to reveal the legs of his long underwear tucked into his socks. He shut his eyes and wiped his forehead, cheeks, and neck with a handkerchief.

After placing the lamp on a table, Amina waited for him to rise so she could help remove his clothes. She looked at him with anxious concern. She wished she had the courage to ask him not to stay out so late—now that his health could no longer shrug off excesses—but she did not know how to express her sad thoughts.

A few minutes passed before he opened his eyes. Then he extracted the gold watch from his caftan and took off his diamond ring to place them both in his fez. When he stood up to remove his cloak and caftan with Amina's assistance, his body seemed as tall, broad, and full as ever, although the hair at his temples had been assailed by gray. When he was putting his head in the neck of his white house shirt, a smile suddenly got the better of him. He remembered how Mr. Ali Abd al-Rahim had vomited at their party that evening and had apologized for his weakness, attributing it to an upset stomach. They had all singled out their friend, upbraiding him and asserting that he could no longer tolerate alcohol, for only a special kind of man could keep on drinking to the end of his life, and so forth. He remembered the anger and vehemence of Mr. Ali in defending himself against this suspicion. How amazing that some people lent importance to such trivial matters.... But if it were not important, then why had he himself boasted in the merry hubbub that he could drink a whole tavern of wine without ill effects?

He sat down again and lifted his feet so that his wife could take off his shoes and socks. Then she disappeared briefly, returning with a basin and a pitcher. She poured the water for him while he washed his face and neck and rinsed out his mouth. Afterwards he sat with his legs folded beneath him, enjoying the gentle breeze flowing between the latticed balcony and the window overlooking the courtyard.

"What an atrocious summer we're having this year!"

Pulling the pallet out from under the bed and sitting cross-legged on it at his feet, Amina replied, "May our Lord be gracious to us." She sighed and continued: "The whole world's a blazing pyre, especially the oven room. The roof terrace is the only place you can breathe in summer—once the sun has set."

She sat there as usual, but time had changed her. She had grown thin, and her face seemed longer, if only because her cheeks were hollow. The locks of hair that escaped from her scarf were turning gray and made her seem older than she was. The beauty spot on her cheek had grown slightly larger. In addition to their customary look of submission, her eyes now revealed a mournful absentmindedness. Her anguish over the changes that had befallen her was considerable, although at first she had welcomed them as an expression of her grief. Then she had begun to wonder anxiously if she might not need her health to get through the remainder of her life. Yes ... and the others needed her to be healthy too, but how could everything be put back the way it was before? And she was older, if not old enough to warrant such a transformation. Still, her age had to make a difference.

Night after night she had stood on the balcony observing the street through the wooden grille. What she could see of the street had not altered, but change had crept through her.

The voice of the waiter at the coffeehouse echoed through their silent room. She smiled and stole a glance at al-Sayyid Ahmad.

She dearly loved this street, which stayed awake all night keeping her heart company. It was a friend but ignorant of the heart that loved it through the shutters of the enclosed balcony. Its features filled her mind, and its evening inhabitants were live voices inhabiting her ears—like this waiter who never stopped talking, the person with the hoarse voice who commented on the events of the day without getting tired or annoyed, the man with the nervous voice trying his luck at cards with the seven of diamonds and the jack, and the father of Haniya—the little girl with whooping cough—who night after night would reply when asked about her, "Our Lord will be able to cure her." Oh ... the balcony seemed to be her special corner of the coffeehouse. Memories of the street paraded before her imagination while her eyes remained fixed on the man's head, which was leaning against the back of the sofa. When the flow of remembered images stopped, she concentrated her attention on her husband. She noticed that the sides of his face were bright red, the way she had grown accustomed to seeing them of late when he returned home. She was uncomfortable about it and asked him apprehensively, "Sir, are you well?"

He held his head up and muttered, "Well, praise God." Then he added, "But the weather's atrocious."

Clear raisin liqueur was the best drink in summer. That was what they had repeatedly told him, but he could not stand it. For him it was whiskey or nothing. Thus every day he had to put up with summer hangovers, and it was a ferocious summer. He had really laughed hard that evening. He had laughed until the veins of his neck were sore. But what had all the laughter been about? He could hardly remember. There seemed to be nothing to relate or repeat. Yet the atmosphere of their party had been charged with such a sympathetic electricity that a touch had sufficed to set off a flash. The moment Mr. Ibrahim al-Far had said, "Alexandria set sail from Sa'd Zaghlul Pasha today heading for Paris," reversing his words, they had all burst out laughing, since they considered the remark an exquisite example of a slip of the tongue caused by intoxication.

They had been quick to add, "He will continue negotiating until he regains his health, when he will set sail for the invitation in response to the London he received from" or "He will receive Ramsay MacDonald from the independence of the agreement" and "He will return with Egypt for independence." They had begun to discuss the anticipated negotiations, larding their comments with whatever jests they saw fit.

Vast as his world of friends was, it really boiled down to three: Muhammad Iffat, Ali Abd al-Rahim, and Ibrahim al-Far. Could he imagine the world's existence without them? The way their faces lit up with genuine joy when they saw him made him happier than anything else could. His dreamy eyes met Amina's inquisitive ones. As though to remind her of something extremely important, he said, "Tomorrow."

With a beaming face she replied, "How could I forget?"

He did not attempt to conceal his pride when he commented, "It's said that the baccalaureate results were awful this year."

She smiled once more to share in his pride and said, "May our Lord make his efforts successful and let us live long enough to see him obtain his degree."

"Did you go to Sugar Street today?" he asked.

"Yes," she replied, "and I invited everyone. They'll all come except the old lady, who excused herself because she's so tired. Her two sons will congratulate Kamal on her behalf."

Gesturing toward his cloak with his chin, al-Sayyid Ahmad said, "Today Shaykh Mutawalli Abd al-Samad brought me amulets for the children of Khadija and Aisha. His wish for me was: 'God willing, I'll make you amulets for your grandchildren's children.'"

Shaking his head, he smiled and continued, "Nothing's impossible for God. Shaykh Mutawalli himself is like iron even though he's in his eighties."

"May our Lord grant you health and strength."

He reflected for a time while he counted on his fingers. Then he observed, "If my father had lived, may God be compassionate to him, he would not have been much older than the shaykh."

"May God have mercy on all those who have departed this life."

Silence reigned until the impact of the reference to the dead had dissipated. As though remembering something important, the man said, "Zaynab's gotten engaged!"

Amina's eyes grew wide. She raised her head and asked, "Really?"

"Yes, Muhammad Iffat told me tonight."

"Who is it?"

"A civil servant named Muhammad Hasan, who is head of the records office in the Ministry of Education."

She commented despondently, "It sounds as though he's advanced in years."

"Not at all," he objected. "He's in his thirties, thirty-five, thirty-six, forty at the most." He continued sarcastically, "She tried her luck with young men and failed. I mean young men with no backbone. Let her try her luck with mature men."

Amina said sorrowfully, "Yasin would have been better for her, if only because of their son."

Al-Sayyid Ahmad shared her opinion, which he had defended for a long time with Muhammad Iffat. In order to conceal his failure, he did not mention that he agreed and said with annoyance, "Her father no longer trusts Yasin, and in truth he's not trustworthy. That's why I didn't insist on it. I was unwilling to exploit our friendship and make her father accept something that would end badly."

Amina mumbled sympathetically, "A youthful mistake can be forgiven."

Her husband felt he could acknowledge some portion of his unsuccessful effort and remarked, "I didn't neglect Yasin's rights but met with no encouragement. Muhammad Iffat told me, 'My first reason for refusing is my concern that our friendship might be exposed to discord.' He also said, 'I would not be able to refuse a request from you, but our friendship is dearer to me than your request.' So I stopped talking about it."

Muhammad Iffat had actually said that, but only to fend off al-Sayyid Ahmad's insistent urging. Because of his friend's high standing with him and in society, al-Sayyid Ahmad had been very keen to restore his bond with Muhammad Iffat, which was severed when their children were divorced. Although he could not hope to find a better wife for Yasin than Zaynab, he was forced to accept the calamity of divorce and remarriage, especially after his friend had told him bluntly at least part of what he knew of Yasin's private life. Muhammad Iffat had even remarked, "Don't tell me we're the same as Yasin. We differ in several respects, and the fact is that I have higher standards for my daughter Zaynab's husband than for her mother's."

Amina inquired, "Does Yasin know what's happened?"

"He'll learn tomorrow or the next day. Do you think he'll mind? He's the last person to be concerned about honor in marriage."

Amina shook her head sadly and asked, "What about Ridwan?"

Al-Sayyid Ahmad replied with a frown, "He'll stay with his grandfather or go with his mother, if he can't bear to be separated from her. May God embarrass those who have caused the boy this embarrassment."

"My Lord, the poor child—his mother one place and his father another. . . . Can Zaynab really bear to be parted from him?"

Her husband replied with apparent disdain, "Necessity has its own laws." Then he asked, "When will he be old enough to come to his father? Do you remember?"

Amina thought for a bit and said, "He's a little younger than Na'ima, Aisha's daughter, and a little older than Khadija's son Abd al-Mun'im. So he must be five, and his father can claim custody in two years. Isn't that right, sir?"

Yawning, al-Sayyid Ahmad replied, "We'll see when the time comes." Then he went on: "He's been married before. I mean her new husband."

"Does he have children?"

"No. His first wife didn't bear any."

"Perhaps that helped endear him to Mr. Muhammad Iffat."

The man retorted angrily, "Don't forget his rank!"

Amina protested, "If it was merely a question of social status no one could match your son, if only for your sake."

He felt indignant and secretly cursed Muhammad Iffat, despite his love for the man. But then he reiterated the point that consoled him: "Don't forget that had it not been for his desire to safeguard our friendship, he would not have hesitated to honor my request."

Amina echoed this sentiment: "Of course, naturally, sir. It's a life-long friendship and not something to be trifled with or taken lightly."

He began yawning once more and muttered, "Take the lamp."

She rose to carry out his order. He closed his eyes for a moment before rising in a single bound, as though to overcome his inertia. He headed for his bed to stretch out. Now he felt fine. How good it was to lie down when exhausted. Yes, his head pulsed and throbbed, but he almost always had some kind of headache. Let him praise God in any case. Being totally at ease was a thing of the past.

"When we are by ourselves," he reflected, "we become conscious of something missing that will never return. It looms up out of the past in a pale memory, like the faint light from the little window in the door."

In any case he should praise God. He would enjoy his life, which others envied. The best thing was to reach a decision about whether to accept his friends' invitation or not. Or should he leave tomorrow's problem till the morrow?

Yasin was a problem not only for tomorrow but for yesterday and today. . . . He was no longer a child, since he was twenty-eight. It would not be difficult to find him another wife, but "God does not change people until they change themselves" (Qur' an, 13:11). When would God's guidance shine forth and encompass the earth so that its light dazzled the eye? Then he would cry out from the depths of his soul: "Praise the Lord." But what had Muhammad Iffat said? That Yasin prowled and patrolled the Ezbekiya entertainment district from top to bottom. . . . Ezbekiya had been another kind of place when he had prowled and patrolled it himself. He was shaken by longing at times to return to its watering holes and revive some memories. Praise God that he had learned Yasin's secret before setting out. Otherwise Satan would have laughed at his embarrassment from the bottom of his mocking heart.

"Clear the way for the next generation," he told himself. "They've grown up. The Australians kept you away from there once. Now it's this Australian mule of a son who does."

2

The early-morning silence was broken by the repeated thumps of dough being kneaded in the oven room and by the crowing of a rooster. Umm Hanafi's corpulent body was bent over the bread bowl. Her face looked full by the light of a lamp atop the oven. Age had not affected her hair or her plumpness, but her appearance had taken on an air of gloom and her features seemed coarser. On a kitchen chair to her right sat Amina, who was spreading bran on the breadboards. They continued the work in silence until Umm Hanafi finished kneading the dough, took her hand from the bowl, and wiped her sweaty brow with her forearm. Then the servant waved her fist, which was covered with dough and looked like a white boxing glove, as she observed, "It'll be a hard day for you, ma'am, but a delightful one. May God grant us many happy days."

Without raising her head from her work, Amina murmured, "We've got to make sure the food's delicious."

Umm Hanafi smiled, gestured toward her mistress with her chin, and said, "Your skill will take care of that." She planted her hands in the bowl once more to resume punching the dough.

"I wish we had contented ourselves with distributing stew to the needy around al-Husayn Mosque."

Umm Hanafi gently scolded her mistress: "No one present will be an outsider."

Amina muttered somewhat nervously, "But there'll be a banquet and a lot of commotion. Fuad, Jamil al-Hamzawi's son, has also earned the baccalaureate—without anyone seeing or hearing anything about it."

But Umm Hanafi kept up her scolding: "It's just an opportunity for us to get together with our loved ones."

How could joy be free from reproach or forebodings? In former times she had reckoned up the years, discovering that Kamal would receive his school certificate at the same time Fahmy received his law degree. That celebration would never take place, and her pious vow could never be honored. Nineteen, twenty, twenty-two, twenty-three, twenty-four ... the prime of his young life, which she had been prevented from witnessing. Instead, it had been earth's lot to embrace him. How heartbreaking what they termed sorrow was!

"Mrs. Aisha will be delighted by the baklava. It will remind her of the old days, my lady."

Aisha would be delighted. So would Amina, her mother, who experienced the succession of night and day, satiation and hunger, wakefulness and sleep, as though nothing had changed.

"Forget your claim to be unable to live on a single day after he died," she thought. "You have lived on to swear by his grave. When a heart is turned upside down, that does not mean the world is too. He seems totally forgotten, until it's time to visit the cemetery. You filled my eye and soul, son. Now they only think of you during the holidays. What has come over them? Everyone's busy with his own affairs, except for you, Khadija. You have your mother's heart and spirit. I even have had to admonish you to be strong. Aisha's not like that. But not so fast! It's not right for me to find fault with her. She's mourned quite enough. And Kamal can't be blamed either. Have pity on their young hearts. Fahmy was everything to me. Your hair has turned gray, Amina, and you look like a ghost. That's what Umm Hanafi says. You'll never be young and healthy again. You're going on fifty and he wasn't twenty yet. Pregnancy with all its cravings, childbirth, breast-feeding, love, hopes . . . and then nothing. I wonder if my husband's head is free of such thoughts. Leave him out of it! 'The grief of men is not like that of women.' That was what you said, Mother, may God make paradise your abode. It tears me apart, Mother, that he's gone back to his old habits, as though Fahmy had never died or all memories of him had evaporated. He's even critical when grief overwhelms me. Isn't he the father as much as I'm the mother? My mother said, 'Poor dear Amina, don't allow such thoughts into your heart. If we could judge people's hearts by comparison with a mother's, all others would seem to be stones. He's a man, and the grief of men is not like that of women. If men gave way to sorrow, they would collapse from the weight of their burdens. It's your duty to cheer him up if you notice he's sad. My poor daughter, he's your bulwark.'"

That affectionate voice had vanished. Its loss had come when their hearts were already filled with grief, so that hardly anyone had mourned for the old lady. Her mother's wisdom had been demonstrated late one night when he had come home drunk and had thrown himself sobbing on the sofa.

"Then you wanted him to recover, even if he forgot his dead son forever. You yourself, don't you forget sometimes? And there's something even more atrocious. It's your enjoyment of life and desire for it. That's what the world is like, so they say. You repeat what they say and believe it. Then how could you have allowed yourself once to resent Yasin's recovery and continuation of his former way of life? Not so fast ... rely on your faith and forbearance. Submit to God's will and to whatever He sends you. You'll always be Fahmy's mother and be called Umm Fahmy. So long as I live I'll continue to be your mother, son, and you'll be my child."

The beats of the dough being kneaded continued as al-Sayyid Ahmad opened his eyes to the early-morning light. He stretched and yawned in a loud, prolonged way—the sound rising like a complaint or a protest. Then he sat up in bed, leaning on hands that rested on outstretched legs. His back seemed curved, and the upper part of his white house shirt was damp with sweat. He began to shake his head right and left, as though to clear the weight of drowsiness from his head. He slipped his feet to the floor and made his way to the bath for a cold shower, which was the only remedy he used to restore balance to his mind and poise to his body. He took off his clothes. As the spray of water hit him, he remembered the invitation he had received the day before. His heart pounded from the combined impact of the memory and the invigorating sensation of the cold water.

Ali Abd al-Rahim had said, "Look again at your former sweethearts. Life can't go on like this forever. I know you better than anyone else."

Should he take this final step? For five years he had resisted it. Had his repentance been merely that of an afflicted Believer? Had it been kept hidden because he feared making it public? Had it been in good faith, even though he had not committed himself fully to it? He did not remember. He did not want to remember. A man going on fifty-five was no youngster. What was there to disturb and upset his thoughts so? He had felt the same way when he had been invited to return to their drinking parties and had agreed, as well as the time he had been asked to rejoin their musical evenings and had accepted. Would he answer this plea on behalf of his former sweethearts in the same way? When had grief ever brought a dead man back to life?

"Did God order us to slay ourselves when those we love depart?"

Grief had almost killed him during the long year of mourning and self-denial. He had drunk no alcohol and listened to no music. Not a single witty remark had escaped from his mouth, and his hair had turned gray. Yes ... that year had been the first time that gray had appeared in his hair. Then he had reverted to drinking and music, out of consideration for his close friends who had renounced their entertainments to honor his grief, or at least that had been how he rationalized it. He had started drinking again both because he could not do without it any longer and because he felt sorry for his three friends. They had not been like the others.

"The others are not to be blamed. They shared in your grief, but then they began to divide their evenings between your sober soirees and their drinking sessions. What was wrong with that? But your three best friends refused to allow themselves more of life than you did. Slowly you returned to everything except the women, since you thought adultery a major sin. At first they did not press you. How you resisted and how you grieved! Zubayda's emissary made no impression on you. You rejected Maryam's mother with sad and resolute dignity. You endured unprecedented pains. You were certain you would never go back. Time after time you asked yourself, 'How can I return to the arms of women entertainers when Fahmy's embraced by the earth?' Oh . . . we are so weak and wretched that we desperately need God's compassion.

" 'Let him continue to grieve who can be sure he will not die tomorrow.' Who came up with this pithy saying? It was either Ali Abd al-Rahim or Ibrahim al-Far. Muhammad Iffat Bey's not good at wise sayings. He rejected my request and married his daughter to a stranger. Then he tried to take me in with his display of affection. He did not renounce his anger but took care not to let me observe it again. But what a man he is! What loyalty and affection! Do you remember how his tears mixed with yours at the cemetery? Yet he's the one who later said, 'I'm afraid you'll become senile if you don't do anything. . . . Come to the houseboat.' When he sensed my hesitation, he said, 'Let it be an innocent visit. . . . No one's going to rip your clothes off and toss you on a woman.' God knows my grief has lasted a long time. When Fahmy passed away, a great part of me died. My best hope in this world vanished. Who can blame me if I'm able to achieve some peace of mind and consolation? Even if it laughs, my heart's still wounded. I wonder what the women are like now? How have five years, five long years, changed them?"

Yasin's snoring was the first thing Kamal noticed when he woke up. He could not keep himself from calling to his older brother, more from a desire to pester him than to awaken him on time. He kept after him persistently until Yasin responded in a complaining and scolding voice like a death cry and turned his huge body over, making the bed creak as though it was groaning with pain. He sighed and opened his red eyes.

In his opinion there was no need for this haste, since neither of them could venture to the bathroom until their father had left it. It was no longer an easy matter to get the first turn in the bathroom. A new regime had been established in the house five years before, when—except for the reception room and the adjacent sitting room furnished with simple furniture as a vestibule—everything from the lower floor had been moved upstairs. Although Yasin and Kamal had hardly welcomed the notion of sharing a floor with their father, they had been forced to comply with his wish to vacate the lower level, where no one set foot, except to entertain a visitor.

Yasin closed his eyes but did not go back to sleep, not merely because it would have been futile but also because an image had flashed through his mind, setting his emotions on fire ... a round face with black eyes at the center of its ivory surface. Maryam! He answered the call of his daydreams and abandoned himself to a spell even stronger than that of sleep.

A few months back she had meant nothing to him and might just as well have never existed. Then he had heard Umm Hanafi tell his stepmother one evening, "Have you heard the news, my lady? Mrs. Maryam's gotten divorced and returned to her mother." At that time he had remembered Maryam, Fahmy, and the English soldier who had been Kamal's friend, although the soldier's name had escaped him. Then he had remembered in turn how lively his own interest in her had been after the scandal. Before he had realized what was happening, a signboard had suddenly lit up inside him. It was like a billboard illuminated at night with the message: "Maryam ... your neighbor ... separated from you by only a wall ... divorced ... and with quite a history behind her. ... Rejoice!" He had tried at once to discourage himself. Her link to Fahmy had deterred and troubled him, prompting him to close the door firmly and repent, if possible, for this passing thought he kept secret.

Later he had run into her and her mother in the Muski. Their eyes had accidentally met, but she had immediately granted him a smiling look of recognition, which could scarcely have been accidental. His heart had been stirred—initially by nothing more than the look but subsequently by the pleasant impression made on him by her ivory complexion, kohl-enhanced eyes, and body pulsing with youth and vitality. She made him think of Zaynab at her prime. He had proceeded on his way with pensive excitement, although after a few steps, as he descended to Ahmad Abduh's subterranean coffeehouse, a sad memory had come to mind and distressed his heart. He recalled Fahmy—what he had looked like and his characteristic ways of speaking and moving. Yasin's passion had subsided and abated, and he had been overcome by a heavy sorrow. He would need to bring everything to a halt . . . but why?

An hour later, after several days, or whenever he asked himself this question, the answer was: Fahmy. But what relation was there between the two of them? He had wanted to get engaged to her once. Why had he not done so? "Your father would not agree. Was that all? It was the initial reason. Then what? Next came the scandal with the Englishman when the faint trace of affection remaining in Fahmy's soul had been erased. Faint trace? Yes, because most probably he had forgotten her. So he forgot her first and spurned her afterwards. . . . Yes, so what relationship was there then between them? None. But! . . . But what? I mean, what about my feelings as his brother? Is there any doubt concerning the sincerity of your feelings for him? Of course not! A thousand times no! Is the girl worth it? Yes! Both her face and her body? Yes! So what are you waiting for?"

From time to time he would catch a glimpse of her at the window and then on the roof . . . repeatedly on the roof.

"Why had she gotten divorced?" Yasin asked himself. "If it was because of some defect in her husband's character, then she was lucky to be divorced. If it was occasioned by some fault of hers, then you're the lucky one."

"Get up, or you'll fall asleep again."

Yasin yawned as he combed his untidy hair with his thick fingers. Then he remarked: "You're fortunate to have that long school vacation."

"Didn't I wake up before you?"

"But you could have kept on sleeping if you'd wanted to."

"As you can see, I didn't want to."

Yasin laughed for no particular reason. Then he asked, "What was the name of the English soldier who was your friend long ago?"

"Oh . . . Julian."

"Yes, Julian."

"What made you ask about him?"

"Nothing!"

Nothing? What ridiculous things we say! Was he not superior to Julian? At any rate Julian had been a transient, and Yasin was a permanent resident. "There's always a hint of a smile in her face for you. Hasn't she noticed how frequently you appear on the roof? Certainly! Remember Julian. She's not a woman who would miss the significance of such a gesture. She responded to your greeting.... The first time she turned her smiling face. The second time she laughed. What a beautiful laugh she has! The third time she gestured to the roofs of the other houses to caution you. 'I'll come back once the sun has set,' that's what I daringly said. Didn't Julian accost her from the street?"

"I really loved the English when I was young. But see how I hate them now."

"Your hero Sa'd Zaghlul has set off to court their friendship."

Kamal exclaimed sharply, "By God, I'll detest them even if I'm the only one who does."

They exchanged a sad look. They could hear the clatter of their father's clogs as he returned to his room, reciting, "In the name of God" and "There is no power or might save with God." Yasin slipped out of bed and left the room yawning.

Kamal rolled over on his side and then stretched out on his back, relaxing. He folded his arms and clasped his hands together under his head. He gazed at his surroundings with eyes that saw nothing.

"Let the summer resort of Ra's al-Barr be happy to have you. Your angelic complexion was not made to roast in the heat of Cairo. Let the sand enjoy the tread of your feet. Let the water and air rejoice in seeing you. Your celebrate your summer resort and praise its beauty. Your eyes show your delight and longing for it. I look at them sadly with a yearning heart and an inquisitive eye. What is this place that has enchanted you and proved worthy of your satisfaction? ... But when will you return and when will your magical voice fill my ears? What's the resort like? I wish I knew. It's said that people there are free as the air, that they meet in the arms of the waves, and that there are as many love affairs as grains of sand on the beach. Many there will get to see your face, but I'm a person whose heartbeats make the walls groan with complaints, since I'm consumed by an inferno of waiting. How impossible it is to forget your face shining with joy when you murmured, 'We're leaving tomorrow.... How beautiful Ra's al-Barr is!' How can I forget my dejection at receiving the warning of separation from a mouth sparkling with radiant happiness, as though I was being administered poison in a bouquet of fragrant flowers. Why shouldn't I be jealous of inanimate objects that make you happy when I can't? They win your affection, which is denied to me. Didn't you notice my dejection when you said farewell? Of course not. You noticed nothing ... not because I was one among many, but, darling, because you didn't notice ... as though nothing caught your attention or as though you were an exotic and unusual creature hovering over ordinary life and observing us from above with eyes that roam through a divine realm beyond our ken. So we stood there face to face—you a torch of dazzling happiness and I ashes of despondent dejection. You enjoy absolute freedom or yield only to laws beyond our comprehension, while I am compelled by an overwhelming force to revolve in orbit around you as though you were the sun and I the earth. Have you found some freedom at the seashore that you do not savor in the villas of al-Abbasiya? Of course not! By the truth of everything you mean to me, you're not like the others. In the garden of the mansion and on the street your feet leave fragrant prints. In the heart of each friend you leave memories and hopes. A young lady welcoming yet inaccessible, you pass between us but remain aloof—as though the East had requested you as a gift from the West on the anniversary of the Night of Destiny, at the end of Ramadan, when prayers are sure to be answered. I wonder what new favor you might grant where the coast is long, the horizon distant, and the beach packed with admirers. What would it be, my hope and my despair?

"Without you, Cairo's a wasteland exuding melancholy desolation and consisting of only the dregs of life and living creatures. Of course it has sights and features, but none that speak to the emotions or stir the heart, for they seem antiquities, memories of an unopened pharaonic tomb. No place in Cairo offers me any solace, distraction, or entertainment. I imagine myself at different times as choking, imprisoned, lost, or wandering aimlessly. How amazing! Did your presence provide me with a hope that separation has banished? Certainly not, my destiny and my doom, but like that aspiration, so long as I remain under your wing, I feel fresh and safe, even if my hope is groundless. Of what use to a person eagerly searching the dark sky is his knowledge that the full moon is shining on the earth somewhere else? None, even if he does not seek any control over the moon. Yet I desire life to its most profound and intoxicating degree, even if that hurts. If you are present as my heart beats, it's because of that fabulous creature, the memory. Before I knew you, I never realized what a miracle it is. Today, tomorrow, or after a lifetime, in al-Abbasiya, Ra's al-Barr, or at the ends of the earth, my imagination will never lose sight of your dark black eyes, your eyebrows which join in the middle, your elegant straight nose, your face like a bronze moon, your long neck, and your slender figure. Your enchantment defies description but is as intoxicating as the fragrance of a bouquet of jasmine blossoms. I will hold on to this image as long as I live. When I die, may it overcome all obstacles and hindrances to become my destiny and mine alone, since I have loved you so deeply. If that is out of the question, tell me what meaning life has for us to seek or what delight there is to yearn for after death.

"Don't claim to have fathomed the essence of life unless you're in love. Hearing, seeing, tasting, and being serious, playful, affectionate, or victorious are trivial pleasures to a person whose heart is filled with love—and from the first look, my heart. Even before my eyes left her, I was certain that this was to be permanent, not transitory. It was one of those fleeting but decisive moments like conception or an earthquake. Oh Lord, I was no longer the same person. My heart collided with the walls of my chest as the secrets of the enchantment revealed themselves. My intellect raced so fast it courted insanity. The pleasure was so intense that it verged on pain. The strings of existence and of my soul vibrated with a hidden melody. My blood screamed out for help without knowing where assistance could be found. The blind man could see, the cripple walked, and the dead man came back to life. I entreated you by everything you hold dear never to leave . . . You, my God, in heaven and she on earth.

"I believe that all my past life has been in preparation for the glad tidings of love. The fact that I did not die young and went to Fuad I School and not some other one, that the first pupil I befriended was her brother Husayn, and . . . and that . . . all of that was just so I would be invited to the mansion of the Shaddad family. What a memory! My heart is almost torn out by the impact of it. Husayn, Isma'il, Hasan, and I were busy discussing various issues when there came to our ears a melodious voice saluting us. I turned around, totally astounded. Who could be approaching? How could a girl intrude on a gathering of young men to whom she was not related? But I quickly abandoned my questions and decided to set aside traditional mores. I found myself with a creature who could not possibly have originated on this earth. She seemed to know everyone but me. So Husayn introduced us: 'My friend Kamal . . . my sister, Aïda.' That evening I learned why I had been created, why I had not died, and why the fates had driven me to al-Abbasiya, to Husayn and the Shaddad family mansion. When did that take place? Unfortunately the date has been forgotten but not the day. It was Sunday, a regular holiday at her French school which coincided with a governmental holiday for state schools, possibly the Prophet's birthday. In any case it was a day of birth for me.

"Of what importance is the date? The calendar has a magic that makes us imagine a memory can be resurrected and revived, but nothing returns. You'll keep on searching for the date, repeating: the beginning of the second year at school, October or November, during Sa'd Zaghlul's journey to Upper Egypt, and before he was exiled for the second time. No matter how much you consult your memory, the evidence, and events of the day, you'll simply end up clinging desperately to your attempt to rediscover that lost happiness and a time that has disappeared forever. If only you had held out your hand when you were introduced, as you almost did, she would have shaken it and you would have experienced her touch. Now you imagine it repeatedly with feelings of both skepticism and ecstasy, for she seems to be a creature with no physical body. Thus a dreamlike opportunity was lost, which—along with that moment—will never return. Then she directed her attention to your two friends, conversing freely with them while you crouched in your seat in the gazebo, racked by the anxiety of a person fully imbued with the traditions of the Husayn district. At last you asked yourself whether there might not be special rules of etiquette for mansions. Perhaps it was a breath of perfumed air originating in Paris, where the beloved creature had grown up. Then you submerged yourself in the melody of her voice, savoring its tones, becoming intoxicated by its music, and soaking up every syllable that slipped out. Perhaps you did not understand, you poor dear, that you were being born again at that very moment and that like a newborn baby you had to greet your new world with alarm and tears.

"The girl's melodious voice remarked, 'We're going this evening to see *The Coquette*.' With a smile, Isma'il asked her, 'Do you like the star, Munira al-Mahdiya?' She hesitated a moment as was fitting for a half-Parisian girl. Then she replied, 'Mama likes her.' Husayn, Isma'il, and Hasan all got involved in a conversation about the outstanding musicians of the day: Munira al-Mahdiya, Sayyid Darwish, Salih Abd al-Hayy, and Abd al-Latif al-Banna.

"Suddenly I was taken by surprise to hear the melodious voice ask, 'What about you, Kamal? Don't you like Munira?'

"Do you recall this revelation that descended on you so unexpectedly? I mean do you recall the natural harmony of it? It was not a phrase but a magical tune that came to rest deep inside you where it sings on silently to an attentive heart, which experiences a heavenly happiness unknown to anyone but you. How astounded you were when greeted by it. It was like a voice from the heavens singling you out to address you by name. In a single draft you imbibed unparalleled glory, bliss, and grace. Immediately afterwards you would have liked to echo the Prophet's words when he would feel a revelation coming and cry out for help: 'Wrap me up! Cover me with my cloak!'

"Then you answered her, although I don't remember how. She stayed a few minutes longer before saying goodbye and departing. The charming look of her black eyes added to her fascinating beauty by revealing an agreeable candor—a daring that arose from self-confidence, not from licentiousness or wantonness—as well as an alarming arrogance, which seemed to attract and repel you at the same time.

"Her beauty has a fatal attraction. I don't understand its essence and I know nothing comparable. I often wonder if it's not the shadow of a much greater magic concealed within her. Which of these two forms of enchantment makes me love her? They're both puzzles. The third puzzle is my love. Although that moment fades farther into the past every day, its memories are eternally planted in my heart because of its associations with place, time, names, company, and remarks. My intoxicated heart circles through them until it imagines they are life itself, wondering somewhat skeptically whether any life exists beyond them. Had there really been a time when my heart was empty of love and my soul devoid of that divine image? At times you were so ecstatically happy that you grieved over the barrenness of your past. At other times you were so stung by pain that you pined for the peace that had fled. Caught between these two emotions, your heart could find no repose. It proceeded to search for relief from various spiritual opiates, finding them at different times in nature, science, and art, but most frequently in worship. From the innermost reaches of your awakened heart there flared up a passionate desire for divine delights. . . . 'People, you must love or die.' That was what your situation seemed to imply as you proudly and grandly strode along bearing the light of love and its secrets inside you, boasting of your elevation over life and other living creatures. A bridge strewn with the roses of happiness linked you to the heavens. Yet at times, when alone, you fell victim to a painful, sick, conscious reckoning of your shortcomings and to merciless brooding about them. These confined you to your little self, your modest world, and the mortal level of well-being

"Oh Lord, how can a person re-create himself afresh? This love is a tyrant. It flies in the face of other values, but in its wake your beloved glistens. Normal virtues do not improve it and ordinary defects of character do not diminish it. Such contrasts appear beautiful in its crown of pearls and fill you with awe. In your opinion, was it in any way demeaning for her to have disregarded the customs most people observe? Of course not ... in fact it would have been more demeaning if she had observed them. Occasionally you like to ask yourself: What is it you want from her love? I answer simply that I want to love her. When life is gushing through a soul, is it right to question what the point is? There's no ulterior motive for it. It's only tradition that has linked the two words: 'love' and 'marriage.' It is not merely the differences of age and class that make marriage an impossible goal for someone in my situation. It is marriage itself, for it seeks to bring love down from its heaven to the earth of contractual relationships and sweaty exertion.

"Someone insists on making you account for your actions and asks what you have gained from falling in love with her. Without any hesitation I reply, 'A fascinating smile, the invaluable gift of hearing her say my name, her visits to the garden on rare blissful occasions, catching a glimpse of her on a dewy morning when the school bus is carrying her off, and the way she teases my imagination in ecstatic daydreams or drowsy interludes of sleep.' Then your madly yearning soul asks, 'Is it absolutely out of the question that the beloved might take some interest in her lover?' Don't give in to false hopes. Tell your soul, 'It is more than enough if the beloved will remember your name when we meet again.'"

"Quick. To the bathroom. Aren't you late?"

Registering his surprise, Kamal's eyes looked at Yasin, who had returned to the room and was drying his head with a towel. Kamal jumped out of bed. His body looked long and thin. He cast a glance in the mirror as though to examine his huge head, protruding forehead, and a nose that appeared to have been hewn from granite, it was so large and commanding. He took his towel from the bed frame and headed for the bathroom.

Al-Sayyid Ahmad had finished praying. Now he lifted his powerful voice in his customary supplications for his children and himself, asking God for guidance and protection in this world and the next. At the same time Amina was setting out the breakfast. Then she went to invite him in her meek voice to have breakfast. Going to the room shared by Yasin and Kamal, she repeated her invitation.

The three men took their places around the breakfast tray. The father invoked the name of God before taking some bread to mark the beginning of the meal. Yasin and then Kamal followed his lead. Meanwhile the mother stood in her traditional spot next to the tray with the water jugs. Although the two brothers appeared polite and submissive, their hearts were almost free of the fear that had afflicted them in former times in their father's presence. For Yasin it was a question of his twenty-eight years, which had bestowed on him some of the distinctions of manhood and served to protect him from abusive insults and miserable attacks. Kamal's seventeen years and success in school also afforded him some security, if not as much as Yasin. At least his minor lapses would be excused and tolerated. During the last few years he had become accustomed to a less brutal and terrifying style of treatment from his father. Now it was not uncommon for a brief conversation to take place between them. An intimidating silence had previously dominated their time together, except when the father had asked one of them a question and the son would hastily answer as best he could, even if his mouth was full of food.

Yes, it was no longer out of the ordinary for Yasin to address his father. He might say, for example, "I visited Ridwan at his grandfather's house yesterday. He sends you his greetings and kisses your hand."

Al-Sayyid Ahmad would not consider such a statement to be impudent or out of line and would answer simply, "May our Lord preserve him and watch over him."

It was not out of the question at such a moment for Kamal to ask his father politely, "When will custody of Ridwan revert to his father, Papa?" In that way he demonstrated the dramatic transformation of his relationship to his father.

Al-Sayyid Ahmad had replied, "When he turns seven," instead of screaming, "Shut up, you son of a bitch."

One day Kamal had attempted to establish the last time his father had insulted him. He had finally recalled that it had been about two years before, or a year after he had fallen in love, for he had begun to date events from that moment. At the time, he had felt that his friendship with young men like Husayn Shaddad, Hasan Salim, and Isma'il Latif demanded a large increase in his pocket money, so that he could keep up with them in their innocent amusements. He had complained to his mother, asking her to request the desired increase from his father. Although it was not easy for the mother to raise such an issue with the father, it was less difficult than it had once been, because of the change that had occurred in his treatment of her after

Fahmy's death. Commending the new ties of friendship to important families with which her son had been honored, she had mentioned the request to her husband. Al-Sayyid Ahmad had then summoned Kamal and poured out his anger on the boy, yelling, "Do you think I'm at the beck and call of you and your friends? Cursed be your father and their fathers too."

Thinking the matter at an end, Kamal had left disappointed. To his surprise, the following day at the breakfast table the man had asked about his friends. On hearing the name Husayn Abd al-Hamid Shaddad, he had inquired with interest, "Is your friend from al-Abbasiya?"

Kamal had answered in the affirmative, his heart pounding.

Al-Sayyid Ahmad had said, "I used to know his grandfather Shaddad Bey. I know that his father Abd al-Hamid Bey was exiled, because of his ties to the Khedive Abbas. . . . Isn't that so?"

Kamal had replied in the affirmative once more, while contending with the strong emotion aroused by this reference to the father of his beloved. He had remembered immediately what he knew of the years her family had spent in Paris. His beloved had grown up in the brilliance of the City of Light. He had been seized by a feeling of renewed respect and admiration for his father along with redoubled affection. He had considered his father's acquaintance with the grandfather of his beloved to be a magical charm linking him, however distantly, to the home from which his inspiration flowed and to the source of everything splendid. Shortly thereafter his mother had brought him the good news that his father had agreed to double his allowance. Since that day Kamal had not been cursed by his father again, either because he had done nothing to merit it or because his father had decided to spare him further insults.

Kamal stood beside his mother on the balcony, which was enclosed with latticework. They were watching al-Sayyid Ahmad walk along the street and respond with dignity and grace to the greetings of Uncle Hasanayn the barber, al-Hajj Darwish, who sold beans, al-Fuli the milkman, Bayumi the drinks vendor, and Abu Sari' who sold seeds and other snacks.

When Kamal returned to his room, he found Yasin standing in front of the mirror, grooming himself patiently and carefully. The boy sat on a sofa between the two beds and studied his older brother's body, which was tall and full, and his plump, ruddy face with its enigmatic smile. He harbored sincere fraternal affection for Yasin, although when he scrutinized his brother visually or mentally he was never able to overcome the sense of being in the presence of a handsome domestic animal. Although Yasin had been the first person to make his ears resound with the harmonies of poetry and the effusions of stories, Kamal, who now thought that love was the essence of life and the spirit, would wonder whether it was possible to imagine Yasin in love. The response would be a laugh, whether voiced or internal. Yes, what relationship could there be between love and this full belly? What could this beefy body know of love? What love was there in this sensual, mocking look? He could not help feeling disdain, softened by love and affection. There were times, though, when he admired or even envied Yasin, especially when his love was troubled by a spasm of pain.

Yasin, who had once personified culture for him, now seemed almost totally lacking in it. In the old days Kamal had considered him a scholar with magical powers over the arts of poetry and storytelling. What little knowledge Yasin had was based on superficial reading confined to the coffee hour, or a portion of it, as he went back and forth, without subjecting himself to effort and strain, between *al-Hamasa*, which was a medieval anthology of poetry, and some story or other, before he rushed off to Ahmad Abduh's coffeehouse. His life lacked the radiance of love and any yearnings for genuine knowledge. Yet Kamal's fraternal affection for his brother was in no way diminished by such realizations.

Fahmy had not been like that. He was Kamal's ideal, both romantically and intellectually, but eventually Kamal's aspirations had reached beyond Fahmy's. He was afflicted by a compelling doubt that a girl like Maryam could inspire genuine love of the sort illuminating his own soul. He was also skeptical that the legal training his late brother had chosen was really equivalent to the humanities he was so eager to study.

Kamal uninhibitedly considered those around him with an attentive and critical eye but stopped short when it came to his father. The man appeared to him to be above any criticism, a formidable figure mounted on a throne.

"You're like a bridegroom today. We're going to celebrate your academic achievements. Isn't that so? If you weren't so skinny, I could find nothing to criticize."

Smiling, Kamal replied, "I'm content to be thin."

Yasin cast a last glance at himself in the mirror. Then he placed the fez on his head and carefully tilted it to the right, so it almost touched his eyebrow. He belched and commented, "You're a big donkey with a baccalaureate. Relax and take time to enjoy your food.

This is your vacation. How can you feel tempted to read twice as much during your school holiday as you do during the academic year? My God, I'm not guilty of slenderness or of association with it." As he left the room with his ivory fly whisk in his hand, he added, "Don't forget to pick out a good story for me. Something easy like 'Pardaillan' or 'Fausta' by Michel Zévaco. Okay? In the old days you'd beg me for a chapter from a novel. Now I'm asking you to provide me with stories."

Kamal rejoiced at being left to his own devices. He rose, muttering to himself, "How can I put on weight when my heart never slumbers?"

He did not like to pray except when he was alone. Prayer for him was a sacred struggle in which heart, intellect, and spirit all participated. It was the battle of a person who would spare no effort to achieve a clear conscience, even if he had to chastise himself time and again for a minor slip or a thought. His supplications after the prescribed prayer ritual were devoted entirely to his beloved.

3

Abd al-Muni'm: "The courtyard's bigger than the roof. We've got to take the cover off the well to see what's in it."

Na'ima: "You'll make Mama, Auntie, and Grandma angry."

Uthman: "No one will see us."

Ahmad: "The well's disgusting. Anyone who looks in it will die."

Abd al-Mun'im: "We'll get the cover off, but look at it from a distance." Then he continued in a loud voice, "Come on. Let's go."

Blocking the door to the stairway, Umm Hanafi protested, "I don't have any strength left to keep going up and down. You said, 'Let's go up on the roof,' so we did. You said, 'Let's go down to the court-yard,' and we did. 'Let's go up to the roof.' So we came up another time. What do you want with the courtyard? . . . The air's hot down there. Up here we have a breeze, and soon the sun will set."

Na'ima: "They're going to take the cover off the well to look in it."

Umm Hanafi: "I'll call Mrs. Khadija and Mrs. Aisha."

Abd al-Muni'm: "Na'ima's a liar. We won't raise the lid. We won't go anywhere near it. We'll play in the courtyard a little and then come back. You stay here till we return."

Umm Hanafi: "Stay here! . . . I have to follow your every step, may God guide you. There's no place in the whole house more beautiful than the roof terrace. Look at this garden!"

Muhammad: "Lie down so I can ride on you."

Umm Hanafi: "There's been enough riding. Pick some other game, by God. God . . . look at the jasmine and the hyacinth vines. Look at the pigeons."

Uthman: "You're as ugly as a water buffalo, and you stink."

Umm Hanafi: "May God forgive you. I've gotten sweaty chasing after you."

Uthman: "Let us see the well, if only for a moment."

Umm Hanafi: "The well is full of jinn. That's why we closed it."

Abd al-Muni'm: "You're a liar. Mama and Auntie didn't say that."

Umm Hanafi: "I'm the one who's right, me and the lady of the house. We've seen them with our own eyes. We waited until they entered it. Then we threw a wooden cover over the opening of the well and weighted it down with stones. Don't talk about the well. Repeat with me: 'In the name of God the Compassionate, the Merciful.' "

Muhammad: "Lie down so I can ride on you."

Umm Hanafi: "Look at the hyacinth beans and the jasmine! Don't you wish you had something like that? All you've got on your roof are chickens and the two sheep you're fattening up for the Feast of the Sacrifice."

Ahmad: "Baa ... baa ... baa."

Abd al-Muni'm: "Fetch a ladder so we can climb up it."

Umm Hanafi: "May God preserve us. The boy takes after his uncle. Play on the ground, not in the sky."

Ridwan: "At our house we have pots of carnations and of red and white roses on the balcony and in the men's reception room."

Uthman: "We have two sheep and some chickens."

Ahmad: "Baa ... baa ... baa."

Abd al-Muni'm: "I'm going to religious kindergarten. What about all of you?"

Ridwan: "I've memorized 'Praise to God ...' "

Abd al-Muni'm: "Praise to God for lamps and meatballs."

Ridwan: "For shame! You're a heathen."

Abd al-Muni'm: "That's what the teacher's assistant chants when he's walking in the street."

Na'ima: "We've told you a thousand times not to repeat it."

Turning to Ridwan, Abd al-Muni'm asked, "Why don't you live with Uncle Yasin, your father?"

Ridwan: "I'm with Mama."

Ahmad: "Where's Mama?"

Ridwan: "With my other grandfather."

Uthman: "Where's your other grandfather?"

Ridwan: "In al-Gamaliya ... in a big house with a special reception room for men only."

Abd al-Muni'm: "Why does your mother live in one house and your father in another?"

Ridwan: "Mama's with my grandfather there and Papa's with my grandfather here."

Uthman: "Why aren't they in one house like my papa and mama?"

Ridwan: "Fate and destiny. That's what my other grandmother says."

Umm Hanafi: "You've pestered him until he's confessed. There's no power or might save God's. Have mercy on him and go play."

Ahmad: "The water buffalo knows how to talk."

Muhammad: "Get down so I can ride on you."

Ridwan: "Look at the sparrow on the hyacinth vine."

Abd al-Muni'm: "Fetch a ladder so I can grab it."

Ahmad: "Don't raise your voice. It's looking at us and hears every word you say."

Na'ima: "How beautiful she is! I know her! She's the sparrow I saw yesterday on our clothesline."

Ahmad: "The other one was on Sugar Street. How could it find its way to my grandfather's house?"

Abd al-Muni'm: "You donkey. The sparrow can fly here from Sugar Street and return before nightfall."

Uthman: "Her family is there, but she has relatives here."

Muhammad: "Get down so I can ride you. Otherwise I'll cry till Mama hears me."

Na'ima: "Why don't we play hopscotch?"

Abd al-Muni'm: "No, let's have a race."

Umm Hanafi: "Without any quarreling between the winner and the loser."

Abd al-Muni'm: "Shut up, water buffalo."

Uthman: "Moo . . . moo."

Ahmad: "Baa . . . baa."

Muhammad: "I'll ride in this race. Get down so I can ride you."

Abd al-Muni'm: "One, two, three . . ."

Al-Sayyid Ahmad Abd al-Jawad welcomed the guests, for whom he had set aside the whole first part of the day. He took his place in the center at the banquet, surrounded by Ibrahim Shawkat, Khalil Shawkat, Yasin, and Kamal. After the meal, he invited the two guests to his bedroom, where they conversed in an atmosphere of affection and friendship, marked by a certain reserve on the host's part and a special politeness on the part of his sons-in-law, stemming from the etiquette the father observed in his relations with his family, even those who did not reside with him, despite the fact that al-Sayyid Ahmad and Ibrahim Shawkat, Khadija's spouse, were of nearly the same age.

The children were invited to their grandfather's room to kiss his hand and receive precious gifts of chocolate and Turkish delight. They presented themselves in order of seniority: Aisha's daughter Na'ima first, then Yasin's son Ridwan, followed by Khadija's son Abd al-Muni'm, Aisha's son Uthman, Khadija's son Ahmad, and Aisha's son Muhammad. Al-Sayyid Ahmad observed strict impartiality in distributing affection and smiles to his grandchildren but took advantage of the absence of observers, except for Ibrahim and Khalil, to relax his customary reserve. He shook the little hands warmly, pinched their rosy cheeks affectionately, and kissed their brows, while teasing this one and joking with that one. He was always careful not to show favoritism, even with Ridwan, whom he loved best.

When alone with one of them he would examine the child with passionate interest, motivated by paternal feelings and additional ones like curiosity. He took great pleasure in tracing the features of grandparents and parents in the boisterous new generation, who had scarcely learned to respect him, let alone fear him. He was captivated by the beauty of Na'ima, who with her golden hair and blue eyes surpassed even her mother's good looks. She graced the family with her beautiful features, some inherited from her mother and others from the Shawkat family. Her brothers Uthman and Muhammad were also handsome but looked more like their father, Khalil Shawkat. They clearly had his large, protruding eyes with the calm, languid look.

By way of contrast, Khadija's sons Abd al-Muni'm and Ahmad had their mother's and maternal grandmother's beautiful small eyes, although they shared the Shawkat complexion. Their noses were exceptionally similar to their mother's or, to be more precise, their maternal grandfather's.

Ridwan could not help but be handsome. His eyes were identical to his father's and therefore like the black, kohl-enhanced ones of Haniya, Yasin's mother. He had the ivory complexion of his mother's family, the Iffats, and his father's straight nose. Indeed, a captivating grace shone in his face.

It had been a long time since al-Sayyid Ahmad's children had been able to cling to him the way his grandchildren did now, without fear on their part or reserve on his. Oh, what days they had been! What memories! Yasin, Khadija . . . and Fahmy, then Aisha and Kamal. He had tickled every one of them under the arms and carried each on his shoulders. Would they remember that? He himself had almost forgotten.

Na'ima, her bright smile notwithstanding, seemed shy and polite. Ahmad would not stop asking for more chocolates and Turkish delight. Uthman stood waiting impatiently for the response to Ahmad's request. Muhammad rushed to the gold watch and the diamond ring inside the fez and grabbed hold of them. Khalil Shawkat had to use force to pry them from his grip. Al-Sayyid Ahmad spent a few moments beset by confusion and anxiety, not knowing what to do, for he was surrounded and even under attack from every side by his beloved grandchildren.

Shortly before the afternoon prayer, the patriarch left the house for his store. His departure allowed the sitting room, where the remaining members of the family were gathered, to enjoy total freedom. It had inherited the role of the abandoned one downstairs and was furnished with the same mat, sofas, and large ceiling lantern. It had become the lounge and coffeehouse for those of the family still living in the old house. No matter how crowded, it had remained tranquil all day long. Now that the only trace of their father was the fragrance of his cologne, it could breathe freely. Their talk grew louder and so did their laughter. Everyone became more animated. The coffee hour once more seemed just like the old days. Amina was sitting cross-legged on a sofa by the coffee utensils. On another couch facing her sat Khadija and Aisha. On a third to the side, Yasin and Kamal were ensconced. Once al-Sayyid Ahmad had left, Ibrahim and Khalil Shawkat joined the party. Ibrahim took a place to the right of their mother-in-law and Khalil one to her left.

Ibrahim had hardly settled there when he addressed Amina affectionately: "God bless the hands that prepared such appetizing and delicious food for us." Then he glanced around the assembly with his languid, protruding eyes as though delivering an oration and continued: "Those casseroles . . . what casseroles! They're marvelous in this house. It's not the ingredients, no matter how delicious and excellent, it's the way they're allowed to cook down, more than anything else. It's an art. It's a miracle. Find me another casserole as delicious as those we had today."

Khadija followed his comments attentively. She was torn between applauding his recognition of her mother's skill and arguing against him, because he was ignoring hers. When he paused to allow his listeners an opportunity to agree with him, she could not restrain herself from saying, "No one would contest that verdict. No one needs to testify on its behalf. But I remember and think it worth consideration that you've filled your belly in your own home repeatedly with casseroles no less skillfully prepared than those we ate today."

Aisha, Yasin, and Kamal all smiled knowingly. Their mother was clearly attempting to overcome her embarrassment and say something that would express her thanks to Ibrahim without offending Khadija. But Khalil Shawkat burst out: "Khadija's right. Her casseroles are a blessing to all of us. You better not forget that, brother."

Ibrahim looked back and forth between his wife and his mother-in-law, smiling apologetically. Then he said, "God forbid that I should fail to acknowledge my indebtedness to my wife, but I was discussing the senior chef." Then he laughed and said, "In any case I was praising the merits of your mother, not mine."

He waited until the laughter provoked by his last remark died down. Then turning toward his mother-in-law, he continued lauding her: "Let's return to the casseroles, although why should we confine our remarks to them? In fact all the other dishes were just as delicious and sumptuous. Take, for example, the stuffed potatoes, the mallow greens, the fried rice with giblets, and the assorted stuffed vegetables. God Almighty, what chickens! How meaty! Tell me, what do you feed them?"

Khadija answered sarcastically, "Casseroles! That's what!"

"I'll have to do penance for a long time and give credit where it is due, but God is forgiving and compassionate. In any case, let's pray that God grants us many more days of celebration. Congratulations on your baccalaureate, Kamal. God willing, you'll have the same good success with your university degree."

Blushing with embarrassment and happiness, Amina said gratefully, "May our Lord give you reason to celebrate for Abd al-Muni'm and Ahmad, for Mr. Khalil to rejoice for Na'ima, Uthman, and Muhammad"—then turning to Yasin—"and for Yasin to rejoice for Ridwan."

Kamal was glancing stealthily at Ibrahim and Khalil. On his lips he had the fixed smile with which he normally concealed his lack of interest in a conversation he did not find to his taste, whenever he felt he ought to participate, if only by paying attention.

The man was talking about food as though still at the table, intoxicated by greed. Food, food, food … why did it deserve all this attention? These two strange men did not appear to have changed with time, as though beyond its reach. Ibrahim today was the same as he had been. He was almost fifty, but the only signs of age were the scarcely noticeable wrinkles under his eyes and at the corners of his mouth or his sedate, serious air, which did not give him the appearance of dignity so much as of lethargy. Not a single hair of his head or of his twisted mustache had gone gray. His full body was still powerful, firm, and free of flab. The resemblance between the two brothers in appearance, state of health, and their languid gaze was great enough to be comical or a subject for mockery. There were only inconsequential differences, like the cut of their hair. Khalil's was long and smooth while Ibrahim's was short. They were both wearing white silk suits, and each had removed his jacket to reveal a silk shirt with gold cuff links gleaming through the buttonholes. Their elite status was obvious from their appearance, but nothing else.

In the course of the seven years during which their two families had been joined by marriage, Kamal had been alone with one or the other of the brothers for periods of time but had never had a conversation of any substance with either of them. But what reason was there for criticism? If they had not been like that, would there have been this successful harmony between them and his two sisters? Fortunately scorn was not incompatible with affection, benevolence, and fondness.

Oh ... it seemed that the conversation about the casseroles had not ended yet. Here was Mr. Khalil Shawkat preparing to have his say: "My brother Ibrahim did not exceed the truth in what he said. May we never be deprived of those hands. The food was certainly worth boasting about."

Amina secretly loved praise and had suffered bitterly because she was so often deprived of it. She was conscious of her tireless exertions, lovingly and voluntarily expended in the service of her house and family. She had often longed to hear a kind word from her husband, but he was not accustomed to bestowing praise on her. If he did, it was brief and limited to a few exceptional occurrences scarcely worth mentioning. With Ibrahim and Khalil on either side of her, she found herself in a pleasant and unusual situation. It truly delighted her but also embarrassed her so much that she felt uncomfortable. To hide her feelings she said, "Don't exaggerate, Mr. Khalil. You have a mother whose cooking would make anyone familiar with it steer clear of all other food."

While Khalil proceeded to reiterate his praise, Ibrahim involuntarily turned his eyes toward Khadija, where they met hers. She was staring at him as though she had expected him to look her way and was prepared for it. He smiled victoriously and told his mother-in-law, "Some people would not concede that to you."

Yasin understood this allusion and laughed out loud. The gathering was quickly engulfed in laughter. Even Amina smiled broadly as her torso shook with suppressed giggles. She concealed her mirth by bowing her head as though to look at her lap. Khadija was the only one whose face remained rigid. She waited until the storm calmed down and then said defiantly, "Our disagreement was not about food and how to cook it. It concerned my right to look after my household myself. And I'm not to be blamed for that."

Those present were reminded of the ancient battle that had flared up during the first year of Khadija's marriage. It had pitted her against her mother-in-law and concerned the kitchen. The issue had been whether there would be a single kitchen for the entire household under the supervision of the Widow Shawkat or whether Khadija would have her own kitchen as she wanted. It had been a serious quarrel threatening the unity of the Shawkat family. News of it had reached her parents' home on Palace Walk, so that everyone knew about it, except al-Sayyid Ahmad. No one dared tell him about it or any of the other disputes that broke out afterwards between the old lady and her daughter-in-law. Khadija had soon realized that she would need to rely on herself alone in the struggle. Her husband was, as she put it, "a slugabed," who was neither for her nor against her. Whenever she prodded him to stand up for her rights, he would entreat her almost playfully, "Lady, spare me the headache." Although he did not come to her defense, he did not silence her either. So she had ventured alone onto the field of battle to oppose the venerable old lady with unexpected daring and stubbornness, which did not disappoint her even in those delicate circumstances.

The old lady had been amazed by the audacity of this girl at whose birth she had assisted. Soon the battle had been joined, and anger had flared up. She had proceeded to remind the girl that had it not been for her own generous interest, Khadija could never have hoped in her wildest dreams to win a husband from the Shawkat family. Although in open rebellion, the daughter-in-law had muzzled her rage and insisted on obtaining what she considered her right, without utilizing her notoriously sharp tongue, for she was restrained by respect for the old lady and by fear that her mother-in-law would complain to al-Sayyid Ahmad.

Her cunning had prompted her to incite Aisha to rebel, but she had found that her lazy sister was cowardly and unwilling to become involved, not from love for their mother-in-law but because she preferred the calm and peace she enjoyed to her heart's content under the tyrannical supervision the old lady imposed on everyone. Khadija had poured out her anger on her sister and accused her of being weak and lazy. Galvanized by her own stubbornness, Khadija had continued her crusade relentlessly and persistently, until the older woman had gotten fed up and grudgingly granted her "gypsy" daughter-in-law an independent kitchen, telling her elder son, "So much for you. You're a weak man, powerless to discipline your wife. You're getting your just reward, which is to be deprived of my cooking forever."

So Khadija had gotten her way, retrieving the copper pots and pans that had been part of her trousseau, and Ibrahim had arranged a kitchen for her according to her specifications. But she had alienated her mother-in-law and severed the ties of friendship that had bound them since Khadija was in the cradle. Amina had not been able to tolerate the idea of a dispute but had waited patiently for everyone to calm down. Then she had set to work on the grande dame with the cooperation of Ibrahim and Khalil until a truce was concluded. Yet what kind of truce had it been? It was a truce that would scarcely come into effect before a new skirmish took place, to be followed by another truce. And so on and so forth. . . . Each of them would hold the other woman responsible. To her dismay, Amina was caught between the two. Ibrahim stood by like a neutral party or an observer, as though the matter did not concern him. Whenever he did choose to intervene, he did so listlessly, contenting himself with repeating some word of advice calmly and even coldly, paying no attention whatsoever to his mother's scolding or his wife's criticism. Had it not been for Amina's dedication and gentleness, the old lady would have complained to al-Sayyid Ahmad. She reluctantly abandoned that notion and set about venting her wrath by complaining at length to everyone she met, whether family or neighbors. She announced for all to hear that her selection of Khadija to be her son's wife had been the biggest mistake of her whole life and that she would just have to bear the consequences.

Smiling as though to lighten the impact of his correction, Ibrahim amended Khadija's statement: "But you weren't satisfied to get what was rightfully yours. You attacked anything you felt like criticizing, if my memory does not mislead me."

Her hair concealed by a brown scarf, Khadija defiantly raised her head. Staring at her husband with scorn and rage, she asked, "Why should your memory mislead you? Do you have any thoughts or concerns to burden it enough to mislead you? If only everyone else could have a memory as calm, contented, and disinterested as yours! Your memory has not betrayed you, Mr. Ibrahim, but it has betrayed me. The truth is that I did not oppose your mother's power. It was of no interest to me, and I had no need for it. Praise God, I know my duties and how to perform them in the best possible way. But I did not like to sit at home while food was carried in from outside, as though we were guests at a hotel. If that weren't enough, unlike someone I know, I could not bear to spend my whole day sleeping or playing, while another person looked after my house."

Aisha realized immediately that she was the target of the comment and laughed before Khadija had finished. As though motivated by compassion, the younger sister commented tenderly, "Do what you think best, and don't worry about other people—or those you know. There's no reason for you to be unhappy now, for you're the mistress of your own destiny—may Egypt achieve that too. You work from dawn to dusk in the kitchen, the bath, and on the roof. At one and the same time you look after the furniture, the chickens, and the children. The maid Suwaydan doesn't dare approach your apartment or pick up one of your children. My Lord . . . why all this exertion when a little would do?"

Khadija responded with a thrust of her chin, while she fought off a smile betraying her pleasure with Aisha's comments. Then Yasin commented, "Some people are born to rule and others to serve."

Revealing his overlapping incisors, Khalil Shawkat smiled and said, "Madam Khadija is a sterling example of a housewife, except that she overlooks her right to relaxation."

Ibrahim Shawkat expressed his total agreement: "That's my opinion exactly. I've told her so repeatedly. Finally I decided to keep quiet to spare myself the headache."

Kamal looked at his mother, who was filling Khalil's cup for the second time. He thought of his father and his dominance. His lips curled up in a smile. Then he looked at Ibrahim with astonishment and commented, "You seem to be afraid of her!"

Shaking his large head, the man replied, "I attempt to avoid trouble whenever I can. Your sister attempts to avoid peace whenever she can."

Khadija shouted, "Listen to this wisdom!" Then pointing at him as though challenging him to disagree, she continued: "You try your best to find a way to sleep."

Giving her a warning look, her mother said, "Khadija!"

Ibrahim patted his mother-in-law on the shoulder and remarked, "This goes on all the time at home . . . but see for yourself."

Yasin was looking back and forth between the powerful, chubby Khadija and the slender, delicate Aisha in a way intended to draw people's attention to them. Then he said incredulously, "You've told us that Khadija works nonstop from dawn till dusk, but where's the evidence of this toil? She looks like the loafer, and Aisha the worker."

To ward off the evil eye, Khadija spread her fingers apart and held up her hand with the palm facing Yasin, reciting, "And from the evil of the envious person in his envy" (Qur'an 113:5).

Aisha was not satisfied with the turn the conversation had recently taken. A look of protest was apparent in her clear blue eyes. Ignoring the point of Yasin's remark and feeling a little jealous, she hastened to defend her slimness: "Plumpness is no longer in fashion nowadays." Sensing that Khadija's head was turning her way, Aisha corrected herself: "Or at least, many think slimness as fashionable as plumpness."

Khadija commented scornfully, "Slenderness is in vogue among women who can't gain weight."

Kamal's heart pounded when the word "slenderness" reached his ears. From his unconscious mind the image of a tall figure with a slender build sprang into his imagination. His heart danced to a spiritual music inspiring raptures. A pure delight captivated him. Within that deep, calm dream he forgot himself, his location, and the time. He did not know how long it was before he became aware of a dark shadow of sadness, which frequently trailed along after his dreams. It did not arrive as an intrusive stranger or an incompatible element but flowed into his splendid dream like one of the threads from which it was woven or a melody forming part of its harmony. He sighed profoundly and then with his dreamy eyes glanced at the faces he had loved for as long as he could remember. They seemed in one way or another to be challenged by her beauty, especially the fair-complexioned one of his sister Aisha. He had once thirsted to drink from the place her lips had touched on the cup. He was embarrassed and almost unhappy to recall that, for he felt he should be devoted to no type of beauty save that of his beloved, even if other varieties might merit his affection and love.

"I don't like slenderness, not even in men," Khadija continued. "Look at Kamal! He ought to gain some weight. Brother, learning's not all there is to life."

Kamal listened to her with a scornful smile. He was examining her body, with its folds of fat and flesh, and her face, which had become so plump that its defects were no longer apparent. He was amazed by the happiness and victory her appearance conveyed but did not feel inclined to debate with her.

Yasin responded with defiant sarcasm: "Then, Khadija, you must like my looks a lot. Don't try to deny it."

His right leg was folded under him while his left one extended to the floor. It was hot and he had opened the collar of his house shirt. Tufts of the thick black hair of his chest could be seen above the wide neck of his undershirt. Khadija cast a penetrating look at him before replying, "But you've overdone it just a tad, and the fat's gone to your brain. So that's an entirely different question!"

As though at a loss for an answer, Yasin sighed and turned to ask Ibrahim Shawkat sympathetically and compassionately, "Tell me how you survive, caught between a wife like this and your mother?"

Ibrahim lit a cigarette, took a drag on it, and exhaled, puffing out his cheeks. He thus joined his brother Khalil, who had not removed his pipe from his mouth except to speak, in polluting the air of the sitting room. Then he responded with apparent disinterest, "I act as though one of my ears was made of clay and the other of dough. This is what I've learned from experience."

Looking at Yasin, Khadija commented in a loud voice that showed how angry she was, "Experience has nothing to do with it. I swear by your life with me that experience hasn't taught you this. The fact is that our Lord gave him a temperament as smooth as Uncle Badr the Turk's ice cream. Even if the minaret of al-Husayn Mosque started shaking, not a hair of his head would be ruffled."

Amina raised her head and gave Khadija a critical, warning look until the daughter smiled and lowered her eyes as if embarrassed. Then Khalil Shawkat said with gentle pride, "This is the temperament of the Shawkat family. It's an imperial one. Isn't that so?"

Although Khadija laughed to lighten the impact of her words, she remarked pointedly, "Unfortunately for me, Mr. Khalil, your mother did not inherit this 'imperial' temperament."

Amina's patience was exhausted, and she shot back, "Your mother-in-law has no equal. She is a lady in every sense of the word."

With a gleam in his protruding eyes, Ibrahim tilted his head to the left to gaze down at his wife. Then, sighing victoriously, he said, "A witness from her own family has testified. God bless you, Mother-in-law." Then he addressed the whole assembly: "You're all aware that my mother's getting on in years. She's at an age when she needs to be treated with consideration and restraint, and my wife knows nothing of the latter."

Khadija was quick to defend herself: "I don't get angry unless there's a reason. I've never been an irritable person. My family's present. You can ask them."

Silence prevailed. The members of her family did not know what to say until a laugh escaped from Kamal. They all looked at him, and he could not keep from saying, "Dear Khadija is the most irritable self-restrained person I've ever known."

Yasin found enough nerve to add, "Or the most self-restrained irritable person, and only God knows for sure."

Khadija waited for the gale of laughter occasioned by these remarks to quiet down before gesturing toward Kamal as she shook her head regretfully. She said, "I've been betrayed by someone I held on my lap more often than I have my own sons, Ahmad and Abd al-Muni'm."

Kamal replied somewhat apologetically, "I don't think I've revealed a secret. . . ."

Amina changed sides to defend Khadija, who appeared to be in trouble. With a smile she said, "Only God the Exalted is perfect."

With equal suavity, Ibrahim Shawkat remarked, "You're right. My wife has virtues that must not be overlooked. God's curse on anger, which strikes the angry person first of all. In my opinion there's nothing in the world worth getting angry about."

"How lucky you are!" Khadija said with a laugh. "That's why— and I don't envy you—no matter how many years pass, you're impervious to change."

For the first time Amina's serious disapproval was evident. To warn Khadija she said, "May our Lord preserve his youth and that of others like him."

Making no attempt to conceal his pleasure at his mother-in-law's prayer, Ibrahim laughingly asked, "Youth?"

Addressing his remarks to Amina, Khalil Shawkat responded, "In our family, forty-nine is considered young."

Amina said apprehensively, "Don't talk like that. Let's be done with it."

Khadija smiled at her mother's evident anxiety, for she knew what motivated it. Any frank expression of praise for a person's health was disliked in the old house, because it showed an ignorance of the dangers of the evil eye. Even Khadija herself would not have referred to her husband's good health if she had not spent the last six years with the Shawkats, who paid little more than lip service to many beliefs, such as the danger of envy and the evil eye. They also delved fearlessly into various subjects, such as the jinn's conduct, death, and ill health, which were not discussed in her old home, because of the residents' anxiety and caution.

The tie between Ibrahim and Khadija was firmer than it appeared on the surface and was not something a casual word or deed would harm. They were a successful couple, and each of them sensed deep inside that he could not do without the other, regardless of flaws. Strangely enough, it was when Ibrahim fell sick once that Khadija was able to reveal the love and devotion she harbored for him.

Yes, there was always some quarrel going on between them, at least from her side. His mother was not her only target. Despite his diplomacy and calmness, she was never at a loss for something to criticize about him—how much he slept, the way he lounged at home instead of going to work, his dismissal of any consideration of a career, his endless chatter, and the way he ignored domestic quarrels and disputes. According to Aisha, days and days would pass when her sister's conversation was totally given over to suspicious and acid remarks about him.

In spite of all this, or perhaps because of it—for an argument may improve a relationship like cayenne pepper, which adds zest to food —their emotional commitment to each other remained strong and uninfluenced by moments of apparent annoyance with each other. It was like a deep current in the water that keeps a steady course, unaffected by surface turbulence or spray. Moreover, it took little effort for her husband to appreciate her exertion, evidence of which was everywhere—in his sparkling residence, delicious meals, smart clothing, and tidy sons.

He would tease her and say, "The truth is that you're a treasure, you gypsy."

His mother's opinion of Khadija's energetic activity was quite different, and she did not hesitate to make it public during their frequent quarrels. She had told her daughter-in-law sarcastically, "This is a virtue for maids to brag about, not ladies."

Khadija had shot back, "The only vocation you people have is eating and drinking. The true master of a house is the person who takes care of it."

In the same scornful tone, the old lady had replied, "If they instilled such ideas in you at home, it was to conceal their opinion that you would never be good for anything except domestic service."

Then the younger woman had screamed, "I know why you're furious with me. I've known ever since I refused to let you push me around in my own home."

The mother-in-law had shrieked, "My Lord, I testify that al-Sayyid Ahmad Abd al-Jawad is a fine man, but he's fathered a she-devil. I deserve to be beaten with a slipper as punishment for picking you."

Khadija had gone off murmuring under her breath so the other woman would not hear, "You certainly deserve to be beaten with a slipper. I won't disagree with that."

Yasin looked at Aisha. Smiling mischievously, he said, "How happy you are, Aisha. You're on good terms with all factions."

Khadija perceived the veiled allusion to her in this remark. Shaking her shoulders disdainfully, she scolded him: "A troublemaker is trying to stir up dissension between two sisters."

"Me? . . . God forbid. God knows my intentions are good."

She shook her head as though in sorrow and replied, "You've never had a good intention."

Commenting on Yasin's remark, Khalil Shawkat said, "We live peacefully. Our motto is: 'Live and let live.' "

Khadija laughed until her gleaming teeth showed. In a tone not free of sarcasm she said, "At Khalil's house, it's one party after another. He's always strumming away on his lute while the lady of the house listens, primps in front of the mirror, or chats with this or that girlfriend through a window or the peephole of the enclosed balcony. Na'ima, Uthman, and Muhammad turn the chairs and pillows into a playground, and if Abd al-Muni'm and Ahmad get fed up with my supervision, they flee to their aunt's apartment, where they join the demolition squad."

Aisha asked with a smile, "In your opinion, is that all there is to our happy home?"

Khadija replied in the same tone, "Or you might be singing while Na'ima dances. . . ."

Aisha said boastfully, "I'm satisfied with the affection of all the neighbors and my mother-in-law."

"I don't see myself confiding in one of these chatterboxes, and as for your mother-in-law, she likes anyone who flatters her and bows down before her."

"We ought to love people. How wonderful it is when people love us too. Then hearts truly speak directly to each other. My friends all fear you. They frequently tell me, 'Your sister doesn't make us feel at home and never tires of putting us down.' " Then, laughingly addressing her mother, Aisha continued: "She still gives people comic nicknames that we joke about at home. Abd al-Muni'm and Ahmad memorize them and repeat them to boys in the neighborhood. That way they become widely known."

Amina smiled again. Khadija, who appeared to be remembering some awkward situations, laughed uneasily. With unconcealed delight, Khalil said, "When you put all of us together, we're a complete ensemble, with a lute player, a vocalist, and a dancer. We only need some more singers and a chorus, but I have my hopes set on my children. It's just a question of time."

Directing his comments to Amina, Ibrahim Shawkat said, "I can testify that your granddaughter Na'ima is a brilliant dancer."

Amina laughed until her pale face turned red. Then she replied, "I've seen her dance. She's charming!"

With an enthusiasm that revealed her well-known affection for her family, Khadija exclaimed, "How beautiful she is! She looks like a picture in an advertisement."

"What a beautiful bride she'll make for Ridwan," Yasin commented.

With a laugh Aisha protested, "But she was the first of the grandchildren. . . . (Oh, I'll never be able to lie about her age the way a mother should.)"

Yasin asked calmly, "Why do people insist on the bride being younger than the bridegroom?"

No one answered, but Amina observed, "Na'ima won't have to wait long to find a suitable husband."

Khadija added, "My Lord, how beautiful she is! I've never seen anyone as beautiful."

"What about her mother?" Aisha asked with a laugh. "Haven't you seen her mother?"

Khadija frowned to lend dignity to her remarks and said, "She's more beautiful than you, Aisha. You can't contest that." Her ironic spirit returned at once, and she continued: "And I'm more beautiful than either of you."

"These people are talking about beauty," Kamal reflected. "What do they know about its essence? They like certain colors: the whiteness of ivory and the gold of precious ingots. If you ask me about beauty I won't speak of a pure bronze complexion, tranquil black eyes, a slim figure, and Parisian elegance. Certainly not! All those are pretty, but they're nothing but lines, shapes, and colors subject to investigation by the senses and open to comparison. Beauty itself is a painful convulsion in the heart, an abundance of vitality in the soul, and a mad chase undertaken by the spirit until it encounters the heavens. Tell me about this, if you can. . . ."

"Why should the ladies of Sugar Street seek the affection of Mrs. Khadija?" Yasin asked, to stir his sister up again, when he noticed that the conversation was going to leave her in peace. "Perhaps she does have some good qualities, as her husband has testified, but in general people are attracted by a pretty face and a sweet tongue."

Khadija threw him a look as if to say, "If you knew what was good for you, you'd quit." Sighing audibly, she remarked, "What more can I ask than God's protection and blessings. I didn't know I had another mother-in-law here."

Then, to Yasin's surprise, she took up the topic again in a serious vein, explaining, "I don't have time to waste on visits. The house and the children consume every moment, especially since my husband pays no attention to either."

In his own defense, Ibrahim Shawkat said, "Fear God and don't exaggerate your role in everything. The truth of the matter is that a man with a wife like mine must take an active, defensive role from time to time, whether to protect pieces of furniture from being dusted and cleaned so much they're almost worn away or children from being pushed beyond their capacities. The most recent incident of this kind, as you know, is her thrusting Abd al-Muni'm into religious school before he's even five."

Khadija retorted proudly, "If I had taken your advice, I would have let him stay home till he came of age. There seems to be some hostility against learning in your family. No, darling, my children will be raised like their maternal uncles. I review Abd al-Muni'm's lessons with him myself."

Yasin asked incredulously, "You review his lessons with him?"

"Why not? Mother went over Kamal's lessons with him in exactly the same way. I sit with him every evening while he recites what he's memorized at school." She laughingly admitted, "That also helps me remember the principles of reading and writing, which I fear I may eventually forget."

Amina blushed from embarrassment and delight. She looked at Kamal as though begging him for a sign that he remembered those bygone nights. He smiled to show how well he did.

"Let Khadija raise her sons the way their uncles were," Amina told herself. "Let one of them follow in Kamal's footsteps as he makes his way to university. Let one of them emulate . . . oh, broken hearts are too weak to bear such dizzying blows. If he had only lived, today he would be a judge or on his way to becoming one. How often he discussed his hopes with you. Or were they your hopes? What has become of all that? If only he had lived, even as an insignificant member of the thronging masses . . ."

Ibrahim Shawkat told Kamal, "We're not as bad as your sister makes out. I sat for the primary certificate in 1895, as Khalil did in 1911. In those days the primary certificate was a major achievement, unlike now, when no one finds it impressive. We didn't continue our education because we had no intention of pursuing a career. In other words, we didn't need a career."

Kamal felt ironic amazement at Ibrahim's words: "I sat for the primary certificate," but answered politely, "This goes without saying."

"How could learning have any intrinsic value for two happy oxen?" he asked himself. "The two of you have provided me with a valuable lesson, teaching me that it's possible to love a person I despise and to wish only the best for someone whose principles in life excite my aversion and disgust. I instinctively hate man's animal nature from the depths of my heart. This emotion became a reality once the heavenly breeze brushed against my heart."

With comic enthusiasm Yasin cried out, "Long live the old primary certificate!"

"We're in the majority in any case." Yasin was annoyed to hear Khalil thrust himself, and by implication his brother, among the holders of the primary certificate, which they had unsuccessfully attempted to obtain, but found himself forced to play along.

Khadija said, "Abd al-Muni'm and Ahmad will continue their studies until they receive university degrees. It will be a new era in the Shawkat family. Listen carefully to the sound of these names: Abd al-Muni'm Ibrahim Shawkat and Ahmad Ibrahim Shawkat. Don't they have the same ring to them as Sa'd Zaghlul?"

Ibrahim laughingly shouted, "Where do you get such wild ambitions?"

"Why not? Wasn't Sa'd Zaghlul Pasha a student at al-Azhar? He went from the student dole to being Prime Minister. One word from him is enough to make everyone sit up and take notice. Nothing's too much for God to achieve."

Yasin asked ironically, "Wouldn't you be satisfied if they were as important as the politicians Adli Yeken Pasha and Abdel Khaliq Sarwat Pasha?"

As though seeking refuge with God, she shouted back, "Traitors? My sons won't be the kind of politicians people chant about night and day to get them removed from office."

Ibrahim took out a handkerchief from his trousers and wiped his face, which had turned a deeper red from the heat and from the perspiration caused by drinking cold water and hot coffee. As he dried his face he said, "If a mother's severity is a factor in the creation of great men, then you can already announce the glory awaiting your sons."

"Would you want me to let them do anything they wish?"

Aisha remarked gently, "I don't remember Mother ever scolding any of us, let alone striking us. Do you?"

Khadija replied sorrowfully, "Mother never resorted to violence because Papa was there. A mention of him was enough to ensure that his commands were obeyed. But at my house—and yours is just the same—the father is present only in name." She laughed when she made this last comment. "What can I do when the situation's like that? If the father's a mother, then the mother must be a father."

Yasin said with delight, "I'm sure you're successful in your paternity. You a father! I've felt this for a long time without being able to put it into words."

Khadija pretended to be complimented and retorted, "Thank you, Miss Bamba Kashar, you seductive songstress."

"Khadija and Aisha," Kamal thought. "What different types. . . . Consider them carefully. Which do you think better suited to be a model for your beloved? . . . Ask God's forgiveness! No one can be a model for my beloved. I can't picture her as a housewife. How impossible it is to imagine that!" His beloved in a housecoat, restraining a child, or supervising a kitchen? "How alarming! How disgusting! She ought to be at ease, oblivious, promenading in a splendid gown through a garden or a park, riding in a car, an angel on a happy, impromptu visit to earth, a unique exemplar of her species, itself unlike any other and known only to my heart. If she is referred to by the same term as these women, it's simply because I don't know the correct one. If her beauty is called by the same name as Aisha's and all the other varieties, that's because I don't know the real name for it. Here is my life, which I consecrate to learning about you. What other thirst for understanding is there beyond that?"

"What do you suppose Maryam's news is?" Aisha asked when she happened to think of her former friend. The name made visibly different impressions on the various people sitting there. Amina's expression changed to reveal her intense annoyance. Yasin pretended not to have heard the question and busied himself with an inspection of his fingernails. Kamal's head swarmed with disturbing memories. It was Khadija who replied coldly, "What do you expect? She's divorced and has returned to her mother."

After it was too late, Aisha realized that she had inadvertently tumbled into an abyss and hurt her mother through a slip of the tongue. Her mother had long believed that Maryam and her mother had not been sincere in their grief for Fahmy and might have actually gloated over the family's misfortune, because of al-Sayyid Ahmad's opposition to the proposed engagement between Maryam and his late son. Khadija had been the first to suggest the idea, and her mother had not hesitated to embrace it uncritically. Amina's feelings toward her longtime neighbor had quickly changed in a way that had led to an estrangement and then a break.

Attempting to apologize for her question, Aisha said nervously, "I don't know what made me ask about her."

With obvious emotion, Amina said, "You shouldn't think about her."

When suspicions had first been voiced about her friend, Aisha had questioned their accuracy. She had argued that the engagement proposal had been kept secret and could not have reached Maryam's home. Thus the girl and her family would have had no reason to rejoice at their sorrow. Her mother had refused to see it that way, on the grounds that it was impossible for an important matter like an engagement to be kept from leaking to the interested parties. Aisha had not insisted on her opinion for long, fearing she would be accused of partiality for Maryam or indifference toward her late brother.

Confronted by her mother's passion, Aisha found herself forced to make up for her slip. She remarked, "No one save God knows the truth, Mother. Perhaps she's innocent."

Contrary to her daughter's expectations, Amina's displeasure grew more intense. There were visible warning signs of anger that seemed out of character for her, since she was known for her calm and self-restraint. In a trembling voice she said, "Don't talk about Maryam, Aisha."

Khadija, who shared her mother's feelings, shouted, "Let's not have anything to do with Maryam and her goings-on."

Aisha smiled in confusion but said nothing. Yasin continued to be engrossed with his fingernails until this violent conversation was concluded. Encouraged by Aisha's statement, "No one save God knows the truth, Mother," he had been on the point of joining in, but had been silenced by Amina's quick answer in that unusual, trembling voice. Yes, he kept his peace and inwardly expressed his thanks for the blessing of silence.

Kamal had followed the conversation with concern, although his face did not betray his feelings. The period during which his love had weathered delicate and adverse conditions had imparted to him enough of an ability to act so that he could conceal his emotions and, if necessary, make people think he felt quite the opposite way. He remembered what he had heard about the alleged gloating of Maryam's family. Although he had never taken the accusation seriously, he recalled the secret message he had conveyed to Maryam and the answer he had brought back to Fahmy. He had kept that old secret, continuing to guard it to honor his promise to his brother, out of respect for Fahmy's wishes. Kamal was amused and astonished that he had only recently grasped the meaning of that message as its ideas took on a new life within him. He had been a stone with obscure inscriptions carved on it, until love had come and solved the riddle.

He did not fail to notice his mother's anger. It was a new phenomenon, to which she had not been subject before the calamity. She was no longer the same. The change was not dramatic or constant, but from time to time she succumbed to angry spells she had never experienced or at least had never yielded to before. What could he say about that? It must be the wounded heart of a mother, about which he knew nothing except for some few insights he had come across in his reading. He felt intense pain for her. But what explained Aisha's conduct or Khadija's? Was it fair to accuse Aisha of insensitivity toward the memory of Fahmy? He could not imagine or admit that. She was a benevolent person with a heart disposed to friendship and affection. Not without reason, she was inclined to think Maryam innocent. Perhaps since her heart was open to everyone, she felt nostalgic for the time when the girl had been her friend. Khadija had been swallowed up by married life. Her interests were limited to being a mother and housewife. She had no need for Maryam or anyone else. The only part of the past that meant anything to her was her attachment to her family and especially to her mother, in whose footsteps she was following. There was nothing strange in that.

"What about you, Mr. Yasin? How long will you remain a bachelor?" Ibrahim Shawkat asked, motivated by a sincere desire to clear the air.

Yasin jestingly replied, "My youth has left me. It's too late for that now."

In a serious tone, which showed he had not understood that Yasin was joking, Khalil Shawkat said, "I got married when I was about your age. Aren't you twenty-eight?"

Khadija was upset by the reference to Yasin's age, for it indirectly revealed how old she was. She addressed Yasin sharply: "Won't you get married and spare people having to talk about your bachelorhood?"

Aiming to please Amina more than anything else, Yasin answered, "Given our experiences of the past few years, it's been necessary for a person to forget about his own desires."

Khadija drew her head back as though a hand were shoving it. She cast him a glance as if to say, "You devil, you beat me." Then with a sigh she remarked, "You're the limit! If you would just say that marriage doesn't suit you, that would be more truthful."

To show her affection for him, Amina commented, "Yasin's a fine man who stays away from marriage only if he's forced to. The fact is that it's time for you to think about getting married again, if only to comply with the teachings of religion."

He had often thought of perfecting his compliance with Islam in this manner, not merely to try his luck again but out of a desire to wipe his honor clean of the blot it had gained when he had been forced, at the instigation of his father, to divorce Zaynab, because that was what her father, Muhammad Iffat, wanted. Then Fahmy had been slain, and Yasin had put off thinking about marriage. Eventually he had grown accustomed to the free life of a divorcé. All the same he meant every word he said when he told Amina, "Some situations are unavoidable. There's a right time for everything."

Their reflections were suddenly interrupted by a screaming hullabaloo and din accompanied by rapid footsteps on the stairs. They looked questioningly at the door to the stairway. It was only a moment before Umm Hanafi appeared on the threshold, frowning and gasping for breath. She cried out, "The children, my lady! Mr. Abd al-Muni'm and Mr. Ridwan are fighting. They threw pebbles at me when I tried to separate them."

Yasin and Khadija rose, rushed to the door, and disappeared up the stairs. They were back again in a couple of minutes. Yasin had

Ridwan by the hand and Khadija was pushing in front of her Abd al-Muni'm, whom she was halfheartedly punching in the back. The others noisily followed them. Na'ima ran to her father, Khalil, Uthman to Aisha, Muhammad to his grandmother Amina, and Ahmad to his father, Ibrahim. Khadija scolded Abd al-Muni'm and warned him he would never see his grandfather's house again. Pointing accusingly at Ridwan, who was sitting between his father and Kamal, the boy began to scream in a tearful voice, "He said they're richer than we are."

Ridwan shouted back, "He's the one who told me that they're richer. He also said they own all the treasures hidden in the old city gate, Bab al-Mutawalli."

Trying to calm his son, Yasin said with a laugh, "Forgive him, son. He's a spitfire like his mother."

Khadija could not help but laugh and asked Ridwan, "Why quarrel over Bab al-Mutawalli when you have, sir, another ancient city gate, Bab al-Nasr, near your grandfather's house. You take that one and don't quarrel."

Ridwan shook his head to show his dissatisfaction and replied, "It's full of corpses, not treasures. Let him have it!"

Aisha spoke up then to implore and tempt them: "Pray by the Prophet; here's a rare opportunity to hear Na'ima sing. What do you think about that suggestion?"

Approval and encouragement came from every corner of the room, and Khalil took Na'ima in his arms to set her on his lap. He told her, "Let all these people hear your voice. My God . . . my God, don't be bashful. I don't like it when you are."

Na'ima was overcome by shyness and buried her face in her father's chest until all that could be seen of her was a halo of gold. Aisha happened to glance around and saw Muhammad attempting unsuccessfully to remove the beauty spot from his grandmother's cheek. She went and brought him back against his will before resuming her encouragement to Na'ima to sing. Khalil too kept after the girl until she whispered that she would not sing unless she could hide behind his back. He gave her permission, and she crept behind him on the sofa, crawling on all fours. A pleased and expectant silence fell on the room. The quiet lasted so long that Khalil almost lost patience, but then a charming, delicate voice could be heard, starting as a whisper. Gradually she gained courage and her tones became increasingly fervent as she sang:

Turn aside here
And come to me,
You whom I love
As you love me.

Small hands began to clap to the music.

4 🖋

"It's time for you to tell me which branch of the university you plan to choose."

Al-Sayyid Ahmad Abd al-Jawad was seated on his bedroom sofa with his legs folded beneath him. At the far end, Kamal sat facing the door with his arms crossed in front of him, cloaked in polite submission. The man would have liked his son to reply, "Whatever you think best, Father," but al-Sayyid Ahmad conceded that choice of specialization at the University was not a matter he could dictate. His son's consent would be an important factor in the selection process. His own knowledge of the topic was also extremely limited, being derived for the most part from occasional discussions at his parties with friends who were attorneys or civil servants. They all agreed that a son should be granted the right to choose which branch of learning to pursue, lest he become discouraged and fail. For all these reasons, the father was not averse to discussing the topic, after confiding his lot to God's care.

"I have decided, Papa, God willing and with your approval, of course, to enroll in the Teachers Training College."

Al-Sayyid Ahmad's head moved in a way that revealed his discomfort. His large blue eyes opened wide. He stared at his son strangely. Then in a disapproving tone he said, "The Teachers College! . . . A free school! Isn't that so?"

After some hesitation Kamal replied, "Perhaps. I don't know."

The father waved his hand scornfully. He seemed to want to tell his son, "You must exercise a little patience and not leap to a decision on something you know nothing about." Then he remarked disdainfully, "It's just as I said. For that reason it rarely attracts students from good families. And then there's the teaching profession. . . . Do you know anything about teaching or is your information limited to the Teachers College? It's a miserable profession, which wins respect from no one. I'm well informed about what's said of such matters, but you're young and inexperienced. You know nothing of the ways of the world. It's an occupation uniting people who have modern educations with the products of traditional religious education. It's one utterly devoid of grandeur or esteem. I'm acquainted with men of distinction and with civil servants who have flatly refused to allow their daughters to marry a teacher, no matter how high his rank."

After belching and exhaling heavily, he continued: "Jamil al-Hamzawi's son Fuad, to whom you used to give your old suits, will attend Law School. He's a smart boy who's done well in school, but he's no smarter than you. I've promised his father to help pay his fees until he's been there long enough to get free tuition. How can I pay for other men's children to go to decent schools when my own son is studying free of charge in a worthless one?"

This grave report on the teacher and his mission came as an alarming surprise to Kamal. What reason was there for all this prejudice? It was not possible to attribute it to the teacher's calling, which was to impart knowledge. Was it based on the absence of tuition fees at the college where teachers were trained? He could not understand how money entered into the question of the value of learning. Why should learning have any worth beyond that of knowledge for its own sake? He believed too deeply in its intrinsic value for his faith to be shaken. He was convinced of the inherent merit of the sublime ideas he came across while reading the works of men he loved and respected, such as the Egyptian authors al-Manfaluti and al-Muwaylihi. He threw his whole heart into living in the ideal world reflected in the pages of their books. Thus he did not hesitate to reject his father's opinion as mistaken, no matter how much he revered the man. He excused this error by attributing it to their backward society and the influence of his father's ignorant friends. He was sorry but could only repeat, with all the politeness and delicacy he could muster, a phrase he had picked up in his reading: "Learning's superior to prestige and wealth, Papa."

Al-Sayyid Ahmad looked back and forth between Kamal and the wardrobe, as though appealing to an invisible person for confirmation of the absurdity of the idea he had just heard. Then he said indignantly, "Really? Have I lived long enough to hear drivel like this? You imply there's a difference between prestige and learning! There's no true knowledge without prestige and wealth. And why are you talking about learning as though it's one thing? Didn't I say that you're young and inexperienced? There are many different types of learning, not just one. Some kinds of knowledge are appropriate for tramps and others belong to the pashas of the world. You need to comprehend this, you ignoramus, before you regret it."

Kamal was convinced that his father had a high regard for religion and consequently for those who made it their profession. Thus he craftily said, "The students who do their advanced training at al-Azhar Mosque don't pay tuition. They become teachers, and no one can despise their fields of learning."

His father gestured scornfully toward him with his chin and said, "Religion's one thing and men who make a career of it are something else."

Deriving strength from his despair for this debate with the man whom he had always been accustomed to obey, he replied, "But, Papa, you revere the religious scholars and love them."

In a voice that was a bit sharp, his father said, "Don't mix things up. I revere Shaykh Mutawalli Abd al-Samad and love him. But I would far rather see you a respected civil servant than a man like him, even if you were to spread blessedness among the people, protecting them from evil with amulets and charms.... Every era has its men, but you refuse to understand."

He examined his son to gauge the effect of these words. Kamal looked down and bit his lower lip. He began to blink, while the left corner of his mouth twitched nervously.

"How amazing!" al-Sayyid Ahmad thought. Why did people insist on things that were clearly bad for them? He came close to exploding with anger but remembered that he was dealing with an issue outside the realm of his absolute sovereignty. He suppressed his rage and asked, "But why are you so enamored of the Teachers College, as though it had a monopoly on all learning? What do you dislike about Law School, for example? Isn't it the institution that graduates important people and government ministers? Isn't it the institution where Sa'd Zaghlul Pasha and men like him studied?"

Then with a despondent look in his eyes, he continued in a subdued voice: "And it was the school that Fahmy, may God be compassionate to him, chose after serious thought and reflection. If his time had not come so early, he would be a public prosecutor or a judge today. Isn't that so?"

Kamal replied emotionally, "Everything you say is true, Papa. But I don't want to study law."

The man struck his hands together and said, "He doesn't want to! Of what relevance to learning and institutions are likes and dislikes? Tell me what attracts you to the Teachers College. I want to know which of its alluring beauties has caused you to fall for it. Or are you a person who loves worthless things? Speak. I'm all ears."

Kamal squirmed, as though summoning all his forces to help him clarify the point his father found so obscure. He realized he had a difficult task before him. He was convinced that his efforts would only earn him more of the sarcastic comments he had already experienced during their argument. Moreover, he did not see himself as having a clearly defined goal he could explain to his father. What could he say? If he thought a little, he would know what he did not want. He was not interested in legal studies, economics, geography, history, or English, although he appreciated the importance of the last two subjects for his pursuits. If he did not want these, what did he desire? The yearnings of his soul would require careful scrutiny before his goals could be ascertained. Perhaps he was not convinced that he could achieve them at the Teachers College but thought this institution the shortest route to them. These yearnings had been aroused by things he had read that could not be classified under a single heading. There had been literary and social essays, religious ones, the folk epic about Antar—that heroic black poet of ancient Arabia, *The Thousand and One Nights*, a medieval anthology of Arabic poetry called *al-Hamasa*, the writings of al-Manfaluti, and the principles of philosophy. His aspirations were probably connected in some way as well to the realm of fantasy Yasin had disclosed to him long ago and even to the legends his mother had poured into his spirit before that. He was pleased to apply the name "thought" to this mysterious world and the title "thinker" to himself. He believed that the life of thought was man's loftiest goal, rising with its luminous character high above the material world. It was superior to prestige, titles, and all other counterfeit forms of greatness. The life of thought was certainly along those lines even if its features were not clearly delineated. He might find it in the Teachers College or his training there might merely be a means of advancing toward it, but he would never turn away from this goal.

It was only fair to acknowledge the strong link connecting the Teachers College to his heart or more precisely to his love. Why was that? There was no link between his beloved and the law or economics, but there were many ties, no matter how slender and concealed, between her and religion, spirituality, morality, philosophy, and other comparable branches of learning that tempted him to drink from their springs. She had similar secret affinities to singing and music. He could hope to gain insight into them through the transport of a musical performance or an outburst of ecstasy. He was aware of all this within him and totally convinced of its truth, but what could he say to his father? Once again he attempted to outfox his father, saying,

"The Teachers College trains people in noble sciences like mankind's history, which is full of lessons, and the English language."

As he spoke, his father scrutinized him. Suddenly al-Sayyid Ahmad's feelings of disdain and anger vanished. As though seeing the lad for the first time, he pondered his son's slender build, huge head, large nose, and long neck. He decided that Kamal looked as strange and eccentric as his ideas sounded. The father's mocking spirit was almost amused by this realization, but his affection and love for the boy restrained his sense of humor. He asked himself, "If his slenderness is a temporary condition and his nose inherited from me, where did he get this amazing head? Isn't it likely that he'll fall prey to someone like me who searches for defects to make the butt of his jokes?"

This upsetting thought increased his affection for his son. When he spoke, his voice sounded calmer, as if he were patiently giving advice: "Knowledge by itself is nothing. The results are what count. The law prepares you for a legal career. All you get from history and its lessons is a miserable job as a teacher. Take time to consider the consequences long and hard." As the tone of his voice became a little sharper, he continued: "All power and might are God's. Lessons, history, and soot like that! Why don't you talk sense?"

Kamal blushed with embarrassment and pain when he heard his father's opinion of the learning and lofty values he cherished. His father had brought them down to the level of soot, comparing them to it. His consolation lay in remembering what he had read in defense of thought and its sanctity and the references to people who disdain learning and prefer to search for profit and status. Oh! . . . those authors must have been debating with men just like his father. But not so fast . . . his father was not one of those stupid people. He was of a grand, distinguished type. He was simply the victim of his time, place, and companions. Would it do any good to argue? Should he try his luck once more, relying on a new stratagem?

"The fact is, Papa, that these disciplines have won the highest respect in advanced nations. The Europeans cherish them and erect statues in honor of persons who excel in them."

Al-Sayyid Ahmad turned his face away, clearly implying: "O God, have mercy." But he was not actually angry. He presumably thought the whole affair a comic surprise beyond his wildest imaginings. When he looked back, he said, "As your father, I want to feel secure about your future. I want you to have a respectable profession. Is there any disagreement about that? What really concerns me is to see you become an esteemed bureaucrat rather than a wretched teacher, regardless of whether a statue is erected like that of our national leader Ibrahim Pasha with his finger in the air. Glory to God! The longer we live, the more amazing are the things we hear and see. What does Europe have to do with us? You live in this country. Does it set up statues in honor of teachers? Show me a single sculpture of a teacher." Then he asked in a disapproving tone, "Tell me, son, do you want a career or a statue?"

Encountering no response save silence and confusion, al-Sayyid Ahmad said almost sadly, "I don't know how some of the ideas in your head got there. I'm inviting you to become one of the great men who shake the world with their distinctions and rank. Do you have some model you look up to that I don't know about? Tell me frankly what you think so I may set my mind at rest and understand what you're after. The truth is that you bewilder me."

He would take a new step and explain some of his feelings, putting his trust in God. He said, "Is it wrong, Papa, to aspire to be like the author al-Manfaluti someday?"

Al-Sayyid Ahmad said with astonishment, "Mustafa Lutfi al-Manfaluti? May God have mercy on him. I saw him more than once in the mosque of our master al-Husayn, but so far as I know he wasn't a teacher. He was much too distinguished for that. He was one of Sa'd Zaghlul's companions and writers. Moreover, he studied at al-Azhar, not at the Teachers College. And his education at al-Azhar had nothing to do with his greatness. He was a gift from God. That's what they say of him. We are discussing your future and the school you ought to enter. Let's leave God's work to God. If you're a gift from God and attain the greatness of al-Manfaluti, why not do so as a prosecutor or a judge?"

In desperate self-defense, Kamal replied, "I don't want to be as famous as al-Manfaluti. I want to be as cultured as he was. I haven't been able to find any college where I can better achieve my objective or at least lay a foundation for it than the Teachers College. That's why I prefer it. I have no special desire to be a teacher. Perhaps the only reason for accepting this profession is that it's the path open to me for the cultivation of thought."

"Thought?" Al-Sayyid Ahmad remembered a verse from a song composed and performed by al-Hamuli:

> *Thought has strayed.*
> *Aid me, tears.*

He had loved it for a long time and in the past had frequently recalled it. Was it this kind of thought his son was striving to develop?

He asked with astonishment: "What is 'the cultivation of thought'?"

Kamal was overwhelmed by confusion. He swallowed and said in a low voice, "Perhaps I don't really know." Then, smiling ingratiatingly, he continued: "If I knew, I wouldn't need to study it."

His father asked incredulously, "If you don't know what it is, what grounds do you have for choosing it? . . . Huh? Are you simply infatuated with a life of humiliation, for no reason at all?"

Kamal mastered his anxiety with great effort and—driven by desperation—defended his pursuit of happiness: "Cultivated thought is something too great to be easily comprehended. Among other things, it searches for the origin of life and its destiny."

His father studied him for a long time in bewilderment before saying, "For this you want to sacrifice your future? The origin of life and its destiny? The origin of life was Adam, and our destiny is paradise or hellfire. Or has there been some new discovery concerning this?"

"Of course not. I know that. What I meant to say was . . ."

His father quickly interrupted: "Have you gone mad? I ask you about your future and you reply that you want to know the origin of life and its destiny. What will you do with that? Open a booth as a fortune-teller?"

Kamal was afraid that if he became baffled and fell silent, he would lose and be forced to accept his father's point of view. Drawing on every ounce of courage he possessed, he said, "Forgive me, Papa. I haven't expressed myself well. I would like to continue my study of literature, begun after I passed the preparatory exam. I want to study history, languages, ethics, and poetry. The future is in God's hands."

As though filling in gaps that Kamal had left in his list, al-Sayyid Ahmad shouted with angry sarcasm, "And to study as well the arts of snake charming, puppetry, crystal gazing, and soothsaying. Why not? O God, have pity on me. Have you really been storing up this surprise for me? . . . There is no might or power save God's."

Al-Sayyid Ahmad became convinced that the situation was far more serious than he had thought. He was at a loss. He began to ask himself whether he had been wrong to allow his son to speak and think freely on this subject. Whenever he had patiently and tolerantly given his son some rope, the boy had dug his heels in and argued in an even more extreme fashion. The father found himself torn between his tyrannical tendencies and his recognition of a son's right to choose a school for himself. He was solicitous for Kamal's future and reluctant to admit defeat, but in an uncharacteristic way—or, more precisely, one that would have been out of character in the old days —he finally let reason have the upper hand.

Thus he returned to the debate and said, "Don't be naïve. There's something the matter with your mind that's beyond my understanding. I ask God to deliver you from it. The future is not an amusing game. It's your life and the only one you'll ever have. Think about the question for a long time. Law School is best for you. I understand the world better than you do. I have friends from all walks of life, and they all agree about Law School. You're a stupid child and don't know what it means to be a prosecutor or a judge. These are the professions that shake the world. It's within your power to attain one of them. How can you reject all this so cavalierly and choose to be . . . a teacher?"

Kamal was distressed and angry, not merely at the insult to the honor of teachers but first and foremost for the sake of learning itself, for what he felt was true learning. He did not think well of occupations that shook the earth. He had often found that the writers who inspired him applied derogatory epithets to them, referring, for example, to their counterfeit grandeur and ephemeral glory. Basing his opinion on what they had said, he believed that the only true greatness lay in the life of learning and truth. Thus all manifestations of majesty and pomp seemed spurious and trivial to him. He refrained from expressing this belief for fear of increasing his father's wrath. He said in a sweet and endearing way, "In any case, the Teachers College is a form of higher education."

Al-Sayyid Ahmad reflected for a time. Then despondently and disgustedly he said, "If you don't feel inclined toward the law—for some people even enjoy being miserable—choose a respectable school like the Military or Police academies. Something's better than nothing!"

Alarmed, Kamal asked, "Should I go to the Military or Police academies after getting my baccalaureate?"

"What other alternative is there, since you don't have the background for medicine?"

At that moment al-Sayyid Ahmad noticed that light reflected from the mirror was dazzling his left eye. He turned to look at the wardrobe and saw rays of afternoon sunshine slipping into the room via the window, which overlooked the courtyard. They had advanced from the wall opposite the bed to fill a portion of the mirror, showing that it would soon be time to leave for his store. He moved a little to get away from the light. Then he exhaled in a manner revealing how uneasy he was and bringing the bad news—or was it good?— that the conversation was about to conclude. He asked glumly, "Isn't there any other school besides these?"

Lowering his eyes in dismay at being unable to satisfy his father, Kamal said, "There's only Commerce left, and I've no interest in it."

Although al-Sayyid Ahmad was annoyed by his son's speedy rejection of that school, he himself felt at best indifferent toward it. He assumed that it only graduated merchants and did not want his son to be a merchant. He had known all along that an establishment like his, although it supplied him with a good living, would not be able to support as comfortably a son who succeeded him, for the income would have to be shared with his other beneficiaries. Therefore he had not attempted to groom one of his sons to take his place.

But this was not the main reason for his lack of interest in the School of Commerce. The fact was that he looked up to the civil service and bureaucrats. He perceived their significance and importance in public life. He had observed this personally with his friends who were civil servants and through contacts with the government relating to his business. He wanted his sons to be civil servants and had prepared them for that career. It was no secret to him that businessmen received only a fraction of the respect that government employees did, even if bureaucrats earned less. He shared this bias, although he would not have admitted it out loud. He was pleased by the deference civil servants showed him and fancied himself to have the mind of a bureaucrat or at least one as good. Who else would be capable of being a merchant and also the equal of a bureaucrat? Why did his sons not have a personality like his? Oh, what a disappointment it was! How he had wished in former times to see one of them become a doctor. He had focused his hopes on Fahmy, until he had been told that the arts baccalaureate did not prepare for the School of Medicine. Then he had contented himself with Law School and had looked forward happily to what would follow. Subsequently he had attached his aspirations to Kamal, selecting the arts section for him and dreaming once more of the successful career to follow Law School. He had never imagined that a struggle between his hopes and fate would result in the death of the genius of the family and in Kamal's insistence on being a teacher. How disappointed he felt!

Al-Sayyid Ahmad seemed genuinely sad when he said, "I've given you the best advice I can. You're free to choose for yourself, but you must always remember that I did not agree with you. Think the matter over at length. Don't be hasty. You still have plenty of time. Otherwise you'll regret your bad choice for the rest of your life. I take refuge with God from stupidity, ignorance, and folly." The man dropped his foot to the ground with a motion that indicated he was preparing to rise and get ready to leave the house.

Kamal stood up politely and modestly and then departed. Returning to the sitting room, he found his mother and Yasin conversing there. He was distraught and dejected after having resisted his father so vigorously, even though the man had been forbearing and lenient. He was also disturbed by the anxiety and sorrow his father showed toward the end of their discussion. He summarized for Yasin the conversation that had taken place in the bedroom. As the older brother listened, his expression was disapproving and his smile sardonic. He wasted no time in advising the teenager that he agreed with their father and was amazed at both the boy's ignorance about the values important in life and his fixation on others that were fanciful or ridiculous.

"You want to dedicate your life to learning? What does that mean? As an insight or maxim in works by al-Manfaluti like his *Reflections* that's brilliant, but in real life it's nonsense that doesn't get you anywhere. You live here and now, not in al-Manfaluti's books. Isn't that so? Books document strange and supernatural matters. For example, you read at times in them a line like Ahmad Shawqi's: 'The teacher is almost like a prophet,' but have you ever encountered a teacher of whom that was true? Come with me to al-Nahhasin School or recall any of your teachers you please. Show me one of them deserving the title 'human being,' let alone that of 'prophet.' What is this learning you desire? Ethics, history, and poetry? All those are beautiful pastimes but worthless in the workaday world. Be careful that an opportunity for a distinguished life does not slip through your fingers. I frequently regret that adverse circumstances prevented me from continuing my education."

Once Yasin followed his father out of the house and Kamal was left alone with his mother, he asked her opinion. She was not normally consulted on a matter like this, but she had followed his conversation with Yasin and knew of al-Sayyid Ahmad's desire for him to go to Law School. She had begun to consider that idea ill-omened, and it made her uncomfortable.

In any case, Kamal knew exactly how to win her approval for his position in the shortest possible time. He told her, "The science I want to study is closely linked to religion. Among its branches are wisdom, ethics, consideration of the attributes of God, and the essence of His revelatory signs and creations."

Amina's face shone as she said enthusiastically, "This is true science, like my father's and your grandfather's. Religious science is the most noble one of all."

She thought for a time as he watched her with a twinkle in his eyes. Then with the same enthusiasm she continued: "Who would ever disparage a teacher? Don't they say, 'I become the slave of anyone who teaches me even a single syllable'?"

Repeating the argument his father had used to attack his choice, as though to elicit her support, Kamal observed, "But they say a teacher has no chance at getting a good position."

She waved her hand disdainfully and replied, "A teacher makes a decent living, doesn't he? What more can you wish for? I ask God that you may have good health, a long life, and sound learning. Your grandfather used to say, 'Learning is more valuable than money.'"

Amazingly, his mother's advice was better than his father's. It was not based on opinion but on sound feelings, which, unlike his father's, had never been corrupted by contact with the realities of worldly life. Her ignorance of the affairs of the world had protected her feelings from corruption. But what value did feelings have, no matter how noble, if they were rooted in ignorance? Was this same ignorance at least partially responsible for his own ideas? He revolted against this kind of logic and to refute it told himself that he knew the good and bad of the world from books. His choice of the good was based on both his beliefs and his thought. Innate and naïve feelings might agree with wise opinions without discrediting the latter in any way. "Absolutely!" he exclaimed to himself.

He did not doubt for a moment that his opinion was correct and noble, but did he know what he wanted? It was not the teaching profession that attracted him. The truth was that he dreamed of writing a book. What book? It would not be poetry. There was poetry in his diary, but it originated with Aïda, who changed prose into poetry, not with any poetic gift of his. Thus the book would be prose. It would be a large, bound volume about the size and shape of the Holy Qur'an, and, like the Qur'an, its pages would have margins filled with notes and commentaries. But what would he write about? The Qur'an embraced everything, did it not? There was no cause for him to despair. He would find his subject one day. It was enough for him to know the size, shape, and style of annotation for the book. Surely a book that would shake the world was better than a civil service position, even if the latter shook the world too. Every educated person knew about Socrates. Who remembered the judges who had presided at his trial?

"Good evening!"

"She's not going to answer," he thought. "That's what I expected. At the beginning, it's always like that . . . has been and ever will be. So she turns her back on you, moving away from the wall beside you to go to the line and check the clothespins. Hasn't she already done that? Of course, but, Maryam, you're trying to be discreet. I understand perfectly. After ten years of chasing women I've become something of an expert. Delight your eyes with her before it gets dark and she's reduced to a shadow. She's put on weight and gotten firmer. She's even more beautiful than when she was a girl. She was pretty as a gazelle back then but did not possess such full hips. Not so fast . . . she still has a maidenlike figure. How old are you, sweetheart? Your family used to claim you were the same age as Khadija, but according to Khadija you're years and years older. My stepmother declares nowadays that you're in your thirties, on the basis of old memories of the type: 'When I was pregnant with Khadija, Maryam was a girl of five,' and so on. What difference does age make? Do you plan to spend your whole life with her? In a few short days, she'll ripen into all the woman you could want—beautiful, alluring, satisfying, and plump. Oh, she looked toward the street and noticed you. Did you see her eyes look at you like a chicken's? I won't budge from here, you beauty. Isn't a young man whose looks, strength, and financial status you know better than that Englishman you once admired?"

"Doesn't your family think a greeting deserves some reply?" he asked.

"She's turned away from you again," he observed. "But wait . . . didn't she smile? Yes, and whatever force allotted beauty to her gave her an enchanting smile. She smiled. You prepared carefully for this final step. No doubt she's been aware of all my previous motions and maneuvers. My time has come . . . and yours too, since luckily you're not a woman afflicted with modesty. That Englishman . . . Julian! Here's a noble stallion standing before you, and his body's ready to carry you away. Don't you hear him neighing?"

"Does your family have no respect for neighbors?" he inquired. "I beg you for a word of greeting. I certainly deserve that."

A faint, delicate voice, which seemed to come from far away, since her face was turned in the other direction, said, "You don't deserve it . . . not like this."

The man knocking at the door had received a reply. The door latch had been lifted. "You won't be charmed by sweet nothings until you've swallowed her scoldings," he counseled himself. "Be steady and firm . . . steady."

Borrowing a phrase from seminary students, Yasin said, "If I have done anything to offend you, I shall never forgive myself as long as I live."

She replied critically, "The roof terrace of Umm Ali the midwife's house is the same height as ours. What would someone think if he saw you standing there while I'm hanging out the laundry?" Then she added sarcastically, "Or do you want to cause a scandal for me?"

"May nothing evil happen to you," he thought. "Were you so cautious when you gazed at Julian in the old days? But not so fast . . . the beauty of your eyes and rump make up for any former or future misconduct."

"May God not spare my life a moment longer," he protested, "if I intended to harm you. I hid under the jasmine arbor until the sun set and did not approach the wall separating our houses until I was certain Umm Ali's roof was vacant."

Then, sighing audibly, he continued: "I have the added excuse that I've gotten in the habit of coming here to enjoy the solitude. When I found just now that no one else was present I was transported by joy. In any case our Lord will shield us . . ."

"Amazing! . . . Why all this effort?"

"That's hardly a naïve question," he thought. "Their questions reflect their experience. She has condescended to converse with you. Congratulations on this conversation."

Out loud he said, "I told myself, 'Nothing could be sweeter than greeting her and hearing her answer.' "

The way she turned her head to look at him revealed even in the semidarkness that she was trying not to laugh. She replied, "Your words are more inflated than your body. I wonder what's behind all this talk of yours?"

"Behind it? Why not come closer to the wall? I have a lot to say. For some time now when I chance to look at the ground on leaving the house I've noticed the shadow of a moving hand. If I look up, I see you glancing down from the wall of the roof terrace. That sight is so beautiful it's unforgettable."

She turned to face him but did not move a step closer. Then she said accusingly, "How dare you look up! If you truly were a good neighbor, as you claim, you wouldn't harm a woman this way. Your evil intentions have become clear from your confession and conduct here."

His intentions really were evil. Was fornication the result of good ones? "These are the kinds of evil intentions you love," he reflected. "You women are the limit. In an hour you'll demand it as one of your rights. In two hours' time, I'll be fleeing, while you pursue me. All the same, tonight's as sweet as jasmine."

"God knows my intentions are good," he declared. "I glanced up because I can't keep myself from looking wherever you are. Haven't you understood that? Haven't you felt it? Your longtime neighbor is speaking out, even if it's rather late."

Mockingly she said, "Speak. Give free rein to your hot air. Raise your voice.... What would you do if your stepmother surprised us on the roof like this?"

"Don't change the subject, bitch. It will be a miracle if I ever convince you," he reflected. "Do you really fear my stepmother? Oh ... one night in this woman's embrace will be worth a whole lifetime."

"I'll hear her footsteps first," he explained. "Let's not get distracted from what we're doing."

"What are we doing?"

"Something so exalted that it defies description."

"It doesn't seem that way to me. Perhaps you're doing it alone."

"Perhaps. Then it's thoroughly heartrending. It's devastating when a heart speaks out and finds no one who will respond. I remember the days when you used to visit our house, those days when we were all like a single family, and I sigh with regret."

Shaking her head, she muttered, "Those days!"

"Return to the past?" he asked himself. "I've made a grave mistake. Don't let painful memories spoil your whole effort. Concentrate on setting aside everything but the present."

He said, "When I finally saw you, I beheld a young woman as beautiful as a flower that blooms by night and illuminates the darkness. I seemed to be seeing you for the first time. I asked myself, 'Could this be our neighbor Maryam who used to play with Khadija and Aisha?' Certainly not! This girl has matured into a perfect beauty. I felt that the world around me had been transformed."

Her tone mischievous once more, she replied, "In the old days your eyes did not take such liberties. You were a neighbor in every sense of the word. But what's left of those days? Everything's changed. We've become like strangers, as though we had never spoken to each other and had not grown up as a single family. This is the way your family wants it."

"Let's not think about that. Don't add to my distress."

"Now you allow your eyes to look anywhere . . . through the window, from the street, and here you are accosting me on the roof."

"What's keeping you from leaving if you really want to?" he wondered. "O light of my darkness, your lies are sweeter than honey."

"This is only a small part of it," he told her. "I'm looking at you even when you don't suspect it. I see you in my imagination more often than you could guess. I tell myself, knowing full well what I say, 'Give me life with her or death.' "

The whisper of a suppressed laugh made his heart tremble. "Where do you find such phrases?" she asked.

Gesturing toward his breast, he replied, "In my heart!"

She moved her foot and caused her slipper to scuff the roof as though she were about to depart. Without quitting her post she said, "Since the discussion has reached the heart, I must leave."

In his ardor, his voice grew louder until he caught himself and lowered it: "No! You must come. Come to me. Now and forever." Then he added sneakily, "To my heart. It and all it possesses are yours."

In a tone of mocking admonishment she advised him, "Don't abuse yourself this way. God forbid that I should deprive you of your heart and its possessions."

"How well do you understand what I'm saying?" he wondered. "When I speak to you, I'm addressing the bitch I love. You're no fool. The memory of Julian makes that clear. Come here, girl. You take after your old lady. I'm afraid I'll light up the darkness with the intense fire flaming inside my body."

"I'll gladly give you my heart and all its possessions," he proclaimed. "Its only happiness is for you to accept it and possess it, if you will belong to it alone."

She answered laughingly, "You crafty fellow, don't you see you want to take rather than give?"

"Where did you learn to talk like that?" he puzzled. "Not even Zanuba, when I was seeing her, could compare. What a cursed place the world would be without you."

"I want you to be mine," he said. "And for me to be yours. What's unfair about that?"

Silence reigned as a look was exchanged by two shadows. Then she said, "Perhaps they're asking now what's keeping you."

Artfully attempting to win her sympathy, he replied, "There's no one in the world who cares about me."

At that, her tone changed and she asked seriously, "How's your son? . . . Is he still with his grandfather?"

"What's behind this question?" he wondered.

"Yes," he answered.

"How old is he now?"

"Five. . . ."

"What's become of his mother?"

"I think she's either married or about to be."

"What a pity! Why didn't you take her back, if only for Ridwan's sake?"

"Bitch!" he thought. "Explain what you're getting at."

"Would you really have wanted that?" he asked.

She laughed gently and replied, "How lucky the man is who brings two people together in a moral way."

"Or immoral?" he wondered.

"I don't look back," he stated.

There ensued a strange silence that seemed thoughtful. Then in a voice that was both tender and admonitory she said, "You better not try to catch me on the roof again."

He answered daringly, "Whatever you command. The roof isn't a safe place. Did you know I have a house in Palace of Desire Alley?"

She called out incredulously, "Your own house! Welcome to the man of property."

He was silent for a time, as though wishing to be cautious. Then he said, "Guess what's on my mind."

"That's no concern of mine."

"Silence, darkness, seclusion . . ." he thought, "what a dreadful effect the gloom has on my nerves. . . ."

"I was thinking," he declared, "of the two adjoining walls of our roofs. What does their image make you think of?"

"Nothing."

"The sight of two lovers clinging together."

"I don't like to hear talk like that."

"The fact that they're next to each other also reminds me that nothing separates them."

"Ha!" This exclamation escaped like an enticing threat.

Laughingly he continued: "It's as though they were telling me, 'Cross over.' "

She retreated two steps until her back touched a sheet hung out to dry. Then she whispered with genuine reproach, "I won't allow this!"

"This! . . . What's 'this'?"

"This kind of talk."

"What of the deed itself?"

"I'm going to leave angry."

"Don't do that. I swear by your precious life . . ."

"Do you mean what you're saying?" he asked himself. "Am I a greater fool than I suspect or are you more clever than I imagine? Why did you mention Ridwan and his mother? . . . Should you allude to marriage? How intensely do you want her? Madly. . . ."

Maryam said suddenly, "Oh . . . what's keeping me here?" She turned around and bent her head down to duck under the wash.

He called after her anxiously, "Are you leaving without saying goodbye?"

She lifted her head high to look back over the laundry and remarked, "Enter 'houses by their doors.' That's my farewell message for you." (Qur'an, 2:189.) She quickly made her way to the stairway door and disappeared through it.

Yasin returned to the sitting room. He excused his long absence to Amina by referring to the heat indoors and then went to his room to don his suit. Kamal watched his older brother with thoughtful amazement, but when he looked back at his mother he found her calm and reassured. She had finished drinking her coffee and was reading the grounds. Kamal wondered how she would react if she knew what had taken place on the roof.

Kamal himself was still perturbed by the scene of the couple conversing privately, which he had accidentally witnessed on following his brother to see what was delaying him. Yasin had done that. Did the memory of Fahmy mean so little to him? He could not imagine that. Yasin had loved Fahmy sincerely and had grieved for him deeply. It was impossible to doubt his sincerity. Moreover, incidents like this were commonplace. Kamal did not know why people always linked Fahmy and Maryam. His late brother had learned of the girl's affair with Julian before it was finished. A long time had passed after that. Fahmy had apparently forgotten her and gone on to loftier and more significant matters. That was all she deserved, for she had never been good enough for him. What Kamal really needed to think about was whether love could be forgotten. He believed it could not, but how did he know Fahmy had loved Maryam in the way Kamal understood and felt the term. Perhaps it had merely been a powerful desire like that currently overwhelming Yasin or even like that outgrown desire Kamal had once felt for Maryam. It had toyed with him when he reached puberty, playing havoc with his dreams. Yes, that had happened. It had afflicted him in two ways: through the equally powerful torments of desire and remorse. Only Maryam's marriage and subsequent disappearance from their lives had rescued him.

Kamal was concerned to know if Yasin was suffering and to what degree remorse was pricking his conscience. No matter what he thought of Yasin's animal spirits and indifference to higher ideals, Kamal could not imagine it had been easy for him. Despite his tolerant view of the whole matter, Kamal felt the annoyance and anxiety of a young man who would not have compromised his ideals for anything in the world.

After putting on his street clothes and grooming himself, Yasin returned from the bedroom. He said goodbye and departed. Before long they heard someone knocking on the door of the sitting room. Certain of the newcomer's identity, Kamal invited him to enter. A young man of his own age appeared. Short and good-looking, he was dressed in a jacket and a floor-length shirt. He went over to Amina and kissed her hand. Then he shook hands with Kamal and sat down beside him. Although he made a point of being polite, his familiar behavior indicated that he was virtually a member of the household. Amina began speaking to him, addressing him quite simply as Fuad and asking about the health of his mother and of his father, Jamil al-Hamzawi. He answered with delighted gratitude for her gracious welcome. Kamal left his friend with Amina to go put on his jacket in his room. When he returned, the two set off together.

6 ❧

They walked along, side by side, toward Qirmiz Alley, avoiding al-Nahhasin Street to keep from passing the store and their fathers. There was enough contrast between tall, skinny Kamal and short Fuad to attract attention.

Fuad asked in a calm voice, "Where are you going tonight?"

Kamal answered excitedly, "Ahmad Abduh's coffee shop."

It was customary for Kamal to pick their destination and for Fuad to acquiesce, even though Fuad was known for his clear, steady mind and Kamal for caprices that seemed ludicrous to his companion. For example, he had repeatedly asked Fuad to accompany him to the Muqattam Hills overlooking the city, to the Cairo Citadel, or to the Tentmakers Bazaar so that they might—as he put it—feast their eyes on the treasures of the past and wonders of the present. The relationship between the two friends was influenced by the difference in class between their families and by the fact that Kamal's father owned the shop where Fuad's father worked. This distinction was accentuated as Fuad grew accustomed to running errands for Kamal's family. In return, he benefited from Amina's generosity, for she did not begrudge him the finest food she had—he often showed up at mealtime—and the most serviceable clothes Kamal no longer needed. From the beginning, their friendship had been marked by Kamal's dominance and Fuad's subservience. Although amity had supplanted these other feelings, their psychological impact had never been totally extirpated.

Circumstances decreed that Kamal found virtually no other companion but Fuad al-Hamzawi during the whole summer vacation. His former classmates in the area had not continued their studies. Some had begun careers once they finished their elementary or competency certificates. Others had been forced to take menial jobs, as a waiter in the coffeehouse on Palace Walk or as an apprentice at an ironing shop in Khan Ja'far, for example. Those two boys had been his classmates in religious primary school. The three of them still greeted each other as old friends whenever they chanced to meet. The words of the two apprentices would be filled with respect because of the distinction the pursuit of knowledge gave Kamal. His greeting would be full of the affection of a modest and unpretentious soul. Kamal's new friends who lived in al-Abbasiya, like Hasan Salim, Isma'il Latif, and Husayn Shaddad, spent their holidays in Alexandria or Ra's al-Barr. Thus Fuad was the only comrade he had left.

They reached the entry of Ahmad Abduh's coffeehouse after walking for a few minutes. They descended to its strange space in the belly of the earth beneath Khan al-Khalili bazaar and sought out an empty alcove. As they sat facing each other at the table Fuad muttered with some embarrassment, "I thought you would be going to the cinema tonight."

His words betrayed his own desire. Although he had almost certainly felt this way even before he stopped by Kamal's house, he had said nothing about his wishes then. He had known he would be unable to change Kamal's mind. Since it was Kamal who paid for their tickets when they saw a film, Fuad's courage was not up to mentioning what he would like until they were ensconced in the coffeehouse, where his words could be understood as an innocent and casual comment.

"Next Thursday we'll go to the Egyptian Club to see Charlie Chaplin. Now we'll play a game of dominoes."

They removed their fezzes and placed them on the third chair. Then Kamal summoned the waiter to order green tea and the dominoes. The subterranean coffeehouse could well have been the belly of an extinct beast buried by an ancient accumulation of rubble except for its huge head, which came up to the level of the earth. Its mouth, gaping wide open, had protruding fangs shaped like an entry with a long staircase. The interior consisted of a spacious square courtyard with large, cream-colored tiles from the village of al-Ma'asara. There was a fountain in the center surrounded by carnations in pots. On all four sides stood benches covered with cushions and decorative mats. The walls were interrupted at regular intervals by cell-like alcoves, without doors or windows. They resembled caves carved into the walls and were furnished with nothing more than a wooden table, four chairs, and a small lamp, which burned night and day and hung in a niche on the back wall. The bizarre setting of the coffeehouse contributed to its character, for there was a sleepy calm about it unusual among coffeehouses. The light was dim and the atmosphere damp. Each group of patrons was isolated in an alcove or on a bench. The men smoked water pipes, drank tea, and chatted idly and interminably. Their conversations had a pervasive, continuous, and languid melody of desire, broken at lengthy intervals by a cough, a laugh, or the gurgling sound of a water pipe.

In Kamal's opinion, Ahmad Abduh's coffeehouse was a treasure for the dreamer and provided much food for thought. Although initially Fuad had been intrigued by its curious attractions, now all he saw in it was a depressing place to sit and be enveloped by damp, putrid air. Yet he was forced to agree whenever Kamal invited him to go there.

"Do you remember the day we saw your brother, Mr. Yasin, when we were sitting here?"

Kamal smiled and replied, "Yes. Mr. Yasin is gracious and easy to get along with. He never makes me feel he's my older brother. I begged him not to tell anyone at home that we meet here, not from fear of my father, for none of us would dare disclose a matter like this to him, but from concern that it might upset my mother. Imagine how alarmed she would be if she learned we frequent this coffeehouse, or any other. She thinks most patrons of coffeehouses are drug addicts and people of ill repute."

"What about Mr. Yasin? Doesn't she know he's a regular?"

"If I told her, she'd say Yasin's an adult and not at risk, whereas I'm still young. It's clear that I'll be thought a child at home until my hair turns gray."

The waiter brought their dominoes and two glasses of tea on a bright yellow tray, which he placed on the table. Then he departed. Kamal took his glass at once and began to drink before the tea had cooled off. He blew on the liquid, took a sip, and then blew again. He sucked on his lip when he burned it, but that did not prevent him from stubbornly and impatiently resuming his attempt to drink, as though condemned to finish in a minute or two.

Fuad observed him silently or gazed at nothing in particular while leaning back in the chair with a dignity that far outstripped his years. His large handsome eyes had a calm and profound look. He did not reach for his glass until Kamal had finished struggling with his. Then Fuad began to sip the tea slowly as he savored its taste and enjoyed its fragrance. After each swallow he murmured, "My God ... how good it is!"

Chafing at the bit, Kamal pressed him to finish so they could start playing. He warned his friend, "I'll beat you today. Luck won't always be on your side."

With a smile Fuad muttered, "We'll see," and began playing.

Kamal brought to the match a nervous intensity that suggested he was embarking on a contest in defense of his life or honor. Fuad calmly and skillfully placed his pieces. His smile never left his lips, whether he was lucky or not and whether Kamal was cheerful or glowering.

As usual Kamal became agitated and shouted, "A stupid move, but a lucky one." Fuad's only response was a polite laugh, calculated not to anger or challenge his friend.

Kamal frequently told himself when enraged, "He's always luckier than I am." Kamal did not display the kind of forbearance appropriate for games and recreation. In fact he manifested the same intensity and zeal in both his serious pursuits and his amusements.

Fuad's superiority over Kamal in dominoes was equaled by his success in school, where he was first in his class and Kamal merely in the top five. Did luck have a hand in that too? How could he explain the success of that young man to whom he felt superior, deep inside? He thought his superiority over Fuad should be evident in their respective intellectual gifts. His way of accounting for his friend's achievements was to observe that Fuad studied all the time. If he had really been as bright as they claimed, he would not have needed to study so much. Kamal also told himself that Fuad avoided sports, whereas he was excellent in more than one. He remarked finally that Fuad limited his reading to schoolbooks. If he thought of reading something other than a school text during the vacation, he chose one that would be helpful for his subsequent studies. Kamal did not limit his reading in any way and did not choose books for their utility. Thus there was nothing strange about the other boy being ranked ahead of him in school. All the same, his grudge against Fuad did not weaken their friendship. He loved him and found such delight and enjoyment in his company that he willingly admitted Fuad's strengths and virtues, at least to himself.

Play continued and the game ended, contrary to initial projections, with a victory by Kamal. He beamed and laughed out loud before asking his opponent, "Another game?"

But Fuad replied with a smile, "That's enough for today." Either he was tired of playing or apprehensive that the proposed match would end in disappointment for Kamal, whose happiness would turn to sorrow.

Kamal shook his head in amazement and commented, "You're a cold fish!" Rubbing the tip of his nose with his thumb and index finger, he added critically, "I'm amazed at you. When you're beaten, you're not interested in avenging your defeat. You love Sa'd Zaghlul but shunned the demonstration to salute him when he became Prime Minister. You seek the blessings of our master al-Husayn but are unruffled by the revelation that his remains may not repose in the nearby sepulcher. You astound me!"

Kamal was intensely annoyed by his friend's icy composure. He could not stand what they termed "being reasonable." He would prefer by far to be "crazy". He remembered the day they were told at school, "The tomb of al-Husayn is a symbol and nothing more."

They had walked home together afterwards. Fuad had repeated the words of the Islamic history teacher. Kamal had asked himself in alarm how his friend was able to deal with this news—as though it did not concern him. Kamal did not brood about it, for he was totally unable to think. How did someone in total revolt against an idea think? He was staggered by the frightful blow, which he felt even in the innermost reaches of his heart. He was weeping for a vision that had faded away and a dream that had evaporated. Al-Husayn was no longer their neighbor. He had never been their neighbor. What had become of all those kisses he had pressed against the door of the sepulcher so sincerely and warmly? What had happened to his exultation and pride in being a close neighbor of the Prophet's grandson? Nothing remained but a symbol in the mosque and desolate disappointment in his heart. He had wept that night until his pillow was soaked, but the revelation had stirred nothing in his reasonable friend save his tongue, which had reacted to the event by repeating their teacher's words. How dreadful it was to be reasonable!

"Does your father know you want to go to the Teachers College?"

When Kamal replied, the sharpness of his tone expressed displeasure with his friend's coldness as well as the pain left over from his interview with his father. "Yes!"

"What did he say?"

Kamal found some relief for his emotions by indirectly attacking his companion. "Alas, my father, like most other people, is crazy about sham forms of success like the civil service, the prosecutor's office, being a judge ... that's all he cares about. I didn't know how to convince him of the grandeur of thought and the lofty values that truly deserve to be pursued in this life. But he left the decision up to me."

Fuad's fingers were toying with a domino when he asked compassionately, "No doubt these are lofty values, but where are they respected as they should be?"

"It's not possible for me to reject a heavenly creed simply because no one around me believes in it."

Fuad replied with a calmness intended to appease his friend: "You show admirable spirit, but wouldn't it be better to plan your future by the light of reality?"

"If our leader Sa'd Zaghlul had taken your advice," Kamal suggested scornfully, "do you suppose he would have thought seriously about going to the British Residency to demand independence for Egypt?"

Fuad smiled as though to say, "Although your argument's sound, it's not fit to serve as a general principle for life." He remarked aloud, "Study law so you'll be sure to have a respectable job. Afterwards you can pursue your cultural interests to your heart's content."

Defiantly Kamal retorted, "God didn't place 'two hearts in a man's breast' [Qur'an, 33:4]. And I must object to your association between legal studies and a respectable job. Isn't teaching a respectable profession?"

Fuad was quick to defend himself resolutely against this suspicion: "I didn't mean that at all. Who would ever say that gathering and distributing knowledge isn't respectable work? Perhaps I was unwittingly repeating what people say ... people, as you suggested, who are dazzled by power and influence."

Kamal shrugged his shoulders in disgust and said with conviction, "A life dedicated to thought is certainly the most exalted type of life."

Fuad nodded his head in agreement but said nothing. He took refuge in silence until Kamal asked him, "What was your reason for choosing Law School?"

He thought a little and then replied, "Unlike you, I'm not in love with thought. I was able to select a branch of the University solely in terms of what it meant for my future. So I chose law."

Was this not the voice of reason? Of course it was, and that infuriated and revolted him. Was it not unfair for him to have to pass the entire summer vacation as a prisoner of this district with no companion besides this reasonable youth? There was another life totally unlike that of this ancient quarter. There were other companions who differed completely from Fuad. His soul yearned for that other life and those other friends ... for al-Abbasiya and its elegant young people. More than anything else he craved the refined elegance, Parisian accent, and exquisite dream of his beloved. Oh ... he wanted to go home to be alone and bring out his diary. He would relive a moment, recall a memory, or record a flight of fancy. Was it not time for him to disband this party and leave?

"I met some people who asked about you."

Tearing himself away from the stream of his reflections, Kamal asked, "Who?"

Fuad replied with a laugh, "Qamar and Narjis!"

Qamar and Narjis were the daughters of Abu Sari', who roasted seeds and other snacks. Kamal remembered the vaulted section of Qirmiz Alley after sunset when the alleys were quite dark. They had fondled each other in a way that combined innocence with sexuality, as they feverishly approached puberty. He could remember all that, but why did his lips pucker up in disgust? That was all relatively ancient history, before the holy spirit had descended on him. He could not recall that flirtation without having his heart boil with anger, pain, and shame, since now it was filled with the wine of pure love.

"How did you come across them?"

"In the crowds at the commemoration of the birth of al-Husayn. I walked along beside them without any hesitation or embarrassment, as though we were all one family touring the sights of the festival."

"You have some nerve!"

"Occasionally. . . . I greeted them and they replied. We talked for a long time. Then Qamar inquired about you."

Kamal blushed a little as he asked, "And then?"

"We agreed I'd tell you and that later we'd all get together."

Kamal shook his head to show his distaste for the idea and said tersely, "Certainly not."

Fuad was astonished. " 'Certainly not'? I thought you'd be happy to meet them in the vaulted alley or the courtyard of a deserted house. Their bodies have filled out. They'll soon be women in every sense of the word. By the way, Qamar was wearing a wrap but no veil. I laughingly told her that if she had been veiled I wouldn't have dared speak to her."

Kamal said emphatically, "Of course not!"

"Why not?"

"I can no longer bear depravity." With a sharpness that betrayed his hidden pain: "I can't meet God in my prayers when my underclothes are soiled."

Fuad suggested innocently, "Then wash and cleanse yourself before you pray."

Shaking his head in exasperation at being taken so literally, Kamal replied, "Water can't wash away sin."

He had wrestled with this issue for a long time. Whenever he had gone to meet Qamar he had been agitated by lust and anxiety, only to return home with a tormented conscience and a grieving heart. At the end of his prayers he would spend a long time fervently requesting forgiveness. Yet he would set off again in spite of himself, to return in torment and beg for forgiveness once more. Those days had been filled with lust, bitterness, and torment, but then the light had burst forth. All at once he had been able to love and pray without any conflict. Why not? Love was a pure drop from the fountainhead of religion.

Fuad said somewhat plaintively, "My encounters with Narjis ended once she was forbidden to play outside."

Kamal asked him with interest, "Didn't that relationship trouble you, since you're a Believer?"

Lowering his eyes in embarrassment, Fuad answered, "Some things can't be helped." Then, as though to conceal his discomfort, he asked, "Will you really refuse to take advantage of this opportunity?"

"Absolutely!"

"Merely on religious grounds?"

"Isn't that enough?"

Fuad smiled broadly and commented, "You always try to bear intolerable burdens."

Kamal replied emphatically, "That's the way I am. There's no need for me to be any different."

They exchanged a long look, which expressed Kamal's determination and defiance and reflected both Fuad's desire not to quarrel and his smile, which was like the sun's fiery rays sparkling merrily on the water. Then Kamal continued: "In my opinion, lust is a base instinct. I hate the thought of surrendering to it. Perhaps it was implanted in us merely to inspire us to struggle against it and to seek to rise above it, so we'll be fit to ascend to the truly human rank. If I'm not a man, I'm a beast."

Fuad hesitated a little. Then he observed calmly, "I think it's not all bad, for it motivates us to get married and have children."

Kamal's heart pounded violently without Fuad being aware of it. Was this what marriage was all about? He knew it was a fact but felt perplexed that people could reconcile love and marriage. It was a problem he did not confront with his love, because marriage had always seemed, for more than one reason, beyond his highest hopes. All the same, it was a problem requiring a solution. He could not imagine any felicitous link between himself and his beloved not based on her spiritual affection and on his ardent aspirations. It would resemble worship more than anything else. Indeed it would be worship on his part. What connection did marriage have to this?

"People who are really in love don't get married."

Fuad asked with astonishment, "What did you say?"

Even before Fuad's question, Kamal realized he had said something he did not intend to. For an awkward moment his confusion was apparent. He tried to remember Fuad's last words before this strange assertion had popped out. Although he had just heard them, it was with some effort that he recalled what Fuad had said about marriage and children. He decided to cover up his slip by adapting the meaning as best he could. So he said, "People who are really in love with ideals superior to life itself don't get married. That's what I meant to say."

Fuad smiled faintly—or perhaps he was trying not to laugh—but his eyes, like deep pools, betrayed none of his sentiments. He simply remarked, "These are serious matters. Talk about them now is premature. Everything in its own time."

Kamal shrugged his shoulders scornfully but confidently and said, "So let's postpone it and wait."

There was a mountain separating him from Fuad, but nonetheless they were friends. It was impossible to deny that the difference between them attracted him to Fuad, although it had repeatedly caused him anguish. Was it not time for him to go home? Solitude and communion with his soul called him. Thought of the diary slumbering in the drawer of his desk stirred the passions of his breast. A person exhausted from putting up with reality seeks relaxation deep inside himself.

"It's time to go home," he said.

7🙰

The carriage made its way along the banks of the Nile until it stopped in front of a houseboat at the end of the first triangle of streets on the road to Imbaba. Al-Sayyid Ahmad Abd al-Jawad descended at once, followed immediately by Mr. Ali Abd al-Rahim. Night had fallen, and darkness blanketed everything. The only exceptions were the widely spaced lights shining from the windows of the houseboats and other vessels lined up along either shore of the river channel downstream from the Zamalek Bridge, and the faint glow of the village at the end of the road, like a cloud reflecting the brilliance of the sun in a sky otherwise dark and heavily overcast.

Al-Sayyid Ahmad was visiting the houseboat for the first time, although Muhammad Iffat had leased it for the last four years, dedicating it to the romantic escapades and parties al-Sayyid Ahmad had denied himself since Fahmy was slain. Ali Abd al-Rahim went ahead to show him the gangplank. When he reached the stairs he warned his friend, "The stairway is narrow and the steps are steep with no railing. Put your paw on my shoulder and come down slowly."

They descended cautiously as the sound of water lapping against the riverbank and the prow of the boat caressed their ears. At the same time their noses were stung by the rank odors of nearby vegetation mixed with the scent of the slit that the floods at the beginning of September were lavishly depositing.

As Ali Abd al-Rahim felt for the doorbell by the entrance, he remarked, "This is a historic evening in your life and ours: the night the old master returns. Don't you think so?"

Tightening his grip on his friend's shoulder, al-Sayyid Ahmad replied, "But I'm no old master. The oldest master was your father."

Ali Abd al-Rahim laughed and said, "Now you'll see faces you haven't glimpsed for five years."

As though wavering, al-Sayyid Ahmad remarked, "This doesn't mean that I'm going to alter my conduct or deviate from my principles." Then after a moment of silence he continued: "Perhaps . . . maybe . . ."

"If you leave a dog in the kitchen with a piece of meat, can you imagine him promising not to touch it?"

"The real dog was your father, you son of a bitch."

Mr. Ali rang the doorbell. The door was opened almost immediately by an aged Nubian servant who stepped aside to allow them to enter and raised his hands to his head in welcome. Once inside they made for the door on the left, which opened on a small vestibule lit by an electric lamp hanging from the ceiling. The walls on either side were decorated with a mirror beneath which a large leather armchair and a small table were placed. At the far end of the room there was another door, which was ajar. Through it could be heard the voices of the guests, and al-Sayyid Ahmad was deeply moved. Ali Abd al-Rahim shoved the door wide open and entered. Al-Sayyid Ahmad followed and had scarcely crossed the threshold when he found himself confronted by his friends, who rose and came forward to greet him joyfully. Their delight was so great it virtually leapt from their faces.

The first to reach him was Muhammad Iffat, who embraced him as he quoted from a popular song: "The beauty of the full moon is shining upon us."

Ibrahim al-Far cited another song title when he hugged him: "Destiny has brought me what I've longed for."

The men then stepped back to let him see Jalila, Zubayda, and a third woman, who stood two steps behind the others. He soon remembered that she was Zanuba, the lute player. Oh ... his whole past had been assembled in a single setting. He beamed, although he appeared slightly embarrassed. Jalila gave a long laugh and opened her arms to embrace him as she chanted, "Where have you been hiding, my pretty one?"

When she released him, he saw that Zubayda was hesitating an arm's length away, although a happy light of welcome illuminated her face. He stretched his arm out to her and she squeezed it. At that same moment she arched her painted eyebrows reproachfully and, referring to yet another song, said in a tone not free of sarcasm, "After thirteen years ..."

He could not help but laugh wholeheartedly. Finally he noticed that Zanuba had not budged. She was smiling shyly, as though she thought their past acquaintance too slight for her to be forward. He held his hand out and shook hers. To encourage and flatter her he said, "Greetings to the princess of lute players."

As they returned to their seats, Muhammad Iffat put his arm around Ahmad's and made his friend sit beside him. He laughingly asked, "Did you just happen to drop by or has passion caught hold of you?"

"Passion caught hold of me, so I just happened to drop by."

At first he had been blinded by the warmth of the reunion and the jests of his friends when they welcomed him. Now his eyes could take in his surroundings. He found himself in a room of medium size with walls and ceilings painted emerald green. There were two windows facing the Nile and two on the street side of the boat. Although the windows were open, the shutters were closed. Hanging from the ceiling in the middle of the room was an electric lamp with a conical crystal shade, which focused the light on the surface of a low table holding the glasses and the whiskey bottles. The floor was covered with a carpet the same color as the walls. On each side of the room there was a large sofa divided in half by a cushion and covered with an embroidered cloth. The corners of the room were filled with pallets and pillows. Jalila, Zubayda, and Zanuba sat on the sofa farthest from the street, and three of the men on the one facing them. The pallets were strewn with musical instruments: lute, tambourine, drum, and finger cymbals. He took his time looking around. Then after sighing with satisfaction he said delightedly, "My God, my God, everything's so beautiful. But why don't you open the windows on the Nile?"

Muhammad Iffat replied, "They're opened once the sailboats stop passing. As the Prophet said, 'If you are tempted, conceal yourselves.' "

Al-Sayyid Ahmad quickly retorted with a smile, "And if you conceal yourselves, be tempted."

"Show us you're still as quick as you used to be," Jalila shouted as if challenging him.

He had intended his words to be nothing more than a joke. The truth was that he was anxious and hesitant about taking this revolutionary step and coming to the houseboat after the long period of self-denial he had observed. There was something more too. A change had taken place that he would have to unravel for himself. He would need to look closely and attentively. What did he see? There were Jalila and Zubayda, each of them as massively beautiful as the ceremonial camel when it set off for Mecca with the pilgrims. He had used that image to describe them in the old days. They had perhaps even added to their mass of fleshly charms, but something had come over them that was almost more easily perceived by his emotions than his senses. No doubt it was associated with the process of aging. Perhaps his friends had not noticed it since they had not been separated from the women as he had. Had he not been affected by age in much the same way? He felt sad, and his spirits flagged. A man's most telling mirror is a friend who returns after a long absence. But how could he pinpoint this change? Neither of the women had a single white hair, for no entertainer would ever allow her hair to turn white. And they had no wrinkles.

"Do you give up?" he asked himself. "Certainly not. Just look at those eyes. They reflect a spirit that's fading, no matter how they sparkle and flash. Fatigue disappears from sight momentarily behind a smile or a jest, but then its full truth is apparent. You can read in that look the obituary for their youth, a silent elegy. Isn't Zubayda in her fifties? And Jalila's several years older. She violently disputes that fact but will never be able to disprove it no matter how often she denies it."

There was a change in his heart too. He felt aversion and repulsion. It had not been that way when he arrived, for he had come in breathless pursuit of a phantom, which no longer existed. So be it. God forbid that he should willingly submit to defeat.... "Drink, let yourself be transported by the music, and laugh. No one will ever force you to do something you don't want."

Jalila said, "I didn't believe my eyes would ever see you again in this world."

He yielded to an overwhelming temptation to ask; "How do you find me?"

Zubayda intervened: "The same as ever. As big and strong as a camel. One white hair shows under your fez. Nothing more than that."

Jalila protested, "Let me answer, because he asked me." Then she told al-Sayyid Ahmad, "You look the way you always did. But there's nothing strange about that. We're all still youngsters."

Al-Sayyid Ahmad discerned her goal. Trying to seem serious and sincere, he replied, "You two have only increased in beauty and good looks. I wasn't expecting this much."

Examining him with interest, Zubayda inquired, "What has kept you away from us all this time?" She laughingly advised him, "If your intentions were at all good, you could have had an innocent rendezvous with us. Can't we ever meet unless there's a bed beneath us?"

Waving his arm in the air to toss back the sleeve of his caftan, Mr. Ibrahim al-Far retorted, "Neither he nor we know how to have an innocent rendezvous with you."

Zubayda grumbled, "I seek refuge with God from you men. All you want a woman for is sex."

Jalila laughed out loud and commented, "Mother's pet, you should thank your Lord for that. Could you have grown so splendidly fat if you had not been content to profit from sex?"

Zubayda told her critically, "Don't interfere with my interrogation of the accused."

With a smile al-Sayyid Ahmad said, "I was sentenced to five years of innocence without labor."

Zubayda pounced on him again and said mockingly, "Alas, poor boy! You deprived yourself of every pleasure, all of them, poor baby, so that the only ones to enjoy were food, drink, music, humor, and staying out till daybreak, night after night."

He answered apologetically, "These things are necessary for a grieving heart, but the other ones . . ."

Zubayda gestured toward him as though to say, "You're hopeless!" Then she remarked, "So, I've learned now that you consider us worse than all the other sins and transgressions put together. . . ."

As though remembering an important matter he had almost forgotten, Muhammad Iffat interrupted her by crying out, "Have we assembled from the ends of the earth just to talk? The glasses are staring down at us, but no one's paying any attention to them. Fill the glasses, Ali. Tune your instrument, Zanuba. And you, the accused gentleman, make yourself more comfortable. Do you think you're at school and can't remove any clothing? Take off your fez and cloak. Don't assume that your interrogation is over, but first all the court officials must get drunk. Then we can resume the interrogation. Jalila insisted that we shouldn't get intoxicated until 'the sultan of good times' arrived. At least that's what she said. This woman esteems you as highly as Satan does a chronic sinner. God's blessing on your relationship with her and hers with you."

Al-Sayyid Ahmad rose to slip out of his cloak, and Ali Abd al-Rahim went to serve as bartender, as usual. A few discordant whispers were emitted by the lute strings as they were being tested. Zubayda crooned gently. With her fingertips Jalila smoothed the strands of her hair and the neck of her dress where it fell between her breasts. Eyes watched Ali Abd al-Rahim's hands with longing as he filled the glasses. Al-Sayyid Ahmad sat down again with his legs tucked beneath him. His eyes wandered over the room and the people in it until they chanced to meet Zanuba's. A smiling look of recognition lit up their eyes. Ali Abd al-Rahim presented the first round of drinks. Then Muhammad Iffat said, "To good health and good love."

Jalila said, "To your return, Mr. Ahmad."

Zubayda said, "To right guidance when it follows error."

Al-Sayyid Ahmad said, "To those I love from whom I've been separated by grief."

They all drank. Al-Sayyid Ahmad raised his drink to his lips. Over the base of the glass he could see Zanuba's face. He was touched by its freshness.

Muhammad Iffat told Ali Abd al-Rahim, "Time for the second round."

Ibrahim al-Far added, "And the third should follow immediately so we can lay the groundwork properly."

As he set to work Ali Abd al-Rahim observed, "A group's servant is their master."

Ahmad Abd al-Jawad found himself watching Zanuba's fingers as she tuned the lute strings. He wondered how old she was, estimating that she was between twenty-five and thirty. He also asked himself why she was present. Had she only come to play the lute or was her Aunt Zubayda preparing to launch her in this profitable career?

Mr. Ibrahim al-Far said that just looking at the water of the Nile made him seasick, and Jalila shouted at him that he had made his mother sick in his day.

Ali Abd al-Rahim asked, "If a woman as big as Jalila or Zubayda were thrown into the water, would she sink or float?"

Al-Sayyid Ahmad answered that she would float, unless there was a hole in her. He wondered what would happen if he felt tempted by Zanuba and told himself that at present it would be a scandal, after five glasses it would be awkward, but after a whole bottle it would become a duty.

Muhammad Iffat proposed they drink to the health of the nationalist leaders Sa'd Zaghlul and Mustafa al-Nahhas, who would be traveling at the end of the month from Paris to London for negotiations. Ibrahim al-Far suggested that they drink a toast to the Labour Party leader Ramsay MacDonald, a friend of the Egyptians.

Ali Abd al-Rahim asked what MacDonald had meant by saying he could solve the Egyptian problem before he finished drinking the cup of coffee he had in front of him.

Ahmad Abd al-Jawad answered that he meant it took an Englishman, on average, half a century to drink a cup of coffee.

Al-Sayyid Ahmad remembered how alienated he had felt by the revolution after Fahmy had been slain and how he had gradually returned to his original pro-nationalist feelings because of the respect and esteem people showered on him as the father of a martyr. In time, he had found that Fahmy's tragedy had even become a source of pride.

Jalila raised her glass in the direction of al-Sayyid Ahmad as she said, "To your health, my camel. I've often asked myself whether you had really forgotten us. But God knows I understood and prayed God would grant you endurance and consolation. Don't be surprised, for I'm your sister and you've been a brother to me."

Muhammad Iffat asked mischievously, "If you're his sister and he's your brother, as you claim, then should you two have done what you used to?"

She emitted a laugh that reminded them of the old days, 1918 or before. She retorted, "Ask your maternal uncles about that, love child."

Glancing at Ahmad Abd al-Jawad slyly, Zubayda said, "I've thought of another reason for his long absence. . . ."

More than one person inquired what it was, while al-Sayyid Ahmad murmured pleadingly, "O God who veils our shortcomings, protect me."

"I suspect he's impotent like other men his age and has used his grief as a convenient excuse."

Shaking her head with all the affectation of a performer, Jalila protested, "He'll be the last to grow old."

Mr. Muhammad Iffat asked al-Sayyid Ahmad, "Which of these two opinions is right?"

Al-Sayyid Ahmad replied suggestively, "The first expresses fear and the second hope."

Jalila said with victorious relief, "You're not a man who disappoints a lady's hopes."

He thought about saying, "It's only when he's tested that a man is honored or despised," but was afraid he would be put to the test or that his statement would be understood as an invitation. Yet whenever he looked closely at them, he was overcome by a wish to hold back and to skip this opportunity. Before coming he would never have thought it possible. Yes, it was undeniable that a change had taken place. Yesterday was gone. Today was different. Zubayda was no longer the same, nor Jalila. There was nothing to justify the risk. He would be satisfied with the brotherly relationship Jalila had acclaimed and expand it to include Zubayda too. He said delicately, "How could a man grow senile when surrounded by such beautiful women?"

Looking at each of the men in succession, Zubayda asked, "Which of you is the oldest?"

Al-Sayyid Ahmad answered inaccurately but with apparent innocence, "I am. I was born just after Urabi's rebellion of 1882."

Muhammad Iffat protested, "Say anything but this. I've heard you were one of Urabi's soldiers."

Al-Sayyid Ahmad replied, "I was a soldier in their bellies, so to speak—just as people now call a child at home a pupil, even before he's started school."

Ali Abd al-Rahim pretended to be astonished and asked, "What was your late mother doing while you were inside a soldier going off to battle?"

After emptying her glass, Zubayda shouted, "Don't evade the question with your jokes. I'm asking you how old you are."

Ibrahim al-Far said challengingly, "Three of us are between fifty and fifty-five. Will you disclose your ages to us?"

Zubayda shrugged her shoulders scornfully and said, "I was born . . ."

She narrowed her kohl-enhanced eyes and looked up at the lamp as though trying to remember, but al-Sayyid Ahmad completed her statement before she could: "After the revolution of Sa'd Zaghlul Pasha in 1919."

They laughed for a long time until finally she waggled her middle finger at them. But it appeared that Jalila did not like the topic of conversation. She yelled, "Let's abandon this smear campaign. What difference does it make how old we are? Let the One who's in charge of the matter worry about it in His heavens. For us, a woman is young so long as she finds a man who desires her and one of you men is a boy so long as he can find a woman who wants him."

Suddenly Ali Abd al-Rahim shouted, "Congratulate me!"

When asked why, he shouted, "Because I'm drunk."

Ahmad Abd al-Jawad said that they ought to catch up before their friend was lost in the land of inebriation, whereas Jalila urged them to let him go on alone as punishment for his haste. Ali Abd al-Rahim retreated to a corner with a full glass in his hand, telling them, "Find another bartender."

Zubayda stood up to look for her wraps and check her handbag to make sure that her container of cocaine was still where she had left it. Ibrahim al-Far seized the opportunity provided by her absence to take the seat beside Jalila. He leaned his head on her shoulder, sighing audibly. Muhammad Iffat went to the windows overlooking the Nile channel and thrust the shutters aside. The surface of the water appeared to consist of a flowing pattern of darkness, except for still streaks of light traced on the undulating river by rays coming from the lamps of other boats where people were staying up late. Zanuba plucked the strings of her lute, and a rollicking tune sprang forth. Al-Sayyid Ahmad gazed in her direction for a long time. Then he rose to refill his glass. When Zubayda returned she sat down between Muhammad Iffat and Ahmad Abd al-Jawad, whose back she thumped.

Jalila's voice was raised in song: "One day you took a bite out of me. . . ."

Now it was Ibrahim al-Far's turn to shout, "Congratulate me!"

Muhammad Iffat and Zubayda started singing along with Jalila once she reached the words: "They brought me an antidote." When Zanuba joined the song, al-Sayyid Ahmad began looking at her again. Before he knew what was happening he was one of the singers too, and Ali Abd al-Rahim's voice lent its support from his corner.

His head still on Jalila's shoulder, Ibrahim al-Far called out, "Six performers and an audience of one: me."

Without stopping his singing al-Sayyid Ahmad told himself, "In the end, she'll comply with my wishes most willingly." Then he mused, "Is tonight to be a passing affair or the beginning of a lengthy relationship?"

Ibrahim al-Far rose unexpectedly and began dancing. The others all started to clap in unison. Then they sang together:

> So take me in your pocket,
> Between your belt and sash.

Al-Sayyid Ahmad wondered whether Zubayda would allow the tryst to take place in her house. When the song and dance were concluded, they vied with each other in trading jests and insults in rapid succession. Ahmad Abd al-Jawad began observing Zanuba's face stealthily whenever he came out with a joke, to judge its impact on her. The merry turmoil intensified, and minutes flew by.

"It's time for me to go," said Ali Abd al-Rahim as he rose to get the rest of his clothes.

Muhammad Iffat shouted at him angrily, "I told you to bring her with you, so the evening wouldn't be cut short."

Raising her eyebrows, Zubayda asked, "Who is this woman you're guarding so carefully?"

Ibrahim al-Far said, "A new girlfriend. A whale of a woman. The madam of an establishment in the Wajh al-Birka entertainment district. . . ."

Al-Sayyid Ahmad asked him with interest, "Who is she?"

Ali Abd al-Rahim answered laughingly as he drew his cloak tightly around him, "Your old friend Saniya al-Qulali."

Al-Sayyid Ahmad's blue eyes grew large and a dreamy look was visible in them. With a smile he said, "Remember me to her and convey my greetings to her."

As he twisted his mustache and prepared to depart, Ali Abd al-Rahim answered, "She asked about you and suggested I invite you to spend an evening at her house, after the time set aside for assignations. I told her, 'His eldest son, may the Prophet's name protect him, has reached an age at which it's considered a duty in their family to frequent Wajh al-Birka and other centers of depravity. Thus if his father came here, he would be in danger of bumping into his son.'"
He grinned from ear to ear, said goodbye, and exited to the vestibule.

Muhammad Iffat and Ahmad Abd al-Jawad followed to see him out. They kept on chatting and laughing together until Mr. Ali left the houseboat. Then Muhammad Iffat touched his friend's arm and asked, "Zubayda or Jalila?"

Al-Sayyid Ahmad answered simply, "Neither one."

"Why? May God spare us evil."

He replied as though convinced, "A step at a time. I'll be content to pass the remainder of this evening in drinking and listening to the lute."

Muhammad Iffat urged him to take another step but did not press him once al-Sayyid Ahmad excused himself. They returned to the disordered room and resumed their seats. Ibrahim al-Far became the bartender. Signs of intoxication were clearly apparent in their flaming eyes, flowing conversations, and animated gestures. Following Zubayda's lead, they sang together: "Why is the sea laughing? . . ."

It was remarked that Ahmad Abd al-Jawad's voice rose until it almost drowned out Zubayda's. Then Jalila narrated some snatches of her romantic adventures.

"Since my eyes fell on you," al-Sayyid Ahmad reflected, "I've had the feeling that tonight will not pass without an adventure. How pretty the young girl is. Young? Yes, since she's a quarter century younger than you."

Ibrahim al-Far lamented the passing of the copper trade's golden age, during the war. With a thick tongue he told them, "Back then you would kiss my hand to get a pound of copper."

Al-Sayyid Ahmad commented, "When you need something from a dog, call him 'mister.'"

Zubayda complained about how drunk she was and rose to try to walk it off, going back and forth. They began to clap to keep time with her staggering steps. They called out in unison the words used to encourage children to walk: "A step at a time. Cross over the doorstep.... A step at a time. Cross over the doorstep." Wine paralyzes the organ that registers sorrow.

Jalila murmured, "That's enough for now." She rose and left the room. She went down the hall to the two cabins, which were opposite each other. She made for the cabin on the Nile side and entered it. Soon they could hear the creaking of her bed as it received her enormous body. What Jalila had done appealed to Zubayda. She followed her lead and headed for the other cabin. The creaking that her bed emitted was even louder.

Ibrahim al-Far said, "The bed has spoken."

From the first cabin a voice made its way to them, singing in imitation of the husky quality of the renowned singer Munira al-Mahdiya: "Darling, come."

Muhammad Iffat got up and answered in song as well: "I'm coming."

Ibrahim al-Far looked questioningly at Ahmad Abd al-Jawad. Quoting a saying of the Prophet, al-Sayyid Ahmad told him, "Unless you're embarrassed, do whatever you want."

The man rose and replied, "There's no need for bashfulness on a houseboat."

The coast was clear. This was the moment for which he had been waiting so long. The young girl put the lute aside. She sat cross-legged with the end of her dress draped over her legs. They silently exchanged a glance. Then she stared off into space. The silence was so charged with electricity that it was unbearable. When she stood up suddenly, he asked, "Where are you going?"

Hurrying through the door, she replied, "The bathroom."

He stood up too and took a seat next to hers. Picking up the lute, he began to strum on it while he wondered whether there was a third cabin.

"Your heart shouldn't pound that way, as though the English soldier were herding you ahead of him in the dark like that night after you'd been with Maryam's mother. Do you remember? Don't dwell on that, for it's a painful memory. She's returning from the bathroom. How fresh she looks!"

"Do you play the lute?"

"Teach me," he answered with a smile.

"You should stick with the tambourine, for you're expert at that."

He sighed and said, "Those days have vanished. How delightful they were. You were just a child! Why don't you sit down."

"She's almost touching you," he noticed. "How sweet the beginning of the chase is."

"Take the lute and play something for me."

"We've had enough singing, performing, and laughing. Tonight I've understood more than ever before why they missed you so much."

He smiled in a pleased way and asked craftily, "But you haven't had enough to drink?"

She agreed and laughed. He sprang like a charger to the table to fetch a half-filled bottle and two glasses. As he sat down he said, "Let's drink together."

"The delightful glutton—her eyes shine with deviltry and magic. Ask her about the third room. . . . Ask yourself whether it's to be just for one night or an affair. Don't wonder about the consequences. Ahmad Abd al-Jawad, no matter how exalted his stature, opens his arms to the lute player Zanuba. She used to serve you platters of fruit. . . . But you have a right to be happy as a reward for your fresh beauty. Conceit has never been one of my failings."

He saw that her palm grasping the glass was near his knee. He reached his hand out to caress it. She silently drew it back to her lap without looking at him. He asked himself whether flirting was in order at this late hour, especially when the host was a man like himself and the guest a girl like her. But he did not abandon his amiable tenderness.

He asked her suggestively, "Is there a third bedroom on the houseboat?"

She gestured toward the vestibule. Ignoring his suggestion, she merely answered, "On the other side."

Smiling and twisting his mustache, he asked, "Wouldn't it be big enough for both of us?"

Politely but without flirtatiousness, she answered, "If you feel sleepy, you'll find it quite large enough for you."

As though astonished, he asked her, "What about you?"

In the same tone she said, "I'm comfortable just the way I am."

He inched closer to her, but she got up and placed her glass on the table. Then she went to the sofa opposite him. She sat there with a serious look of silent protest sketched on her face. The man was amazed at her attitude. His enthusiasm waned, and he felt that his pride was under attack. He looked at her with a forced smile and then asked, "Why are you angry?"

She kept silent for a long time, her only response being to fold her arms across her chest.

"I'm asking why you're angry."

She answered tersely, "Don't ask questions to which you already know the answer."

He guffawed abruptly to proclaim his disdain and disbelief. Then he rose, filled both glasses, and handed one to her, telling her, "Lighten your spirits."

She took the glass courteously but set it on the table. "Thank you," she murmured.

After retreating to his place he sat back down, raised his glass to his lips, and drained it in one gulp. Then he laughed uproariously.

"Could you have anticipated this surprise? If it were possible to backtrack a quarter of an hour ... Zanuba, Zanuba, just plain Zanuba ... can you believe it? Don't let yourself be flustered by the blow. Who knows? Perhaps this is the fashion in coquetry now in 1924, you provincial has-been. How have I changed? ... Not in any way. It's Zanuba. Isn't that her name? Clearly every man meets at least one woman who resists his advances. Since Zubayda, Jalila, and Maryam's mother are all wild about you, who is there but Zanuba, this dung beetle, to resist you? Endure it to overcome it. In any case the matter's not a catastrophe. Oh, look. See how pretty and firm her leg is. What a solid base she has. You don't think she's really rejected you, do you?"

"Have a drink, sweetheart."

In a voice both polite and determined she replied, "I will when I feel like it."

He fixed his eyes on her. Then he asked suggestively, "When do you think you'll feel like it?"

She frowned in a way that showed she understood his allusion but did not respond.

With a sinking feeling al-Sayyid Ahmad asked, "Doesn't my affection meet with any acceptance?"

Bowing her head to hide her face from his eyes, she begged him, "Won't you stop that?"

He was overcome by a surge of anger, which came in reaction to his sense of being rejected. In astonishment he asked her, "Why did you come here?"

Pointing to the lute lying on the sofa not far from him, she protested, "Because of this."

"Only? . . . There's no conflict between that and what I'm proposing."

Vexed, she asked him, "Against my will?"

Prey to the disquieting feelings of disappointment and annoyance, he said, "Of course not, but I don't see any reason for you to refuse."

She said coldly, "Perhaps I have some reasons."

He laughed loudly and dryly. Then, exasperated, he said sarcastically, "Maybe you're afraid of losing your virginity."

She glared at him for a long time and then said furiously and vengefully, "I only accept a man I love."

He would have laughed again but restrained himself. He was tired of these sad, mechanical laughs. He stretched his hand out to the bottle and impulsively poured himself half a glass. But he left it on the table. He began to look anxiously at the woman, not knowing how to extricate himself from the fix he had created himself.

"That viper and daughter of a viper only accepts a man she loves," he reflected. "Does that mean anything more than that she falls in love with a different man every night? It will be hard for you to save face after this disaster tonight. The gentlemen are inside, and you're at the mercy of this pampered musician. . . . Flay her with your tongue. . . . Kick her. . . . Shove her into the cabin against her will. . . . The best thing would be to turn your back on her and leave this place immediately. Our eyes have looks fierce enough to humble proud necks. . . . How charming hers is. Don't try to dispute her beauty. When a person loses his head, he will surely suffer."

"I didn't expect such harshness," he said.

He frowned and came to a decision. His face was scowling as he rose. Shrugging his shoulders disdainfully, he said, "I thought you would be gracious and charming like your aunt, but I was wrong. I have only myself to blame."

He heard the gentle smack of her lips as she cleared her throat in protest, but he went to get his cloak, which he put on rapidly. He was fully dressed in less than half the time he usually required to satisfy his taste for elegance. He had made his decision and was angry, but his despair was not yet total. Part of him still rebelliously refused to believe what had happened or at least found it easy to doubt. He picked up his walking stick but watched from one moment to the next for something to occur that would prove him wrong and satisfy the hopes of his wounded pride. She might suddenly laugh and thus slip back the veil of her bogus objection. She would rush to him, deploring his anger. She could leap in front of him to prevent him from leaving. When a woman cleared her throat in protest like that it was frequently a maneuver to be followed by her surrender. But none of these possibilities came to pass.

She remained sitting there, staring off into space, ignoring him as though she did not see him. So he quit the room for the vestibule and went from there to the entrance and on to the road, sighing with regret, sorrow, and rage. The fresh autumn air gently flowing through his garments, he walked along the dark road until he reached the Zamalek Bridge. There he got in a taxi and sped away. His intoxication and brooding thoughts made him oblivious to the world around him. When he began to pay attention he was already in Opera Square. As the vehicle circled around it on the way to al-Ataba al-Khadra Square, by the light of the lamps he chanced to see the wall of the Ezbekiya Garden. He fixed his eyes on it until a turn hid it from view. Then he closed his eyes, for he felt a stinging pain deep within his breast. He was conscious of a voice like a moan inside him, crying out in his silent world. It was praying God's mercy for his darling lost son. He did not dare express the prayer with his tongue, lest God's name be mentioned by one soaked in wine.

When he opened his eyes again, two large tears flowed down.

8 ❧

He did not know if what had gotten hold of him was a devil to be pelted with stones or a noxious disease. He had gone to sleep hoping the evening's foolishness, which he attributed to his inebriation, was finished. There was no question that drinking caused foolish behavior capable of spoiling pleasures and upsetting delights. When the morning light found him, he was tossing about restlessly in bed. The spray of the shower on his naked body dispelled thought from his mind and made his heart pound. He could see her face before his eyes. The whisper of her lips resounded in his ears, and the vibration of pain returned to his heart.

"You dwell on your romantic fantasies like an adolescent. People around you on the street greet you respectfully, saluting your dignity, piety, and neighborliness. If they only knew that you return their greetings mechanically while you dream of a girl who is an entertainer, a lute player, a woman who offers her body's favors for sale every night ... if they only realized this, they would surely treat you to a scornful and pitying smile instead of a greeting. Once the viper says yes, I'll drop her with disdain and relief. What's come over me? What do I want? Are you getting senile? Do you remember the ravages time has visited on Jalila and Zubayda? That foul havoc was discovered by your heart, not discerned by your senses. But not so fast. Beware of being taken in by your imagination, for it will feed you like a tasty morsel to destruction. . . . It's all a question of that one white hair. What other reason could a lowly lute player have had for scorning you? Spit her out like a fly that slips into your mouth when you're yawning. Alas, you know you won't spit her out, if only because of a desire for revenge. I need to regain my respect, that's all. The girl must say yes. Then you can abandon her with no regrets. She hasn't enough attractions to merit the struggle. Do you remember her legs, her neck, and the carnal look in her eyes? If you had treated your pride with a spoonful of patience, you would have won enjoyment and delight that very evening. What cause is there for all this anguish? I'm in pain. Yes, I'm suffering. I'm oppressed by the humiliation I've encountered. I threaten to scorn her, but when I think of her, my body blazes with desire. Have some shame. Don't make yourself a laughingstock. I ask you to swear by your children, those who remain and the one departed. Your first wife, Haniya, was the only woman to leave you. You chased after her, and what did you gain from that? Don't you remember?

"The brawlers in the wedding procession dance, get drunk, assault people, and rove around. Then they apply their sticks liberally to the lamps, bouquets of roses, oboes, and guests, till shrieks drown out the trills of joy. That's the kind of man you should be. Be the brawler of the houseboat, and slay your enemies with indifference and neglect. How weak your enemies are, yet how powerful. . . . A yielding leg scarcely able to walk can crush immovable mountains. How atrocious September is, if it's hot, because of the humidity. How charming the evenings are, especially on a houseboat. Comfort follows distress.

"Think about your position and consider which way to go. What's fated to happen will become manifest. To advance is bitter and to withdraw terrifying. You used to see her all the time when she was a fresh young thing. She awakened nothing in you then. You passed by her as though she did not exist. What new development has there been to cause you to shun the ones you loved and love the one you shunned? She's no more beautiful than Zubayda or Jalila. If her looks provided her aunt with any competition, she would not let the girl accompany her. Yet you desire her with all your might. Oh! What's the use of being haughty? 'I only accept a man I love.' May you have a lizard for a lover, you bitch.

"Your pain's so great it's almost stifling. No one demeans a man as successfully as he does himself. . . . Will you go to the houseboat? That's not the most scandalous thing you could do. What about her house? Zubayda will be there: 'Welcome, do come in. Have you finally returned to your lair?'

"How should I answer her? 'I haven't returned to you. I want your niece.' What nonsense! Enough of this prattle. . . . Have you lost your mind? Enlist the support of al-Far or Muhammad Iffat. Al-Sayyid Ahmad Abd al-Jawad seeks a go-between for . . . Zanuba! Wouldn't it be better for you to leech this contaminated blood that's drawing you down to disgrace?"

Night had fallen on al-Ghuriya and the doors of its shops were locked when Ahmad Abd al-Jawad walked back toward his store, which was already closed. His steps were slow and his eyes searched the street and the windows. Two windows at Zubayda's house were lit up, but he could not know what was going on behind them. He walked some distance before retracing his steps. Then he continued on to Muhammad Iffat's residence in al-Gamaliya, where the four friends met each evening before heading off to their party together.

Addressing Muhammad Iffat, al-Sayyid Ahmad remarked, "How delightful nights are on the houseboat. My heart is yearning for it."

Muhammad Iffat laughed triumphantly and said, "It's yours for the asking anytime you want."

Ali Abd al-Rahim added, "You're really longing for Zubayda, you pimp."

Al-Sayyid Ahmad shot back earnestly, "Certainly not."

"Jalila?"

"The houseboat. Nothing else."

Muhammad Iffat asked him craftily, "Would you like it to be an evening limited to us men or should we invite our girlfriends from the old days?"

Al-Sayyid Ahmad laughed to admit his rout. Then he said, "Invite the ladies, you crafty son of a bitch. Let it be tomorrow, for it's getting late now. But I won't do anything more than enjoy the company and the fellowship."

"Ahem," said Ibrahim al-Far.

Quoting the words of a favorite song, Ali Abd al-Rahim recited, "I'm an accomplice against myself."

Muhammad Iffat said sarcastically, "Call it whatever you like. There are many names for it, but they all refer to the same act."

The next day he seemed to be discovering the coffeehouse of al-Sayyid Ali for the first time. He felt drawn there late in the afternoon and took a seat on the bench under the little window. When the owner came over to welcome al-Sayyid Ahmad, as though to justify this first visit to the establishment he told the man, "I was returning from some errands and experienced an urge for some of your refreshing tea."

"It appears that it will be anything but easy to repeat this visit. . . . Slowly, not so fast! Do you want to disgrace yourself in front of everyone? What's the use of this anyway? Would you truly like her to see you through the shutters so she can make fun of your downfall? You don't realize what you're doing to yourself. No matter how much you exhaust your eyes and dizzy your brain, she'll never show herself to you. What's even more upsetting is that she's watching you with amusement from the window. Why did you come? You want to feast your eyes on her. Confess. You wish to survey her supple body, see her smile and wink, and watch her hennaed fingers. What's the point of all this? Nothing comparable has ever happened to you before, not even with women superior to her in beauty, splendor, and renown. Have you been condemned to suffering and humiliation for the sake of such a worthless item? She'll never reveal herself, no matter how much you stare. You've attracted attention to yourself ... al-Sayyid Ahmad Abd al-Jawad at the coffeehouse of al-Sayyid Ali, peeping out through a little window. How you have fallen! Do you think she hasn't divulged your secret? Perhaps all the members of the troupe have heard it. Possibly Zubayda herself is aware of it. Maybe everyone knows.

" 'He held out his hand adorned with its diamond ring, but I brushed him aside. When he pleaded with me, I resolutely rejected this Mr. Ahmad Abd al-Jawad whom you praise so highly.'

"How you have fallen. The most apalling ignominy into which you can slip—no, which you insist on sliding into, since you realize better than anyone else the humiliation and disgrace your shameful act will bring—will be for your friends as well as Zubayda and Jalila to learn your secret. So what are you doing? It's a fact that you're skillful at masking your distress behind a joke, but once the waves of boisterous laughter roll away, the bitter reality will be revealed. This is painful, but what's most troubling is that you want her. Don't try to deceive yourself. You want her so badly you could die.

"What do I see?" he asked himself, looking at a wagon that stopped in front of the performer's home. The door opened without delay, and Ayusha the tambourine player came out, dragging behind her Abduh, who played the zitherlike qanun in their ensemble. The others followed. He realized they were going to a wedding. While he watched the door with an eagerness both mournful and passionate, he was painfully aware of the pounding of his heart. He recklessly stretched his head up, ignoring the people around him. Laughter rang out from the house. Then the lute in its rose-colored case appeared moments before its owner burst from the house in a gale of laughter. She placed the lute at the front of the wagon and climbed up with the help of Ayusha. She sat in the middle, so that all he could see of her was a shoulder visible in a gap between Ayusha and blind Abduh.

Al-Sayyid Ahmad clenched his teeth from both longing and annoyance. He followed the wagon with his eyes as, swaying back and forth, it set off down the street. The sight left a profound feeling of despair and humiliation in his breast. He asked himself whether he should get up and pursue them but did not move a muscle. He did nothing more than tell himself, "Coming here was crazy and stupid."

On the appointed evening he went to the houseboat in Imbaba. He had not been able to decide what to do, although he had mulled the matter over at length. He finally resolved to try to deal with his problems by exploiting the circumstances and opportunities that presented themselves. It was enough for him to be sure of seeing her, at first in the company of the others and then alone at the end of the evening. He would be able to size up the situation again and renew his advances, this time calling into play every form of enticement. He entered the boat somewhat timidly and in a condition that would have aroused his laughter and sarcasm had he observed it in someone else and understood the reasons for it.

He found his comrades there with Jalila and Zubayda but saw no trace of the lute player. He was welcomed warmly and had scarcely removed his cloak and fez to sit down when cheerful laughter rang out around him. Because he was habituated to it, he was able to blend into that happy atmosphere. He conversed, jested, and flirted, while combating his anxiety and setting aside his concerns. Yet his fears— like a pain that disappears temporarily when treated with an anesthetic—lay concealed beneath the mirthful current and did not dissipate. He kept hoping that a door would open and she would appear or that one of them would say something to explain her absence or to predict her speedy arrival. As the minutes dragged by wearily, his hopes faded, enthusiasm waned, and serene expectations became clouded.

"Which do you suppose was the chance occurrence: her presence the day before yesterday or her absence today? I won't ask anyone. The evidence suggests that your secret has been safely kept. If Zubayda knew, she wouldn't hesitate to make a disgraceful scandal out of it."

He laughed a lot and drank even more. He asked Zubayda to sing "My mouth laughs, but my heart of hearts weeps." Once he almost closeted himself with Muhammad Iffat to reveal what he sought. Another time he was on the verge of testing the reaction of Zubayda herself but restrained himself and escaped from that crisis with his secret and honor intact.

When Ali Abd al-Rahim rose at midnight to go to his girlfriend's establishment in Wajh al-Birka, he also got up, to everyone's surprise, to return home. They tried in vain to dissuade him or to get him to stay just one more hour. He departed, leaving behind him astonished and disappointed friends, whose hopes, aroused by his arrival at the designated time, had not been realized.

That Friday he set off for the mosque of al-Husayn shortly before the time for communal prayer. As he was walking down Khan Ja'far Street he saw her proceed from Watawit Alley to the street running by the mosque. Oh! . . . his heart had never pounded that way before. That was followed immediately by the total paralysis of all his psychic faculties. In a daze, he imagined incorrectly that he had stopped walking and that the world around him was silent as a tomb. He resembled an automobile that, although vibrationless, continues to move because of its momentum after its engine has been turned off and its roar silenced. When he came to his senses, he discovered that she had gotten far ahead of him. Without any deliberation or consideration he followed after her at once. He passed by the mosque without turning in. Staying some distance back, he pursued her to New Street. What did he hope for? He did not know. He was acting blindly and impulsively. Never before had he followed a woman on the street, not even when he was young. He began to feel anxious and wary. Then an idea both ironic and alarming caught him off guard. What if Yasin or Kamal should discover the secret of this surreptitious pursuit?

He took care to keep the distance between them as great as ever. His eyes feasted ravenously on her charming body while he was overcome by successive waves of passion and pain. Then he saw her leave the street to enter a goldsmith's shop belonging to an acquaintance of his named Ya'qub. He slowed his steps to allow time to plan. His feelings of anxiety and wariness increased. Should he not go back the way he had come? Should he walk past the store without paying any attention to her? Should he look inside and see what would happen?

He gradually drew closer to the store, and only a few paces remained when a daring thought occurred to him. Without any hesitation he quickly put it into action, ignoring the seriousness of its possible consequences. He would leave the flow of pedestrian traffic on the street to mount the sidewalk, where he would saunter past the store, anticipating that the owner would see him and, as usual, invite him in. Then he would accept the invitation. He proceeded according to this plan until he reached the store. Then he glanced inside as though by accident. His eyes met those of Ya'qub, who immediately called out to him, "Welcome to al-Sayyid Ahmad. Please come in."

Al-Sayyid Ahmad smiled amiably and made his way inside, where the two men shook hands warmly. The proprietor invited him to have a glass of carob sherbet, which he graciously accepted. He took a seat at the end of a leather sofa in front of the table on which the scales were placed, giving no indication of being aware of the presence of a third person in the store until he sat down. Then he saw Zanuba. She was standing opposite the proprietor and turning an earring around in her hands. He pretended to be astonished, and their eyes met. Since she smiled, he did so too. Then he placed his hand on his breast in greeting and said, "Good morning. How are you?"

Looking back at the earring, she said, "Fine, may our Lord be good to you."

Mr. Ya'qub was proposing to trade her the earrings for a bracelet, with the balance in cash, but they disagreed about the amount. Al-Sayyid Ahmad seized the opportunity provided by her involvement in the negotiations to feast his eyes on her cheek. It did not escape his attention that their haggling offered him a chance to intervene on her behalf. Perhaps, maybe . . . But not knowing what he had in mind, she spoiled his plan by returning the earring to the goldsmith and announcing that she had decided definitively against the exchange. She asked him to repair the bracelet instead. Then she said goodbye to him, nodded at al-Sayyid Ahmad, and left the shop. She accomplished all this more rapidly than he thought necessary. He was taken aback and upset. Listless embarrassment gained control of him. He tarried there with the proprietor, exchanging the usual pleasantries until he had drunk his glass of carob sherbet. Then he asked leave of the man and departed.

With profuse shame he remembered the communal prayer service he had almost missed. He was hesitant about going to the mosque, for he lacked the courage to proceed directly there following his pursuit of a woman during the time set aside for prayer. Had not his frolic terminated the requisite state of ritual cleanliness? Did it not render him unfit to stand before his Compassionate Lord? In pain he sadly gave up the idea of going to prayers and walked the streets aimlessly for about an hour. Then he returned home, reflecting once more on his sin. But even in those sensitive moments filled with regret, his mind never closed the door on Zanuba.

That evening he called on Muhammad Iffat early, before the other friends arrived, so that he could speak to him in private. He told his friend, "I have a favor to ask of you. Tomorrow evening invite Zubayda to the houseboat."

Muhammad Iffat laughed and said, "If you want her, why all this beating around the bush? If you had asked for her the first night, she would have opened her arms to you in the warmest possible welcome."

With some embarrassment al-Sayyid Ahmad replied, "I want you to invite just her."

"Only? What a selfish man you are, thinking of no one but yourself. What about al-Far and me? Why not make it a night to remember forever. We'll invite Zubayda, Jalila, and Zanuba too."

With apparent distaste Ahmad Abd al-Jawad asked, "Zanuba?"

"Why not? As a reserve to be tapped in case of need, she's perfectly adequate."

"How much it hurts me to hear that," al-Sayyid Ahmad said to himself. "So how could she, that chip off the old block, reject me and why?"

"Haven't you discerned my aim yet?" he asked his friend. "The fact is that I don't intend to come tomorrow night."

Surprised, Muhammad Iffat exclaimed, "You ask me to invite Zubayda! You say you won't come! What are these riddles?"

Al-Sayyid Ahmad laughed loudly to conceal his confusion. Then he felt forced to say almost desperately, "Don't be a mule. I asked you to invite just Zubayda so Zanuba would be left alone in the house."

"Zanuba, you son of a gun."

After laughing long and hard he asked, "Why all this trouble? Why didn't you ask for her that first night on the houseboat? If you had moved a finger, she would have flown over and stuck to you like glue."

Despite his painful resentment, he smiled inanely. Then he said, "Carry out my instructions. That's all I want."

Twisting his mustache, Muhammad Iffat appropriated a phrase about idolatry from the Qur'an: "Feeble are the one who seeks and the one sought" (22:73).

With extreme earnestness Ahmad Abd al-Jawad requested, "Let this be a secret between us."

9 ❧

The street was empty and pitch black when he knocked on the door at about nine o'clock. It opened after a while, but the person inside remained hidden. Then a voice that made his heart tremble asked, "Who is it?"

He replied calmly, "Me."

Entering without being invited, he closed the door behind him and found himself face to face with her. She stood on the bottom step, holding out her hand with the lamp, and gave him a surprised look before muttering, "You!"

He stood there silently for a time, and his faint smile revealed his apprehension and anxiety. Encountering no objection or anger on her part, he felt courageous enough to ask, "Is this how you welcome an old friend?"

She turned away and started back up the stairs saying, "Come in."

He followed her quietly, concluding from her having opened the door herself that she was alone and that the position of the maid Jaljal, who had died two years before, remained vacant. He accompanied her to the vestibule, where she hung the lamp on a nail near the door. She went on alone into the reception room, where she lit the large lamp hanging from the ceiling. This served to confirm his hunch. She came back out, gestured to him to enter, and vanished.

Proceeding into the room, he took a seat on the middle sofa, where he had been accustomed to sit in the old days. Removing his fez, he placed it on the pillow that divided the seat in half. He stretched his leg out as he cast a questioning look at his surroundings. He remembered the place as though he had only left it a day or two before. There were the three sofas, the armchairs, the Persian carpet, the three tables inlaid with mother-of-pearl. . . . Things were much as they had been. Could he remember the last time he had sat there? His memories about the music room and the bedroom were clearer and firmer, but he could not forget the first meeting he had had with Zubayda in this room, in exactly this spot. He could recall everything that had transpired. Back then no one had been more sure of himself and relaxed than he was. When would she return? What impact had his visit made on her? How overbearing would her conceit be? Had she realized that he had come because of her and not her aunt?

"If you fail this time, you can kiss the whole affair goodbye."

He heard the muffled tread of slippers. Then Zanuba appeared at the door in a white dress decorated with red roses. She wore a spangled sash and was bareheaded, and her hair was arranged in two thick braids that hung down her back. He greeted her ... erect, smiling, and optimistic because of the care she had taken to adorn herself. She acknowledged his presence with a smile and motioned for him to sit down. She took a place on the sofa halfway down the wall on his right, as she said with mild astonishment, "Welcome. What a surprise!"

Al-Sayyid Ahmad smiled and asked, "What kind of surprise, I wonder?"

Raising her eyebrows enigmatically, with no hint as to whether she was in earnest or in jest, she replied, "Pleasant, of course."

"Since we've allowed our feet to carry us here," he reflected, "we must put up with whatever style of flirtation she chooses, whether delicate or heavy-handed."

He scrutinized her body and face calmly, as though to isolate in them the features that had tormented him and played havoc with his dignity.

They were both silent until she turned to look at him. Although she said nothing, the motion of her head suggested a polite inquiry, as if saying, "We're at your service."

Al-Sayyid Ahmad asked her slyly, "Will we have to wait long for the sultana? Hasn't she finished dressing yet?"

She gave him a strange look, narrowed her eyes, and then said, "The sultana's not at home."

Pretending to be amazed, he inquired, "Where do you suppose she is?"

Shaking her head and smiling mysteriously, she answered, "Your guess is as good as mine."

He thought about her reply a little and then said, "I would have supposed she kept you informed of her whereabouts."

She waved her hand modestly and said, "You think too highly of us." Then, laughing, she continued: "The time of military rule is over. If you want, you're in a much better position to keep abreast of her activities than I am."

"Me?"

"Why not? Aren't you an old friend of hers?"

Treating her to a deep, eloquent, smiling look, he said, "An old friend and a stranger are much the same. I wonder if your former friends keep up with you?"

She raised her right shoulder and made a face, proclaiming, "I have no friends, neither old nor new."

He started toying with one end of his mustache and responded, "Talk like that would only fool a person totally lacking in sense. A man with any wits about him could not imagine men seeing you and not rushing to become your friends."

"That's what gracious men like you might imagine, but that's all it is—figments of your imagination. You provide the evidence that I'm right. Although you're an old friend of this house, were you ever moved to provide me with a share of that friendship?"

He frowned in confusion. After some hesitation he said, "At that time I was . . . I mean, there were circumstances . . ."

She snapped her fingers and said sarcastically, "Perhaps it was those same circumstances, alas, that have kept the others away from me too."

In a quick, theatrical gesture he reared back against the sofa. Then he looked down his large nose at her, shaking his head as though asking God to rescue him. Finally he commented, "You're a puzzle. I hereby confess that I'm helpless before you."

She hid the smile his praise had inspired and pretended to be astonished as she said, "I absolutely do not understand what you mean. It's clear that we're mountains apart. The important thing is that you said you came to see my aunt. Is there any message I can give her when she returns?"

Al-Sayyid Ahmad laughed briefly. Then he replied, "Tell her, 'Ahmad Abd al-Jawad came to complain about me and didn't find you in.'"

"To complain about me? What have I done?"

"Tell her that I came to gripe about the harsh treatment you meted out to me. It's not becoming to a beautiful woman."

"What a perfect remark for a man who makes everything grist for his jokes and banter. . . ."

He sat up straight and said earnestly, "God forbid that I should make you the subject of my jokes or banter. I'm serious about my complaint. I think you understand the allusion perfectly well, but are flirting the way beautiful women do. They have every right to flirt, but they also have a duty to show mercy."

She pursed her lips and said, "Amazing!"

"It's not amazing at all. Do you remember what happened yesterday in the shop of Ya'qub the goldsmith? Was this stiff reception all that a person merits who is as proud of your friendship as I am and who has known you for as long? I wish, for example, that you had appealed to me to assist you in your negotiations with the goldsmith. I would have liked for you to give me a chance to put my expertise to work for you or for you to go even one step further and leave the whole matter to me, as though the bracelet were mine or its owner my good friend...."

She smiled and raised her eyebrows in confusion. Then she said tersely, "Thanks."

He breathed in deeply, filling his wide chest. "A man like me is not satisfied with thanks," he said eagerly. "What good does it do a hungry man you turn away to tell him, 'May God provide'? A hungry man wants something to eat, food that's tasty and appealing."

She folded her arms across her breast and pretended to be astonished. Mockingly she asked, "Are you hungry, my master, sir? We have mallow greens and rabbit that will melt in your mouth."

He laughed loudly and said, "Fine! It's a deal. Mallow greens and rabbit supplemented by a glass of whiskey ... then we'll amuse ourselves with some lute music and dancing and stretch out together for an hour while we digest the food."

She waved her hand at him as though to tell him to back off. Then she said, "My God! If we don't speak up, he'll try to bring in his donkey too. Keep your distance."

He folded the fingers of his right hand into a fist, which looked like a tightly puckered mouth. He began to raise and lower it deliberately, as he said oratorically, "Girl, don't waste precious time in talk."

Shaking her head, she replied proudly and flirtatiously, "You should say rather, 'Don't waste valuable time with middle-aged men.'"

Al-Sayyid Ahmad rubbed his broad chest with the palm of his hand in a gesture of friendly challenge. She shook her shoulders laughingly and said, "Even if ..."

"'Even if'? What a baby you are! I won't rest easy till I teach you what you need to learn. Fetch the mallow greens, rabbit, whiskey, lute, and the sash for your dance outfit. Come on. Let's go!"

Bending the index finger of her left hand, she placed it by her left eyebrow as she wiggled the other one. She inquired, "Aren't you afraid the sultana will take us by surprise?"

"Never fear. The sultana won't return tonight."

She gave him a sharp, suspicious look and asked, "How do you know?"

He realized that he had said more than he should have and for a time almost fell prey to confusion. He rescued himself by saying adroitly, "The sultana would not stay out this late except for an emergency requiring her to stay over till morning."

She gazed at his face for a long time without speaking. Then she shook her head in a clearly ironic way and said with complete assurance, "How cunning middle-aged men are! Everything about them grows weaker except their guile. Do you think I'm a fool? Certainly not, by your life! I know the whole story."

He began playing uneasily with one end of his mustache again. He asked her, "What do you know?"

"Everything!"

She paused a little to increase his discomfort. Finally she continued: "Do you remember the day you sat in the coffeehouse of al-Sayyid Ali and peeked through the window? At that time your eye stared so intensely at the wall of our house that you dug a hole in it. When I got in the wagon with the other members of the troupe I asked myself, 'Do you suppose he'll follow along behind us yelling like a kid?' But you were craftier and waited for a better opportunity."

The man bellowed with laughter until his face grew even redder. Then, announcing his surrender, he said, "God, forgive us."

"But you forgot to be wise yesterday when you saw me at Khan Ja'far. You followed me and even entered Ya'qub's store after I did."

"Were you aware of that too, you niece of Zubayda?"

"Yes, prince of lovers, although I never imagined you would enter the store while I was inside. Before I knew what was happening there you were sitting on the sofa, even more daring than a lustful jinni. When you pretended to be astonished to see me, I almost let you have it with my tongue, but the circumstances forced me to be polite."

Striking his hands together, he laughingly asked, "Didn't I say you're a puzzle?"

She went on speaking, intoxicated by victory and delight: "And one night what do I know but the sultana tells me, 'Get ready, we're going to Muhammad Iffat's houseboat.' So I proceed to get ready. But afterwards I hear her say, 'It's al-Sayyid Ahmad who suggested the party.' So I smell a rat and tell myself, 'Al-Sayyid Ahmad doesn't suggest something merely out of the goodness of his heart.' I understand the trick and stay home, pretending to have a headache."

"How unfortunate I am! I have fallen into the clutches of a merciless person. Is there anything else?"

"Not much more . . . just the invitation for this evening, an invitation solely for the sultana."

"You couldn't have done any better if you were an experienced fortune-teller."

"How sweet your words are! Ape the preachers, you sinner."

"May God forgive you!" He laughed out loud and with gentle delight observed, "You understood what was up this time as well, but you stayed in. You didn't leave the house or hide yourself. . . ."

Before finishing his sentence he rose, went to her, and sat down beside her. He took the edge of her spangled sash and kissed it, saying, "My God, I testify that this beautiful creature is more delightful than the tunes of her lute. Her tongue's a whip, her love's an inferno, and her lover's a martyr. Tonight will have an importance for all of history."

She pushed him away and remarked, "Don't try to take me in with your chatter. Away! Go back to your place."

"From now on nothing will ever separate us."

She abruptly jerked her sash out of his hand and rose to step aside. Standing an arm's length away, she gazed at him curiously and silently, as though to reconsider some important matters. Then she said, "Why don't you ask what made me refrain from going to the houseboat the day Muhammad Iffat invited us, at your suggestion?"

"In order to stoke the flames of passion."

She gave three short laughs in succession and then was silent for a long time. Finally she said, "Not a bad idea, but a bit passé. Isn't that so, prince of sinners? The truth will remain a secret until I decide to reveal it in my own good time."

"I'll offer my life in exchange for it."

For the first time she smiled with genuine pleasure. Following her ironic glances, there was now a tender look in her eyes, like the calm after a storm. Her appearance proclaimed that a new strategy was being unveiled along with a new idea. Drawing a step closer to him, she gracefully stretched her hand out to his mustache, which she began to twist carefully. In a tone he had not heard her use before she said, "If you offer your life in exchange for this, what will be left for me?"

He felt the kind of deep repose he had not experienced since that unsuccessful night in the houseboat. It was as though he was winning a woman for the first time. He removed her hands from his mustache and held them between his large palms. Affectionately and gratefully he said, "I'm more delirious than words can say, mistress of all creation. May you be mine forever and ever. Death to anyone who refuses you anything you hope or ask for. Complete your benefactions to me and prepare our party. Tonight is unlike any other one. It deserves to be celebrated until dawn."

Stroking the palms of his hands with her fingers, she said, "Tonight really is unlike any other, but you'll have to be satisfied with just a little."

"A little! Is there to be a rebuff after all this tenderness? I can't wait patiently for you any longer."

He began to caress her hands. He unfolded her palms and admired the rose color of the henna with which they were decorated. She unexpectedly asked him in a laughing voice, "Do you read palms, old man?"

He smiled and said jokingly, "I'm renowned for my predictions. Would you like me to read your palm for you?"

She nodded in agreement, and he began to ponder her right hand, pretending to think deeply. With great interest he remarked, "I see a man who will be of great significance to you."

Laughing, she asked, "In a licit way, do you suppose?"

He raised his eyebrows as he continued to scrutinize her palm. Without even the slightest indication that he was not totally in earnest he replied, "No, illicitly!"

"I take refuge with God! How old is he?"

Not raising his head but looking up at her, he said, "That's not clear, but judged by his abilities, I'd say he's in the prime of youth."

She said slyly, "I wonder if he's generous."

"Oh!" he reflected. "It wasn't your generosity that pled your case with them in the old days."

"His heart's unfamiliar with stinginess."

She thought a little and then asked, "Would he be happy for me to stay on as a flunky in this house?"

"The calf is down," he told himself. "Go fetch the knives."

"No. He'll make you a lady without a peer."

"I wonder where I'll be living, under his wing."

"Not even Zubayda," he warned himself, "made you do this. There'll be no end of talk about you."

"In a beautiful apartment."

"An apartment!"

He was amazed by her tone of disapproval. Astonished, he asked her, "Wouldn't you like that?"

Pointing to her palm, she asked, "Don't you see flowing water there? Look carefully."

"Flowing water! Do you want to live in a bathhouse?"

"Don't you see the Nile? A houseboat or a sailboat?"

"Four or five pounds a month all in one blow, not to mention the other expenses. Oh," he reflected, "it doesn't pay to fall in love with lowlife."

"Why choose such an isolated place?"

She came so close to him that their knees were touching and said, "Your rank is not inferior to Muhammad Iffat's. And if you love me as much as you claim, then my luck should not be inferior to the sultana's. You would be able to pass your evenings there with your friends. That's my dream. Make it come true."

He put his arms around her waist and stood there, silently enjoying the softness and reassurance of her touch. Then he told her, "Whatever you want is yours, light of my life."

To thank him she placed her hands on his cheeks. Then she said, "Don't think you're going to give and get nothing in return. Always remember that it's for your sake that I'm leaving this house where I've spent my whole life. I won't be able to return. And remember that if I ask you to make me a lady, it's only because it's not appropriate for your mistress to be anything less than that."

His arms squeezed her waist toward him until her breast was pressed against his face. Then he said, "I understand perfectly, light of my eyes. You'll have everything you want and more. I want to see you the way you want to be. Now, prepare our celebration for us. I would like my life to begin with this night."

She grasped his arms. Smiling apologetically, she said gently, "When we're in our houseboat on the Nile."

He cautioned her, "Don't drive me crazy. Can you withstand my assault?"

She stepped back and said in a tone between entreaty and ultimatum, "Not in this house where I've worked as a servant. Wait till we're united in the new home, yours and mine. Then I'll be yours forever. Not before then.... I ask it for the sake of our new life together."

10

"Good news, God willing," Ahmad Abd al-Jawad repeated to himself when he saw Yasin coming into his store. This visit was unusual and unexpected, reminding him of the time Yasin had come to discuss the intention of his mother, since deceased, to marry for the fourth time. Al-Sayyid Ahmad was sure his son had not called merely to say hello, pass the time of day, or chat about some routine matter he could bring up at home. No, Yasin would not visit him at the store unless the issue was serious.

After shaking hands with his son he invited him to have a seat and said "Good news, God willing."

Yasin sat down near his father, who was behind the desk. The young man turned his back on the rest of the shop, including Jamil al-Hamzawi, who stood by the scales weighing a customer's goods. The young man looked at his father uneasily, confirming al-Sayyid Ahmad's suspicions. The proprietor closed the ledger in which he had been recording some figures and sat up straight in preparation for what was to come. The half-open safe was visible to his right. Above his head a photograph of Sa'd Zaghlul as Prime Minister was hung on the wall under an old framed inscription reading: "In the name of God."

Yasin's visit to the store was not a random one but the result of thoughtful deliberation. He considered this the safest place to present his proposal to his father. The presence of Jamil al-Hamzawi and of any customers who happened to be there should safeguard and protect him if his father's wrath were provoked. Yasin still took every precaution to avoid angering his father despite the security age afforded him and the good treatment he ordinarily received.

With great courtesy he said, "Please grant me a little of your precious time. Were it not absolutely necessary, I would not have dared to trouble you. But I am unable to undertake a step without your guidance and consent."

Al-Sayyid Ahmad smiled to himself at this extravagant display of courtesy and began to gaze apprehensively at his huge, handsome, fastidious son. He cast a comprehensive glance over him, taking in the young man's mustache, twisted just like his father's, dark blue suit, shirt with starched collar and blue bow tie, ivory fly whisk, and gleaming black shoes. In honor of this interview with his father, Yasin had altered his normal attire in only two respects. He had hidden the tip of his silk handkerchief, which usually peeked out from his jacket pocket, and had straightened his fez, which he ordinarily wore slanted to the right.

"He says he can't take a step without my guidance. . . . Bravo! Was he guided by me when he learned to drink or when he roved through the Wajh al-Birka entertainment district, which I forbade him? Did he consult me the night he assaulted the maid on the roof? Bravo! Bravo! What's behind this sermon from the pulpit?"

"Naturally, this is the least that one would expect from a reasonable person like you. I hope it's good news, God willing."

Yasin glanced around quickly at Jamil al-Hamzawi and the customers. Then he brought his chair closer to the desk and, summoning all his courage, said, "I've decided, with your consent and approval, to perfect my religious observance by marrying."

This was a genuine surprise, although unexpectedly a happy one. "But not so fast," al-Sayyid Ahmad reflected. It would be a pleasant surprise only under certain conditions. He would have to wait until he heard the most important part of the proposal. Were there no reasons for concern? Yes, there were: that introduction—so profusely polite and ingratiating—and his choice of the store as the setting for their talk. These warning signs could not escape an astute observer. Al-Sayyid Ahmad had long hoped his son would remarry and for this reason had urged Muhammad Iffat to allow Zaynab to return to Yasin. On concluding his prayers he would entreat God each time to grant Yasin good sense and a good wife. If he had not been apprehensive that his son would cause him and his friends embarrassment—as he had with Muhammad Iffat—al-Sayyid Ahmad would not have hesitated to find him another wife. Now he would bide his time to see if his fears were to be realized.

"An excellent decision. . . . I'm in full agreement with it. Have you selected any particular family?"

Yasin lowered his eyes for a moment. Raising them, he said, "I have found what I was seeking . . . an honorable family well known to us, because we have long been neighbors. The head of the household was one of your worthy acquaintances."

Al-Sayyid Ahmad arched his eyebrows inquisitively but said nothing. Yasin continued: "The late Mr. Muhammad Ridwan."

"No!" The word escaped from the father before he could gain control of himself. It popped out in a groan of protest, which he felt obliged to justify in order to conceal the true reason for his feelings. He had no trouble in finding an explanation: "Hasn't his daughter been divorced? Are there so few women in the world that you're willing to marry a divorcée?"

This objection did not come as a surprise. He had been expecting it ever since he had resolved to marry Maryam. He hoped he could overcome his father's opposition, which he imagined would focus on the superiority of a virgin over a divorcée or dislike for a woman who might remind them of Fahmy's tragedy. He had faith in his father's good sense and was optimistic that it would ultimately dismiss these two minor objections. Indeed he was relying heavily on his father's approval to defeat the genuine opposition he anticipated from his stepmother. He was at such a loss to counter it that he had thought of leaving his father's house and marrying as he saw fit. He would elope and present them all with a fait accompli. He could not bear the thought of angering his father, or he would have done that, even though it would have been hard for him to ignore the feelings of his second mother, who had been much more of a mother to him than his own. He felt he should do his utmost to sway her and convince her that he was right.

Yasin answered his father, "There are plenty of women in the world, but she's destined and fated to be mine. I'm not looking for wealth or prestige. A good family and an upright character are enough for me."

If al-Sayyid Ahmad found anything to console himself in the midst of these painful and awkward matters, it was having his undisputed opinion of his son confirmed again. How typical this was of Yasin! He was a man, or beast, who brought problems with him, whether coming or going. Had he conveyed good news or glad tidings he would not have been Yasin. Al-Sayyid Ahmad's opinion and estimation of his son would have been overturned.

"Perhaps he can be excused for not seeking a wife with wealth or prestige, but is the girl of good character? The mule is not to be blamed, for he quite naturally appears to know nothing about the conduct of the mother of the girl he wishes to marry."

Al-Sayyid Ahmad knew about her conduct from personal experience. Perhaps other men had preceded and followed him. What could he do? The girl might be well behaved, but it was certain her mother and home environment were less than ideal. It was sad, but he could not state his opinion openly, since he would be unable to provide the evidence needed to support his views, which would presumably be received with disbelief and annoyance by anyone hearing them for the first time. Worse still, he was afraid that allusion to these matters would motivate Yasin to investigate them thoroughly. Eventually the young man would find some evidence implicating him—al-Sayyid Ahmad. The result would be a scandal to end all scandals.

The issue was delicate and awkward. There was also a sharp thorn concealed within it—the old story linking her to Fahmy. Had Yasin forgotten that? How could he overlook the fact that he wanted to marry the girl his late brother had once sought? Surely this was odious behavior. Yes, it was, although he felt confident that Yasin's sentiments for his late brother were sincere. The harsh logic of life provided an excuse for people like Yasin. Desire was a blind and merciless tyrant. Al-Sayyid Ahmad knew that better than anyone.

The father frowned to make his displeasure clear to his son and said, "I'm upset with your choice. I don't know why. The late Mr. Muhammad Ridwan was really a fine man, but his paralysis prevented him from supervising his household for a long time before his death. I don't intend this observation to cast suspicions on anyone. Certainly not! But it's something that has been said and possibly some people have repeated it. So? The most important thing with me is that she's been divorced. Why was she divorced? This is one of many questions for which you must learn the answer. It's not right for you to trust a divorcée until you've investigated everything about her thoroughly. Perhaps that's what I was trying to say. The world's full of girls from good families."

Encouraged by his father's tone, which was one of discussion and counsel, Yasin said, "I've investigated, and others have too. I've discovered that the husband was at fault. He already had a wife and concealed that from them. Besides, he wasn't wealthy enough to support two households at the same time and was of bad character."

" 'Bad character'! Who's talking unashamedly about bad character? The mule's providing you with rare material for a whole evening's worth of jokes."

"So you've concluded your search and investigation," he said.

Evading the piercing eyes of his father, Yasin said with embarrassment, "This was an obvious first step. . . ."

Looking down, the man asked, "Didn't you realize that the girl is associated with painful memories for us?"

Seized by confusion, as his color drained, Yasin said, "It was impossible for me to overlook that, but theirs was an imaginary relationship with no foundation. I know for certain that my late brother was interested in her for only a few days and then forgot all about the affair. I'm almost positive he later felt relieved his efforts had failed, once he became convinced that, contrary to what he had imagined, the girl was not interested in him."

Was Yasin telling the truth or defending himself? His late brother had confided in him. Yasin was possibly the only person who could rightfully claim special knowledge about Fahmy's personal affairs. If only he was sincere! Yes, if only he was telling the truth, then al-Sayyid Ahmad would be delivered from a torment that kept him awake whenever he recalled it. He was afraid he had stood in the way of his deceased son's happiness. He often worried that his son had died brokenhearted or angry at his tyranny and obstinacy. These ideas had long gnawed at his heart. Did Yasin wish to relieve him of that?

With a sorrow deeper than Yasin could have imagined, he asked his son, "Are you really sure of what you're saying? Did he admit that to you?"

For only the second time in his life Yasin observed his father wilt. The first time had been the day Fahmy was killed. Al-Sayyid Ahmad entreated his son, "Tell me the whole truth without any sugarcoating. This matter interests me more than you can imagine." He was about to admit his pain but held the confession back, even though it was on the tip of his tongue. "The whole truth, Yasin!"

With no hesitation, the young man replied, "I'm certain of what I say. He told me himself. I heard it with my own ears. There's absolutely no doubt about it."

In other circumstances, this statement, or even a more eloquent one, would not have sufficed to convince him that Yasin was telling the truth. But he was eager to believe his son. Thus he accepted Yasin's words and believed them. His heart was filled with deep gratitude and a pervasive feeling of peace. At that moment at least, the question of Yasin's marriage no longer troubled him. He was silent for a time, enjoying the tranquillity that overflowed his heart.

Only slowly and gradually did his attention return to his predicament. After being blinded by emotion he could once more see Yasin clearly. Al-Sayyid Ahmad began thinking about Maryam, her mother, Yasin's marriage proposal, his own duty, and what he could and could not say. Then he told his son, "Whether or not that's true, I would like you to treat this question with deep thought and circum-

spection. Don't be in too great a hurry. Allow yourself time to consider and reflect. It's a question of your future, reputation, and
happiness. I'm ready to choose another bride for you, if you promise
me as a man of honor that you won't make me regret intervening on
your behalf. So? What do you think?"

Yasin was silent as he thought it over. He was discouraged by the
conversation's awkward turn, for it was fraught with embarrassing
complications. His father was speaking with amazing self-restraint,
but his anxiety and dissatisfaction were apparent. If Yasin insisted on
having his way, the discussion could well create a lamentable split
between them. But should he retreat in order to avoid this eventuality? Certainly not! He was no longer a child. He would marry any
woman he wanted. If only God would help him retain the affection
of his father. Yasin said, "I don't want to impose another burden on
you. Thank you, Papa. All I hope for is your consent and approval."

Al-Sayyid Ahmad waved his hand impatiently. Rather sharply he
said, "You refuse to open your eyes to the wisdom of my advice."

Yasin begged him warmly, "Don't get angry, Papa. Swear to God
you won't get angry. Your approval's a boon I can't bear to be denied. Let me try my luck. Pray I'll be successful."

Ahmad Abd al-Jawad realized that he would have to accept the
situation but did so mournfully and despondently. Perhaps Maryam
was an honorable girl who would be a good wife, despite her mother's wildness. But it was beyond doubt that Yasin had not succeeded
in choosing the most suitable bride or the finest family.

The matter was in God's hands. He could no longer simply dictate
as he saw fit, without fear of rejection. Yasin was a responsible adult.
Any attempt to impose his ideas on his son would only make Yasin
rebel. Al-Sayyid Ahmad would just have to give in and ask God that
it would end well.

He advised and cautioned his son, while Yasin responded with
affectionate apologies, until there was nothing more for either of
them to say.

Yasin left the shop convinced that he had obtained his father's
consent and approval, but he knew the most serious obstacle awaited
him at home. He also knew he would be moving. Merely thinking of
adding Maryam to that household would be a form of insanity. He
hoped to leave peacefully without causing any hard feelings or resentment. It was not easy for him to ignore the wishes of his stepmother or to appear ungrateful for her affection and care. He had
never imagined that fate would force him to adopt this strange atti-

tude toward home and family, but the situation was complicated and his options limited. His only viable alternative was marriage. Amazingly, he had grasped intuitively the feminine strategy working to entrap him. It was an ancient one that could be summarized in two words: seduction and evasion. But desire for the girl had gotten into his blood and had to be satisfied by any means available, even matrimony. It was equally astonishing that although he knew as much of Maryam's history as the others in his family—except, naturally, his father—this knowledge did not restrain or discourage him, for he was dominated by lust.

He told himself, "I won't worry about what's over and done with. I wasn't responsible for it. She'll begin a new life with me. That's when my responsibilities commence. I have unlimited confidence in myself. If my hopes turn out to be groundless, I'll cast her away like a worn-out shoe."

His decision had not been based on careful thought. What thinking he had done had been to justify his wild and unruly passions. He was accepting marriage this time as a substitute for the affair he had been denied. This did not mean that he harbored any antipathy to marriage or that he was using it only as a temporary expedient to attain his goal, for his soul, despite its restlessness, longed for wedded life and a stable home.

These ideas passed through his mind when he took his place beside Kamal at the coffee hour, that gathering he was presumably attending for the last time. With great regret he cast his eyes around the room with it sofas, colored mats, and large lantern hanging from the ceiling. As usual Amina was seated with her legs folded under her on the sofa between the doors to al-Sayyid Ahmad's bedroom and the dining room. Despite the heat, she was bent over the brazier, preparing the coffee. Her white scarf came down over her lavender housedress, which revealed how thin she had become. She was cloaked in a stillness at times stained by sorrow—like seawater that during a momentary calm becomes transparent enough to reveal what is beneath the surface.

Yasin felt sad and uneasy as he prepared to reveal his plan, but there was no alternative. After drinking his coffee, which seemed tasteless, he said, "By God, Mother, there's a question for which I want your advice." The glance he exchanged with Kamal revealed that the latter already knew what the subject would be and was equally concerned about its possible outcome.

"Good news, son?" Amina asked.

Yasin answered tersely, "I've decided to marry."

A look of happy interest appeared in her small honey-colored eyes. "That's a fine idea, son," she commented. "You shouldn't postpone it any longer." There was an inquisitive look in her eyes, but instead of voicing her question she said, as though trying to induce him to confess if there was any secret about it, "Speak to your father or let me. He'll be able to find you another wife better than the first."

With more solemnity than his stepmother thought the subject warranted, Yasin replied, "Actually, I have spoken to my father. There's no need for me to impose a new burden on him, for I've selected someone myself. Father has agreed, and I hope I may have your consent as well."

She blushed with embarrassment and delight at the importance he was attaching to her opinion. Then she replied, "May our Lord help you obtain everything good. As soon as you want, set up house on the first floor, which we've abandoned. But who's the fine girl you've decided to take for your wife?"

Yasin exchanged another glance with Kamal. Then with difficulty he said, "A neighbor. Someone you know."

With her eyebrows contracted in a thoughtful frown, she stared off into space, moving her index finger, as though counting out their neighbors to herself. Then she said, "You perplex me, Yasin. Won't you speak up and set my mind at rest?"

Smiling wanly, he answered, "Our closest neighbors. . . ."

"Who?" The word escaped from her in alarmed denial. She stared at his face. With a gloomy expression he lowered his head and pressed his lips together.

Her voice trembling, she asked once more as she pointed behind her with her thumb, "Them? Impossible! Do you mean what you're saying, Yasin?"

His only response was glum silence. She screamed, "What dreadful news! Those people who gloated over our greatest misfortune?"

He could not keep from crying at her, "I entreat you to swear to God you won't repeat that. It's false, imaginary. If my heart felt for a moment . . ."

"Naturally, you defend them. But it's a defense that won't deceive anyone. Don't wear yourself out trying to convince me of such an absurdity. My Lord! Why is a catastrophe like this necessary? They're riddled with defects and vices. Is there one good point to justify this outrageous selection? You said you'd obtained your father's consent.

The man doesn't know anything about these matters, so you should say you duped him."

Yasin entreated her, "Calm down. I hate nothing more than making you angry. Calm yourself and let's talk quietly."

"How can I listen to you when you've given me this harsh slap? Say the matter's nothing more than a silly joke. Maryam? The girl's no good. You know that as well as anyone. Have you forgotten her scandalous past? Have you really forgotten that? Do you want to bring that girl into our home?"

Exhaling, as though to rid his breast of its sorrow and turmoil, Yasin said, "That's not at all what I said. Whether we live here or not is unimportant. What's really important to me is for you to examine the question seriously, setting aside your prejudice."

"What prejudice, fellow? Have I accused her falsely? You say that your father consented. Did you tell him about her scandalous flirtation with the English soldier? My Lord, what's come over children from good families?"

"Calm down. Let's have a quiet conversation. What's the use of all this agitation?"

She shouted at him with a sharpness that would have been totally alien to her in the old days, "I can't be calm about a matter threatening our honor." In a tearful voice she continued: "And you're insulting the memory of your precious brother."

Swallowing, Yasin said, "My brother? May God be merciful to him and grant him a spacious abode in paradise. This question doesn't reflect on his memory in any way. Believe me, I know what I'm saying. Don't disturb his repose."

"I'm not the one disturbing him. You are, since you want that girl. You know it, Yasin. You can't deny it." With great emotion she added, "Perhaps you wanted her even back then."

"Mother!"

"I'm no longer sure of anything. How could I be, after this betrayal? Has the world become so small and desolate that the only girl you can find to marry is one who made your brother's heart bleed? Don't you remember how sad he was when we all heard the story of the English soldier?"

Yasin spread his arms out in supplication, saying, "Let's postpone this conversation to another time. I'll prove to you that when my late brother heeded the call of his Lord there was no trace of emotion left for this girl. As for now, the atmosphere is no longer appropriate for a conversation."

She shouted angrily at him, "It's inconceivable that there should ever be an appropriate atmosphere for me to hear talk like this. You have no respect for Fahmy's memory!"

"I wish you could imagine how sad your words make me."

Her wrath reached its ultimate peak as she yelled, "What sadness? You never grieved for your brother! There were strangers who grieved for him more than you did."

"Mother!"

Kamal attempted to intervene, but his mother silenced him with a gesture of her hand. She cried out, "Don't call me 'Mother.' I've been a mother to you, but you never were a son to me or a brother to my son."

It was impossible for Yasin to stay any longer. He rose sadly and dejectedly, leaving the sitting room for his bedroom. Kamal soon joined him there, no less sad and dejected. He asked his older brother, "Didn't I warn you?"

Frowning, Yasin said, "I won't stay in this house another minute."

With alarm Kamal told him, "You've got to excuse her. You know my mother's changed. Even Father occasionally closes his eyes to her failings. It's just a flash of anger that will soon die down. Don't take her words seriously. That's all I ask."

Sighing, Yasin said, "I don't hold it against her, Kamal. I won't forget all the happy years because of one bad hour. As you said, she's to be excused. But how can I show her my face morning and evening when this is what she thinks of me?"

After some moments of gloomy silence, Yasin continued: "Don't think that Maryam broke our late brother's heart. Fahmy asked permission to marry her one day and Father refused. Fahmy set the matter aside and finally forgot all about it. How is the girl to be blamed for that? And why am I to blame if I want to marry her, six years after all that happened?"

Kamal said hopefully, "You haven't said anything that's not true, and Mother will quickly accept it. I trust your talk of leaving the house was merely a slip of the tongue...."

Shaking his head sadly, Yasin said, "I'm the one most distressed by my departure. But I'll leave sooner or later, for it's impossible to move Maryam in here. Don't think of my departure in any light but this. I'll move to my house in Palace of Desire Alley. Fortunately, my mother's apartment is still vacant. I'll stop by to see Father at the store and explain my reasons for leaving, omitting anything that might upset him. I'm not angry. I'm leaving the house most regretfully. I'll miss everyone here, starting with Mother. Don't be sad. The stream will return to its banks shortly. No one in this family has a vengeful heart, and your mother's is the purest of all."

He went to the wardrobe, opened it, and began looking at his clothes and belongings. He hesitated a little before executing his decision. Turning toward Kamal, he said, "I'm going to marry this girl. The fates have decreed that for me. God knows, I'm convinced that I'm not betraying Fahmy's memory. You recall, Kamal, how much I loved him. Why shouldn't I? If anyone gets hurt by this marriage, it will be me."

II ≈

A servant girl led Yasin into the parlor and then disappeared. He was visiting the home of the late Mr. Muhammad Ridwan for the first time ever. Spacious and with a high ceiling, the room was like those in his father's house. Its latticed balcony overlooked Palace Walk, and its two windows opened on the side alley where the door of the house was located. There was a small carpet on the floor. Couches and armchairs were lined up along the walls. The door and windows were hung with gray velvet curtains, which had grown pale with age. In a large black frame on the wall facing the door there was an inscription reading: "In the name of God." At the center of the wall to the right, above the main sofa, was a portrait of the late Mr. Muhammad Ridwan, showing him in the prime of life. Yasin picked the first couch on his right and sat down. He carefully examined the place until his eyes came to rest on the face of Mr. Muhammad Ridwan, who appeared to be looking at him with Maryam's eyes. Yasin smiled contentedly and started to flick his ivory fly whisk at nothing in particular.

A problem confronting him since he had first thought of coming to ask for Maryam's hand was the absence of any men in her house and his failure to obtain a female representative from his family. He had come alone, like "a branch cut from the family tree," as he put it. This embarrassed him a little, since he was a man who had absorbed from his milieu a pride in family and kin. All the same, he was confident that Maryam had prepared the way for him with her mother. The mere announcement of his visit would suffice to reveal the reason for it and to create a fine atmosphere for the performance of his mission.

The maid put in another appearance, carrying a coffee tray, which she placed on the table in front of him. As she retreated, she informed him that the senior mistress was on her way. He wondered if the junior mistress knew of his visit. What impact would it have on her delicate soul? He was going to carry her and her beauty off to Palace of Desire Alley, no matter what. Who would have thought that

Amina could get so angry? She used to be as meek as an angel. "May God destroy grief!" he thought.

His father had grown angry too when Yasin had confessed at the store that he had left home. But it had been a compassionate anger, revealing how upset and sad he was.

"I wonder if Amina will tell him about Maryam's past. The anger of a bereaved mother is a frightening thing, but Kamal promised to persuade her to keep quiet about it. Back at Palace of Desire Alley you encountered the first happy surprise of this stormy affair . . . the death of your late mother's former lover, the fruit seller. His place has been taken by a watchmaker. To the grave!"

He heard someone at the door clear her throat. As he rose he turned his eyes in that direction. In no time at all he saw Mrs. Bahija. She was making her entrance sideways, since only one panel of the door was open and the space would not have been wide enough for her had she come in straight. Without meaning to, he observed the lines demarcating the divisions of her voluminous body. He could not help but marvel when her hips came into view, for their crest almost reached the middle of her back, while their bottom flowed down over her thighs. They were like inflated balloons.

She advanced toward him with steps slowed by the extraordinary weight of her flesh and flab. Then she extended a soft white hand, which emerged from the sleeve of her loose white dress. She was saying, "Welcome! Welcome! You honor and illumine us."

Yasin shook her hand politely and remained standing until she had seated herself on the nearest sofa. Then he sat down. He was seeing her up close for the first time. Her long-standing ties to his family and the status of matriarch she had acquired over the years because of her age and prestige had kept him, when he saw her at a distance in the street, from scrutinizing her the way he did other women. Thus, it seemed he was making a new discovery. The dress she was wearing covered her body from her neck down to her feet, which she had concealed in white socks despite the warm weather. The sleeves of her dress reached to her wrists, and her head and neck were enveloped in a white scarf, the ends of which spread over her breast and back. She presented a modest appearance suiting the occasion and fitting her age, which was close to fifty, so far as Yasin knew. Yet she also appeared to be in splendid health, suggesting a mind at rest and a youthful heart. One thing he noticed was that her face was free of makeup, although he knew her reputation for loving to show herself off to advantage. For that reason she had long been the established authority in the whole quarter for everything relating to feminine taste in clothes and cosmetics. He remembered how Amina had once defended this woman whenever anyone criticized her excesses of self-adornment but over the past few years had attacked Bahija for the most trifling reasons, accusing her of immodesty and of disregard for the decorum appropriate to her age.

"A noble step, Yasin Effendi."

"May God be generous to you." He almost ended his words with "Auntie," but at the last minute an instinctive fear prevented him, especially since he had noticed that she had not called him "my son," as he would have expected.

"How are all of you?" she asked. "Your father, Fahmy's mother, Khadija, Aisha, and Kamal?"

Feeling embarrassed because she had inquired about people who were hostile to her for no clear reason, he answered, "They're all fine. It's hoped you're in good health."

No doubt she was thinking of the cold reception she had received in his father's home after Fahmy's death. After a lifelong friendship she had been forced to stop visiting his family. What rude treatment! No, it had been the beginning of a cold war. His stepmother had soon announced her "feeling" that Maryam and her mother had not grieved sincerely for Fahmy. May God not bring any more evil, why? She had said it was inconceivable that they would not have heard back then in one way or another about al-Sayyid Ahmad's refusal to allow Fahmy to ask for Maryam's hand. If they had not heard, they could have deduced it. And if they knew about it, they would inevitably hold a grudge against Fahmy's family. She frequently repeated that she had heard Maryam at the funeral lament Fahmy's passing by saying, "I'm sorry you didn't get to enjoy your youth." Amina interpreted this to mean: "I'm sorry you didn't get to enjoy your youth, because your family stood in your way," adding to that interpretation whatever else her sorrow and grief dictated. No stratagem had succeeded in weaning her from her "feeling." Her behavior toward Maryam and Umm Maryam had quickly been transformed, and relations had been severed.

Still under the influence of his embarrassment and uneasiness, he said, "God curse the devil!"

Endorsing his sentiments, Bahija said, "A thousand curses! I've frequently asked myself what I did to be treated the way I have been by Mrs. Umm Fahmy, but I keep on praying that she may find some consolation, the poor lady. . . ."

"May God reward you magnificently for your noble manners and good heart. She's truly in a pitiful state and in need of consolation."

"But how am I at fault?"

"You're not. It's the devil, God's curses on him."

The woman shook her head as though she were an innocent victim and was silent for a time until she happened to turn to the cup of coffee, which seemed to be sitting forgotten on the tray. Gesturing toward it, she asked, "Haven't you drunk your coffee yet?"

Yasin raised the cup to his mouth and drained it. Putting it back on the tray, he cleared his throat a little and then began his spiel: "I've been distressed by the events ending the friendship between our two families, but there has been nothing I could do. We need to set that aside and let time take care of it. The fact is I didn't mean to arouse sad memories. That's not why I came. My visit has another purpose, one as far removed as possible from sad memories."

Bahija tossed her head as though to drive away sad thoughts. Then she smiled to show she was ready to hear something new. Her toss of the head and smile resembled a musician's change of key to introduce the vocalist and a new section of the song.

Put at ease by her smile, Yasin said, "My own life is not lacking in sad memories from my past. I refer to my first attempt at marriage. God did not grant me success in finding a proper wife. But I don't want to dwell on that. The fact is that I've come as a result of my decision—putting my trust in God—to turn over a new page in my life, anticipating nothing but good from my resolve. . . ."

Their eyes met, and he found a gratifying reception for his words. Had he been well advised to mention his first marriage? Would not news of the real reasons for the failure of that marriage have reached this woman?

"Don't worry," he told himself. "Her beautiful face gives every indication of unlimited tolerance. Her beautiful face! Aren't her features pretty? They certainly are. If it were not for the difference in age, she would be more beautiful than Maryam. Without any doubt she was more beautiful when she was young. No! She's more beautiful than Maryam, despite the difference in age. She really is!"

"I suspect you've guessed what I have in mind. I've come to ask for the hand of your daughter, Miss Maryam."

Her radiant face was illuminated by a smile in which pulsed a new vitality. She answered, "All I can say is: Welcome and welcome again. An excellent family and an excellent man. Last time we were unlucky and fell victim to a person of no character. This time a man seeks Maryam who can truly make her happy. By the grace of God she will be able to make him happy. Regardless of the separation occasioned by that misunderstanding we've been a single family for a long time."

Yasin was so delighted that his fingers began adjusting his bow tie with quick, unconscious strokes. With a blush on his handsome bronze face he said, "I thank you from the bottom of my heart. May God reward the sweetness of your words. As you observed, we are one family in spite of everything, and Miss Maryam is a girl who adorns our whole district with her lineage and character. May God grant each of us consolation with the other for our past misfortunes."

She murmured, "Amen," and sighed. Then she approached the table with her glorious body. She took the coffee tray and called Yasmina. Holding the tray, she turned around to give it to the maid, who was hurrying in. Suddenly Maryam's mother looked back to tell him, "We've enjoyed your visit," and surprised him staring at her massive hips. He was at once aware that he had been caught in a compromising position. He quickly lowered his eyes so that she would assume he had been looking at the floor, but it was too late. . . . He was rattled and began to ask himself what she would think of him.

After she sat down again he peeked at her stealthily and glimpsed her delicate smile, which seemed to say, "I saw you!" To hell with his eyes that did not know how to be modest. . . . He wondered what was going through her head. Yes, she was trying to pretend that she had not seen anything, but her attitude subsequent to her smile also implied: "I saw you!" The best solution would be for him to forget this blunder. But would Maryam become like her mother one day? When would that day come? The mother had qualities fate rarely handed out. What a woman she was! The best way to rid himself of these thoughts and disperse the cloud of suspicion would be to break the silence.

He said, "If my request meets with your approval, you will find me ready to discuss the important details at your convenience."

She laughed briefly but with an incandescence that made her face seem gentle and youthful. She said, "Why wouldn't we accept, Yasin Effendi? As the saying goes: Seek a neighbor with good lineage. . . ."

Blushing, he replied, "You enslave me with your graciousness."

"All I've said is the truth, with God as my witness."

After a brief silence, she asked, "Is your household in agreement?"

A serious look came into his eyes for a moment. Then he laughed listlessly through his nostrils. He said, "Let's not talk about my household and its affairs."

"May God shelter us from evil, why?"

"Not everything at home is as I would like."

"Haven't you consulted al-Sayyid Ahmad?"

"My father has given his consent."

She clapped her hands together and said, "Now I understand. Fahmy's mother? Isn't that so? She was the first to come to mind when you brought up the topic. Naturally, she hasn't agreed. So? Glory to the One who never changes. Your father's wife is a strange woman."

Shrugging his shoulders dismissively, he said, "That's neither here nor there."

She complained, "How often I've asked myself what I did wrong. How have I harmed her?"

"I don't want to abandon our current conversation for one that will only cause headaches. Whatever her doubts are, the important thing is for me to accomplish my goal. The only issue that concerns me is your consent."

"If you don't have room at your house, ours is at your disposal."

"Thanks! I have my own house in Palace of Desire Alley, out of this quarter altogether. As far as my father's house goes, I moved out of it some days ago."

She struck her breast with her hand and cried out, "She evicted you!"

Laughing, he replied, "Not at all. The matter did not reach that pass. It's just that my choice upset her for reasons from the past connected to my late brother." He gave her a look that suggested they both knew what he was referring to. "Since I could never find a truly convincing way to deal with her objections, I thought it appropriate to prepare a new home for my married life."

Raising her eyebrows and shaking her head somewhat dubiously, she asked, "Why didn't you stay at home until the wedding?"

He laughed to acknowledge his defeat and said, "I preferred to move away for fear the disagreement would become worse."

She commented ironically, "May our Lord resolve the dispute. . . ."

Before finishing, she rose again and went to the window overlooking the alley. She opened the shutter to let in the late-afternoon sunshine, for the door of the balcony no longer admitted sufficient light to illuminate the room. Although he was trying to be cautious, he caught himself, despite his good intentions, gazing stealthily at the precious treasure of her rump, which loomed up like the dome of a shrine as she knelt on the sofa and leaned over the window ledge to fasten back the shutters. The amazing sight he witnessed then made a vivid impression on his soul. His throat felt dry, and he wondered why she had not called the maid to open the window. How could she have permitted this unquestionably suggestive vision to appear before his eyes, which she had so recently caught in a suspicious look? Why and how? How and why? When it came to women, Yasin was perceptive and leery. He was aware of a doubt loitering at the threshold of his consciousness, not wanting to come in and not wanting to disappear. Wary because of the seriousness of the situation, he quickly closed his eyes. Either he was crazy or she . . . she was. Was there some other possibility? If only someone would extricate him from this dilemma. . . .

She straightened up, put her weight back on the ground, and then turned away from the window to regain her seat. Before she whirled around, he was quick to raise his eyes to the inscription of "In the name of God," in order to pretend to be engrossed in examining it. He did not turn his head toward her until the creaking of the couch informed him that she was seated. Then their eyes met. The crafty, smiling look of her eyes put him on notice that it was impossible to hide anything from her. She might just as well have told him in so many words, "I saw you!" For a time he felt agitated and confused. Everything seemed a puzzle to him. He was afraid of being unfair to her and of laying himself open to her accusations. He thought the best thing would be to watch his every move, for any slip could precipitate a scandal.

"The weather's still rather warm and humid. . . ." Her voice sounded calm and natural and showed her desire to banish the silence.

He said with relief, "Yes, it certainly is."

He was reassured but in his imagination could still see the vision he had had of her at the window. Against his better judgment, he found himself mulling it over with fascination. He wished he had stumbled across something like that on one of his romantic excursions. If only Maryam had a body like her mother's! Was it not for something like this that the Qur'an said, "Let those who have aspirations compete"? (83:26.)

She assumed that his silence indicated he was brooding over her comment about his disagreement with his stepmother and almost playfully advised him, "Don't trouble your mind about it. There's nothing in the world worth worrying about." Then she waved her hands and head, making her body quiver in a special way, as though she wished to encourage him to spurn his cares.

He smiled obediently and murmured, "That's true."

All the same, he was doing his best to gain control of himself. Yes, something momentous had happened. Although it appeared to be nothing but a movement of her body meant to express her disdain for trivial worries and to encourage him to feel the same way, it was extremely significant, for it was clear evidence of wanton and licentious flirting. This gesture had escaped in a moment of forgetfulness. It interrupted the modest decorum she had observed with him throughout their interview and unintentionally disclosed her true nature. Or was it intentional? He could not decide between the two, but he no longer doubted that he was in the presence of a woman truly worthy of being the mother of a daughter with a past like Maryam's. Nothing could make him change his mind, for this flirtatious, dancing motion was not one a well-behaved woman would ever exhibit. His alarm lasted only for a fleeting moment and was quickly replaced by a sensation of sly and sensuous joy. He began to recall where and when he had seen this gesture before.... Zanuba? . . . Jalila, the night she surprised his father by storming into the men's reception room at the Shawkat residence during Aisha's wedding. Yes, that was it!

It occurred to him that despite her age the mother might be more desirable and delightful than Maryam. Submitting to his natural drives, he told himself that he should test her out and if possible not hold anything back. He felt like laughing at the novelty of the idea. He would be traveling a rugged path he had never taken before, but he had never been one to restrain his passions. Where would this conduct lead him? Would it be possible to give Maryam up for her mother? Certainly not! He had no intention of doing that. But imagine a dog that finds a bone on its way to the kitchen. Would it be ashamed to take the bone? In any case, these were all just thoughts, flights of imagination, and hypotheses. Let him wait and see. They smiled at each other in the silence that once more had come between them. Her smile was apparently that of a host greeting a guest, but his was flavored with whispers of suffocating lust.

"You've brought light to our home, Yasin Effendi."

"Madam, there's no shortage of light in your home. You illuminate the town and everything in it."

She laughed and threw her head back as she said softly, "May God be good to you, Yasin Effendi."

He should have returned to the conversation about his proposal or asked permission to leave, naming a date when they could continue their discussion, but he began to cast peculiar glances at her, some long and some short, without cease. The silence was frightening. His looks conveyed messages that no one with eyes could miss. He had to convey all his thoughts to her through these looks alone to discover her reaction.

"Look before you leap, and down with High Commissioner Allenby. Let her receive my fiery glance and tell me, if she's sincere, what madman could ignore her naughty intentions and assert her innocence. See how she raises and lowers her eyes absentmindedly but at the same time with a suspicious clarity of understanding. You can now say that the floodwaters have reached Aswan and that the sluice gate must be opened. While you're asking for her daughter's hand? After today anyone who doesn't believe in insanity must be insane. At present I desire you more than anything else. *'Après moi le déluge.'* The way you look certainly does nothing to discourage my hopes."

"Do you live alone in the Palace of Desire?"

"Yes."

"My heart goes out to you."

It was a phrase that either a devil or an angel might have uttered. Was Maryam listening behind the door?

"You've experienced loneliness here in your house. It's unbearable."

"Truly unbearable!"

She suddenly put her hand up to her scarf and jerked it from her head and neck, saying apologetically, "Excuse me. It's hot."

Her head in its orange kerchief and her spotless neck could now be seen. He gazed at her neck for some time with increasing anxiety. Then he looked at the door as though to ask who might be lurking behind it. God help the suitor who came asking for the hand of the daughter and fell into the clutches of the mother.

In response to her apology he said, "Make yourself comfortable. You're in your own house. There's no stranger present."

"I wish Maryam were home so I could break the good news to her."

His heart pounded as if directing him to attack. He asked, "Where is she?"

"With friends in al-Darb al-Ahmar."

"Farewell, reason!" he thought. "Your daughter's fiancé wants you and you want him. May God be merciful to anyone who thinks well of women. This woman must not have any sense. She's been our neighbor all my life, and I'm only finding out who she is today . . . a madwoman . . . a fifty-year-old adolescent."

"When will Miss Maryam return?"

"Late in the afternoon. . . ."

Wickedly he said, "I feel my visit's lasted too long."

"It's not a long visit, for you're at home."

With equal naughtiness he inquired, "I wonder whether I may hope you'll return my call."

She smiled broadly as though to tell him, "I understand what's behind this invitation." Then she bowed her head with embarrassment, although the theatrics of her gesture did not escape him.

He did not concern himself with that but started to describe the location of his house and of his apartment within that building. Her head bowed, she smiled silently. Was she not conscious of wronging and injuring her daughter in the clearest possible way?

"When will you honor me with a visit?"

She mumbled as she raised her head, "I don't know what to say."

Confidently and firmly he said, "I'll answer on your behalf. Tomorrow evening. You'll find me waiting for you."

"There are matters we must take into account."

"We'll deal with all of them . . . at my house."

He rose at once and started to go toward her, but she gestured for him to keep his distance and looked toward the door to caution him.

"Tomorrow evening," she said, as though her only goal was to avert his attack.

12

The house in Palace of Desire Alley came to know Bahija as a persistent visitor. Once darkness spread its veil, the lady draped herself in her wrap and proceeded to al-Gamaliya, heading for the home that had once belonged to Yasin's mother, Haniya. There she found Yasin waiting for her in the only furnished room of the apartment. They never referred to Maryam, except once when Bahija said, "I wasn't able to keep the news of your visit from Maryam, because our maid knows you. But I told her you had mentioned your interest in asking for her hand once the obstacles blocking your way in the family circle were overcome."

He was too astonished by her remark to care to comment and merely expressed his agreement and approval. Together they embarked on a life of sensual gratification. Yasin found the custodian of the treasured rump submissive to his every whim, and he himself was as free from inhibitions as a wild stallion. The hastily and frugally furnished room was not an ideal location for an affair, but Yasin went out of his way to create an attractive atmosphere by providing an ample supply of food and drinks so that their trysts would go well. He assaulted her repeatedly with an appetite that knew no limit or moderation.

Shortly before the first week had run its course Yasin began to feel bored. His lust was once more acting out the same cycle he had experienced before, as the remedy became an ailment. At least it did not come as a surprise to him. From the beginning he had harbored no good intentions whatsoever for that curious relationship and had not expected it to last. He obviously thought this romance in the parlor was no more than a passing fling but found that the woman was becoming attached to him. She wanted him and hoped he would be so satisfied with her that he would abandon the idea of marrying her daughter. He saw no alternative to humoring her, lest he put his pleasure at risk. He believed that time bore the sole responsibility for returning everything to normal.

Matters quickly sorted themselves out, probably faster than he had imagined possible. He had gone along with her, thinking that the novelty of her charms would be enough to sustain her appeal for several weeks or a month, but he must have miscalculated. Although her appearance was seductive, it had caused him to commit the greatest folly of a life littered with them. Her years lay concealed behind that beauty like a fever disguised by rosy cheeks. The pounds and pounds of flesh treasured in layers under the folds of her clothes were, as he put it, not quite as appealing when seen stripped naked, for nothing records the effects of a sad life so graphically as the human body. He even told himself, "Now I understand why women are crazy about clothes."

Considering all this, it was hardly strange that he referred to her as a "plague" once he tired of her attentions or that he should resolve to end their relationship. As his mad infatuation with her mother faded, Maryam regained her previous place in his affections. In fact, she had never lost it but had been overshadowed by this unexpected outbreak of passion—like the moon obscured by a fleeting cloud. How amazing! His desire for Maryam was no longer merely a response to his insatiable lust for women, even if that was the dominant factor. His interest in her was also furthered by his longing to start a family, an eventuality he considered both desirable and predestined.

Yasin reluctantly counseled himself to be patient until Bahija returned to her senses, assuming that she would tell him one day, "We've had enough fun. Now go to your bride." But his hopes found no echo in her. She visited him persistently night after night, growing ever more overwhelming and intense. He sensed that as time passed she was beginning to believe he was rightfully hers, as though he had become her property and the pivot around which her life revolved.

She did not think of the affair as a trivial or humorous escapade, and the frivolous, fickle, and reckless character she displayed convinced him that her aberrant behavior with him at their first meeting had not been an isolated phenomenon. Feeling that she was cheap, he scorned her. To his critical eyes her defects were magnified until he was totally disgusted with her. He decided to get rid of her at the first opportunity, although he was eager to avoid any rude conduct that would strew the path to Maryam with obstacles.

One time he said, "Doesn't Maryam ask what has become of me?"

With a reassuring toss of her head, she answered, "She knows perfectly well that your family's opposed."

After some hesitation he said, "I'll tell you frankly that we used to converse occasionally on the roof and that I assured her repeatedly of my determination to marry her, regardless of opposition from any quarter...."

She gave him a piercing look and asked, "What are you trying to say?"

With feigned innocence he replied, "I mean she's heard that assurance from me and knows of my subsequent visit. She needs to be offered some convincing explanation for my disappearance."

With a nonchalance that stunned him, she said, "It won't harm her if you don't.... Not every discussion leads to a marriage proposal, and not every proposal leads to a marriage. She knows all that perfectly well." Then she continued in a low voice: "It won't hurt her to lose you. She's a young woman in her prime. She'll have a suitor tomorrow if not today."

Bahija seemed to be apologizing for her selfishness or else pointing out that it was she, not her daughter, who would be harmed by losing him. Her statement only made him more uneasy and annoyed. If that were not enough, he began to nourish fears about the effects of an affair with a woman twenty years his senior, because of the notion popular at the time that associating with a mature woman would rob a man of his youth. Thus the hours they spent together were charged for him with such tension and circumspection that he detested them.

He was in this state of mind when he ran into Maryam one day on New Street. He went up to her without any hesitation, greeted her, and walked along beside her as though he was one of her relatives. She frowned nervously, but he told her that he had been working to achieve his father's consent, which he finally had won, and that he was preparing his dwelling in Palace of Desire Alley for them. He apologized for the length of his absence, citing his many chores. Then he told her, "Inform your mother that I'll visit her tomorrow to make arrangements for the wedding."

He went off, happy that he had seized this unexpected opportunity. In his joyful exuberance he was indifferent to Bahija's possible reaction. That evening she arrived at her regular time, but devastated and agitated.

Even before she removed her veil she shouted at him, "You've sold me out, by hook and by crook."

Then she plopped down on the bed and nervously yanked off her veil. She said, "It never occurred to me that you could be so deceitful, but you're a sneaky coward like every other man in the world."

Gently and apologetically Yasin said, "It wasn't the way you imagine. The truth is that I met her by accident."

Scowling, she shouted, "Liar! Liar! By the truth of the One capable of making me see anything desirable in you, do you think I'll ever believe you again after what's happened?" Then she repeated his words in a sarcastic parody: " 'The truth is that I met her by accident.' What kind of accident, buster? Let's suppose it really was an accident. Why did you speak to her in the street in front of all the passersby? Wasn't that the act of a wicked traitor?" Returning to her parody, she said, " 'The truth is that I met her by accident.' "

Somewhat ill at ease, he said, "I suddenly found myself face to face with her. My hand stretched out to greet her. It wasn't possible for me to ignore her after our conversations on the roof. . . ."

Her face pale with rage, she screamed, " 'My hand stretched out to greet her.' A hand doesn't reach out until you extend it. May your hand and you both be struck down. What you're saying is that you stretched your hand out to her to get rid of me."

"I had to greet her. I'm a man with feelings."

"Feelings? Where are they? You traitor and son of a traitor, may you choke on your feelings." After swallowing she continued: "What about your promise to come make all the arrangements for the wedding? Did that slip away from you too like your hand? . . . Speak, Mr. Sensitivity!"

With extraordinary calm he answered, "Everyone in the neighborhood knows I left my father's home in order to marry your daughter. It was impossible for me to ignore that when talking to her."

She yelled sharply, "You could have invented any excuse you wanted, if you'd had a mind to. You're not a person who is short on lies. But you wanted to get rid of me. That's the truth of it."

Avoiding her eyes, he said, "Our Lord knows of my good intentions."

She cast a long look at him and then asked defiantly, "Would you have me believe that you allowed yourself to be coerced into making this promise to her?"

Recognizing the danger of admitting that, he lowered his eyes and took refuge in silence. Panting with rage, she yelled, "You see! You're a liar, just as I said." Then she shrieked, "See? See? Traitor! Son of a traitor!"

After some hesitation he responded, "A secret can't remain hidden forever. Imagine what people will say if they find out about our affair. Indeed, imagine what Maryam will say. . . ."

She ground her teeth in her fury and said, "You swine! Why didn't you mention any of these reservations the day you stood before me slobbering like a dog? Oh, the male sex! Red-hot hell will be too mild a punishment for you."

He smiled a little and would almost have laughed had he not been restrained by cowardice. Then he said gently and affectionately, "We've had a wonderful time. I'll always remember it fondly. That's enough anger and bitterness. Maryam is your daughter and you more than anyone else desire her happiness."

She shook her head scornfully and said, "Are you the one to make her happy? May the walls be my witness: The poor girl doesn't know the kind of devil she's marrying. You're the lecherous son of a debauchee. May our Lord repay her for the mess she's getting herself into."

He said with the composure he had maintained from the beginning, "Our Lord will be able to set everything right. I have a sincere desire for a good marriage with a good wife."

She said derisively, "I'll cut my arm off if you're speaking the truth. We'll see. Don't cast any aspersions on my qualities as a mother. My daughter's happiness is more important to me than any other consideration. If you had not deceived and betrayed me, I would have been glad to hand you to her like a dirty shoe."

Yasin wondered whether the crisis was over. He was waiting for her to put on her veil and bid him farewell, but she did not budge. Time passed. She was sitting on the bed, and he was on the chair facing her. He had no idea how or when this strange and tense meeting would end. He stole a look at her and found her gazing at the floor, so lost and resigned that his fond feelings for her were momentarily revived.

"Will she start raving again? That's not unlikely. But it appears that she's aware of her delicate situation with regard to her daughter and will honor its demands."

Before he knew what was happening she had removed the wrap from around her shoulders and chest, mumbling, "It's warm." Then she scooted along the bed to the end, where she leaned back against the headboard. She stretched her legs out, paying no attention to her shoes, the heels of which were sinking into the folds of the comforter. She still appeared lost in her reflections. Did she simply have nothing more to say?

In a tone notable for its gentleness, he asked her, "Would you permit me to call on you tomorrow?"

She ignored his question for a minute. Then she threw him a look like a curse and replied, "You will be most welcome, you chip off the old block."

He smiled with satisfaction, although he felt her glances scorching his face. After a moment she said, "Don't think I'm a fool. I reconciled myself to this conclusion sooner or later. It's just that you've speeded it up in a way that . . ." Then she finished with a combination of resignation and scorn: "Whatever we have to do. . . ."

He did not believe her but pretended to. He told her that he was sure it was true and hoped she would forgive him and not harbor ill feelings. She did not bother to listen and made her way back to the edge of the bed. Then she threw her feet to the ground, stood up, and began to pull her wrap around her. She said, "I leave you in the hands of God."

He rose silently and went ahead of her to the door to open it. He led the way out but was caught off guard by a blow falling on the nape of his neck. Then the woman passed by him to the stairs, leaving him stunned, his hand spread over the place where she had hit him. Grasping hold of the railing, she turned back and said, "May you live to receive many more. You've hurt me much more than that. Don't I have a right to satisfy my craving for vengeance, even if only with a slap, you son of a bitch?"

13 ✌

"Al-Sayyid Ahmad, please excuse me if I tell you frankly that you're spending money recklessly these days."

Jamil al-Hamzawi said that in a tone blending subservient politeness with friendly informality. Although fifty-seven, he was strong and in good health. His hair was speckled with gray, but time had not decreased his energy in any respect. He still spent the whole day in constant motion, looking after the store and its customers, just as he had since he started working there, back when the business was first established. Over the years he had gained secure rights and the respect due him for his industry and honesty. Ahmad Abd al-Jawad considered him a friend. The affection he had shown his employee recently by helping enroll Fuad in Law School had only increased al-Hamzawi's loyalty and inclination to speak up frankly when necessary to avoid some harm or realize some gain.

Referring perhaps to their brisk sales in the frantic market, Ahmad replied in a reassuring tone, "Business is great, praise God."

Smiling, Jamil al-Hamzawi answered, "My our Lord multiply and sanction it. But I repeat what I've said of you, that if you had embraced the mores of the merchant along with his profession, you would be a wealthy man today."

Ahmad grinned with satisfaction and shrugged his shoulders. He earned a lot and spent a lot. How could he regret the pleasures he gained from life? He had never lost track of the need to keep his income and expenditures in balance and always kept a reserve on hand. Aisha and Khadija were both married. Kamal was beginning the final stage of his schooling. Why should he not enjoy some of the good things life had to offer? But al-Hamzawi was not overstating the case when he accused his boss of squandering money, for in fact he had been anything but economical and judicious of late. His expenses took many forms. Gifts devoured a substantial sum. The houseboat was squeezing him dry. His mistress was demanding sacrifices of him. In short, Zanuba was pushing him to spend money extravagantly, and he was allowing himself to be manipulated, putting up little resistance. He had not been like that in the past. Of course he had spent lavishly, but no woman had ever been able to sway him from a steady course or to force him to spend recklessly. Back then he had been confident of his powers. He had not cared much whether he responded to all his mistress's requests. If she was coy with him, he would pretend to lose interest in her, for he was proudly aware of his youthful virility. Nowadays, desire for his lover had subjected his will to hers and made the expenses appear trivial to him. He seemed to have no object in life beyond retaining her affection and winning her heart. But how vainglorious her affection was! What a refractory heart she had! The truth of his situation was not hidden from him, and he felt saddened and hurt by it. He remembered his salad days with longing and sorrow, although he did not acknowledge that they had departed. Yet he did not lift a finger to make any serious attempt to resist. That was beyond his power.

Al-Sayyid Ahmad told Jamil al-Hamzawi with apparent irony, "Perhaps you're wrong to consider me a merchant." Then with resignation he added, "Only God is well-to-do."

Some people came in, and al-Hamzawi was busy looking after them. No sooner was al-Sayyid Ahmad left to his own reflections than he noticed a person who, after filling the doorway to capacity, was strutting toward him. This was a surprise. He recalled at once that he had not laid eyes on this figure for four years or more. Moved solely by politeness, he rose to greet her, saying, "Welcome to our honored neighbor."

Maryam's mother held out a hand covered with a corner of her wrap as she said, "Thank you, al-Sayyid Ahmad."

He invited her to sit down, and she took the chair she had used on a day that was now part of history. He sat back down wondering about this new development. He had not seen her since she came to call on him at the store a year after Fahmy's death, when she had attempted to get him to resume his visits to her house. He had been amazed at her daring then. Not having recovered from his grief, he had treated her gruffly and bade her farewell coldly. Why was she coming back today? He looked her over and found her unchanged. She was plump and elegant, wearing a fragrant perfume. Her eyes sparkled over the top of her veil. But her finery could not conceal the advance of time and the lines under her eyes. She reminded him of Jalila and Zubayda. How heroically these women risked their lives in the battle for life and youth. . . . Amina had only too quickly fallen prey to her sorrows and allowed her bloom to fade.

Bahija brought her chair close to the desk and said in a low voice, "Excuse me, al-Sayyid, sir, for this visit. Necessity has its own laws."

Looking dignified and grave, al-Sayyid Ahmad immediately replied, "Welcome to you. Your visit is an honor and a favor for us."

Smiling, she answered in a tone that revealed her gratitude, "Thank you. Praise to God I've found you in good spirits and good health."

He in turn thanked her and prayed that she would be well and strong. Then she was silent for a few moments before saying with concern, "I've come for an important reason. I was told he had consulted you in due time and received your consent. I refer to Yasin Effendi's request to marry my daughter Maryam. Was I correctly informed? This is what I've come to discover."

Ahmad Abd al-Jawad lowered his eyes to keep her from reading in them his resentment at her words. He was not deceived by her pretense at concern for his consent. Let her try her wiles on some other man unfamiliar with what lay hidden behind them. He for one knew beyond the shadow of a doubt that it was all the same to her whether he gave his consent or withheld it. Did she not realize why he had not accompanied Yasin on his visit to her? Even so, she had come to force him to proclaim his approval and for some other reason, which would shortly be revealed.

He looked up at her with calm eyes and said, "Yasin told me of his plan and I wished him success. Maryam has always been like a daughter to us."

"May God grant me the blessing of your being favored with a long life. This marriage tie will be a prestigious honor for us."

"I thank you for your compliment."

She said fervently, "I'm pleased to tell you frankly that I postponed announcement of my consent until I could be certain of yours."

"Bitch!" he exclaimed to himself. "She probably announced her approval even before seeing Yasin."

"Mrs. Umm Maryam, I can only repeat my thanks."

"For that reason, the first thing I told Yasin Effendi was: 'Let me be sure your father agrees before anything else, for every other consideration is negligible compared to his wrath.'"

"My God, my God!" She had no sooner stolen the mule than she was busy throwing ropes around his master.

"Coming from you, such a noble statement is hardly unusual."

With triumphant enthusiasm she continued her verbal offensive:

"Al-Sayyid, sir, you're a man after our own heart, the best anyone would boast of in our whole quarter."

The guile of women and their coquetry—how fed up he was with both. Could she possibly imagine that he was wallowing in the dust to pursue the affections of a lute player once scorned by drunkards?

He replied modestly, "God forgive me."

In a sad tone, her voice rising enough so that he was afraid those at the far end of the store would hear her, she said, "I was very sad to learn he had left his father's home."

Al-Sayyid Ahmad shook his head to caution her not to speak too loudly. Before she could say anything more, he commented with a frown, "The fact is, his conduct angered me. I was amazed he had done such a stupid thing. He should have asked my advice first, but he carried his belongings to Palace of Desire Alley. Only then did he come apologize to me! A juvenile prank, Mrs. Umm Maryam. . . . I lectured him, ignoring his alleged disagreement with Amina. That was a silly reason for him to give in an attempt to justify even more foolish behavior."

"By your life, that's exactly what I told him. But Satan is ingenious. I also advised him that Mrs. Amina is not to be blamed. May our Lord console her for her sufferings. In any case, from someone like you, al-Sayyid, sir, pardon can be hoped."

With a flick of his wrist he seemed to say, "Let's drop this."

She commented ingratiatingly, "But I'll only be satisfied with a full pardon and your approval."

"Pshaw!" If only he could tell her frankly how disgusted he was with all of them: her, her daughter, and the great mule.

"Yasin's my son in any event. May God guide him to the right path. . . ."

She leaned her head back a little and left it there while she savored the pleasures of success and victory. Then she continued in a gentle voice: "May our Lord be gracious to you, al-Sayyid Ahmad. On my way over, I asked myself, 'Do you suppose he'll disappoint me and send me away empty-handed? Or will he treat his old neighbor the way he used to, in the past?' Praise God, you always live up to people's expectations. May God extend your life and enjoyment of health and strength."

"She thinks she's pulling the wool over my eyes," he told himself. "And she's entitled to. You're a failure as a father. Your best son has died, the second's a loss, and the third is headstrong. This has all happened over my dead body, you bitch."

"I can't thank you enough," he said.

Bowing her head, she observed, "Whatever I've said of you is far less than you deserve. How frequently I confessed that to you in the past. . . ."

"Oh, the past! Close that door, by the life of the mule whose acquisition you've come to record." He spread his hand across his chest to express his thanks.

She said dreamily, "Why not? Didn't I love you more than any man before or after you?"

This was what she wanted. Why had he not realized it from the first moment? "She hasn't come for Yasin or Maryam but for me. No, you've come for your own sake, you whom time has not changed in any respect save to deprive you of youth. But not so fast. . . . Can you really bring back a day that's over and done with?"

He allowed her remark to pass without comment, limiting himself to a smile of thanks. She grinned so broadly that her teeth were visible through her veil.

Somewhat critically she said, "It seems you don't remember a thing. . . ."

He wanted to apologize for his apparent disinterest without hurting her feelings. He said, "I no longer have a mind in my head capable of remembering anything."

She cried out sympathetically, "You've grieved far more than you should. Life can't tolerate or allow this, when you—if you'll excuse me for saying it—are accustomed to a pleasant life. The grief that would affect an ordinary man one carat has a twenty-four-carat impact on you."

"It's a sermon intended to benefit the preacher," he reflected. "If only Yasin was as easily satiated as I am. Why do I find you repulsive? You're certainly more obedient than Zanuba and incomparably less expensive. It seems my heart has developed a will to suffer."

With a combination of humility and cunning he asked, "How can a grieving heart laugh?"

As though glimpsing a ray of hope she quickly said with enthusiasm, "Laugh so your heart may laugh. Don't wait for it to laugh first. It's out of the question to think it will laugh all by itself after it's suffered from depression for such a long time. Resume your old life. Its joy, now slumbering, will return to you. Search out the things that delighted you in previous times as well as your former lovers. How do you know that there are no hearts that have stayed true to you, yearning for you, despite your long avoidance of them?"

Despite his better judgment his heart was transported by such delight that his thoughts strayed. This really was the way people ought to speak to Ahmad Abd al-Jawad. Words like these, accompanied by the tinkling of glasses, had caressed his ears during their parties. If only the lute player heard praise like this, perhaps she would curb her excesses. "Too bad it's someone you loathe who is praising you," he brooded.

In a tone that gave no hint of his secret delight, he said, "Those days have passed."

She reared back in protest and said, "By the Lord of al-Husayn, you're still a young man. . . ." Smiling modestly, she continued: "You're a camel and as handsome as the full moon. Your time isn't up and never will be. Don't consider yourself old prematurely. Or let others make that decision, for they may see you in a different light than you do yourself."

He replied politely but in a tone that graciously expressed his desire to terminate their conversation: "Rest assured, Mrs. Umm Maryam, that I'm not killing myself with grief. I've found various amusements to distract me from my sorrow."

Her enthusiasm waning a little, she asked, "Does that suffice to raise the spirits of a man like you?"

"My soul aspires to nothing more," he answered contentedly.

He seemed to have flustered her, but she pretended to be at ease as she said, "Thank God I've found you with the peace of mind and tranquillity I wish for you."

Then there was nothing more to say. She rose and held out a hand covered with the end of her wrap. They shook hands and, preparing to depart, she said, "I hope I leave you in good health."

She left, averting her eyes because she was unable to conceal their disappointed look.

14 ✑

The Suarès omnibus' went down al-Husayniya Street, and then its two emaciated horses began to traverse the asphalt of al-Abbasiya Street, as the driver goaded them on with his long whip. Kamal was sitting at the front of the vehicle at the end of a bench close to the driver. With a slight turn of his head the boy could see al-Abbasiya Street stretching out in front of his eyes. It was wider than the streets he was used to in the old part of town and so lengthy that it appeared to have no end. The surface was level and smooth, and the houses on either side were huge with spacious grounds and lush gardens.

He admired al-Abbasiya greatly, and the love and respect he harbored for that area bordered on reverence. The underlying reasons for his admiration were the district's cleanliness, its careful planning, and the restful calm reigning over its residences. All these characteristics were alien to his ancient and noisy district. His love and respect were attributable to al-Abbasiya's being the homeland for his heart and the residence for his love, since it was the location of his beloved's mansion.

During the past four years he had come this way repeatedly with an alert heart and fine-honed senses. Thus he had everything memorized. Wherever he looked, he found an image that was familiar enough to be the face of an old friend. All of the region's landmarks, sights, side streets, and many of its residents were associated in his mind with thoughts, emotions, and fantasies which in their totality had become the central focus of his life and the hub of his dreams. Wherever he turned he found an invitation for his heart to prostrate itself in prayer.

He removed from his pocket a letter he had received two days earlier. It had been sent by Husayn Shaddad to inform him of his friend's return from the beach. Hasan Salim and Isma'il Latif had also come home. Kamal was invited to meet them at Husayn's house, and the Suarès was taking him there. He looked at the letter with an eye that was dreamy, thankful, loving, reverent, adoring, and devoted, but not merely because it had been sent by his true love's brother. Kamal assumed that before Husayn wrote this letter the paper had been placed somewhere in the house. Her beautiful eye might have seen it as she passed or her fingers could have touched it, even accidentally. His hunch that the paper had lain near her transformed the letter into a symbol of something divine, which his spirit desired and his heart sought.

He read through the letter for the tenth time until he reached the sentence: "We returned to Cairo on the evening of October first." Without his knowing it, she had been in the capital for four days. Why had he not realized that? Why had he not sensed her presence there, whether by instinct, emotions, or intuition? How had the desolation that had enveloped him all summer long been able to spread its dark shadow over these four blessed days? Had his unbroken despair rendered him insensitive and dull? At any rate, his heart was throbbing now, and his spirit was soaring blissfully. He was looking down from a towering pinnacle. From that vantage point the world's features seemed encircled by diaphanous and luminous halos, like reflections of things in the angelic world. His mind was aflame with vital energy, intoxicating delight, and drunken exaltation. But even at this moment he was haunted by pain, which for him was as constant an accompaniment to the happiness of his love as an echo is to sound. In the old days when his heart was empty of love and oblivious, the Suarès had carried him along this same route. What feelings, hopes, fears, and expectations had he experienced then? All he could remember of life before love was a set of bare-bones memories, which seemed worthless to him now that he had recognized the value of love. But he also longed for them whenever the pain was too great. Yet his mind was so overwhelmed by love that these previous memories almost seemed figments of his imagination. He had begun to date his life by love, saying, "That happened before love, or B.L., and this took place after love: A.L."

The vehicle stopped at al-Wayliya, and Kamal put the letter back in his pocket. He got out and headed for Palaces Street, his eyes fixed on the first mansion on the right, at the edge of the desert. Viewed from the exterior, this two-story mansion seemed a massive, lofty structure. It fronted on Palaces Street, and behind it there was a spacious garden. The tops of tall trees were visible over a gray wall of medium height that surrounded both the mansion and its garden, tracing out a vast rectangle, which extended into the desert. This image was imprinted on the pages of his mind, for he was captivated by the residence's majesty and enchanted by its magnificence. Its grandeur appeared to him to testify to the worth of the owner. Some of the windows that he could see were shuttered and others were hidden by curtains. This seclusion and reserve seemed to symbolize his beloved's distinction, purity, inviolability, and mystery, ideas reinforced by the expansive gardens and the desert, which stretched out to the horizon. Set here and there through the garden were towering palm trees. Ivy vines scrambled up the sides of the house, and intertwining jasmine branches sprawled over the garden walls. This vegetation besieged his heart with clusters of memories like fruit on a tree. They whispered to him of ecstasy, pain, and devotion. They were a shadow of the beloved, a breath from her spirit, and a reflection of her features. Joined to what he knew of the family's exile in Paris, they provided an atmosphere of dreamy beauty. They were comparable to his love in their lofty sanctity and allusions to the mysterious world of the unknown.

As he approached the gate of the mansion, he saw the doorman, the cook, and the chauffeur sitting together on a nearby bench, as they usually did in the afternoon. When he reached them, the doorman stood up and announced: "Husayn Bey is waiting for you in the gazebo."

Kamal went in, greeted by the blend of fragrances from the jasmine vines and from the carnations and roses in pots arranged on either side of the steps, which were a short distance inside the gate and led to a large veranda. Kamal veered off to the right on a side path between the mansion and the garden wall. It conveyed him to the top of the garden near the back porch of the house.

The walk through these sacred precincts was an ordeal for his pounding heart. He was treading underfoot a surface her feet had once traversed. His reverence was so great he could scarcely continue. He would have liked to stretch his hand out to the wall of the mansion to seek its blessing, as he had once at the sepulchre of al-Husayn, before he learned it was nothing but a symbol. In what area of the mansion might his beloved be disporting herself at the moment? What would he do if she favored him with one of her fascinating glances? If only he would find her in the gazebo, then his eye would be rewarded for all its forbearance, longing, and sleeplessness.

He looked around the garden and back to the rear wall, where the desert began. From the street side of the house, the afternoon sun was striking the tops of the trees, the palms, the sprays of jasmine covering the walls in every direction, and the circles, squares, and crescents of assorted flowers and roses, which were separated by paths of stone mosaic. Kamal went down the center walk that led to the gazebo in the middle of the garden. Husayn Shaddad was visible in the distance along with his two guests, Hasan Salim and Isma'il Latif. They were sitting on rattan chairs grouped around a circular wooden table on which glasses were set beside a water jug. Hearing cries of joy from Husayn, Kamal realized that they had noticed his arrival. His friends immediately stood up to greet him, and he embraced each of them, for they had been separated all summer long.

"Praise God for your safe arrival."

"We've missed you a lot."

"How brown your faces have gotten. Now there's no difference between you and Isma'il."

"You're the European among us darker types."

"Soon everything will return to normal."

"We were asking ourselves why we don't get tans from the sun in Cairo."

"Who is brave enough to expose himself to the sun in Cairo— except someone wanting to get sunstroke?"

"What's the secret of this tanning process?"

"I remember we had an explanation of it in one of our courses; yes, perhaps in chemistry. Over the years we studied the sun in different subjects like astronomy, chemistry, and physics. In which of those do we find an explanation for tanning?"

"This question is moot. We're done with our secondary studies."

"So give us news of Cairo, then."

"No, you've got to tell me about Ra's al-Barr, and then Hasan and Isma'il need to tell us about Alexandria. Just wait. There's time for every topic."

The gazebo was nothing more than a round wooden roof supported by a massive post. The ground there was covered with sand and encircled by pots of roses. Its furnishings were limited to the wooden table and the rattan chairs. The young men sat near the table in a half circle facing the garden. They were obviously happy to be reunited, as the summer had separated them, except for Hasan Salim and Isma'il Latif, who usually spent the summer in Alexandria. They laughed at the slightest provocation and occasionally just on looking at each other—as if recalling comic memories. Kamal's three friends were wearing silk shirts and gray trousers, but he had on his lightweight gray suit. He considered the visit to al-Abbasiya a formal occasion. In his own district, he roamed everywhere content to put a jacket over his ankle-length shirt.

The surroundings spoke to Kamal's heart and shook it deeply. He had been smitten by love in this gazebo. Only this garden shared his secret with him. He was fond of these friends both out of friendship and because they were part of the saga of his love. All these things talked to his heart of love. He wondered when she would appear. Could the gathering conclude without his ardent eyes catching a glimpse of her? To compensate himself, he cast long looks at Husayn Shaddad whenever he could, regarding him with more than a friend's eye. The young man's relationship to Kamal's beloved lent him a mysterious enchantment. In addition to love, Kamal came to harbor admiration, veneration, and wonder for his friend. There was a marked resemblance between Husayn and his sister. It was visible in his black eyes, tall slender build, and thick, straight black hair as well as in his gestures and postures, which were distinguished by gracious refinement. The only major differences were his large hooked nose and his fair complexion, tanned by the summer sun.

Since Kamal, Husayn, and Isma'il had been successful in the baccalaureate examination that year—although admittedly the first two were seventeen and the third twenty-one—they discussed the examination and related issues pertaining to their futures. Isma'il Latif raised the topic. When he spoke, he craned his head up as though to conceal his short stature and light build—compared with those of his three companions. All the same, he was muscular and sturdy. The caustic, ironic look of his narrow eyes, his sharply pointed nose, his thick eyebrows, and his strong wide mouth were sufficient warning to anyone tempted to attack him.

Isma'il said, "We were one hundred percent successful this year. Nothing like this has ever happened before, at least not where I'm concerned. I ought to be in my final year at the University like Hasan, who began Fuad I School with me the same day. When my father saw my number listed in the newspaper among the students who passed, he said sarcastically, 'I wonder whether God will let me live long enough to see you graduate from the University.' "

Husayn Shaddad commented, "You're not far enough behind to justify your father's despair."

Isma'il said ironically, "You're right. Two years in each grade is hardly remarkable." Then, addressing Hasan Salim, he continued: "And probably you're already planning what you'll do when you finish University."

Hasan Salim was in the final year of Law School. He realized that Isma'il Latif was inviting him to announce his goals for the future. But Husayn Shaddad answered Isma'il first: "There's no reason for him to worry about that. He'll surely land a position in the judiciary or the diplomatic corps."

Hasan Salim emerged from his haughty silence. His handsome face with its fine features had an argumentative look. He asked defiantly, "Why should I believe you?"

He prided himself on his industry and intelligence and he wanted everyone to acknowledge them. No one disputed that, but likewise no one was forgetting he was the son of Salim Bey Sabry, superior court judge. To have a father like that was a distinction far more significant than intelligence and industry.

Husayn Shaddad avoided any reference that would rile his friend and said, "Your superior success is the guarantee you're seeking."

Isma'il Latif would not let him enjoy this praise. He said, "And there's your father. I reckon he's far more important than good grades."

Hasan met the attack with unexpected nonchalance. Either he had grown tired of Isma'il's teasing, since they had been together almost every day all summer long, or he had started to think his friend a chronic complainer whose comments should not be taken seriously. The friendship linking the young men did not rule out bickering and wrangles, which occasionally became intense but did not weaken their relationship.

Glaring at Isma'il mockingly, Hasan Salim asked, "What about you? What have your agents been able to come up with for you?"

Isma'il laughed out loud, revealing his sharp teeth, yellow from smoking, which he had been one of the first to embrace in secondary school. He answered, "An unsatisfactory result. Medicine and Engineering didn't accept me, because my overall average was too low. That left only Commerce and Agriculture. So I chose the former."

Kamal was upset that his friend had ignored the Teachers College, as though it was not worth considering. All the same, since he could have attended Law School and there was no dispute about its high status, his choice of the other instead seemed so noble that it helped console him for his lonely sorrow.

Husayn Shaddad laughed in a charming way that showed off his attractive mouth and eyes. He said, "Oh, if only you had chosen Agriculture! Imagine Isma'il out in the fields spending his life with farm laborers. . . ."

Isma'il answered with conviction, "That's not for me, not even if the fields were in downtown Cairo, on Imad al-Din Street."

Then Kamal looked at Husayn Shaddad and asked, "And you?"

Husayn looked off into the distance thoughtfully before he replied, granting Kamal an opportunity to scrutinize him. How fascinated he was by the idea that Husayn was her brother—that his friend kept her company in their home the way he had once lived together with Khadija and Aisha. It was hard for him to picture that. Husayn sat with her, conversed with her, spent time alone with her, and touched her.

"Touches her? He has meals with her! I wonder how she eats? Does she make little noises with her lips? Does she eat regional specialties like mallow greens or beans in oil? That's difficult to imagine too. What's important is that he's her brother."

Kamal could touch the hand that touched hers. If only he might inhale the fragrant perfume of her breath at one remove from her brother. . . .

Husayn Shaddad replied, "Law School on a provisional basis."

Was it not conceivable that Husayn would become friends with Fuad Jamil al-Hamzawi? Why not? Law School was no doubt a truly admirable institution, since Husayn was enrolling in it. Attempting to convince people of the value of his own idealism would be foolhardy now.

Isma'il Latif commented sarcastically, "I didn't know some students enroll in school 'on a provisional basis.' Please explain this to us."

Husayn Shaddad answered seriously, "All the schools are the same to me. None has anything that I find especially attractive. Of course I want to learn, but I don't want to work. Nowhere at the University will I get the knowledge I want free from professional ties. Since I haven't succeeded in discovering anyone in our house who agrees with me, I find myself obliged to meet them halfway. I asked them which school they would choose. My father commented, 'Is there anything besides Law?' So I said, 'Let it be Law.'"

Imitating his tone and gestures, Isma'il Latif exclaimed, "On a provisional basis!"

They all laughed. Then Husayn Shaddad continued: "Yes, on a provisional basis, you quarrelsome fellow. For it's possible, if things turn out the way I want, that I may cut short my studies in Egypt and go to France, even if I have to study law there. Then I could sip freely from the springs of culture. There I could think, see, and listen. . . ."

Still imitating his friend's tone and gestures, as though to complete what had been left unsaid, Isma'il Latif added, "And taste, touch, and smell."

After they had laughed, Husayn Shaddad went on: "Rest assured that my intentions aren't what you suspect."

Kamal believed him wholeheartedly and felt no need for any substantiation, not only because he thought too highly of his friend to doubt him but also because he believed that the life Husayn was bent on enjoying in France would by its very nature transport the soul. Obvious as this point was, Isma'il and others like him, who believed only in things countable and visible, could hardly be expected to grasp it. Husayn had long excited Kamal's dreams. Here was another of those dreams, remarkable for its expansive beauty. This was a dream rife with food for the spirit and for the mind, for hearing and seeing.

"How often I've had this dream," Kamal thought, "both waking and sleeping. After all my aspirations and efforts, the dreaming process has led me to the Teachers College." Then he asked Husayn, "Do you really mean what you said about not wanting to work?"

With a dreamy look in his handsome black eyes, Husayn Shaddad answered, "I'm not going to be a speculator on the stock market like my father. I couldn't stand a life that consisted of uninterrupted work for the sake of making money. I will never be a civil servant. A career as a bureaucrat is slavery disguised as earning a living. I have more than enough to live on. I want to live as a tourist in the world. I'll read, see, hear, and think, moving from the mountains to the plains and back again."

After watching him throughout the discussion with a scornful look softened by his aristocratic reserve, Hasan Salim objected, "A civil service career need not be simply a way of earning a living. I, for example, won't need to work to earn a living, but it's important for me to work in a noble profession. A man must have a career. A dignified occupation is a goal worth achieving for its own sake."

Isma'il endorsed Hasan's statement: "This is true. Even the very richest people aspire to careers in the judiciary, the diplomatic corps, and the civil service." Then, turning toward Husayn Shaddad, he added, "Why don't you select one of these careers for yourself, since they're within your grasp?"

Kamal also addressed Husayn: "The foreign service would provide you with a distinguished profession and opportunities for travel."

Hasan Salim said importantly, "It's hard to get into."

Husayn Shaddad replied, "The foreign service no doubt has extraordinary advantages. For the most part it's a ceremonial career. It would accommodate my desire to avoid the servitude of work. It's a form of tourism and provides free time. It would allow me to have my desired spiritual life dedicated to the pursuit of beauty. But I think I won't attempt it, not because it's so selective, as Hasan points out, but because I doubt I'll continue my formal studies through to the end."

Laughing wickedly, Isma'il Latif said, "I can't help thinking that you want to go to France for reasons that have nothing to do with culture. And you're right."

Husayn Shaddad laughed and shook his head to deny the allegation. "Certainly not!" he said. "You're thinking of your own passions. My distaste for schooling has other reasons. The first is that I'm not interested in studying law. The second is that no one branch of the University can provide me with the variety of disciplines and arts I wish to learn—like theater, painting, music, and philosophy. And if you enroll in some branch, you'll have to cram your head with dust in order to come across a few specks of gold, if you find any at all. In Paris you're allowed to attend lectures in all the different areas of learning without being tied down to a schedule or an examination. That way you can have a beautiful, spiritual life."

Then, as though to himself, he added in a low voice, "Perhaps I'll marry there, so I can spend my life as a tourist both in reality and in my imagination."

Hasan Salim's face gave no indication that he was following this discussion with any serious interest. Isma'il Latif raised his bushy eyebrows, leaving it up to his eyes to disclose the sly irony surging within his breast. Only Kamal seemed enthusiastic and touched. He had nourished these same hopes. His differed only in nonessential details. He was not interested in tourism or getting married in France, but how he longed for learning not confined to a schedule or an examination. . . . That would obviously be far superior to the dirt he would cram into his head at the Teachers College in hopes of coming away with a few atoms of gold. Paris? It had been a beautiful dream for him ever since he learned that his beloved had spent part of her childhood there. It still beckoned Husayn with its magic and fascinated Kamal with its diverse promises. But what cure was there for his passionate hopes?

After some hesitation he said apprehensively, "It seems to me that the school coming closest to offering what you want, if only to a limited degree, is the Teachers College."

Isma'il Latif turned toward him somewhat anxiously and asked,

"What have you selected? Don't say the Teachers College! My Lord, I'd forgotten that you're almost as foolish as Husayn."

Kamal smiled so broadly that his large nostrils were flexed. He answered, "I've enrolled in the Teachers College for the reasons mentioned."

Husayn Shaddad looked at him with interest. Then, smiling, he said, "No doubt your cultural passions got the better of you while you were wrestling with this choice."

Isma'il Latif told Husayn accusingly, "You bear a great deal of responsibility for encouraging these passions of his. The truth is that you talk a lot and read little, while this poor boy takes the matter seriously and reads himself blind. Look at your evil influence on him. In the end it's driven him to the Teachers College."

Ignoring Isma'il's interruption, Husayn continued: "Are you sure that the Teachers College has what you want?"

Delighted by this first inquiry about his school free of scorn or derision, Kamal said enthusiastically, "It's enough for me to be allowed to study English. Then I can use it as a way of learning a limitless number of things. Besides that, I think it will provide an excellent opportunity for studying history, education, and psychology."

Husayn Shaddad thought a little. Then he said, "I've met many teachers and observed them at close range in my tutorial sessions. They were not good models for the cultured man; but the antiquated instructional program's responsible for that."

With undiminished enthusiasm Kamal said, "All I need are the tools. True cultural development depends on the man, not the school."

Hasan Salim asked, "Do you plan to become a teacher?"

Although Hasan phrased this question politely, it made Kamal uncomfortable. Hasan's politeness was deeply ingrained, and he only abandoned it as a last resort or when an adversary attacked. His courtesy was a natural result of his composure and aristocratic upbringing. So it was difficult for Kamal to determine whether his friend's question was really free of scorn and derision.

Kamal shrugged his shoulders as he said, "That's inevitable, since I'm determined to study what I want."

Isma'il Latif was covertly scrutinizing Kamal, looking at his head, nose, long neck, and skinny body. He must have been trying to judge the impact this sight would have on schoolchildren, particularly the naughtiest ones. He could not keep himself from muttering, "By my life, it'll be a catastrophe."

Revealing his affection for Kamal, Husayn Shaddad continued: "The job's a secondary consideration for people with ambitious goals. And we mustn't forget the elite group of prominent figures who graduated from this school."

The University discussion ended there, and the young men were silent. Kamal attempted to fuse his spirit with the encompassing garden, but the discussion had made such a lively impression on him that he had to wait for its effect to wear off. He happened to notice the jug of ice water on the table. An old fantasy came to mind, one that had made him joyous on occasions like this. It consisted of filling a glass and drinking from it while he imagined that his lips were touching a place on the rim brushed by hers. He went to the table, filled a glass from the jug, and drank. As he sat down again, he concentrated on himself, anticipating some change in his state of consciousness, if he were lucky enough to achieve his goal. A magical force he had never experienced would radiate from his spirit. He would succumb to a divine intoxication transporting him to the heavens of bliss. But, alas, he finally had to satisfy himself with the pleasure he received from the adventure and his delicious hope.

Kamal began to wonder anxiously, "When will she come?" Was it possible for this promising moment to be added to the three months of their separation? His eyes returned to the jug. He recalled a conversation he had once had with Isma'il Latif about it, or rather about its ice water, which was the only refreshment they were served at the Shaddad mansion.

During their talk, Isma'il had mentioned the strict economies observed in the mansion from roof to basement and had asked if that was not a form of stinginess. Kamal had refused to allow the reputation of his beloved's family to be questioned or tarnished and had defended them against this accusation. He had cited their luxurious lifestyle, servants, employees, and their two automobiles: the Minerva and the Fiat, which Husayn virtually monopolized. Once all of that had been taken into account, how could they be accused of parsimony?

Never at a loss for an impudent remark, Isma'il had distinguished between different types of stinginess. He thought that since Shaddad Bey was a millionaire in every sense of the word, he had a duty to surround himself with all the trappings of prosperity. Yet Shaddad

Bey limited his family to what, in his circle, constituted the bare necessities. The principle observed without deviation by every member of the family was not to tolerate the expenditure of one millieme except when it was appropriate and necessary. The servants received low wages and ate cheap food. If one broke a dish, the price was deducted from his pay. Husayn Shaddad came from the only family that did not provide an allowance for its sons. They did not want him to get used to squandering money. His father might buy some stocks and bonds for him in honor of a holiday but would not give him spending money. And the dear son's visitors were served nothing but ice water. Was this not stinginess, no matter how aristocratic?

Kamal remembered that conversation while looking at the jug. He wondered with alarm, as he had before, whether it was possible for any defect to attach itself to his beloved's family. His heart refused to believe that. It rejected the possibility that perfection could be flawed in any respect, no matter how slight. All the same, he imagined that a feeling close to relief was mischievously whispering to him, "Don't be frightened. Isn't this shortcoming, if it exists, a factor bringing her closer to your level, if only by a little?"

Although skeptical and dubious about Isma'il's claims, Kamal found himself unintentionally reflecting on the vice of stinginess. He classified it into two types. One was despicable, but the other was a wise policy providing an excellent foundation for a person's financial life. To term systematic care in spending stinginess or a vice would be an extravagant exaggeration. Why not proceed in this manner, since it was compatible with the erection of palaces, the acquisition of automobiles, and the display of prestigious luxuries? Why worry when it applied to noble souls cleansed of all wickedness and baseness?

Kamal was roused from his reflections by Isma'il Latif's hand, which grasped his arm and shook it. Then he heard Isma'il tell Hasan Salim, "Watch out! Here's the Wafd Party representative. He'll answer you."

Kamal realized at once that they had begun discussing politics while he was daydreaming. Political discussion . . . how tiresome and yet how pleasant it was. Isma'il called him the Wafd Party representative. Perhaps he was being sarcastic. So let him make fun of anything he wanted. Kamal had imbibed the nationalist ideology of the Wafd Party from Fahmy, and in his heart it was associated with his brother's sacrifice and death as a martyr.

He looked at Hasan Salim and said with a smile, "My friend, since you are dazzled by nothing save true majesty, what have you said about Sa'd Zaghlul?"

Hasan Salim gave no sign of interest in discussing majesty. Kamal had not expected any other reaction. For a long time he had struggled with his friend only to be rebuffed by Hasan's—and perhaps also his father the superior court justice's—stubborn and arrogant view of Sa'd Zaghlul, whom Kamal almost venerated. In Hasan Salim's opinion, Sa'd was nothing but a populist agitator. Hasan repeated this characterization with provocative disdain and scorn, which were at odds with his normal gentle courtesy. He made fun of Sa'd Zaghlul's policies and rhetorical flourishes. He extolled the majesty of Adli, Tharwat, Muhammad Mahmud, and other members of the Liberal Constitutionalist group, who, in Kamal's eyes, were traitors or Englishmen in fezzes.

Hasan Salim answered calmly, "We were discussing the negotiations, which lasted only three days before being halted."

Kamal said enthusiastically, "That was a patriotic stance truly worthy of Sa'd. Since the demand for our national rights was not negotiable, it became necessary to terminate the negotiations. And Sa'd pronounced his immortal words: 'We were invited here to commit suicide, but we refused. This is all that happened.' "

Finding politics a fit topic for banter, Isma'il Latif observed, "If he had agreed to commit suicide, his life would have been crowned with the most exalted service he could have rendered his country."

Hasan Salim waited for Isma'il and Husayn to stop laughing before he said, "How have we benefited from this bon mot? Patriotism is nothing for Sa'd but a rhetorical device to seduce the masses. 'We were invited here to commit suicide,' and so on and so forth. 'I like to speak the truth,' and so on. . . . words and more words. There are men who say nothing but work silently. They are the ones who achieved the only boon the nation has won in recent history."

Anger flared up in Kamal's heart, and he would have exploded had he not been restrained by his respect for Hasan and for his age. Kamal was amazed that a young man like Hasan should follow the deviant political views of his father, a member of the old guard.

"You belittle the importance of words, as though they had none. But in fact the most significant and noteworthy events of human history can ultimately be traced back to some statement. The grand phrase contains hope, power, and truth. We proceed through life by the light of words. And Sa'd Zaghlul is not merely a wordsmith. His record is full of achievements and stands."

Husayn Shaddad ran his long thin fingers through his black hair as he said, "Leaving Sa'd out of it, I agree with what you said about the value of language."

Hasan paid no attention to Husayn Shaddad's interjection. Addressing Kamal, he remarked, "Nations survive and advance with brains, wise policies, and manpower—not through speeches and cheap populist agitation."

Isma'il Latif looked at Husayn Shaddad and asked sarcastically, "Don't you think a man who wears himself out talking about the betterment of this country is like a person attempting to inflate a punctured balloon?"

Kamal turned to Isma'il in order to address Hasan indirectly and to tell him things he would otherwise be reluctant to say. Venting his wrath, Kamal said, "Politics means nothing to you, but occasionally your jokes express so clearly the viewpoint of a faction who claim to be Egyptians that you could be their spokesman. They express their despair that the nation will ever progress, but it stems from contemptuous snobbery, not from a zealous ambition for reform. If politics were not an expedient way of satisfying their greed, they would shun it, like you."

Husayn Shaddad laughed pleasantly. He put his hand on Kamal's arm and squeezed it, saying, "You're a stubborn debater. I like your enthusiasm, even if I don't share your faith in politics. You know I'm uncommitted politically. I don't belong to the Wafd Party or the Constitutionalists, not because I scorn them like Isma'il Latif, but because I'm convinced that politics corrupts the mind and heart. You have to rise above it before life can appear to you as an endless opportunity for wisdom, beauty, and tolerance instead of an arena for combat and deceit."

Kamal was reassured to hear Husayn speak out, and his fury abated. He was ecstatic whenever Husayn agreed with him and broad-minded whenever they disagreed. Even so, he felt that Husayn's defense of political neutrality was nothing more than an excuse for his lack of patriotism. Kamal had never resented that in his friend or regarded it as a failing, although he did with Isma'il. If Kamal ever thought of it as a shortcoming, his goodwill, forbearance, and tolerance allowed him to overlook it.

Picking up on Husayn's ideas, Kamal said, "Life is all of that. It's composed of struggle, deceit, wisdom, and beauty. Whenever you neglect one aspect, you lose an opportunity to perfect your understanding of it as well as your ability to influence it in a positive way. Never scorn politics. It's half of life, or the whole of life if you consider wisdom and beauty to be above life."

As though by way of apology, Husayn Shaddad answered, "So far as politics is concerned, I'll tell you frankly that I don't trust any of those men."

Kamal asked him almost cajolingly, "What made you lose confidence in Sa'd Zaghlul?"

"No, let me ask what should make me trust him? Sa'd or Adli, Adli or Sa'd, how silly it all is.... Yet even though Sa'd and Adli are equivalent for me politically, I can't say the same of them as men. I can't ignore Adli's distinguished family lineage, prestige, and culture. Sa'd—don't get angry—is nothing but a former seminarian from al-Azhar."

Oh, how it hurt Kamal whenever his friend let slip some hint of his sense of superiority over the Egyptian people. Kamal was extremely sad, for it seemed that Husayn felt superior to him or—and this was even more devastating and bitter—that his words reflected the feelings of the whole family. Yes, when Husayn talked to Kamal, he left his friend with the impression that he was talking about a people to which neither of them belonged. Was that caused by an error of perception on Husayn's part or was it flattery? Strangely enough, this attitude of Husayn's did not anger Kamal in its general implications nearly so much as it saddened him because of what it implied specifically about Kamal. It did not excite a feeling of class hostility or patriotism in him, for these emotions were put to flight by his friend's guileless grin, which revealed his sincerity and benevolence. They were decisively routed by a love uninfluenced by opinions or events.

Despite their friendship, Hasan Salim's attitude toward the common people enraged Kamal's sense of patriotism, even though Hasan's aloofness and haughtiness were no more pronounced than Husayn Shaddad's. Not even Hasan's polite manner of speaking or his reserve in expressing his feelings mediated for him with Kamal, who considered them a form of cleverness serving to double his friend's responsibility and to reinforce his solidarity with the aristocracy in opposition to the people.

Addressing Husayn, Kamal asked, "Do I need to remind you that true majesty is not determined by whether a person wears a turban or a fez and is poor or rich? It seems to me that politics occasionally forces us to debate self-evident truths."

Isma'il Latif commented, "What I admire in Wafdists like Kamal is their intense partisan spirit." Then, looking around at his friends, he continued: "And what I despise about them is also their party loyalty."

Laughing, Husayn Shaddad said, "You're lucky. No matter what political opinion you advance, no critic can ever object to it."

Then Hasan Salim asked Husayn Shaddad, "You claim you're above politics. Do you insist on that even with regard to the former Khedive?"

Their eyes were directed toward Husayn with cheerful defiance, since his father's support for the former Khedive, Abbas Hilmi II, was well known and since it was for this reason that he had spent several years in exile in Paris. But Husayn said nonchalantly, "These matters are no concern of mine at all. My father was and still is a supporter of the Khedive. I'm not required to embrace his views."

His eyes sparkling with amusement, Isma'il Latif asked, "Was your father one of those who shouted, 'God lives! Abbas arrives'?"

Husayn Shaddad said with a laugh, "I've never heard about this, except from you. The indubitable truth is that there was nothing between my father and the Khedive beyond friendship and loyalty. Besides, as you all know, there's not a single party calling for the return of the Khedive today."

Hasan Salim said, "The man and his era have become part of history. The present situation can be put in these few words: Sa'd Zaghlul refuses to allow anyone else, no matter how fine or wise, to speak in the name of Egypt."

Immediately after receiving this blow, Kamal retorted, "The present situation can be summed up in even fewer words: No one in Egypt is able to speak for her except Sa'd. The people's support for him is great enough to achieve our goals in the end."

Kamal folded his arms across his chest and stretched out his legs until the tip of his shoe touched the table leg. He was planning to continue his remarks, but they heard someone close behind them ask, "Budur, don't you want to say hello to your old friends?"

Kamal's tongue was paralyzed. His heart leapt so violently that it shook his chest in a fashion that initially alarmed and almost hurt him. Then, quicker than a flash of lightning, an overwhelming and intoxicating happiness took hold of him. The effect on him was so great that he almost had to close his eyes. He discovered that every notion pulsing through his soul was directed heavenward. He rose with the others and turned around. He saw Aïda standing a step away from the gazebo, holding the hand of Budur, her little sister, who was three years old. The girls were looking at them with calm smiling eyes. After a wait of three months or more, here she was. Here was the original of the portrait that filled his spirit and body during his waking and sleeping moments. Here she was, standing before him, bearing witness to the fact that the limitless pain, the indescribable happiness, the searing periods of wakefulness, and the dreams spinning him through the skies could, in the final analysis, all be traced back to a charming human being whose feet left prints in the garden. He gazed at her, and her personal magnetism attracted his emotions so totally that he lost all sense of time, place, people, and self. He was once more reduced to a spirit swimming through the void toward his beloved. He perceived her—more with his spirit than his senses —in an enchanting intoxication, a musical rapture, and a lofty splendor. His sight grew weak and feeble. The force of his spiritual reaction seemed to have affected all his vital functions. Thus his senses and his faculties were transported to a semiconscious state approaching annihilation. Therefore, his beloved was more easily observed in his memory than in real life. When he was in her presence, he could scarcely see anything. Later she would appear to his memory with her slender figure, bronze face as beautiful as the moon, and thick black hair cut in a boyish bob, the bangs coming down over her forehead like the teeth of a comb. In her dark eyes there was a look as tranquil, gentle, and majestic as the dawn. He saw this picture in his memory, not with his senses. It was like a magical melody that so absorbs us when we hear it that we are unable to recall anything about it, until it comes back to us as a happy surprise in the first instants when we awake or during a moment of contentment. Then it reverberates deep within our consciousness in a perfectly harmonious manner.

Kamal hopefully wondered whether she would change her usual procedure and shake hands with them. Then he would feel her touch, if only for that one time in his whole life. But she greeted them with a smile and a nod of her head.

In her voice, which by comparison made even the most beloved melodies seem worthless, she asked, "How are all of you?"

They vied with each other to greet and thank her and congratulate her on her safe return.

Then, her slender fingers toying with Budur's hair, she told the girl, "Shake hands with your friends."

Budur sucked in her lips and bit them as she looked around shyly. Then she fixed her eyes on Kamal, and they both smiled. Knowing of the affection between them, Husayn Shaddad said, "She's smiling at the one she loves."

"Do you really love this fellow?" Aïda asked. Then, pushing her sister toward the young man, she said, "So greet him."

Blushing with happiness, Kamal held his hands out to her. She approached him, and he lifted her up. He began to kiss her cheeks with longing and emotion. He was delighted by her love and proud of it. In his arms there was a fragment from the body of the family. When he hugged this part of them, he was embracing the whole family. Was it possible for a worshipper to contact his beloved without some mediation like this? The strange resemblance between this child and her older sister was nothing short of magical. The person contentedly nestled against his breast seemed Aïda herself at an earlier stage of life. Once she had been as young, small, and generous with her affections as Budur. "Ponder that," he advised himself.

Let him rejoice in this pure love. Let him find happiness in embracing a body she embraced and in kissing a cheek she kissed. Let him dream until his mind and heart were transported. He knew why he loved Budur, Husayn, the mansion with its garden and servants. He loved them all for Aïda's sake. What he did not understand was his love for Aïda.

Looking back and forth from Hasan Salim to Isma'il Latif, Aïda asked, "How was Alexandria?"

Hasan replied, "Splendid!"

Then Isma'il asked, "What makes you always want to go to Ra's al-Barr?"

In a pleasant voice with a musical ring, she answered, "We've spent several summers in Alexandria, but the only resort we really enjoy is Ra's al-Barr. The one other place as calm, unpretentious, and congenial is your own home."

Laughing, Isma'il said, "Unfortunately we don't care for calm."

How happy this scene made Kamal ... and this conversation and this voice. "Think about it," he advised himself. "Isn't this happiness? A butterfly, like the dawn breeze, saturated in delightful colors, sipping the nectar of the flowers ... that's what I am." If only this moment could last forever.

Aïda said, "We had an enjoyable trip. Hasn't Husayn told you about it?"

In a disapproving tone Husayn said, "No, they've been arguing about politics."

She turned toward Kamal to say, "Here's someone who wants to talk about nothing else."

"Her attention comes to you as a grace," Kamal reflected. "Her look's so pure it reveals her angelic spirit. I'm revived by it like a sun worshipper soaking up radiant light. If only this moment would last forever."

"I wasn't responsible for initiating the discussion today."

Smiling, she said, "But you seized the opportunity...."

He grinned in surrender. Then she turned her eyes on Budur and cried out, "Are you planning to fall asleep in his arms? That's enough greeting for you."

Budur was embarrassed and buried her head against his chest. He started stroking her back fondly.

But Aïda threatened: "Then I'll leave you and go back alone."

Budur lifted her head and held out her hand to her sister, mumbling, "No." Kamal kissed her and set her on the ground. She ran to Aïda and grasped her hand. Aïda looked at each of them in turn, waved goodbye, and went back the way she had come. They resumed their seats and continued their conversation.

Aïda's visits to the gazebo in the garden were like this. They were brief, happy surprises, but Kamal appeared content. He felt that his patience during the long summer months had not been in vain. Why did not people commit suicide to attempt to hold on to happiness just as they killed themselves to escape from suffering?

"It's not necessary for you to travel around the world like Husayn if you wish to find pleasure for your senses, intellect, and spirit. It's possible for you to acquire all of those in a fleeting moment without stirring. How does a human being obtain the power to effect all this? What's happened to the political feud, the heated debate, the furious quarrel, and the class conflict? They've melted away and vanished at a look from your eyes, O beloved. What distinguishes dream from reality? I wonder which of them I'm roaming through now."

"Soccer season starts soon."

"Last season belonged to the Ahli team. They were unrivaled."

"The Mukhtalat team was defeated, but it's got some outstanding players."

Kamal sprang to the defense of Mukhtalat—much as he defended Sa'd Zaghlul—to block the attacks of Hasan Salim. All four of them played soccer, but they differed in their skill and enthusiasm. Isma'il was by far the best and stood out among them like a professional playing with amateurs. Husayn Shaddad was the weakest player. Kamal and Hasan were in the middle. The exchange between Kamal and Hasan heated up. The former attributed Mukhtalat's defeat to bad luck, the latter thought it showed the superiority of Ahli's new players. The controversy continued, since neither of them would give in.

Kamal wondered why he always found himself on the other side from Hasan Salim, whether they were discussing the Wafd Party and the Liberals or the Mukhtalat team and Ahli. Among musicians Kamal preferred Hijazi, but Hasan liked Mukhtar. In cinema, the former enjoyed Charlie Chaplin, while the latter favored the dapper French comedian Max Linder.

Kamal left his friends shortly before sunset. As he walked along the path beside the house heading for the gate he heard a voice cry, "There he is."

Enchanted, he looked up and saw Aïda at one of the first-floor windows. She was pointing him out as she held Budur, who sat on the window ledge. Kamal stopped below them, looking up with a smiling face at the child, who waved her small hand at him. He also glanced from time to time at the face in whose form and expressions his hopes for life and the afterlife were vested. His heart was colliding drunkenly with his ribs. Budur waved to him once more, and Aïda asked her, "Are you going to him?"

The little girl nodded yes, and Aïda laughed at this wish that would not be realized. Encouraged by her laughter, Kamal examined her carefully, losing himself in the beautiful coloration of her eyes and in the exquisite meeting point of her eyebrows. He recalled the reverberation of her throaty laughter and the inflections of her warm voice until he was sighing with emotion and passion. Since the situation obliged him to speak, he asked his beloved, "Did she think of me at the beach?"

Moving her head back a little, Aïda said, "Ask her yourself. What you two think of each other is none of my business." Then before he could utter a word, she added, "Did you remember her?"

"Oh," he thought. "This is like Fahmy reviewing lessons with me on the roof while Maryam listened."

"She was never absent from my thoughts," he answered fervently.

A voice called to the girls from inside. Aïda straightened up and lifted Budur in her arms. As she was about to leave she made this final comment: "What an amazing love!" Then she disappeared from the window.

15 ❧

Amina and Kamal were the only remaining patrons of the coffee hour, and even he left the house before sunset. Then his mother stayed on there by herself or called Umm Hanafi to keep her company until it was time for bed. Yasin had left a void behind him. Although Amina tried not to mention him, Kamal felt isolated by his brother's departure, and the delightful enjoyment he had found in this gathering was spoiled. In the old days coffee had been an excuse for conversation. Now it was everything to the mother. She drank so much that, without her realizing it, preparation and consumption of the coffee became her sole entertainment. She would drink five, six, or even ten cups in succession.

Kamal anxiously kept track of her excesses and cautioned her about the consequences. She answered him with a smile as though to say, "What would I do if I weren't drinking coffee?" In a confident and assured tone she told him, "There's nothing harmful about coffee."

They sat facing each other, she on the sofa between the doors to the bedroom and the dining room, Kamal on one between the entries to his bedroom and his study. She was bent over the coffeepot, which was half buried in the brazier's coals. He was silent and staring vacantly into space. Suddenly she asked, "What are you thinking about, I wonder? You always look as though you're thinking about something important."

He sensed the criticism in her tone and replied, "The mind constantly finds things to occupy it."

She looked up questioningly at him with her small, honey-colored eyes. Then she said somewhat shyly, "It's been ages since we found time for a conversation."

"Really?" he wondered. That past was gone forever—the era of religious lessons and stories about prophets and demons, when he had been insanely devoted to her. That era had come to an end. What would they discuss today? Except for meaningless chatter there was absolutely nothing for them to say to each other. He smiled, as though to apologize for both past and future silences.

Then he said, "We talk to each other whenever we have something to discuss."

She replied gently, "People who want to talk set no limits on their conversations, but you seem always to be absent or absentminded...."

After reflecting a bit she added, "You read a lot. You read as much during your vacation as when you're in school. You never get enough rest. I'm afraid you've worn yourself out."

In a tone that indicated he did not welcome this interrogation, Kamal answered, "There are many hours in a day. Spending a few of them reading won't wear anyone out. It's nothing but a pastime, even if it's a beneficial one."

After some hesitation she observed, "I'm afraid reading's the reason you seem so quiet and preoccupied...."

"No," he thought. "It's not reading. If only you knew how it distracts me from my discomfort." Something else had been absorbing him, and he could not escape from it even when he was reading. His was a condition without a cure that she or anyone else could provide. He was sick with love, devoted but at his wits' end, not knowing what to wish for beyond his suffering.

Slyly ˙he said, "Reading's like coffee. There's nothing harmful about it. Don't you want me to become a scholar like my grandfather?"

Delight and pride shone in her pale, oval face. She answered, "Of course. I wish that wholeheartedly, but I want to see you in good spirits all the time."

Smiling, he said, "I'm in as good spirits as you could wish. So don't trouble your mind with idle speculation."

He had noticed that her concern for him had increased in recent years more than was necessary or desirable. Her devotion, solicitude, and apprehension about anything that might harm him—or that she imagined might—had begun to engage her mind to a degree that made him uncomfortable, prompting him to defend his freedom and dignity. Yet he never lost sight of this development's causes, which included Fahmy's death and the misery she had endured. Thus Kamal never overstepped the bounds of affection and politeness in defense of his independence.

"I'm happy to hear that from you, if it's really true. All I desire is your happiness. I prayed for you today at the shrine of our master al-Husayn. I hope God may answer my prayer."

"Amen."

He watched her raise the coffeepot to fill her cup for the fourth time. The corners of his mouth spread open in a faint smile. He remembered how a visit to the mosque of al-Husayn had once seemed an impossible dream for her. Now she visited it whenever she went to the cemetery or to see her two daughters on Sugar Street. But what an oppressive price she had paid for this limited freedom. He too nourished impossible dreams. What price would be exacted from him if he was to fulfill them? Yet, any payment, no matter how great, would seem insignificant if he could.

Emitting a forced laugh, he observed, "The visit to al-Husayn is certainly linked to unforgettable memories. . . ."

Smiling, she felt her collarbone, which she had broken during her first trip there, and said, "And to lasting results."

With a modicum of enthusiasm Kamal said, "You're not a prisoner in the house as you once were. You've gained the right to visit Khadija, Aisha, and our master al-Husayn as often as you want. Imagine what you would have missed if Father had not relaxed the rules."

She looked up at him with confused embarrassment, for the reference to a distinction she had won as a result of losing a child troubled her. Then she bowed her head despondently, as if to say, "I wish I had remained as I was and kept my son." She did not air the feelings raging in her breast for fear of upsetting Kamal. Apologizing for the freedom she enjoyed, she said, "My occasional excursions are not for my entertainment. I go to al-Husayn to pray for you. I visit your sisters to reassure myself about them and to resolve the problems no one else seems able to handle."

He had no difficulty guessing which problems she meant. Knowing she had visited Aisha and Khadija that day, he asked, "Anything new at Sugar Street?"

Sighing, she answered, "The usual."

He shook his head sadly. Then with a smile he remarked, "Khadija has a gift for quarreling."

Amina responded sorrowfully, "Her mother-in-law told me that any conversation with her threatens to end badly."

"It seems her mother-in-law is growing senile too."

"Her age is excuse enough. But what's your sister's excuse?"

"Did you side with her or with the truth?"

Amina laughed in a way that suggested she knew only too well what he meant. She sighed again and said, "Your sister has a hot temperament. She is quick to bridle at even the most sincere advice. And woe to me if I'm polite to her mother-in-law out of respect for her age and status. Then she'll ask me with fiery eyes, 'Are you for me or against me?' There is no strength or might save from God. 'For me or against me!' Are we at war, son? Strangely enough, at times her mother-in-law is at fault, but Khadija carries the fight to such extremes that she ends up in the wrong."

It would be impossible for anything to make Kamal angry at Khadija. She had been and still remained his second mother and an inexhaustible source of affection. How did his sister Aisha compare with her—beautiful, giddy Aisha who had absorbed all the characteristics of the Shawkat family?

"What did the investigation reveal?"

"This time the argument began with the husband, and that's unusual. When I entered their quarters, they were having a violent dispute. I was amazed that something had agitated the good man and intervened to make peace. Then I learned the cause for all of it. She had made up her mind to dust the apartment, but he was still sleeping at nine. So she insisted on rousing him, and he woke up angry. Feeling obstinate for once, he refused to get out of bed. His mother heard the row and was quick to come. Then the fires flared. This quarrel was scarcely concluded before another one broke out, because Ahmad returned from playing in the street with mud on his shirt. She hit him and wanted him to take a bath. The boy appealed to his father for help, and the man came to his rescue. So a second fight broke out in one morning."

Laughing, Kamal asked, "What did you do?"

"I tried my best but did not succeed. She scolded me for a long time because I had attempted to mediate. She told me, 'You should have taken my side the way she stood up for him.' "

Sighing a third time, she continued: "I told Khadija, 'Don't you remember how you saw me act when I was with your father?' She answered sharply, 'Do you think there's another man in the whole world like Father?' "

Uninvited, the vision of Abd al-Hamid Bey Shaddad and his wife, Saniya Hanim, popped into Kamal's imagination. They were walking side by side from the veranda to their Minerva automobile, which was parked by the gate of the mansion. They did not seem a master and his servant but two equal friends conversing easily with each other, with her arm draped over his. When they reached the vehicle, the bey stepped aside to allow the lady to climb in first.

"Will you ever get to see your parents act like this?" he wondered. "What a silly idea!"

The couple walked with an air of distinction befitting the parents of his beloved. Although her mother was as old as his, she was wearing an expensive coat, which was a marvel of taste, elegance, and style. Her face was unveiled and attractive, although it did not compare with the angelic countenance of her daughter. There emanated from her a fragrant perfume and a captivating elegance. He wished he knew what they discussed and their manner of agreeing and disagreeing, if they ever did differ. He was eager to learn about this life, which was linked to his beloved's by the firmest ties and bonds.

"Do you remember," he asked himself, "how you gazed at her—like a worshipper viewing great priests and high church dignitaries?"

He told his mother calmly, "If Khadija's character was more like yours, she would be assured a happy life."

She smiled with delight, although her pleasure ran afoul of a bitter truth—namely, that her disposition, no matter how mild, could not always guarantee her happiness. Then with the smile still on her lips to conceal her gloomy thoughts, which she was apprehensive he might detect, she said, "God alone is the guide. May our Lord make you even more sweet-tempered than you are, so you'll be a person loving others and loved by them."

He quickly asked her, "What do you think of me?"

With conviction she replied, "You're already like that and better."

"But how can angels love you?" he wondered. "Call up her blissful image and contemplate it a little. Can you imagine her unable to sleep or left prostrate by love and passion? That's too remote even for a fantasy. She's above love, for love is a defect remedied only by the loved one. Be patient and don't torment your heart. It's enough that you're in love. It's enough that you see her. Her image shines into your spirit and her dulcet tones send intoxicating delight through you. From the beloved emanates a light in which all things appear to be created afresh. After a long silence, the jasmine and the hyacinth beans begin to confide in each other. The minarets and domes fly up over the evening glow into the sky. The landmarks of the ancient district hand down the wisdom of past generations. The existential orchestra echoes the chirps of the crickets. The dens of wild beasts overflow with tenderness. Grace adorns the alleys and side streets. Sparrows of rapture chatter over the tombs. Inanimate objects are caught up in silent meditation. The rainbow appears in the woven mat over which your feet step. Such is the world of my beloved."

"I went by al-Azhar on my way to al-Husayn and ran into a large demonstration with people chanting slogans. It reminded me of the past. Has something happened, son?"

He answered, "The English do not wish to leave peacefully."

With a look of anger sparkling in her eyes she said sharply, "The English ... those Englishmen! When will God's just vengeance fall on them?" She had felt a similar aversion to Sa'd Zaghlul himself for a long time, until Kamal had finally convinced her it was impossible to detest a person Fahmy had loved. With obvious anxiety she asked, "What do you mean, Kamal? Are we returning to the days of suffering?"

He replied resentfully, "Only God knows!"

Her discomfort was apparent in her facial contractions. She said, "May God preserve us from suffering. We'll leave them to the wrath of Almighty God. This is the best policy. To throw ourselves to destruction is madness. Let us take refuge with God."

"Don't alarm yourself. Death is inescapable. People die for one reason or another—or for none at all."

She responded indignantly, "I don't deny that what you say is true, but I dislike your tone."

"How should I talk?"

With compelling emotion she said, "I want you to state that you agree it's sinful for a man to risk his life."

Trying to hide his smile, he gave in: "I agree."

She looked at him skeptically and begged, "Say that with your heart, not your tongue."

"I'm speaking with my heart."

"What an enormous gap there is between ideal and reality," Kamal thought. "You zealously strive for the ultimate in religion, politics, thought, and love, but mothers think only of their children's security. What mother would want to bury a son every five years? The quest for ideals in life necessarily requires sacrifices and martyrs. Body, mind, and spirit are sacrificed. Fahmy gave up a promising life in return for a magnificent death. Will you be able to meet death as heroically as he did? You would not hesitate to make this choice, even though that would crush your unfortunate mother's heart. A death that would drain blood from one wound to stanch others ... what a love it would be! Yes, but as you know, Aïda, the love between me and Budur is not of that kind. The truly amazing love is mine for you. It testifies on behalf of the world against pessimistic adversaries. It has taught me that death is not the most atrocious thing we have to dread and that life is not the most splendid thing we can desire. I have learned that some facets of life are so rough and repulsive that death is sought instead and some so smooth and sustaining that immortality is desired. How captivating are the world's appeals to you in its indescribable voice, not too high or low—like a violin playing the middle note of a scale—resonant and pure as a light (if you can imagine this) colored sky blue and pulsing with conviction. These calls are an invitation to the empyrean."

16

"Next Thursday, putting my trust in God, I'll get married."

"May our Lord grant us success."

"I'll be successful if I please my father."

"Your father isn't angry at you, praise God."

"The only guests will be family members. You won't find anything there to upset you."

"Fine, fine!"

"I wish Mother would come, but . . ."

"It's not our fault. The important thing is for the evening to pass quietly."

"Naturally. That hasn't escaped me. I know your tastes as well as anyone. There will be nothing to the wedding beyond the marriage contract and some refreshments."

"Fine. May our Lord guide you to the right path."

"I've asked Kamal to give my greetings to his mother and to request her not to deprive me of the benefit of her prayers and to forgive me. . . ."

"Of course. Naturally."

"Please let me hear you say again that you're not angry with me."

"I'm not angry at you. By God I hope you're destined to find success and prosperity. God hears our prayers."

Matters did not turn out according to the wishes of al-Sayyid Ahmad. He was forced to go along with his son for fear of jeopardizing their relationship. His heart was too tender for him to quarrel seriously with Yasin, let alone to sever ties with him. Al-Sayyid Ahmad had agreed to hand over his eldest son to Bahija's daughter and to sanction by his presence the wedding that would bring his former mistress into the family circle. He had rejected Amina's attempt at intervention when she had declared her wish that Fahmy's brother and sisters should be prevented from attending Yasin's marriage to Maryam.

He had told her in a peremptory tone, "That's a silly idea. Some men marry their brother's widow, in spite of their love and devotion for him. Maryam wasn't married to Fahmy. She wasn't even engaged to him. It's ancient history, from six years ago. I won't deny that he's made a poor choice, but for a mule he's got good intentions. He's hurting himself more than anyone else. He could have found a better family, and the girl's divorced. It's in God's hands. Yasin bears full responsibility for this."

Amina had fallen silent, as though accepting his arguments. Although she had acquired from her time of suffering some measure of courage about voicing her opinion in front of her husband, she did not have enough nerve to oppose him. Thus when Khadija visited her to say that Yasin had invited her to his wedding and that she was thinking of using ill health as an excuse for declining, Amina had disagreed and advised her to accept her brother's invitation.

Thursday arrived, and al-Sayyid Ahmad Abd al-Jawad went to the home of the late Mr. Muhammad Ridwan, where he found Yasin and Kamal waiting to greet him. They were soon joined by Ibrahim and Khalil Shawkat, who were accompanied by Khadija and Aisha. Maryam's family was represented by only a few women, and al-Sayyid Ahmad felt reassured that the day would indeed pass tranquilly.

On his way to the parlor, he encountered familiar landmarks, ones he had seen previously in radically different circumstances. He was besieged by memories, which provoked various forms of disgust and vexation within him, because of the silent mockery of the new role he had come to perform—that of the dignified father of the bridegroom. He was secretly cursing his son, who had landed him and himself—if he would only realize it—in a fix. The fact that the marriage was actually taking place tempted him to reconsider the situation and to hope that God had created the daughter from another pattern than her mother's and that Yasin would find Maryam an excellent wife, in every sense of the word, and be spared reckless behavior like her mother's. Then he asked God to conceal things best forgotten.

Yasin was handsome in his finery and obviously happy, despite the simplicity of the reception honoring his wedding. The secret of his good spirits was the presence of his brother and sisters. He had been apprehensive that their mother might influence one of them to stay home. Would it have been possible to dispense with Maryam for their sakes? Certainly not ... He loved her. Since she had offered him no route to her save marriage, this wedding was inevitable. The objections of his father and stepmother were misplaced. Yasin was unimpressed by the threat of dire consequences. Furthermore, Maryam was the first woman he had desired to marry on the basis of a prior knowledge of her character and appearance. For this reason he was optimistic about the prospects for the marriage, hoping that it would establish a lasting conjugal life for him. That much was true. He felt he would be a good husband and that she would make a good wife for him. In time he was sure Ridwan would have a happy home in which to grow up and mature. Yasin had drifted around a lot, and it was time for him to settle down. Had the circumstances attending his wedding been different, he would not have hesitated to celebrate it with a party offering many delights and pleasures. He was not so old, poor, or ill at ease with parties that he would ordinarily be content with this dreary reunion, more like a funeral than a wedding. But one should not judge the situation too hastily, for necessity has its own laws. He would dedicate this abstinence to Fahmy's memory.

Maryam's reunion with Khadija and Aisha, after a separation of several years, was an emotional one, no matter how reserved or awkward. They exchanged kisses and compliments. Their lengthy conversation ranged far and wide but sidestepped the past, as far as possible. The first moments were the most strained. Each of the women expected old memories relating to the rupture and the development of bad feelings between them to be dredged up in a negative or critical fashion. These first delicate moments passed safely, and Maryam adroitly steered the conversation toward Khadija's clothes and Aisha's slender figure, which she had retained even after bearing three children. Maryam and her mother asked about "the mother." They were told that she was well, and nothing more was said about her.

Aisha looked at her longtime friend with an eye filled with tender affection, for her heart was always ready to love. If she had not felt apprehensive about the consequences, she would have turned the conversation to memories of the past, in order to laugh over them to her heart's content.

Khadija stealthily scrutinized Maryam. Although she had not thought of her former friend for years, news of her marriage to Yasin had inspired a flood of bitter comments. She had reminded Aisha about the incident with the Englishman, wondering aloud what could have blinded and deafened Yasin. Yet Khadija's emotional commitment to her family was so intense that it took precedence over everything else and prevented her from criticizing Maryam within earshot of members of the Shawkat family. Not even Khadija's husband was exempted. She cautioned her mother: "Whether we like it or not,

Maryam is going to become part of our family." There was nothing strange in this attitude, for Khadija, even after giving birth to Abd al-Muni'm Shawkat and Ahmad Shawkat, still considered the Shawkats strangers, to a certain degree.

The marriage clerk arrived early in the evening, and the wedding contract was drawn up. Cool drinks flavored with fruit syrup were passed around and a single whooping trill of joy resounded. Yasin received their congratulations and good wishes. The bride was summoned to meet her "senior master," al-Sayyid Ahmad, and the family of her new husband. Escorted by her mother, Khadija, and Aisha, she kissed her father-in-law's hand and shook those of the others. Then al-Sayyid Ahmad presented her with the wedding gift, a set of gold bracelets studded with small diamonds and emeralds. The family gathering lasted a long time, with the guests starting to leave, one after the other, at about nine. Then the carriage arrived to take the couple to Yasin's house in Palace of Desire Alley, where he had prepared the third floor to receive his bride. Everyone thought that, for better or for worse, the curtain had fallen on Yasin's second marriage.

But two weeks after this wedding the home of the late Mr. Muhammad Ridwan witnessed another nuptial party, one considered truly bizarre by the residents of al-Sayyid Ahmad's home, of Sugar Street, of Palace of Desire Alley, and of the whole Palace Walk neighborhood. Without any prior warning, people learned to their total amazement that Bahija was marrying Bayumi, who sold fruit drinks. Everyone was stunned by this. It seemed they were realizing for the first time that Bayumi's shop stood at the head of the alley where the Ridwan residence was located and that it lay directly beneath one of the venerable latticed balconies of the house. Confronted by this fact, they could only wonder. And people had every reason to be amazed, for the bride was the widow of a man known during his lifetime for his goodness and piety and she was considered one of the respectable ladies of the district, even though she was fond of personal adornment. And she was fifty. The bridegroom was a common fellow who wore unpretentious ankle-length shirts and sold carob- and tamarind-flavored drinks in a small shop. He was only forty. He had also been married for twenty years and had fathered nine children. All these factors provoked gossip. Without any reserve whatsoever people waded into the subject of the events that must have preceded the wedding but which had passed undetected by any-

one. When and how did these things happen? How did they develop
to the point of culminating in matrimony? Which of the two parties
had initiated the relationship and which had accepted the invitation?

Uncle Hasanayn, the barber, whose establishment was on the other
side of the street, next to the ancient building housing the public
cistern, reported that he had frequently seen Mrs. Bahija standing in
front of Bayumi's stall, consuming a carob drink. Perhaps they had
exchanged a few words then, but, being a kindly man, the barber had
never suspected anything. Asking God's forgiveness, Abu Sari', who
sold roasted snacks from a shop that closed later than other ones,
said he had occasionally noticed men slipping into her house by night
but had not known Bayumi was one of them. Darwish, who sold
cooked beans, had some things to say, as did al-Fuli, the milkman.
Although they pretended to pity the man with all those children and
to criticize him bitterly for being so stupid as to marry a woman old
enough to be his mother, they were secretly envious of his luck and
resented his ascent from their class by means of this unorthodox ploy.
Following those comments there was a great deal of talk about the
extent of his expected inheritance from the house and a possible treasure trove of jewelry.

The households of al-Sayyid Ahmad, of Sugar Street, and of Palace
of Desire Alley were severely shaken. "What a scandal!" everyone
exclaimed. Al-Sayyid Ahmad was so angry that members of his immediate family were too terrified to speak to him for several days
running. From that time on, Bayumi the drinks vendor would surely
have a right to consider al-Sayyid Ahmad his relative. "Curses on
Yasin and his lusts!" Bayumi the drinks vendor had become his "uncle," and everyone's nose had been rubbed in the dirt.

When the information reached Khadija, she shouted, "What awful
news!" Then she asked Aisha, "Who could ever fault Mother after
this? Her heart is never wrong."

Yasin swore to his father that the event had taken place without
his knowledge or his wife's. It had made his wife sadder than anyone
could possibly imagine. But what could she do?

The scandal did not stop there, for the moment Bayumi's first wife
heard the news, she went berserk and stormed out of her home like
a lunatic, pushing her children in front of her. She swooped down on
Bayumi in his store, and a fierce battle broke out between them as
words, hands, feet, shrieks, and screams were employed within the
sight and hearing of their children, who began to howl and implore
people at hand and passersby to help. Soon a crowd had collected in

front of the store—pedestrians, shop owners, women, and children. When they separated the couple and forced the woman back into the street, she came to rest under Bahija's balcony. Her dress was ripped, her wrap in shreds, her hair disheveled, and her nose bloody. She reared her head back to look up at the shuttered windows before unleashing a tongue like a whip with poisoned, weighted ends.

Worse still, when she left her post there, she headed for al-Sayyid Ahmad's store, because he was the father-in-law of her husband's new stepdaughter. She begged him tearfully and oratorically to use his influence to convince her husband to mend his sinful ways. Although seething with rage and chagrin at his plight, al-Sayyid Ahmad heard her out. Then he delicately tried to make her understand, so far as he was able, that this whole affair was beyond the scope of his influence, contrary to her expectations. He kept at it until he persuaded her to leave his store. He was furious but, even so, thought long and hard about Bahija's motives for this strange marriage, especially since he was certain it would not have been hard for her to find a way to gratify any desire she might have felt for Bayumi the drinks vendor without exposing herself and her family to the disturbing consequences of marriage. Why had she committed this folly, paying no attention to the man's wife and children and wantonly disregarding the feelings of her daughter and her daughter's new family, as if she had gone insane? Was it not a gloomy feeling of growing old that had made her seek refuge in marriage? Indeed she was sacrificing many of her possessions in her pursuit of the happiness that fleeting youth had once secured for her. He brooded over this idea sorrowfully and despondently. He remembered his own humiliation at the hands of Zanuba the lute player. She had refused him so much as an affectionate glance until he had set her up in the houseboat. That humiliation had shattered his self-confidence and had made him, despite his apparent serenity, frown back at time, since it had begun to frown at him.

In any event, Bahija did not have long to enjoy her marriage. By the end of the third week she was complaining of a sore on her leg. When she had a medical examination she was diagnosed as being diabetic and taken to Qasr al-Ayni Hospital. Reports of the gravity of her condition were heard for several days. Then the appointed hour overtook her.

17

Holding a small bag under his arm, Kamal stood in front of the Shaddad family mansion. He was wearing an elegant gray suit, and his black shoes were gleaming. With his fez perched securely on his large head, he looked tall and thin. Protruding from his shirt, his neck seemed nonchalant about supporting this large head and huge nose. The weather was pleasant, although occasionally a chilly breeze announced that December was on its way. The scattered, sparkling white clouds moved across the sky languidly, veiling the morning sun from time to time. Kamal stood there expectantly, his eyes directed toward the garage. Then the Fiat emerged, driven by Husayn Shaddad, who turned it around on Palaces Street and came to a halt beside Kamal. He stuck his head out the window and asked his friend, "Haven't they come yet?"

He blew the horn three times. Opening the door, he said, "Come sit next to me."

Kamal was content to put the bag inside. He muttered, "Be patient." Then Budur's voice reached him from the garden. Turning in that direction, he saw her advance at a gallop with Aïda trailing behind. Yes, his beloved was approaching, her exquisite figure clad in a stylish short gray dress. A blue silk smock hid the top part of her dress but revealed the girl's pure, bronze forearms. The black halo of her hair encircled the back of her neck and her cheeks and swung with a flowing motion as she walked. The strands of her bangs were plastered to her forehead. In the middle of the black oval there was a face of moonlike beauty, lovely in a way both chic and angelic. It seemed the serene ambassador of the kingdom of happy dreams.

Kamal felt held in place by an overpowering magnetic force. He was in a state between dreaming and waking, conscious only of a sense of gratitude and a pulsing ecstasy. With light prancing steps she approached, like a beautiful melody in bodily form, until she was near enough for him to inhale her Parisian perfume. When their eyes met, a cheerful smile that was tempered by aristocratic reserve could be detected in her eyes and on her pursed lips. Kamal responded with an anxious grin and a bow of his head.

Husayn told her, "You and Budur sit in the back seat."

Kamal moved to open the rear door of the automobile and stood there at attention like one of the household help. He was rewarded with a smile and a word of thanks in French. He waited for Budur and his beloved to climb in. Then he closed the door and slipped onto the front seat beside Husayn, who blew the horn once more as he looked toward the mansion. The doorman immediately arrived with a small basket, which he placed next to Kamal's bag in the space between the two young men. Laughingly tapping the basket and the bag, Husayn asked, "What good is an excursion without food?"

As the engine started it emitted a groan of protest. Then the car dashed off along al-Abbasiya Street. Husayn Shaddad was telling Kamal, "I know a lot about you, and today will permit me to add fresh information concerning your stomach. I suspect that despite your slenderness, you're a glutton. Do you think I'm mistaken?"

Smiling and more delighted than one would think humanly possible, Kamal answered, "Wait and see for yourself."

A single automobile was carrying all of them on a shared adventure almost impossible to imagine except in dreams. Kamal could hear his wishes whisper, "If only you were sitting in the back seat and she was in front, your eyes could have watched her all they wanted during the whole trip, free of supervision."

"Don't be greedy and ungrateful," he cautioned himself. "Bow down in praise and thanksgiving. Liberate your head from thought, free yourself from the stream of desires, and devote all your attention to experiencing the present moment. Isn't an hour worth a whole lifetime or even more?"

"I wasn't able to invite Hasan and Isma'il to join us on this excursion."

Kamal did not speak but gave his friend a questioning look. His heart was throbbing with joy and embarrassment at being singled out for this distinction.

Then Husayn continued apologetically: "The car, as you can see, isn't big enough for everyone."

In a faint voice Kamal replied, "That's clear."

Smiling, his friend observed, "When it's necessary to choose, you should pick the person who most resembles you. And there's no doubt that our interests in life are close. Isn't that so?"

Kamal's face reflected the happiness overflowing his heart, and he said, "Of course." Then, laughing, he added, "Except that I'm content with spiritual journeys, whereas it appears that you won't be satisfied until your spiritual trip takes you all around the physical world."

"Don't you long to see the world?"

Kamal thought a little before saying, "It seems to me that I have a natural love of staying put. I flinch at the thought of travel. I mean because of the commotion and upheaval, not because of the sights and the chance to explore. If it were feasible, I would like to have the world parade past while I stand here."

Husayn Shaddad laughed in an endearing way that came straight from his heart. He said, "Stay aloft in a balloon, if you can, and watch the world revolve beneath you."

Kamal savored Husayn's charming laugh for some time. The image of Hasan Salim came to mind, and he compared these two different versions of the aristocracy: one remarkable for charm and cheerfulness, the other characterized by reserve and arrogance. Regardless of these differences, both were distinguished.

Kamal observed, "Fortunately, mental journeys don't require any movement at all."

Husayn Shaddad raised his eyes with apparent skepticism but abandoned the topic. He said joyfully, "What's important for us now is to take a short trip together, united by our tastes, which are so similar."

Before Kamal knew what was happening, a sweet voice behind him said, "In short, Husayn's as fond of you as Budur is."

Perfumed with love and set to music by her angelic voice, this sentence penetrated Kamal's heart and sent him into an inebriated ecstasy. It was like a magical melody emerging suddenly in the middle of a song, rising above customary expectations in an unimagined way to leave the listener perched between rationality and delirium.

"The beloved is recklessly playing with the vocabulary of love. She sprinkles you with it, little realizing that she is pouring flammable magnesium on a blazing heart." He recalled the sound of her words in order to re-create their resonant love within him. Affection is an ancient melody but seems marvelously fresh in each new rendition. "My God, I'm perishing from an excess of happiness," he thought.

Commenting on his sister's words, Husayn said, "Aïda's able to translate my thoughts into her special feminine language."

The vehicle sped along to al-Sakakini, then down Queen Nazili Street, followed by Fuad I Street. From there it crossed over the Nile to Zamalek at a speed Kamal thought insane.

"There are a few clouds in the sky, but we need even more if we're to have a comfortable day at the pyramids."

The miraculous voice was then heard, apparently addressing Budur: "Wait till we get to the pyramids. Then you can sit with him all you want."

Laughing, Husayn asked, "What does Budur want?"

"She desires, my dear sir, to sit with your friend."

" 'Your friend'! Why not say 'Kamal'? Why not grant that name a happiness beyond the aspirations of its owner?"

Husayn told him, "Yesterday Papa heard her ask me, 'Is Uncle Kamal coming with us to the pyramids?' So he wanted to know who Kamal was. When I told him, he asked her, 'Do you want to marry Uncle Kamal?' She told him quite plainly, 'Yes.'"

Kamal looked around, but the little girl had leaned back to hide her face against her sister's shoulder. Before turning his head away, Kamal fortified himself with a fleeting glance at the superb face of his beloved. He said, "If she's serious, she better not forget her promise."

When their automobile reached the Giza road, Husayn accelerated, and the roar of the engine increased so much that no one felt like talking. Kamal welcomed this opportunity to be alone with his thoughts and to enjoy his happiness. The day before, their family had discussed him, and the head of the household had suggested he should marry the little girl.

"Oh, what a warbling, flowery happiness! Memorize every word said. Replenish your soul with her Parisian perfume. Stock your ears with these calls of doves and gazelles. Perhaps you will be able to return to these experiences if you're troubled again by sleepless nights. The words of the beloved lack the wisdom of philosophers and the glittering insights of fine authors, and yet they shake you to the core and cause springs of happiness to well up in your heart. This is what makes happiness a mystery baffling the most brilliant minds. All you who breathlessly pursue happiness, I've come across it in a casual remark, a foreign phrase, in silence, and even in nothing at all. My Lord, how huge these giant trees are on both sides of the road! Their lofty branches form a canopy overhead, creating a lush green sky. There's the Nile flowing along with a brilliant coat of pearls supplied by the sun's decorative rays. When did I last see this road? On a trip to the pyramids when I was in the third year of secondary school. Each time I promise myself I'll return here alone. Behind you is sitting the person who has inspired you to see everything in a new way, even the traditional style of life in the ancient quarters of the city. Would you wish for anything beyond your present condition? Yes, for the automobile to continue racing along like this forever. . . . O Lord! Is this the aspect that always escaped you when you were wondering what you desired from love? The inspiration of the hour has revealed it to you, impossible though that seems. Rejoice in this preordained moment. There are the pyramids, looking small in the distance. Soon we'll stand at the foot of the largest one, like an ant at the base of a towering tree."

"We're going to visit the tomb of one of our original ancestors."

Kamal laughed. "To recite the opening prayer of the Qur'an in his memory in hieroglyphics," he joked.

Husayn remarked ironically, "A nation whose most notable manifestations are tombs and corpses!" Pointing to one of the pyramids, he continued: "Look at all that wasted effort."

Kamal replied enthusiastically, "Immortality!"

"Oh, as usual, you'll spare no effort to defend Egypt. Your patriotism's chronic. We differ in this. I might actually prefer to be in France instead of Egypt."

Hiding his pain behind a tender smile, Kamal answered, "There you'll find that the French are one of the most patriotic nations in the world."

"Yes, patriotism is an international disease. But I love France itself and I admire qualities of the French people unrelated to nationalism."

This kind of talk really saddened Kamal, but it did not cause resentment, since it came from Husayn Shaddad. He occasionally became vexed with Isma'il Latif on account of his arrogance. Hasan Salim angered Kamal at times with his haughtiness. But Husayn Shaddad always met with Kamal's approval, no matter what.

The automobile stopped near the foot of the great pyramid and at the end of a long line of empty vehicles. Many people could be seen here and there scattered in small groups. Some were riding donkeys or camels and others were climbing the pyramid. There were also the vendors and the donkey and camel drivers. The expanse of land seemed vast and limitless, but the pyramid shot up in the center like a legendary giant. On the far side, beyond the downward-sloping plateau, the city of Cairo was visible with the tops of its trees, a thread of water, and the roofs of its large buildings. Where were Palace Walk and Kamal's ancient house in all of that? Where was his mother, who would be putting out water for the chickens now, near the jasmine arbor?

"Let's leave everything in the car, so we'll be free to scout around."

They got out of the automobile and set off in single file: Aïda, Husayn, Budur, and finally Kamal, who was holding his young friend's hand. They walked around the great pyramid, admiring it from every direction. Then they went into the desert. The sand made it hard to walk and hindered their progress, but the refreshing breeze blew gently. The sun alternately hid and reappeared. Clusters of clouds spread along the horizons, sketching on the celestial canvas spontaneous pictures, which the hand of the wind altered at will.

Filling his lungs with the air, Husayn exclaimed, "Beautiful! Beautiful. . . ."

Aïda said something unintelligible in French. Kamal with his limited knowledge of that language assumed that she was translating her brother's comment. Using foreign words was a common practice for her, one that softened his extreme identification with the national tongue, Arabic, and imposed itself on his taste as a characteristic of feminine beauty.

Looking at everything around him, Kamal was moved and said, "Truly beautiful, praise to God Almighty."

Laughing, Husayn commented, "You always find God or Sa'd Zaghlul in everything."

"I think we have no quarrel concerning the first of those two."

"But your insistence on mentioning Him gives you an especially religious flavor, as though you were a scholar of religion." Then, in a tone of surrender, he continued: "What's strange about that since you're from a religious district?"

Was there any sarcasm lurking behind this statement? Was it possible that Aïda felt the same way? What did they really think of the ancient Islamic district at the heart of Cairo? How did residents of al-Abbasiya view Palace Walk and al-Nahhasin?

"Should you be embarrassed?" Kamal wondered. "Not so fast. . . . Husayn demonstrates scarcely any interest in religion and the beloved even less. Didn't she say once that she attends classes in Christianity at Mère de Dieu School, goes to mass, and sings their hymns? But she's a Muslim! A Muslim despite the fact that she knows nothing worth mentioning about Islam. . . . What do you think of this? I love her. I love her to the point of devotion. Despite the pricking of my conscience, I confess that I love her religion, while asking forgiveness from my Lord."

Husayn gestured toward the beauty and splendor surrounding them. Then he said, "This is what really attracts me. You're wildly patriotic, but compare the splendors of nature with demonstrations, Sa'd Zaghlul and Adli, and trucks packed with soldiers."

Smiling, Kamal replied, "Both nature and politics are splendid."

As though the association of ideas reminded him of an important event, Husayn said suddenly, "I almost forgot. Your leader has resigned." Kamal's only response was a sad smile.

Intending to provoke him, Husayn said, "He resigned after losing both the Sudan and the constitution. Isn't that so?"

With a calm attributable solely to the company in which he found himself, Kamal answered, "The assassination of Sir Lee Stack Pasha was a blow directed at Sa'd's government. . . ."

"Let me repeat for you what Hasan Salim said: 'This attack is a manifestation of the hatred that some people, including the killers, harbor for the English. Sa'd Zaghlul is more responsible than anyone else for inciting this hatred.' "

Kamal suppressed the rage ignited within him by Hasan Salim's opinion. With the composure mandatory when he was in the presence of his beloved he said, "This is the English view. Haven't you read the telegrams printed in the newspaper, in *al-Ahram*? No wonder the Liberal Constitutionalists are repeating it. One of Sa'd's proudest achievements is that he aroused hostility against the English."

With a look of criticism or warning in her eyes and a fetching smile, Aïda intervened to ask, "Are we here to picnic or to politick?"

Kamal gestured toward Husayn as he said apologetically, "There's the one responsible for bringing up this subject."

Laughing and combing his silky black hair with his slender fingers, Husayn said, "I thought I'd offer you my condolences for the resignation of your leader. That's all there is to it." Then he asked in a serious tone, "Didn't you take part in the momentous demonstrations that erupted in your district during the revolutionary era?"

"I was too young!"

In a voice not free of gentle irony, Husayn observed, "In any case, the way you hid in that pastry shop during a demonstration must be considered participation in the revolution."

They all laughed. Even Budur imitated the others. Their quartet was composed of two horns, a violin, and a whistle. After a moment of silence, as though coming to Kamal's defense, Aïda said, "It's enough that he lost his brother."

Feeling pride pulsing through his heart because of their sympathy, Kamal said, "Yes, we lost the best of our family."

She asked with interest, "He was in Law School; isn't that so? How old would he be if he were alive today?"

"He'd be twenty-five. . . ." Then he continued in a mournful voice: "He was a genius in every sense of the word."

Cracking his knuckles, Husayn said, "Was! This is what you reap from patriotism. How can you cling to it after that?"

Smiling, Kamal said, "The time will come when we're all referred to in the past tense. But what a difference there is between one form of death and another!"

Husayn cracked his knuckles once more without comment. Kamal's words seemed to mean nothing to him. What had made them discuss politics? It was not fun anymore. Partisan hostilities distracted people from the English. Down with all of it! A person who had caught a whiff of paradise should not trouble himself with terrestrial cares, not even momentarily.

"You're walking with Aïda in the desert near the pyramids. Ponder this ravishing fact and shout it aloud until the pyramid builders hear you. The beloved and her suitor are strolling together over the sand. The lover's rapture is so intense that the breeze might almost carry him off, while the beloved amuses herself by counting pebbles. If love's malady were contagious, I would not mind the pain. The wind is agitating the fringes of her dress, raking the halo of her hair, and penetrating her lungs. How fortunate it is! Spirits of lovers who float over the pyramid, bless this procession. They admire the beloved and pity the lover. They repeat with the voice of time the phrase: 'Nothing save love is stronger than death.' You see her but a few feet from you. Yet in truth she's as far removed as the horizons, which you imagine touching the earth, even though they are part of the sky and soar high overhead. How my soul wishes I could feel her touch on this excursion, but it seems you'll journey through this earthly existence before you experience that. Why aren't you courageous enough to throw yourself on the sand and kiss her footprints? Take a handful of sand from them for use in an amulet to ward off the pains of love during thought-filled nights. But alas! Everything indicates that the only contact with the beloved will be through singing hymns of praise or via insanity. So sing your psalms or go insane."

He felt a small hand tug at his. He looked down at Budur, who held her arms up to him, asking to be carried. He leaned over and lifted her, but Aïda protested: "No. It seems fatigue's getting the best of us. Let's rest a little."

On a boulder at the top of the slope leading to the Sphinx they sat down in the same order they had observed while walking. Husayn stretched his legs out and planted his heels firmly in the sand. Kamal sat with his legs crossed, holding Budur beside him. Aïda, seated to the left of her brother, took out her comb, which she ran through her hair. Then she smoothed her bangs with her fingers.

Husayn happened to notice Kamal's fez and asked his friend critically, "Why are you wearing a fez on this outing?"

Kamal removed it and placed it on his lap, saying, "I'm not used to going anywhere without it."

Husayn laughed and said, "You're a fine example of a conservative!"

Kamal wondered whether he was being praised or faulted and wished to force his friend to clarify the point, but Aïda leaned forward a little and turned toward Kamal to have a look at his head. He forgot what he was up to and anxiously concentrated all his attention on his own head. Now that it was bare, its huge size was obvious, and his short cropped hair, free of any attempt at styling, was exposed. Her beautiful eyes were gazing at him. What impression did he make on her?

The musical voice asked, "Why don't you let your hair grow out?"

It was a question he had never considered before. Fuad Jamil al-Hamzawi had his hair cut just like his and so did all their comrades in the ancient quarter. Yasin had not been seen with hair long enough to brush or a mustache until he had found employment. Could Kamal imagine encountering his father every morning at the breakfast table with long hair?

"Why should I?"

Husayn asked thoughtfully, "Wouldn't it look better?"

"That doesn't matter."

Laughing, Husayn commented, "It seems to me that you were made to be a teacher."

"Praise or blame?" Kamal wondered. "In any case, your head's to be congratulated for receiving this heavenly attention."

"I was created to be a student."

"Good answer. . . ." Then, with a rising inflection of voice to show he was asking a question, Husayn continued: "You haven't told me the whole story of the Teachers College yet. What do you think of it after almost two months?"

"I hope it will be a serviceable introduction to the world I desire. I'm currently trying to learn the meaning of difficult words like 'literature,' 'philosophy,' and 'thought' from the English professors."

"This is the cultural discipline we want. . . ."

Kamal answered apprehensively, "But it seems human culture is a stormy ocean. We need to know the limits. We must learn more clearly what we want. It's a problem. . . ."

Husayn's interest was apparent in his handsome eyes. He said, "For me, there's no problem. I read French stories and plays, with some help from Aïda to understand the difficult passages. I also listen with her to selections from Western music, some of which she plays expertly on the piano. Recently I've been reading a book that summarizes Greek philosophy in an easy way. All I want is mental and physical forms of tourism, but you also wish to write. That forces you to learn boundaries and goals."

"The worst part is that I don't know exactly what I'm going to write about."

Aïda asked pleasantly, "Do you want to be an author?"

Swept by a tidal wave of happiness rarely experienced by human beings, Kamal answered, "Perhaps."

"Poetry or prose?" Then, leaning forward so she could observe him, she added, "Let me see if I can tell by looking at you."

"I've exhausted all the resources of poetry in my intimate exchanges with your dream vision," he reflected. "Poetry is your sacred tongue. I won't try to make a living from it. My tears have drained its wells during dark nights. How happy I am to have you look at me . . . and how wretched! I revive under your gaze—like the earth, which burgeons with life when the sun shines down on it."

"A poet. Yes, you're a poet."

"Really? How do you know?"

She sat up straight, and a laugh like a whisper escaped from her. She replied, "Physiognomy is too instinctive a science to be explained."

"She's bluffing!" Husayn said, laughing.

She retorted, "Not at all. If you don't like the idea of being a poet, then don't be one."

"Nature has made the female bee a queen," Kamal reflected. "The orchard is her palace. The flower's nectar is her drink. Honey is her product. And the reward earned by a person passing her throne is . . . a sting. But she denied Husayn's accusation."

She had another question for him: "Have you read any French stories?"

"Some by Michel Zévaco, in translation. You know I can't read French."

She said enthusiastically, "You won't be an author until you master French. Read Balzac, George Sand, Madame de Staël, and Pierre Loti. After that write your story."

Kamal said disapprovingly, "A story? That's a rather marginal art form. I aspire to do serious work."

Husayn said earnestly, "In Europe the story is considered a serious art form. Some writers there concentrate on it to the exclusion of all other types of writing. This is the way they've achieved the status of immortals. I'm not throwing praise around blindly. The French professor confirmed that."

Kamal shook his large head skeptically, and Husayn resumed speaking: "Be careful not to make Aïda angry. She's a reader who delights in French stories. In fact, she's one of their heroines."

Kamal leaned over a little to observe her reaction to Husayn's comment, seizing this opportunity to fill his eyes with the gorgeous sight. Then he asked, "How did that happen?"

"She gets all caught up in the stories, and her head is crammed with an imaginary life. Once I saw her strutting in front of a mirror. When I asked her what she was doing, she said, 'Aphrodite used to walk like this along the beach at Alexandria.' "

Frowning and smiling at the same time, Aïda said, "Don't believe him. He's more immersed in the world of the imagination than I am. But he's not satisfied until he accuses me of things that aren't true."

"Aphrodite?" Kamal wondered. "What's Aphrodite compared with my beloved? By the truth of your perfection, I'm sad to have you imagine yourself in any form but your own."

He commented sincerely, "You're not to blame. The heroes of al-Manfaluti and Rider Haggard have made a big impression on my imagination."

Husayn laughed delightedly and cried out, "How fitting it would be for all of us to be united in a single book. Why should we stay here on the ground, since we're so drawn to the world of the imagination? It's up to you. Bring this dream to reality. I'm not a writer and don't want to be, but you would be able to bring us together, if you so desired, in one book."

"Aïda in a book of which you would be the author ..." Kamal marveled to himself. "Worship, mysticism, or insanity?"

"And me?" Budur's voice burst out suddenly in protest. The three others roared with laughter.

Husayn cautioned Kamal: "Don't forget to reserve space for Budur."

Hugging the little girl affectionately, Kamal said, "You'll be on the first page."

Aïda looked off to the horizon and asked, "What will you write about us?"

He did not know what to say. He hid his confusion with a feeble laugh, but Husayn replied for him: "Like all the other authors, he'll write a violent love story ending with death or suicide. They kick your heart around, but it's all a game to them."

"I hope only it's the hero who meets this end," Aïda said with a laugh.

"The hero is unable to imagine his beloved perishing," Kamal thought. He asked, "Is it mandatory that it should end with death or suicide?"

"That's the normal ending for a passionate love story."

"When one is fleeing from pain," Kamal reflected, "or trying to hold on to happiness, death seems a valid goal."

Then he said ironically, "A very distressing business!"

"Haven't you learned that? It seems you haven't been in love yet."

"There comes a moment in the lives we lead," Kamal told himself, "when weeping serves the purpose of the anesthetic in a surgical operation."

Husayn continued: "To me the important thing is that you save a place in your book for me, even if I'm out of the country."

Kamal gave him a long look and asked, "Are you still seduced by the notion of traveling?"

A serious note crept into Husayn Shaddad's voice as he said, "Every moment! I want to live. I want to be everywhere, far and wide, high and low. Then let death come, after that."

"What if it came before?" Kamal wondered. "Could that happen? What of the sorrow that's almost killing you? Have you forgotten Fahmy? A life isn't always judged by its length. Your life, Fahmy, was a brief moment, but it was complete. Otherwise, what's the use of virtue and immortality? But you're sad for another reason. It's hard for you to contemplate dispassionately separation from your friend who is so keen to travel. What will your world be like after he's left? What will become of you if his trip separates you from the mansion of your true love? How deceptive today's smiles are. She's at hand now. Her voice tickles your ear, and her perfume your nose. But can you stop the wheel of time? Will you spend the rest of your life circling round her mansion at a distance, like the fabled lunatic lovers of old?"

"If you want my opinion, you should postpone your travels until you've finished your studies."

Aïda said eagerly, "That's what Papa has told him repeatedly."

"It's sound advice."

Husayn asked sarcastically, "Is it necessary for me to memorize civil and Roman law in order to savor the beauty of the world?"

Still addressing Kamal, Aïda said, "Father has heaped scorn on Husayn's dreams. He hopes to see his son in the judiciary or working in finance like him."

"The judiciary, finance! I'm not going to join the judiciary. Even if I get my degree and seriously consider choosing a profession, my interest will be in the diplomatic corps. And as for money, do you want more? We're already unbearably rich."

"How amazing that a man's wealth can be unbearable," mused Kamal. "Long ago you thought you would be like your father and own a safe similar to his. Wealth is no longer one of your dreams, but don't you wish you could liberate yourself from material concerns to embark on spiritual adventures? How wretched life is when it's devoted solely to earning a living."

"No one in my family understands my hopes. They think I'm a spoiled child. My mother's brother once said sarcastically so I could hear, 'Wouldn't you have expected the only boy in the family to turn out better than this?' Why should they feel like this? It's because I don't worship wealth and prefer living to making money. You see? Our family believes that any effort not leading to an increase in wealth is a foolish waste of time, and you find them dreaming of titles, as though they were a lost paradise. Do you know why they love the Khedive Abbas II? Mama has often told me, 'If only Our Effendi Abbas had stayed on the throne, your father would have been named a pasha long ago.' Precious money is scorned and spent with abandon if a prince honors us with a visit." Then, laughing, he added, "Don't forget to record these foibles if you ever get around to writing the book I proposed."

He had scarcely finished speaking when Aïda told Kamal, "I hope you won't be influenced by the prejudices of my disrespectful brother and slander our family in your book."

Kamal replied in a worshipful tone, "God forbid that I should ever

say anything against your family. Moreover, there's nothing disgraceful in what he alleged."

Aïda laughed triumphantly, and Husayn smiled with relief, although his eyebrows were raised in mock astonishment. Kamal felt
that Husayn was not totally sincere in his attack on his family. He
did not question Husayn's statement that he did not worship wealth
and preferred living to making money. Yet Kamal imagined that Husayn's comments about the Khedive, titles, and entertaining princes
had slipped out as boastful criticism, not just boasts or criticism. Husayn appeared to be bragging about these things with his heart but
condemning them with his mind. Or perhaps he resented them but
saw nothing wrong in mentioning them to a friend whom they would
dazzle and fascinate, even if he deplored them too.

Smiling calmly, Husayn asked, "Which of us is to be the book's
central character? Me, Aïda, or Budur?"

Budur cried out, "Me!"

Hugging her, Kamal said, "Agreed." Then he told Husayn, "This
will remain a secret until the book is born."

"What title will you give it?"

"Husayn Around the World!"

Except for Budur, they all roared with laughter at this parody of
the title of a farce, *The Barbarian Around the World*, which was playing
at the Majestic.

Inspired by that, Husayn asked him, "Have you found your way
to the theater yet?"

"No, the cinema's enough for now."

Husayn told Aïda, "The author of our book is not allowed to stay
out after nine P.M."

Aïda replied captiously, "Still, he's better than people who are allowed to circle the planet."

Then she turned toward Kamal and, with a tenderness capable of
eliciting his agreement regardless of what she proposed, she said, "Is
it really wrong for a father to want his son to grow up to be as
vigorous and respected as he is? Is it wrong for us to pursue money,
titles, and higher things?"

"Stay as you are," thought Kamal, "and wealth, prestige, and lofty
ideals will pursue you. Everyone will want to kiss the ground you
walk on. How can I answer, when the response you desire entails
my destruction? Alas for your heart, Kamal; it wishes for something
you're forbidden."

"There's nothing wrong with that." Then, after a short pause, he added, "On condition that the person's temperament is congenial to it."

"What temperament would not be congenial to that? The strange thing is that Husayn does not renounce this refined life out of an ambition for something superior to it. No, my good man, he dreams of living without any lifework, in idle unemployment. Isn't that amazing?"

Laughing sarcastically, Husayn asked, "Don't the princess you adore live that way?"

"Because there's no life above theirs to aspire to. What are you compared with them, lazybones?"

Husayn turned toward Kamal and in a voice tinged with anger said, "The precept followed in our family is to work to increase our fortune and to become friends with influential people in hopes of obtaining the rank of bey. Once that is achieved, you need to redouble your efforts to expand your fortune and befriend the elite so you will be promoted to pasha. Finally you make ingratiating yourself with the princes your supreme goal in life. You have to content yourself with that, since joining the royal family is not an objective you attain by effort or ingenuity. Do you know how much the prince's last visit cost us? Tens of thousands of pounds were wasted on buying new furniture and rare curios from Paris."

Aïda protested: "That money was not spent to curry favor with the prince just because he's a prince, but because he's the Khedive's brother. The motive for flattering him was our loyal friendship for him and his brother. It wasn't fawning ingratiation. And it's an honor no intelligent person could reject."

But Husayn obstinately persisted: "At the same time, Papa keeps on consolidating his ties to politicians like Adli, Tharwat, and Rushdi, who cannot be accused of loyalty to the Khedive. Doesn't that show he accepts the prevailing wisdom that the end justifies the means?"

"Husayn!" Aïda shouted her brother's name in a voice Kamal had never heard before. It was full of haughty, disdainful censure, as though she wanted to warn Husayn that such things should not be said, at least not in the presence of an outsider. Kamal's face blushed with embarrassment and pain. The happiness that had momentarily hovered over him at being included in the activities of this beloved family dissipated. Her head was erect, her lips were knit, and her eyes betrayed a frown, which she had not allowed to reach her forehead. The impression she gave was one of anger—the anger of a highborn queen. Kamal had never seen her emotional before. He had

not imagined that she had feelings. He gazed at her face with astonishment and relief but felt so uncomfortable he wished he could in-
vent an excuse to avoid continuing this conversation. After a few
seconds he recovered and began to observe the beautiful, regal anger
on her queenly face. He admired her flaming pride, domineering
scorn, and frowning superiority.

As though speaking for Kamal's edification, Aïda proclaimed, "Papa's friendship with the men you mentioned has a long history prior
to the Khedive's deposition."

Kamal wished sincerely to drive away this cloud. He playfully
asked Husayn, "If that's the way you feel, why do you look down
on Sa'd Zaghlul for having been a student at al-Azhar?"

Husayn laughed in his untroubled way and replied, "I hate fawning
over the nobility, but that doesn't mean I respect the masses. I love
beauty and despise ugliness. Sadly enough, beauty is rarely found
among common people."

Aïda interjected in an even voice, "What do you mean by 'fawning
over the nobility'? It's contemptible behavior for someone who does
not belong to this class. But I think we do. When we attempt to
ingratiate ourselves with other members of our class, they reciprocate
it."

Kamal volunteered to answer, saying fervently, "That's the indis-
putable truth."

Husayn rose at once and said, "We've rested long enough. Let's
walk some more."

They got up to resume their excursion, heading for the Sphinx.
The sky was partly overcast. Groups of clouds spread out from the
horizons to meet and veil the sun with a translucent curtain. The
sun's light appeared gleaming white through this covering and fell to
earth with a graceful purity.

As they walked along they met parties of students and mixed
groups of European men and women. Perhaps wishing to placate
Aïda indirectly, Husayn told her, "The European women are looking
at your dress with great interest. Are you satisfied?"

She smiled with contented pride. Raising her head with charming
conceit, she said in a voice that revealed her secure self-confidence,
"Naturally!"

Husayn laughed and Kamal smiled. Then the former told the latter,
"Aïda is considered an authority on Parisian taste throughout our
whole district."

Still smiling, Kamal said, "Naturally."

Aïda rewarded him with a soft, tender laugh, like the cooing of a dove. It cleansed his heart of the residue left behind by the bizarre aristocratic squabble.

"The wise man," Kamal cautioned himself, "is the one who knows where his foot will fall before he moves it. Recognize how far below these angels you are. The beloved, who looks down at you from the clouds, feels superior even to her own relatives. What's strange about that? She should not have relatives or a family. Perhaps she selected them to be intermediaries between her and her devotees. Admire her composure and rage, her humility and arrogance, her forwardness and reserve, as well as her satisfaction and anger. They are all attributes of hers. So quench your heart's thirst with love. Look at her. The sand impedes her steps. She is not so light-footed here. She has lengthened her stride. Her torso sways like a bough intoxicated by a dying breeze. Yet she affords the eyes a new vision of graceful walking so beautiful that it equals in loveliness her normal manner of strolling down the mosaic paths of the garden. If you turn back, you'll see her charming footprints in the sand. Rest assured that they constitute landmarks on the mysterious road, providing guidance toward the heights of love and the illuminations of happiness. During your previous visits to this desert you spent all your time playing and leaping about. You were oblivious to the perfumed scents of the hidden meanings here, because your heart's bud had not yet blossomed. Today, its petals are moist with the dew of longing—those droplets of delight and pain. If you have been deprived of your peaceful ignorance, you have been granted a heavenly anxiety, which brings the heart to life and makes light sing."

"I'm hungry," Budur complained.

Husayn said, "It's time for us to turn back, don't you think? If we keep on this way, it will be so far that anyone who isn't hungry yet will be starved by the end."

When they reached the automobile, Husayn got out the bag and the basket with the food. He placed them on the hood of the car and started to open the lid of his basket, but Aïda suggested that they should eat on one of the blocks of the pyramid. They went there and climbed up on one of the bottom stones. Putting the food in the center of the block, they sat at the edge with their feet hanging over. Kamal spread out a newspaper that was in his bag and placed on it what he had brought—two chickens, potatoes, cheese, bananas, and oranges. Then he watched Husayn's hands remove the angelic picnic from their basket: elegant sandwiches, four glasses, and a thermos.

Although the food Kamal had brought was more substantial, it appeared—to him at least—to lack the elegant flourish of theirs. He was beset by apprehension and embarrassment. Husayn gazed appreciatively at the chickens and asked if Kamal had brought any silverware. Kamal extracted knives and forks from the bag and began to slice up the chickens. Then Aïda removed the stopper from the thermos and started filling the glasses with a golden liquid.

Kamal was so surprised that he could not keep from asking, "What's that?"

Aïda laughed but did not reply. Winking at his sister, Husayn said quickly, "Beer."

"Beer!" Kamal exclaimed fearfully.

Pointing to the sandwiches, Husayn said defiantly, "And ham."

"You're making fun of me! I don't believe this."

"No, believe and eat. What a skeptic you are! We've brought the best food and the most delicious drink."

Kamal's eyes proclaimed his astonishment and alarm. He was tongue-tied, for he did not know what to say. What troubled him most was the fact that this food and drink had been obtained from their home and thus with the knowledge and consent of their parents.

"Haven't you ever had these before?"

"That's a question needing no reply."

"Then you'll taste them for the first time, and the credit is ours."

"Impossible."

"Why?"

"Why! . . . Another question needing no reply."

Husayn, Aïda, and Budur raised their glasses and drank some beer. The first two smiled at Kamal as though to say, "You see. It didn't do anything to us."

Then Husayn said, "Religion, huh? A glass of beer doesn't make you drunk, and ham is delicious and good for you. I don't see the wisdom of letting religion intrude on questions of diet."

Kamal's heart felt bruised by these words, but in a tone as amiable as ever he said critically, "Husayn, don't blaspheme."

For the first time since they started eating Aïda spoke: "Don't think ill of us. We only drink beer to whet our appetites. Perhaps Budur's participation will satisfy you of our good intentions. And ham's very tasty. Try it. Don't be a Hanbali fundamentalist. There are enormous opportunities for you to obey religion in more important ways than this."

Although her words did not differ in any essential way from Husayn's, they brought peace and balm to his wounded heart. Her words also found in him a soul totally committed to doing nothing to upset them or hurt their feelings. He smiled with gentle forbearance and, picking up some of his own food, said, "Let me eat the food I'm accustomed to and do me the honor of sharing it."

Husayn laughed. Gesturing toward his sister, he told Kamal, "We agreed at home to boycott your food if you boycotted ours, but it seems we did not properly appreciate your situation. Therefore, in your honor, I'm going to withdraw from that agreement. Perhaps Aïda will follow my example."

Kamal looked hopefully in her direction, and she said with a smile, "If you promise not to think ill of us."

Kamal answered delightedly, "Death to anyone who thinks ill of you."

They ate with great appetite, Husayn and Aïda first. Then Kamal, encouraged by watching them, followed suit. He served Budur her food himself. She was content with one sandwich and a piece of chicken breast. Then she turned her attention to the fruit. Kamal could not resist the temptation to observe Husayn and Aïda surreptitiously as they ate, in order to see how they handled their food. Oblivious to his surroundings, Husayn devoured his food as though he were alone. Even so, he did not lose his distinguished air and thus represented in Kamal's eyes the beloved aristocracy acting spontaneously. Aïda revealed new dimensions of elegance, grace, and refinement whether in cutting the meat, in grasping the sandwiches by the tips of her fingers, or in the movements of her lips as she chewed. All this took place in an easy, relaxed manner, without any affectation or embarrassment. The truth was that Kamal had been looking forward to this moment expectantly and incredulously, as though skeptical that she ate food like other human beings. Although his knowledge of the type of food she was consuming troubled his religious sensibilities greatly, he found in its novel and unusual nature, compared with what people he knew ate, a parallel to the eater herself, and this helped calm his questioning, perplexed imagination. Two contradictory feelings alternated within him. At first he was uneasy to see her undertake this activity in which both men and animals share. Then he felt somewhat relieved, since this activity brought the two of them closer together, if only a little. But he was still not free of questions. He was forced to wonder whether she also participated in other natural human functions. He could not deny that, but it was hard for him to accept. Therefore he refused to answer, although he experienced a sensation he had not known previously, one containing a silent protest against the laws of nature.

"I admire your feeling for religion and your moral idealism."

Kamal looked at his friend cautiously and suspiciously. So Husayn affirmed, "I'm speaking sincerely, not making a joke."

Kamal smiled shyly. Then he pointed at the remaining sandwiches and beer as he said, "Despite all this, your celebrations in the month of Ramadan are beyond description. Lights are lit, the Qur'an is recited in the reception hall, the call to prayer rings out in the gentlemen's parlor. Isn't that so?"

"My father celebrates the nights of Ramadan out of love, respect, and veneration for the traditions my grandfather observed. He and Mama are also scrupulous about fasting."

Aïda said with a smile, "I am too."

With an earnestness he meant to be sarcastic Husayn said, "Aïda fasts one day out of the whole month and sometimes gives up by afternoon."

Aïda retorted in revenge, "Instead of fasting, Husayn eats four meals a day during Ramadan: the three normal ones and then the meal before daybreak reserved for fasters."

Husayn laughed, and food would have fallen from his mouth if he had not reared his head back quickly. He said, "Isn't it strange that we know so little of our religion? What Papa and Mama know about it is hardly worth mentioning. Our nurse was Greek. Aïda knows more about Christianity and its rituals than she does about Islam. Compared with you we can be considered pagans." Then, addressing Aïda, he added, "Kamal reads the Qur'an and works about the life of the Prophet."

In a tone giving a hint of admiration she said, "Really? Bravo! But don't think any worse of me than is absolutely necessary, for I've memorized more than one Qur'an sura."

Kamal murmured dreamily, "Marvelous, extremely marvelous. Which one, for example?"

She stopped eating to try to remember. Then with a smile she replied, "I mean I used to know some chapters by heart. I'm not sure how much I've retained. . . ." Then, raising her voice as though she had found what she was searching for, she continued: "Like the sura which speaks of God's unity and so forth."

Kamal smiled, since the sura she referred to, number one hundred twelve, had only four verses. He handed her a piece of chicken breast, which she took gratefully, although she confessed she was eating more than she normally would.

She said, "If people ate all their meals at picnics, no one would be slender anymore."

Kamal said hesitantly, "The women in my part of town don't want to be slim."

Husayn agreed with him and commented, "Mama herself feels that way, but Aïda considers herself a Parisian."

"God forgive my beloved her scorn," Kamal brooded. "Like the skeptical notions you read, she deeply troubles your believing soul. But will you be able to confront your beloved's scorn for Egypt and Islam with the same criticism and anger you employed against those skeptical ideas? Of course not! Your soul harbors nothing but the purest love for her. You love even her defects. Defects! She has no defects, even if she makes light of religion and does things it forbids. In someone else, those would be defects. What I fear most is that from now on no beautiful woman will be able to please me unless she takes her religion lightly and performs forbidden acts. Does that make you apprehensive? Ask God's forgiveness for yourself and for her. Say that it is all amazing, as amazing as the Sphinx. How much your love and the Sphinx resemble each other. Each of them is an eternal riddle."

Aïda emptied what was left from the thermos into the fourth glass. Then she asked Kamal seductively, "Won't you change your mind? It's just a refreshing drink...."

He smiled with apologetic thanks. Husayn grabbed the glass and raised it to his mouth, saying, "Me instead of Kamal." With a moan he continued: "We've got to stop or we'll die of overeating."

When they concluded their meal, only half a chicken and three sandwiches remained. Kamal, who thought he would distribute the leftovers among the young boys prowling about, saw Aïda put her sandwiches back in the basket along with the glasses and thermos and felt obliged to return the rest of his food to the bag. He happened to recall Isma'il Latif's comments about the parsimonious spirit of the Shaddad family.

Husayn jumped to the ground and said, "We have a pleasant surprise for you. We've brought a phonograph and some records to help our digestion. You'll hear some European music selected by Aïda and also Egyptian pieces like 'Guess What,' 'After Dinner,' and 'Turn Aside Here.' What do you think of this surprise?"

18 ⌒

December was half over, and the weather was still relatively mild, although the month had begun with windstorms, rains, and bitter cold. Kamal approached the Shaddad family mansion with happy deliberate steps, his neatly folded overcoat thrown over his left arm. His elegant appearance suggested that he had brought his coat to perfect the splendor and respectability of his attire rather than to guard against a change in the weather, especially since it was so mild. The late-morning sun was brilliant. Kamal thought their gathering would take place in the garden gazebo rather than the parlor, where they met in cold weather, and that consequently he might have an opportunity to see Aïda, who was only allowed to visit them in the garden.

If winter deprived him of a chance to meet her outside, it did not prevent him from seeing her at the window that overlooked the path to the garden or on the balcony surveying the entrance to the mansion when he arrived or left. He might catch a glimpse of her resting her elbows on the ledge or holding her chin in her hand. He would look up and bow devoutly. She would return his greeting with a delicate smile so sparkling that it lit up his dreams both day and night. Hoping to see her, he glanced stealthily at the balcony when he entered the grounds of the mansion and then at the window as he walked along the path. But he did not find her in either spot. Indulging himself in the hope that he would meet her in the garden, he headed for the gazebo, where he saw Husayn sitting unaccustomedly alone. They shook hands, and Kamal's heart rejoiced with delighted affection as he looked at the handsome face, since Husayn was a kindred spirit.

Husayn welcomed him in a merry, untroubled way: "Greetings to the teacher! Overcoat and fez! Next time don't forget your scarf and stick. Welcome, welcome!"

Kamal removed his fez and placed it on the table. Throwing his coat on a chair, he asked, "Where are Isma'il and Hasan?"

"Isma'il has gone to the country with his father. So you won't see him today. And Hasan telephoned me this morning to say he'll be at least an hour late, because he's copying some lecture notes. You know he's a model student like you. He's determined to get his degree this year."

They sat on neighboring chairs, with their backs to the house. The fact that they would be alone presaged for Kamal a quiet conversation with no dissension. It would be a harmonious and thoughtful meeting lacking the tedious but delightful debates unleashed by Hasan Salim and the stingingly sarcastic comments tossed off ad nauseam by Isma'il Latif.

Husayn continued: "I, to the contrary, am a rotten student. I listen to the lectures attentively, since I'm able to concentrate on them, but I can hardly bear to read my textbooks. I've often been told that studying law requires rare cleverness. They should rather say it requires denseness and patience. Like others motivated by ambition, Hasan Salim's a diligent student. I've often wondered what makes him push himself beyond normal human endurance, working and staying up late. As the son of a superior court judge he could have contented himself with doing just enough to pass, confident that his father's influence would guarantee him the kind of position he desires. The only explanation I can find is pride, which makes him want to succeed and drives him on relentlessly. Isn't that so? What do you think?"

Kamal replied sincerely, "Hasan's a fine young man who deserves praise for his character and intelligence."

"I heard my father say once that his father's an extraordinary and fair judge, except when it comes to political cases."

This opinion coincided with Kamal's own prejudice, since he knew that Salim Bey Sabry favored the Liberal Constitutionalists. He said sarcastically, "That means that he has a brilliant legal mind but is unfit to judge."

Husayn laughed loudly and then said, "I forgot I was speaking to a Wafdist."

Shrugging his shoulders, Kamal answered, "But your father isn't one! Imagine Salim Bey Sabry judging conspiracy and murder charges against Wafdists like Abd al-Rahman Fahmy or al-Nuqrashi . . ."

Had his opinion of Salim Bey Sabry been well received by Husayn? Yes, that could be seen clearly in his handsome eyes, to which prevarication and hypocrisy were alien. Perhaps Husayn's appreciation of this criticism could be attributed to the rivalry—no matter how muted by refined manners and decorum—that often arises between peers. Shaddad Bey was a millionaire, a wealthy man with status and prestige, who also had a long-standing relationship with the Khedive Abbas. Salim Bey Sabry, on the other hand, was a superior court judge for the largest judicial circuit in a land where official titles inspired people to veneration. It was inevitable that high rank and vast wealth should occasionally look askance at each other.

Husayn gazed at the vast garden calmly but sadly. The palms had been stripped of their hanging fronds, the rose bushes were denuded, the lush green of the vegetation had faded, and the smiles of the flowers had disappeared from the mouths of the buds. The garden appeared to be plunged in grief over the advent of winter. Gesturing toward the view, he said, "See what winter has done. This will be our last meeting in the garden. But you're one of winter's admirers."

Kamal really was fond of winter, but he loved Aïda more than winter, summer, fall, and spring put together. He would never be able to forgive winter for depriving him of the happy reunions in the gazebo. Yet he agreed: "Winter's a brief, beautiful season. In the cold overcast conditions and the drizzle there's a vitality to which the heart responds."

"It seems to me that winter's advocates are normally energetic and industrious. You're that way, and so is Hasan Salim."

Kamal rejoiced at this praise but wished most of it had been reserved for him. "I only expend half my energy on school assignments," he said. "The life of the intellect ranges far beyond school."

Husayn nodded his head approvingly and commented, "I don't think there's a school that could use up all the hours you devote to study each day. By the way, I think you're overdoing it, although occasionally I envy you. Tell me what you're reading now."

Kamal was delighted by this kind of conversation. Next to Aïda, it was what he loved best. He answered, "I can tell you my reading has become more systematic. It's no longer a question of reading anything I want—stories in translation, selections of poetry, or critical essays. I've begun to proceed in a slightly more enlightened manner. I recently started spending two hours every evening at the National Library. There I look up the meanings of deep and mysterious words in the encyclopedia, terms like 'literature,' 'philosophy,' 'thought,' and 'culture.' As I read, I jot down the names of books I come across. It's an extraordinary world. My soul dissolves in it from eager curiosity."

Husayn listened with attentive interest, leaning back in his rattan chair and putting his hands in the pockets of his dark blue English

jacket. On his broad lips there was a pure smile of empathy. He said,
"That's really beautiful. Once you asked me what you should read.
Now it's my turn to confer with you. Do you see clearly where
you're heading?"

"Gradually. . . . It seems I'm moving toward philosophy."

Husayn raised his eyebrows and said with a smile, "Philosophy?
That's a provocative word. Be careful not to mention it within
Isma'il's hearing. I've thought for a long time that you're destined for
literature."

"Don't feel bad about it. Literature's a lofty form of entertainment,
but that's not enough for me. My primary goal is the truth. What is
God? What is man? What is the spirit? What is matter? Philosophy
gathers all these together into a single, luminous, logical synthesis—
as I've recently learned. That's what I crave with all my heart. This
is the real journey. Compared with it, your trip around the world is
secondary. Imagine! It will allow me to find a satisfactory answer to
all these questions."

Husayn's face lit up with enthusiasm and desire as he said, "That's
really extraordinary. I won't hesitate to accompany you into this
magical world. In fact, I've read some chapters about Greek philosophy, even if I didn't get much out of that. I don't like plunging into
things the way you do. I pluck one flower here and another there.
Then I flit back and forth. Let me tell you frankly that I fear philosophy will terminate your relationship with literature, for you're not
satisfied with learning about something. You want to think and to
write. I believe it won't be possible for you to be a philosopher and
a literary figure at the same time."

"Nothing will separate me from literature. Love of truth is not
incompatible with the enjoyment of beauty. But work is one thing
and relaxation another. I've determined to make philosophy my work
and literature my relaxation."

Husayn laughed suddenly. Then he said, "So that's how you're
going to duck out of your promise to write a story uniting all of us
inside the covers of a book."

Kamal could not help but laugh too. He answered, "But I hope to
write about 'man' one day. So you'll be part of that."

"I'm not nearly as interested in 'man' as I am in our individual
personalities. Wait till I report you to Aïda."

When Kamal heard this name, his heart pounded with recognition,
affection, and desire. He felt intoxicated, as if overwhelmed by a
lively and expressive tune. Did Husayn really think the matter mer-

ited Aïda's censure? How ignorant he was! How could it have escaped him that there was no emotion Kamal felt, idea he pondered, or desire he nurtured that did not have the splendor of Aïda and her spirit glistening across its horizons.

"You wait. Time will show that I won't renege on my commitment so long as I live." Then after a moment he asked in a serious voice, "Why haven't you thought about being a writer? Your circumstances leave you free to devote yourself to this art."

Husayn shrugged his shoulders disdainfully and replied, "I should write so people can read? Why shouldn't people write so I can read?"

"Which of the two is of greater importance?"

"Don't ask me which is more important. Ask which is more pleasant. I consider work the human curse, but not because I'm lazy. Certainly not! Work is a waste of time. It imprisons the individual and gets in the way of living. A life of leisure is the happy one."

Kamal gave him a look that indicated he did not take his friend's words too seriously. Then he said, "I don't know what life a man would have if it weren't for work. An absolutely empty hour is certainly more tedious than a year filled with work."

"What wretchedness! The very truth of your statement confirms how miserable things are. Do you think I'm able to enjoy absolute leisure? Certainly not, alas. I still while away my hours with useful and necessary tasks. But I hope one day to achieve a state of total inactivity."

Kamal started to answer Husayn, but a voice behind them asked, "I wonder what they're talking about." Once this voice, this pretty melody, came within earshot his heart began to vibrate. The response came from deep inside him. Her words and his heart seemed to be different harmonious elements of a single tune. His soul was immediately freed of its bounding thoughts, and an absolute emptiness pervaded it. Was this the kind of total emptiness Husayn dreamt of? It was nothing in itself, but happiness pervaded it.

He turned around to watch as Aïda, preceded by Budur, approached from a short distance and came to a halt in front of them. Aïda was wearing a dress the color of cumin and a blue wool jacket with gilded buttons. Her bronze complexion was so clear it had the depth of a cloudless sky and the purity of distilled water.

When Budur rushed to him, he caught her in his arms and hugged her, as though attempting to conceal by that embrace the ecstasy of love he felt. Just then a servant hastened up. He stopped in front of Husayn and said politely, "Telephone."

Husayn rose, excused himself, and retreated to the men's parlor, followed by the servant.

Thus Kamal found himself alone with her for the first time in his life. Budur's presence did nothing to detract from the intimate atmosphere. He wondered apprehensively whether Aïda would remain or depart. But she advanced a couple of steps to stand under the roof of the gazebo, on the far side of the table from him. He gestured for her to sit down, but she smilingly declined with a shake of her head. So he stood up and lifted Budur onto the table. He caressed the young girl's head anxiously as he devoted all his attention to taming his emotions and mastering his feelings. A period of silence ensued, during which the only sounds to be heard were the rustling of the branches, the whispering of the dry leaves scattered about, and the chirping of the sparrows. To his eyes the earth, sky, trees, and distant wall separating garden from desert—not to mention the bangs of his beloved falling over her forehead and the extraordinary sparkle and contrast of her eyes—all seemed a joyous vision from a happy dream. He could not tell for certain whether these things were really before his eyes or if it was an imaginary scene glimmering in his memory —until the melodious voice crooned, "Don't bother him, Budur."

His response was to clasp Budur to his breast as he said, "If this is what it means to be bothered, I love it."

He gazed at Aïda with eyes full of myriad desires, enjoying himself, free this time of any supervision. He studied her carefully as though to grasp her secrets and to print her features and expressions on the surface of his imagination. He so lost himself in the vision's magic that he seemed in a daze or stupor. Before he knew what was happening she asked, "Why are you looking at me like that?"

When he emerged from his daze, his eyes clearly showed his confusion. She smiled and asked, "Do you want to say something?"

Did he want to say something? He did not know what he wanted. He really did not understand what he wanted. He inquired in turn, "Did you see that in my eyes?"

With a mysterious smile on her lips she replied, "Yes."

"What was it you saw in them?"

She raised her eyebrows in mock astonishment and said, "That's what I want to know."

Should he reveal his closely held secret and tell her straightforwardly, "I love you," without regard to the consequences? But why divulge it? What would become of him if, as was most likely, this confession ended the friendship and affection between them forever?

As he pondered this question, he noticed a daring, self-satisfied, and supremely confident look in her eyes. Free of embarrassment or confusion, this glance seemed to fall on him from above, even though their eyes were at the same level. That made him uncomfortable and even more hesitant. He wondered what lay behind it. So far as he could see it was inspired by a feeling of disdain or perhaps by a sense of sport—as though she were an adult looking at a child. There was also evidence of a feeling of superiority that could not be justified merely by the difference in age between them, for she was only two years older at the most. The towering mansion on Palaces Street might look down on the old house on Palace Walk in just this way. But why had he not glimpsed it in her eyes before? She had never been alone with him. This was the first time he had had an opportunity to look at her closely. These ideas hurt and saddened him, causing his intoxication to fade away.

Budur held her hands out to him asking to be picked up, and so he lifted her in his arms. Then Aïda said, "How amazing! Why does my little sister love you so much?"

Looking at her eyes, he answered, "Because I harbor the same amount of love for her, or even more."

Aïda asked skeptically, "Is that a law?"

"The proverb says, 'Hearts communicate directly with each other.'"

She rapped on the table as she inquired, "Suppose a beautiful girl is loved by many men—should she love all of them? What sense would your law make in this case?"

This enchanting discussion made him oblivious to everything including his troubles. He replied, "She should then love the one who loves her most sincerely."

"How can she pick him out from the others?"

"If only this conversation could last forever," he wished.

"I refer you once more to the proverb: 'Hearts communicate directly with each other.'"

Her brief laugh sounded like a string being plucked. She remarked defiantly, "If this were true, no sincere lover would ever be disappointed in love. Is that correct?"

Her statement shocked him, as though reality was catching up with a man who relied on logic alone. If his reasoning was right, he would have been the happiest person alive with his love and his beloved. But was he anywhere near that blissful state? The long history of his love had embraced some moments of deceptive hope. These had illuminated the dark corners of his heart with an imaginary happiness after a sweet smile granted by the beloved, a passing remark open to wishful interpretation, or a cheerful dream concluding a night of pensive insomnia. His fantasies had drawn strength from maxims he revered, like: "Hearts communicate directly with each other." Thus he had been able to cling to his false hope with all the determination of a desperate person, until reality brought him back to his senses with this sarcastic and definitive statement like bitter medicine. With it, he could cure his future of lying hopes and learn exactly where he stood.

When he offered no response to the question with which she had challenged him, his beloved tormentor cried out victoriously, "I win!"

Silence reigned once more. Again he heard the rustling of the branches, the whispering of the dry leaves, and the chirping of the sparrows, but this time they encountered the tepid response of a disappointed heart. He noticed that her eyes were scrutinizing him more keenly than necessary and that her glance was increasingly daring and self-confident, as though she were toying with him. She looked like anything but a woman engrossed in a romantic conversation. He felt a cold, gnawing sensation in his heart. He wondered whether he had been destined to be alone with her like this so his dreams could be demolished in one blow.

She noticed his anxiety and laughed carelessly. Pointing to his head, she teased him: "You don't seem to have started to let your hair grow out."

He said tersely, "No."

"That doesn't appeal to you?"

Grimacing scornfully, he answered, "No."

"We told you it would look better."

"Does a man have to look handsome?"

Astonished, she replied, "Everyone likes people to look nice, whether they're men or women."

He felt tempted to repeat one of the phrases he had memorized, like: "The beauty of men is in their deeds," but realized that a statement of this kind coming from a person resembling him would only meet with sarcastic mockery from his beloved. He attempted to conceal his heart's pain with a forced laugh and said, "I don't agree with you."

"Or perhaps you flee from beauty the way you flee from beer and ham."

He laughed to relieve his despair and grief. Then she continued:

"Hair is a natural covering. I believe your head needs it. Don't you realize that your head is very large?"

" 'The two-headed boy!' Have you forgotten that old taunt?" he asked himself. "What misery!"

"Yes, it is."

"Why?"

Shaking his head disapprovingly, he answered, "Ask it yourself. I don't know."

She laughed faintly, and they were silent.

"Your beloved is beautiful, fascinating, and captivating but—as is appropriate—also all-powerful. Taste her power and discover the different varieties of pain."

She gave no sign of having mercy on him. Her beautiful eyes kept climbing up his face steadily until they fixed on . . . yes, his nose. Deep inside he felt a convulsion that caused his hair to stand on end and his eyes to look down. He waited fearfully. He heard her laugh and looked up to ask, "What's so funny?"

"I remembered some hilarious things I came across in a famous French play. Haven't you read *Cyrano de Bergerac?*"

"The best time to scorn pain is when it's boundless," he advised himself.

Calmly and disdainfully he said, "There's no need to be polite. I know my nose is bigger than my head. But I beg you not to ask me why again. Ask it yourself, if you want."

Then Budur suddenly stretched out her hand and grabbed his nose. Aïda burst into laughter. She leaned her head back. He too could not help but laugh. To hide his confusion he asked the little girl, "And you, Budur—does my nose terrify you?"

They heard Husayn's voice as he came down the steps from the porch. Aïda suddenly changed her tone. She warned him entreatingly, "Don't be angry at my little joke."

Husayn returned to the gazebo and sat down again in his chair, inviting Kamal to be seated. After some hesitation Kamal, placing Budur on his lap, followed his friend's example. But Aïda did not stay long. She took Budur and bade them farewell. As she departed she gave Kamal a significant look, as though to stress her warning not to get angry. Kamal felt little appetite for resuming his conversation with Husayn and confined himself to listening or pretending to listen. From time to time he volunteered a question or an exclamation of surprise, appreciation, or disparagement, simply to show that he was present. Luckily for Kamal, Husayn harked back to a familiar topic requiring little concentration: his desire to go to France and his father's opposition, which he hoped to overcome shortly.

Kamal's heart and mind were preoccupied with the new look Aïda had displayed in the minutes they were alone or almost alone together. Her visage had been disdainful, sarcastic, and harsh. How cruel she had seemed! She had toyed with him mercilessly. Like a cartoonist confronting the human form with his brush, she had focused her jests on him to produce a caricature extraordinary for both its ugliness and its accuracy. In a daze, he recalled her appearance. Although pain flowed like poison through his spirit, spreading a dark stain of dejection and despair, he felt no resentment, anger, or contempt. Was this not a new attribute of hers? Certainly! Like her infatuation with French or her taste for beer and ham, it was one of her essential characteristics, no matter how strange, and therefore worthy of her, although in someone else it would be considered a flaw, an indulgence, or a sin. It was no fault of hers if one of her attributes produced pain in his heart or despair in his soul. The guilt was his, not hers. Was she responsible for giving him an enormous head or a huge nose? In her jests had she deviated from the truth and the reality? She had not and therefore was blameless. He deserved to suffer. It was his duty to accept this with ascetic resignation, like a devotee who believes implicitly in the fairness of a divine decree, no matter how harsh it appears, because the decree has been issued by the perfect beloved whose attributes and acts are beyond suspicion.

In this fashion Kamal fought his way out of the brief but violent ordeal that moments before had overwhelmed him. He felt hurt and tortured, but the strength of his fond fascination with the beloved was in no way affected. He had just experienced a new kind of pain, that of bowing to the harsh verdict passed against him. Previously he had learned, also from love, the different pains associated with separation, forbearance, leave-taking, doubt, and despair. He had learned as well that some pains are bearable, some enjoyable, and others constant, no matter how many sighs and tears are sacrificed to them. It seemed that he had fallen in love in order to master the dictionary of pain. By the glow of the sparks flying from his colliding pains he could see himself and make fresh discoveries.

"It's not merely God, the spirit, and matter you need to learn about. What is love? What are hatred, beauty, ugliness, woman, and man? You must learn about all of these too. The ultimate stage of damnation reaches up to the first level of salvation. Laugh as you remember or remember as you laugh that you were about to reveal your secret to her. Recall, as you weep, that the hunchback of Notre Dame terrified his beloved when he leaned over to comfort her. He, the hunchback, never elicited her sincere affection until he was breathing his last. 'Don't be angry at my little joke.' She even begrudges you the consolation of hopelessness. If the beloved would only speak openly, then we might leave the inferno of uncertainty and content ourselves with the tomb of despair. It's out of the question for despair to eradicate love from my heart, but it could save me from lying dreams."

Husayn turned to ask why he was so quiet but noticed someone approaching. Looking back, he exclaimed, "Here's Hasan Salim. What time is it now?"

Kamal twisted around and saw Hasan approaching the gazebo.

19

Hasan and Kamal left the mansion of the Shaddad family around 1 P.M. Kamal was going to say goodbye to his friend in front of the gate, but Hasan asked, "Won't you walk a little with me?"

His invitation willingly accepted, Hasan, whose head barely reached his friend's shoulder, set off along Palaces Street with the lanky Kamal, who wondered what the purpose was, especially since the hour was more suitable for dining and resting than a stroll. Before he knew what was happening, Hasan had turned to ask him, "What were you talking about?"

Although the question only increased his curiosity, he answered, "Different subjects as usual . . . politics, culture, and so on."

It was a genuine surprise when Hasan said in his calm, level voice, "I mean you and Aïda."

Kamal was astonished. Seconds passed without his attempting to reply. Then gaining control of himself he asked, "How did you know? You weren't there?"

Without any change of expression, Hasan Salim said, "I arrived while you were talking. It seemed best to leave so I wouldn't interrupt your conversation."

Kamal wondered whether he would have done the same thing if he had found himself in Hasan's position. He felt even more perplexed, sensing that he was on the verge of an animated conversation with many ramifications. "I don't know why you felt you should go off," he said. "If I had noticed, I wouldn't have let you."

"There are standards of polite behavior. I admit I'm very sensitive in this regard."

"Aristocratic etiquette!" Kamal told himself. "How alien it seems!"

"Excuse me," Kamal said, "if I tell you frankly that you're being overly meticulous."

Hasan's delicate smile tarried on his lips for only a second. He seemed to be waiting for something. When the wait became too long he asked, "Yes? What were you talking about?"

How could refined manners sanction such an interrogation? Kamal briefly considered asking Hasan this but elected to use an approach more compatible with his respect for the young man. This respect was based more on Hasan's personality than on their difference in age. Thus he continued: "The matter's too simple to warrant all this, but I wonder how much I'm obliged to say."

Hasan was quick to respond apologetically, "I hope you won't think I'm intruding or poking my nose into your personal affairs. I have reasons that justify my asking this question. I'll tell you things I haven't had occasion to mention before. All the same, counting on our friendship, I believed you wouldn't be offended by my question. I hope you won't misinterpret it."

The tension was eased. Kamal was pleased to hear tender words of this kind from Hasan Salim, the person he had long considered a shining example of aristocracy, nobility, and grandeur. In addition, he was even more eager than Hasan to enjoy an elevated conversation about anything related to his beloved. If it had been Isma'il Latif asking the question, the issue would not have required so much hemming and hawing over what was or was not necessary and was or was not proper. Kamal would have told him everything, as they laughed. But Hasan Salim never dropped his reserve and did not confuse friendship with intimacy. So there was nothing wrong in letting him pay the price for his reserve.

"Thanks for your good opinion of me," Kamal replied. "You can be sure that if there were anything worth telling I would not keep it from you. We just talked for a short time about some ordinary matters. That's all there was to it. But you've aroused my curiosity. May I ask you, if only to expand my horizons, what reasons justify your inquiry? I won't insist, naturally. In fact, I'm prepared to withdraw my question if it's inappropriate."

With customary calm and moderation, Hasan Salim said, "I'll answer your question but ask you to wait a little. It seems you don't care to brief me on your talk with her. And this is no doubt your right. I don't consider it an offense against the duties of friendship. But I would like to direct your attention to the fact that many are misled by Aïda's words and interpret them in a manner bearing no relationship to reality. For this reason, they cause themselves unnecessary problems."

"Go ahead and spit it out, Hasan," Kamal wished. "There are portents of foul weather in the air. A whirlwind's going to carry off the remnants of your stricken heart. You're the one who's been deceived, my friend. Don't you know that nothing but modesty keeps me from telling you everything? If it makes you feel any better, go ahead and strike me with your thunderbolts."

"I haven't understood a single thing you've said," Kamal protested.

Hasan raised his voice a little to explain: "The most gracious expressions flow easily and freely from her. A young man listening to her words assumes that she attaches some special significance to them or that they are prompted by some measure of affection. But they're nothing but pretty phrases she addresses to anyone she's conversing with, privately or in public. Thus many people have been duped. . . ."

"The cat's out of the bag," Kamal reflected. "Your friend's been afflicted by the same malady that has broken you. But who is he to claim he knows the most secret mysteries? He really makes me mad!"

Smiling and pretending to be unperturbed, Kamal said, "You seem very confident of what you're saying."

"I know Aïda extremely well. We've been neighbors for a long time."

The name he was too awestruck to use in secret, let alone to mention to others, had been pronounced carelessly by this infatuated young man, as though it belonged to some member of the swarming masses. This daring of Hasan's lowered him several notches in Kamal's heart while raising the young man by as many in his imagination. The sentence "We've been neighbors for a long time" plunged into Kamal's heart like a dagger, for it excluded him from serious consideration as effectively as distance does a traveler.

In a polite tone but with ironic insinuation, Kamal asked Hasan, "Isn't possible that you've been deceived like the rest?"

Hasan drew his head back haughtily and said with great certainty, "I'm not like the others!"

How Hasan's arrogance infuriated him. . . . How angry Kamal was at the good looks and self-confidence of this coddled son of the eminent superior court judge whose rulings in political cases were suspect. . . . A "ha" escaped from Hasan, like the tail end of a laugh, although there was nothing in his look to suggest amusement. It was his way of preparing for a change from a haughty voice to a more gracious tone.

"She's an exceptional girl," he said, "without a flaw, although occasionally her appearance, conversation, and amiable nature leave her open to suspicions."

Kamal was quick to respond enthusiastically, "In both appearance and reality she's beyond criticism."

Hasan bowed his head gratefully as though to say, "Well done." Then he remarked, "That's what anyone with sound judgment and insight must see. Yet there are matters that have troubled a few minds. To make myself clear I'll cite examples. People misconstrue the fact that she visits in the garden with friends of her brother Husayn, thus challenging our cultural traditions. Some question her practice of conversing with these young men and befriending them. Still others fancifully imagine that there must be a weighty secret behind her innocent custom of pleasantly trading jokes with them. Do you get my meaning?"

With the same enthusiasm as before Kamal said, "Naturally I understand what you mean, but I fear your suspicions are exaggerated. I mean I've never been suspicious of any of her actions. Her conversation and little jokes are obviously innocent. Moreover, she did not receive a totally Egyptian upbringing. So she shouldn't be expected to observe all our traditions and shouldn't be blamed for deviating from them. I suspect that's what the others think too."

Hasan shook his head as though wishing he believed Kamal's opinion of their friends. Kamal did not bother to comment on Hasan's silent observation. He was happy with his defense of his beloved and delighted by the opportunity to declare his belief in her chastity and innocence. It was true that his enthusiasm was insincere, but not because he harbored reservations he was hesitant to make public. He had long believed his beloved was beyond suspicion. Yet he lamented his happy dreams based on the assumption that there was a secret meaning behind her jests and delicate hints. Hasan was banishing those dreams, much as the recently concluded conversation in the gazebo had. Although Kamal's wounded heart was struggling secretly to cling to them, if only by a slender thread, he went along with Hasan Salim publicly, accepting his friend's opinion in order to cover his own tracks, conceal his sense of defeat, and demolish his rival's claim to be the authority on the beloved's true nature.

Hasan continued: "It's not surprising that you should understand, for you're a bright young man. As you said, the fact is that Aïda's innocent, but excuse me if I tell you frankly about a trait that may seem peculiar to you. Perhaps it's her own fault to a great degree if she's misunderstood. I refer to her penchant for being the 'dream girl' of all the young men she meets. Don't forget that it's innocent. I tell you I've never encountered a girl more protective of her honor than she is. But she's crazy about reading French novels, frequently refers to their heroines, and has her head filled with an imaginary world."

Kamal smiled to reassure him, wishing to suggest in this fashion that he was hearing nothing new. Then driven by a desire to provoke Hasan, he said, "I learned this some time ago when we had a conversation—she, Husayn, and I—on this very subject."

He was finally able to make Hasan abandon his aristocratic composure. Hasan's face showed his astonishment, as he asked with apparent alarm, "When was that? I don't remember being present! Did someone tell Aïda she wanted to be everyone's 'dream girl'?"

With victorious relief, Kamal gazed at the changes affecting his friend. Afraid of carrying it too far, he said cautiously, "That wasn't mentioned in so many words but was implied during a conversation about her infatuation with French novels and her immersion in the world of the imagination."

Regaining his calm and equilibrium, Hasan was silent for a time, as though attempting to collect his thoughts, which Kamal had momentarily succeeded in scattering. He seemed hesitant. Eventually Kamal realized that Hasan wanted to know everything about his conversation with Aïda and Husayn. When had it occurred? What had made them discuss those sensitive topics? Would he spell out exactly what had been said?

But Hasan's pride restrained him from asking. At last he said, "So you can vouch for the accuracy of my view. Unfortunately many people do not understand Aïda's conduct the way you do. They don't comprehend the important truth that she loves a person's love for her, not that person."

"If the fool knew what had actually happened," Kamal thought, "he wouldn't waste all this effort. Doesn't he know I don't even aspire to have her love my love? Look at my head and nose. Reassure yourself!"

In a voice not free of sarcasm Kamal said, " 'She loves a person's love for her, not that person'—what a philosophy!"

"It's the truth, and I'm certain of it."

"But you can't know for certain that this is always the case."

"Yes, I can, even with my eyes closed."

Falling prey to his sorrow, Kamal asked with sham astonishment, "Can you be sure that she does not love one person or another?"

Confidently and contentedly Hasan replied, "I can confirm with total certainty that she does not love any of the men who occasionally imagine she does."

"Only two types of people have a right to speak with such confidence," Kamal reflected, "the believer and the fool. And he's no fool. There's nothing new in what you're hearing. So why does it hurt? The truth is that I've felt enough pain today for a full year of love."

"But you can't prove she doesn't love anyone."

"I didn't say that."

Kamal looked at him as though consulting a diviner and then asked, "So you know she's in love?"

Nodding his head in agreement, Hasan said, "I invited you on this walk to tell you."

Kamal's heart sank in his chest—as though in attempting to flee from pain it had drowned in pain's waves. Until then he had suffered because it was impossible for her to love. Now his tormentor was affirming that she was in love, that the beloved loved, that her angelic heart was subject to the laws of passion, affection, desire, and longing—all directed at one individual. Of course, his intellect, but not his emotions, had occasionally allowed for that possibility, but in the way it accepted death—as an abstract thought, not a cold reality affecting his own body or that of a loved one. For this reason the news took him by surprise, as if the concept and its actual existence were being revealed to him at the same time.

"Reflect on these realities," he counseled himself. "Admit that there are pains in this world you never imagined, despite your expertise in pain."

Hasan continued: "I told you at the beginning that I have my reasons for this conversation with you. Otherwise I wouldn't have intruded into your personal affairs."

He would be consumed by the sacred fire to the last speck of ash.

"I'm sure that's true. I'm interested to hear what you have to say."

Hasan's feeble smile revealed that he was hesitant to utter the decisive words. So Kamal tried to be patient but finally, although his heart dimly perceived the distressing truth, he prodded his friend: "You said you know she's in love...."

Flinging off his hesitation, Hasan said, "Yes. Our relationship gives me a right to assert this."

"Aïda's in love, O celestial realms. The strings of your heart contract to accompany a dirge. Does her heart harbor the same feelings for this happy young man that yours does for her? If this truly were possible, the best thing would be for the world to burst asunder. Your companion isn't lying, for handsome young men from distinguished families don't lie. The most you can hope for is that her love is of a different kind than yours. If this catastrophe is inevitable, it's some consolation that Hasan's the one. It's also comforting to find that sorrow and jealousy do not blot out the reality standing before you —this wealthy, enchanting, marvelous fellow."

As though pressing the trigger of a revolver he knew was empty, he remarked, "You seem extremely confident that she's in love this time with the person himself, not with his love for her."

Another "ha" escaped from Hasan to express his certainty. He glanced swiftly at Kamal to see if he was convinced. Then he said, "Our conversation—mine and hers—was definitely not a talk that could be understood in more than one manner."

"What kind of conversation was it?" Kamal wondered. "I'd trade my whole life for a single word of it. I've learned the truth and am quaffing the torment down to the dregs. Do you suppose he heard the ravishing voice tell him, 'I love you'? Did she say it in French or in Arabic? The fires of hell burn with torment like this."

He said calmly, "I congratulate you. It seems to me that each of you is truly worthy of the other."

"Thanks."

"But I wonder what prompted you to reveal this precious secret."

Hasan raised his eyebrows as he said, "When I discovered you talking together, I was afraid you might be taken in, like many others, by some statement of hers. So I decided to tell you the truth quite candidly, because I hated for you of all people to be deceived."

"Thank you," murmured Kamal, moved by the lofty sentiments of the gifted young man whom Aïda loved and who had hated to let Kamal be deceived and therefore had slain him with the truth. Was it not possible that jealousy had been among the motives inducing Hasan to tell Kamal his secret? But had he no eyes to see Kamal's head and nose?

Hasan picked up the conversation again: "She and her mother frequently visit our residence. Then we have opportunities to talk."

"Alone?" This question slipped out unconsciously, and he regretted it. Feeling uneasy, he blushed.

Hasan replied quite simply, "At times."

How he wished he could see her in this role, that of a woman in love. He had never imagined it in his wildest dreams. What did the glow of passion and affection look like in her dark eyes, which cast him patronizing glances? Although fatal to the heart, it would be a vision to light up the mind with a firebrand of sacred truth justifying an eternal curse on any skeptic.

"Your spirit flutters like a trapped bird wishing to fly free. The world is a crossroads of ruins. It would be pleasant to leave it. But even if you're certain their lips have met in a rose-red kiss, you can look forward to the pleasure of absolute freedom in the whirlpool of madness."

Driven by a suicidal desire he could no more resist than understand, he asked, "How can you agree then to let her mingle with Husayn's friends?"

Hasan hesitated a little before replying, "Perhaps I'm not totally comfortable with it, but I find no real reason to take offense. She's always in full view of her brother and all the others. Then there's her European upbringing. I concede that I've occasionally thought of mentioning my annoyance to her, but I'd hate to have her accuse me of jealousy. She'd love to make me jealous! Naturally you know about these feminine wiles. I'll admit I don't relish them."

"No wonder," mused Kamal, "that the demonstration of the earth's revolution on an axis and around the sun swept myths away and left people feeling dizzy."

"As though she's deliberately baiting you," he said.

Hasan replied confidently, "If I ever need to, I can always make her defer to me."

This sentence and the tone in which it was uttered enraged Kamal to the point of insanity. He wished he could think of some pretext to attack Hasan and to roll him in the dust. Kamal would be strong enough to do it. He looked down on Hasan from above, and their difference in height seemed even greater than it actually was. If she could love someone that short, why could she not love someone a little younger than she was? He felt he had forfeited the world. Hasan invited him to dine with his family, but Kamal excused himself with thanks. Then they shook hands and parted.

He returned home feeling listless, dejected, and despondent. He wanted to be alone to brood over the events of the day, pondering them until their implications became clear. Life seemed clad in mourning weeds. But had he not known from the first that this was a hopeless love? What extra nuances had these events supplied? In any case, his consolation was that while other people talked of love, he loved with all his heart. No one else would be capable of the kind of love that illuminated his heart. This was where his distinction and superiority lay. He would not relinquish his dream of long standing to win his beloved in paradise where there were no artificial distinctions. He would not have a large head or a huge nose there.

"In heaven Aïda will be mine, by virtue of celestial law."

20 ❧

He seemed not to exist anymore. She ignored him so totally that it
could only have been by design. He first realized this a week after he
had spoken with Hasan Salim on Palaces Street, when he met his
friends Friday morning at the gazebo in the gardens of the Shaddad
mansion. They were all conversing when Aïda arrived as usual, accompanied by Budur. She stayed for a while, chatting with this one
and joking with that one, without paying any attention to Kamal.
Initially he assumed his turn would come. But when he grew tired of
waiting and noticed she did not want to look him in the eye or at
least was avoiding his glance, he abandoned his passive stance and
commented on something she had said in order to force her to address him. But she kept on talking and ignored him. Although no
one else appeared to have noticed his abortive maneuver, because
they were engrossed in what the beloved was saying, that did not
soften the blow he had received without knowing what could have
provoked it. Since he was predisposed to deny what had happened
to him, he hid his suspicions. He began to watch for opportunities to
try his luck again, though he was extremely apprehensive. When
Budur attempted to escape from Aïda's grasp and waved her free
hand at Kamal, he went to take the little girl in his arms. But Aïda
dragged Budur closer to her, protesting, "It's time for us to go." Then
she said goodbye and retraced her steps.

Oh, what was the meaning of this? Aïda was annoyed with him
and had come for the sole purpose of displaying her anger. But what
was she blaming him for? What sin had he committed? What lapse,
great or small, was he responsible for? Sneering at logic, anxiety
shattered the certainties of his world.

At the time, he was able to gain firm control of himself so that his
worries would not be exposed. He knew how to keep his head and
played his normal role to perfection, concealing from his friends' eyes
the impact of this crushing blow.

After the gathering broke up, he told himself it was best to face
the truth, no matter how bitter. He would have to admit that Aïda
had deprived him, for one day at least, of the benefits of her friend-

ship. There was a tiny recording device in his loving heart, and no whisper, thought, or glance of the loved one escaped it. This mechanism even detected her intentions and could anticipate events still remote. Let the cause be whatever it was or let there be no cause— as though this was a disease defying medical treatment—in either case he felt like a leaf ripped from the twig by a violent wind and cast into an oozing heap of refuse.

He found his thoughts hovering around Hasan Salim, who had ended their conversation with the words: "If I ever need to, I can always make her defer to me." But she had come today as usual. Kamal had suffered from her snub, not her absence. Moreover, he and Hasan had parted on good terms. There would have been no reason for Hasan to ask her to ignore Kamal. And she was not a person to take orders from any man, no matter who. Besides, Kamal had done nothing wrong. Lord of the heavens, what was the secret behind this censure? At their meeting in the gazebo Aïda had spoken harshly and mercilessly and had mocked Kamal's head, nose, and dignity. But these remarks had not lacked an affectionate, jesting quality, and the session had ended with something like an apology. Although it had dashed any hope he had nourished for his love, still his love had always been hopeless. When they met today, he had been ignored, ostracized, and condemned to silence and death. It would have been better for the loved one to treat her devotee harshly or cruelly than for her to pass by him as though he did not exist. How wretched! A new entry had been added to the dictionary of pains he carried in his breast. Here was a new levy imposed by love—and how oppressive its levies were! In this manner he paid for the light that both illuminated and scorched him.

He was enraged. It was very hard to obtain nothing but this haughty cold-shoulder treatment in return for his enormous love. He was painfully aware that the only expression his anger could find was love and loyalty and that the one way to counteract the blow was prayerful supplication. If his soul had stood accused by anyone else, even by Husayn Shaddad, Kamal would not have hesitated to sever ties, but since the plaintiff was the beloved, all the slivers of anger sped back to his chest. His hostility was poured out on a single target, Kamal. A desire for revenge drove him to inflict punishment on the defendant, Kamal. He sentenced himself to a life of renunciation. A pervasive, sad, obstinate feeling directed him to avoid her forever. He had enjoyed her friendship. Indeed he had considered it a blessing beyond his wildest dreams, even though the force of his love overwhelmed heavens and earth. More than all that, he had enjoyed his despair at ever being loved by her and had forced his unruly cravings to be satisfied with a sweet smile or a kind word, even if these came in parting. But to be ignored by her saddened, baffled, and disoriented him, leaving him alienated from the entire world. In this manner he was afforded an opportunity to feel what a dead man might if still conscious.

His thoughts churned away mercilessly during his waking hours that whole week he was separated from the Shaddad mansion. He kept brooding about his failure, which he agonized over repeatedly —in the morning at home having breakfast with his father, walking along the street with senses that only appeared to be functioning, at the Teachers College listening absentmindedly to a lecture, reading in the evening with scant attention, or humbly begging entry to sleep's ideal realm. Early in the morning when he opened his eyes, these thoughts were ready to fight for control of him, as though they had been lying in ambush at the threshold of consciousness or had awakened him out of an insatiable urge to devour him. Yes, how hideous the soul is when it turns on its master.

On Friday he went to the palace of love and torment, arriving slightly ahead of the appointed hour. Why had he been looking forward so impatiently to this day? What did he hope to gain from it? Did he wish to find some indication, even if only a feeble pulse, that would let him think life had not yet departed from hope's body? Did he dream of a miracle that would unexpectedly cause his beloved to be friendly again for no conceivable reason, exactly as she had grown angry? Or was he trying to stoke the fires of hell so that he might taste cold ashes all the sooner?

He proceeded to the garden along the path strewn with memories. Then he saw Aïda seated on a chair, holding Budur on the edge of the table in front of her. There was no one else in the gazebo. He stopped walking and thought of going back outside before she noticed him. But he rejected this idea defiantly and scornfully. He advanced on the gazebo, driven by a strong desire to face his punishment and to strip the veil from the puzzle that had slain his security and peace of mind. This lovely, gracious creature, this ethereal spirit disguised as a woman—did she realize what her harshness had done to him? Would her conscience rest comfortably once he complained about his suffering? Her tyrannical hold over him resembled the sun's over the earth, which was destined to orbit in a prescribed path. If it drew too close to the sun they would fuse together, but if the earth retreated too far, it would be annihilated once and for all.

She could bestow one smile on him, and he would salve all his pains with it. He approached her, deliberately treading heavily so she would hear. She turned her head around inquisitively, but then her face seemed to go blank. He stopped a little more than a meter from where she was sitting, bowed his head humbly, and with a smile said, "Good morning."

She nodded her head slightly but did not speak. Then she looked straight in front of her.

There was no longer any doubt that hope was a rigid corpse. He imagined she would shout, "Take your head and nose away so they don't obscure the light of the sun." Budur waved to him. He glanced down at her beautiful and radiant face and went toward her to mask his defeat with her innocent affection. She grabbed hold of his arms, and he leaned over to kiss her cheek warmly and gratefully.

Then the voice that in the past had opened the portals of celestial music for him said roughly, "Please don't kiss her. A kiss is not a hygienic greeting."

A disconcerted laugh escaped from him, he knew not how or why. He became quite pale. At first dumbfounded and in a stupor, he finally responded incredulously, "It's not the first kiss, so far as I remember."

She shrugged her shoulders as if to say, "That changes nothing."

"Oh!" Was he to begin a new week of torture without getting to utter a word in self-defense?

"Allow me to ask what secret is behind this bizarre change? I've been wondering all week long and have been unable to find an answer."

She did not seem to have heard him and consequently did not bother to reply.

With his voice betraying his anxiety and pain, he continued: "What really makes me sad is that I'm innocent. I've done nothing to deserve this punishment."

She still seemed determined to remain silent, but he was afraid Husayn would arrive before she was coaxed into speaking. In a voice combining complaint with entreaty he quickly said, "Doesn't an old friend like me deserve at least to be informed of his offense?"

She raised her head, cast him a sideways look as gloomy as storm clouds, and said angrily, "Don't pretend you're innocent!"

"O Lord of the heavens, can sins be committed unconsciously?"

he asked himself as he mechanically patted Budur's hands, with which she was attempting to draw him close to her, for she understood nothing of what was going on.

"Alas, my suspicions are correct," he said jerkily. "This is what my heart told me, but I couldn't believe it. You think I've done something wrong. Isn't that so? But of what offense are you accusing me? By your life, tell me. Don't wait for me to confess, for the simple reason that I've committed no crime against you. No matter how much I search the recesses of my soul, life, and past I can find no intention, word, or deed meant to harm you. I'm amazed that you don't realize how self-evident this is."

She replied scornfully, "I'm not the kind of girl who's taken in by theatrics. Ask yourself what you said about me."

With alarm he asked, "What have I said about you? To whom did I say it? I swear to you ..."

She cut him off in exasperation: "I'm not the least bit interested in your oaths. Save them for yourself. The oaths of slanderers are not to be trusted. The important thing is for you to remember what you said about me."

He tossed his overcoat on a chair as though preparing to throw himself into the debate and stepped away from Budur to free himself from her innocent attempts to monopolize his attention. Then he said so heatedly that his words had the ring of truth, "I've never said anything about you I would be embarrassed to repeat now in your hearing. I have never said anything bad about you in my whole life. I wouldn't be able to, if you only realized.... If one of our friends has told you something about me that's angered you, then he's a despicable liar who doesn't deserve your trust. I'm ready to confront him in your presence so that you can see for yourself whether he's telling the truth or, more precisely, lying. You have no defects, so how could I mention any? You've really been unfair to me."

She commented sarcastically, "Thanks for this praise, which I don't deserve. I don't think I'm that flawless ... if for no other reason than that I haven't received a totally Egyptian upbringing."

This last phrase skewered his mind, for he remembered saying it in his conversation with Hasan Salim when defending his beloved from the doubts Hasan had raised. Had Hasan repeated it in a manner that had stirred her doubts about Kamal's good intentions? The noble Hasan Salim ... would he do such a thing? How Kamal's head was spinning. ...

His eyes eloquently expressing his shock and sorrow, he said,

"What do you mean? I admit I said that, but ask Hasan Salim to tell you—he's got to tell you—that I said those words when I was praising your virtues."

She glared at him coldly and asked, "My virtues? And is my wish to be everyone's 'dream girl' a virtue?"

Kamal cried out with panic and rage, "He said that about you, not I. Won't you stay and let me challenge him in front of you?"

She bitterly and ironically pursued her interrogation: "And is my flirting with you another of my virtues?"

Feeling desperately unable to defend himself from this flood of accusations, he said, "You flirt with me? Where? When?"

"In this gazebo! Have you forgotten? Do you deny you left him with that impression?"

He was hurt by the sarcasm with which she asked, "Have you forgotten?" He perceived at once that Hasan Salim—how stupid it all was—had nourished suspicions about their tête-à-tête and had shared his doubts with his sweetheart or had ascribed them to Kamal in order to investigate them by this dirty trick of which he was the victim.

He said sadly and indignantly, "I deny it. I deny it with all my force and sincerity. I only regret trusting Hasan."

She said haughtily, as though she considered this last sentence a dig at her, "He always deserves that."

Kamal was beside himself. He imagined the Sphinx had raised its awesome stone paw, unmoved for thousands of years, to bring it down on him, crushing him and burying him beneath it forever.

In a trembling voice he said, "If it's Hasan who told you these lies, then he's a common liar. He's the one slandering me. It's not me slandering you."

A stern expression was visible in her eyes. She asked sharply, "Do you deny that in his presence you criticized my association with Husayn's friends?"

Was this the way an aristocratic patrician distorted a person's words? Deeply moved, he said, "Absolutely! That never happened. God knows I didn't. But he claimed something quite stupendous. He said . . . he said you love him. He said that if he wanted to, he could prevent you from associating with us. I never meant . . ."

She interrupted him scornfully and rose, proudly holding herself erect as the halo of her black hair fluttered around her uplifted face. "You're raving! It doesn't matter to me what people say. I'm above all this. In my opinion my only error is in bestowing my friendship indiscriminately."

As she spoke she put Budur down on the ground and took her hand. Then, turning her back on Kamal, Aïda left the gazebo.

He called after her entreatingly, "Wait a moment please, so . . ."

But she was already far away, and his voice was louder than it should have been. He imagined that the whole garden had heard him. The trees, the gazebo, and the chairs all seemed to be staring at him scornfully. He closed his mouth and rested his hand on the edge of the table. He leaned over as though his tall torso was bowed by the force of defeat.

He was not alone long. Husayn Shaddad soon appeared with his usual cheerful expression and greeted Kamal in his normal, sweet, innocent fashion. They sat down on neighboring chairs. Isma'il Latif came a little later. Finally Hasan Salim arrived. He made his way to them with unhurried steps and an arrogant bearing.

Kamal wondered anxiously whether Hasan had observed them from a distance as he had that previous time. When and how would Hasan learn what had been said in their stormy final conversation? Kamal's rage and jealousy swelled within him like a ruptured appendix. He promised not to allow any adversary to gloat over him. He would not expose himself to anyone's mockery or feigned affection. He would not let them see any evidence of the turmoil within him. He threw himself into the current of the conversation, laughing at Isma'il Latif's observations, commenting at length on the formation of the new Ittihad or Union Party, on the deserters who had left Sa'd Zaghlul and the Wafd Party, and on the role of Nashat Pasha in all of that. In brief, he played his part to perfection until the meeting concluded peacefully.

When Kamal, Isma'il, and Hasan left the Shaddad mansion at noon, it seemed that Kamal could not restrain himself any longer. He told Hasan, "I'd like to speak to you."

Hasan replied calmly, "Go ahead."

Kamal looked apologetically at Isma'il and said, "Alone."

Isma'il was ready to leave them, but Hasan gestured for him to stay, saying, "I keep nothing from Isma'il."

This tactic infuriated Kamal, for he glimpsed behind it a dubious ploy, which was cause for concern. All the same he said nonchalantly, "So let him hear us. I don't have anything to hide from him either."

He waited until their steps had carried them some distance from the Shaddad mansion. Then he said, "Before you came today, I happened to meet with Aïda in the gazebo alone. We had a bizarre conversation from which I gathered that you had communicated to her part of the conversation you'll recall we had on Palaces Street. But my comments had been so distorted and mutilated that she assumed I had attacked her unfairly and unjustly."

Hasan repeated the words "distorted and mutilated," his lips deformed by anger. Then, casting Kamal a glance to remind him that he was addressing Hasan Salim, not just anyone, Hasan said coldly, "It would be good for you to choose your words carefully."

Kamal replied passionately, "That's just what I did. The truth is that her comments left no room for doubt that you wished to cause trouble between us."

Hasan became pale with anger but did not yield to it. In a voice he made as cold as possible he observed, "I'm sad I had a good opinion of your understanding and comprehension of things." Then he continued sarcastically: "Won't you tell me what I might gain from this alleged trouble? The fact is you're jumping to conclusions without any deliberation or thought."

Kamal's anger intensified, and he shouted, "You have allowed yourself to be tempted into disgraceful behavior."

At this point Isma'il intervened to say, "My suggestion is that you postpone this conversation to another time when you'll both be in better control of your nerves."

Kamal said determinedly, "The matter's too clear for there to be any need for debate. He knows it and so do I."

Isma'il interjected once more, "Tell us what you said to each other in the gazebo. Perhaps we . . ."

Hasan interrupted haughtily: "I refuse to be put on trial."

Even though he knew full well that Hasan would lie, Kamal gave vent to his anger: "Anyway, I told her what happened, so she could see who was telling the truth."

His face pale, Hasan shouted, "We'll let her compare the words of a merchant's son to those of the son of a superior court judge."

Kamal darted toward him with a clenched fist, but they were separated by Isma'il, who was the strongest of the three despite his diminutive build.

Isma'il said resolutely, "I won't allow this. Each of you is a friend and the respectable son of an honored father. Let's renounce foolish conduct like this, which is better suited to children."

Kamal returned home feeling rebellious, agitated, and hurt. He stamped his feet angrily on the pavement. Inside him there was a wild conflagration. He had received potentially lethal blows to his heart and honor with regard to his beloved and his father. What else was there for him in the world? What of Hasan, whom he had respected more than any other comrade, admiring his rectitude? . . . In a single hour Hasan had been transformed into a vituperative slanderer. The fact was that, angry as Kamal was, he could not believe his own accusation wholeheartedly and unequivocally. He still kept reflecting about it, asking himself whether it was not possible that there was some secret explanation for that painful scene? Had Hasan distorted Kamal's words or could Aïda have misconstrued them and read more into them than she should have? Had she surrendered to wrath too quickly? But the comparison between the son of a merchant and the son of a superior court judge cast Kamal into an inferno of anger and pain, which conspired to make his attempt to be fair to Hasan an exercise in futility.

The next time Kamal went to the Shaddad mansion at the customary hour for their weekly reunion, Hasan was absent, having excused himself because something had come up. After the session disbanded, Isma'il Latif informed Kamal that he—Hasan—was very sorry for what he had blurted out in a moment of pique about "the merchant's son and the son of the superior court judge" and that he believed Kamal had made serious accusations based on fanciful deductions. Hasan hoped that this untoward incident would not end their friendship and had asked Isma'il to convey this message to Kamal orally.

Later Kamal received a letter from Hasan to the same effect, emphasizing the request that they should put the past behind them when they met and forget about it. The letter concluded with the statement: "Remember everything you did to offend me and what I did to offend you. Perhaps you will be as convinced as I am that each of us was in the wrong and that therefore it would not be right for either of us to reject his friend's apology." This letter made Kamal feel better for a while. Yet he noticed the contrast between Hasan's customary arrogance and this delicate and unexpected apology. Yes, it was unexpected, since he had never imagined that Hasan would apologize for any reason. What had made him change? Their friendship would not have had this huge an impact on his comrade's pride. Perhaps he, Hasan, wished to restore his own reputation for civility more than he wished to reclaim their friendship. Perhaps he also wanted to keep the quarrel from growing any more virulent lest news of it reach Husayn Shaddad, for that young man might be indignant at having his sister embroiled in the dispute or angry for his own sake if he heard what had been said about "the merchant's son and the son of the superior court judge," since Husayn was also the son of a businessman. Any of these would have been plausible reasons and more logical, given Hasan's character, than an apology influenced by nothing but their friendship.

Whether he made peace with Hasan or continued to be his enemy seemed insignificant to Kamal. The important thing was to know whether Aïda had decided to conceal herself. She no longer wandered by when they were sitting in the garden. She was not visible at the window. She did not appear on the balcony. Counting on her pride, Kamal had told her what Hasan had said about being able, if he chose, to prevent her from visiting them. Kamal had done that to shore up her determination to visit the gazebo, so he would not be deprived of seeing her. But in spite of that she disappeared as though she had quit the house altogether, indeed the whole district. Why not say the whole world, which had become insipid? Was it possible that this separation would last forever? He hoped it was her intention to punish him for a time and then pardon him. If only Husayn Shaddad would mention some reason for her absence and dispel his fears. . . . He wished with all his heart for one of these eventualities and bided his time, but his wait was long and fruitless.

Whenever he went to visit the mansion he approached it with anxious eyes, as he wavered between hope and despair. He would steal a glance at the front balcony and another at the window overlooking the side path. Then on his way to the gazebo or the men's parlor he would gaze at the rear balcony. As he sat with his friends, his long reveries featured the happy surprise that just did not take place. When they split up after their conversation, he would keep looking stealthily and sadly at the window and the balconies, especially at the window over the side path, for it frequently served as a frame for his beloved's image in his daydreams. Then he would depart, gulping down his despair and puffing out his distress. He became so despondent that he would have asked Husayn Shaddad the secret behind Aïda's disappearance had it not been for the traditions of the ancient quarter, with which his mentality was saturated. Thus he said nothing but began to wonder anxiously about the extent of Husayn's knowledge of the circumstances leading to the disappearance of the beloved.

Hasan Salim made no reference to the past, and his face gave no indication that he thought about it at all. Yet doubtless at each session that brought them together, he saw a living witness to his victory: Kamal. This thought hurt Kamal a good deal. He suffered a lot and felt the torment penetrating his marrow. The delirium of suffering affected his thinking. His worst agonies stemmed from the grief of separation, the bitterness of defeat, and the anguish of despair. Even more atrocious than all of these was his sense of abasement at being expelled from the garden of her good graces and deprived of the beloved's melodies and illuminations. As his spirit shed tears of grief and sorrow, he began to repeat, "You deformed creature, what are you compared with those blissful fellows?" What meaning would life have if she persisted in concealing herself? Where would his eyes find light or his heart warmth? What rapture was there for his spirit to enjoy? So let the beloved appear at whatever price she stipulated. Let her appear and love anyone she pleased, Hasan or someone else. Let her appear and mock his head and nose as much as her sense of humor and her playfulness wanted. His craving to contemplate her form and to hear her voice exceeded the human norm—so what then of a pleasant look to remove the resentment, despair, and desolation from his breast and to cheer a heart deprived of happiness as a blind man is deprived of the light? Let her appear even if she ignored him, for in that case, although he would be denied the pleasure of being acknowledged by her, he would not miss the happiness of seeing her and thus of seeing the world her magnificent light revealed. Otherwise, life would be nothing but successive moments of pain racked by insanity. Her withdrawal from his life was equivalent to extracting the spine from a body, which, having once known a balanced perfection, is then reduced to a sentient blob.

His pain and anxiety made him restless. He could not bear to wait for Friday to come, and he would go with friends to al-Abbasiya and circle around the mansion at a distance, on the chance that he might see her at a window, on a balcony, or as she walked when she thought she was far from his eyes. One of the consolations of waiting patiently in his home on Palace Walk was despair. In his feverish condition hovering near the shrine of the beloved was comparable to putting sticks of dynamite around a pillar of flame. He never saw her. Several times he saw one of the servants going or coming on the street. Then he would follow the fellow with amazed and curious eyes, as if asking the fates why they singled out this person to be near the beloved, to associate with her, and to observe her in various different modes—whether lying down, singing, or daydreaming. Why should all this good fortune befall a man who lived in her prayer niche with a heart oblivious to her worship.

On one of his jaunts he witnessed Abd al-Hamid Bey Shaddad and his treasured wife as they left the mansion to get into the Minerva automobile, which was waiting for them at the gate. Thus he saw the two happy individuals whom, more than anyone else in the whole world, Aïda venerated and respected. They occasionally gave her orders, which she had to obey. This precious mother had carried Aïda in her belly for nine months. Doubtless Aïda had once been a fetus and then a newborn, like those creatures Kamal had stared at for a long time when they first appeared in Aisha's and Khadija's beds. No person knew more about the childhood of his beloved than this happy and precious mother.

The pains would remain, or at least their effects would not be erased, so long as he wandered through life's labyrinth. To what avail were those nights in January when he buried his eyes, flowing with tears, in the pillow? He spread out his hands in prayer to the Lord of the heavens, pleading with total commitment, "O God, tell this love to be as cold as ashes, just as You commanded the fire burning Abraham: 'Be cold and safe'" (Qur'an, 21:69). He wished that love was concentrated in one location in the human being, for perhaps then it could be surgically removed the way a diseased limb is amputated. With a humble heart he uttered her beloved name to hear it echo in the silent room, as though someone else had summoned her. To revive a dream of lost happiness, he imitated her voice speaking his name. He ran his eyes over the pages of his diary to confirm that what had happened was a reality, not a figment of his imagination.

For the first time in years he thought regretfully of his life before love, as if he were a prisoner harking back to memories of lost freedom. Yes, he could think of no condition more like his than the prisoner's. Yet prison bars seemed easier to break and less confining than love's invisible shackles, which take total control over the heart's emotions, the mind's thoughts, and the body's nerves and then refuse to let go.

One day he wondered whether Fahmy had experienced this kind of torment. Memories of his late brother haunted him like a mournful song sighing in the hidden recesses of his soul. Kamal remembered how once in Fahmy's presence he had recounted Maryam's flirtation with the British soldier Julian. Kamal had plunged a poisoned dagger into his brother's heart, recklessly and carelessly. He summoned Fahmy's face into his conscious memory, recalling his brother's deceptive composure at the time. Then he re-created the contractions of pain on that handsome face when Fahmy had gone off by himself. He invented the plaintive monologues Fahmy had no doubt indulged in, like Kamal now, with moans and groans. Kamal felt the pain in his own heart and concluded: "Fahmy felt something worse than a bullet in his heart, even before the lead ripped into his chest."

Strangely enough, Kamal found that the political activities of the day presented an enlarged version of his life. When he read about developments in the newspapers he could have been reading about the events at Palace Walk or on Palaces Street. Like Kamal, Sa'd Zaghlul was as good as imprisoned and the victim of outrageous attacks, unjust charges, and the treacherous betrayal of friends. They had suffered because of contacts with people distinguished both by the loftiness of their aristocratic backgrounds and by the baseness of their deeds. The personal distress of the great nationalist leader also resembled the vanquished state of the nation. Kamal felt the same emotion and passion about the political situation as he did about his personal condition. He might just as well have been referring to himself when he asked of Sa'd Zaghlul, "Is this unjust treatment appropriate for such a sincere man?" He might easily have meant Hasan Salim when he said of Ahmad Ziwar Pasha, who replaced Sa'd Zaghlul as Prime Minister, "He has betrayed our trust and resorted to unfair tactics to gain control." Aïda could have been on his mind when he said of Egypt, "Has she dismissed the one man she could trust at a time when he was busy defending her rights?"

21 ❦

The Shawkat residence on Sugar Street did not enjoy the blessings of peace and quiet, not merely because the three floors were crowded with members of the Shawkat family but because of Khadija most of all. The elderly matriarch resided on the bottom floor, and Khalil, Aisha, and their children—Na'ima, Uthman, and Muhammad—were on the top one. But the uproar for which they were responsible was nothing compared with that raised by Khadija, whether it came from her directly or was provoked by her. Various changes in the management of the household had been made with an eye to confining the reasons for disputes to the narrowest possible limits. Khadija, who had been given her own living quarters and kitchen, had also ousted her mother-in-law's chickens from the roof so that she could raise chickens there herself and establish a modest garden patterned after the one on the roof of her childhood home. All these steps should have lessened domestic turmoil a great deal, but it had not decreased, or only to an imperceptible degree.

On this particular day Khadija's normally contentious spirit was afflicted by a certain listlessness. There seemed to be no secret about the reason, for Aisha and Khalil had come to help relieve the crisis. Yes, it was a crisis—one Khadija had precipitated. The two brothers sat on a sofa in the living room and the two sisters, their wives, were on the opposite one. They all looked serious, and Khadija was frowning. They exchanged eloquent glances, but no one wished to address the subject that had brought them together.

Finally, in a tone both plaintive and resentful, Khadija said, "Every household has quarrels like these. That's the way the world has been since our Lord created it. But there's no reason to broadcast our troubles to everyone and especially not to people who ought to be spared idle gossip. But she wasn't satisfied until she transformed our private affairs into public scandals. I can only trust in God and His blessings."

Ibrahim shifted around inside his overcoat as though trying to get comfortable on the sofa. Then he laughed briefly in a manner that left the others in doubt as to the exact import. Khadija looked at him suspiciously and asked, "What do you mean, 'ha-ha'? Is there nothing in the world that can make an impression on your heart?"

She turned away as though despairing of any assistance from him. Then, addressing Khalil and Aisha, she continued: "Are you happy that she went to see my father at the shop to complain about me? Is it right to drag men—especially ones like my father—into women's disputes? No doubt he was annoyed by her visit and complaint. If he wasn't so polite, he would have told her that frankly. But she kept at him until he promised to come. What disgusting conduct! My father wasn't made for petty matters like these. Do you approve of this behavior, Mr. Khalil?"

Khalil frowned disapprovingly and said, "My mother made a mistake. I told her so frankly, and she poured out her anger on me. But she's an old lady. You know people her age need to be treated with flattery and discretion, almost like children. Fine...."

Ibrahim interrupted him irritably: " 'Fine, fine'!... How many times are you going to repeat 'Fine'? I'm sick of it. As you observed, Mother's an old lady, but her blow has landed on a person who refuses to show any mercy."

Khadija glared at him with a scowling face and flaring nostrils. She exclaimed, "God! God! All that's left is for you to repeat these outrageous comments in front of Papa."

Expressing his regret with a wave of his hand, Ibrahim answered, "Papa isn't here yet. And if he does come, it won't be to listen to me. I'm just stating the truth, which everyone acknowledges and even you can't deny. You can't bear my mother and can't stand the sight of her. I take refuge in God. Why is all this necessary, reverend lady? With a little discretion and cleverness you would be able to hold her in the palm of your hand. But the moon would be easier to obtain than your moderation. Can you deny a word I've said?"

She looked back and forth from Khalil to Aisha in order to draw their attention to this screaming injustice. They seemed to be wavering between truth and personal safety. At last Aisha, although she was apprehensive about the result, muttered, "Mr. Ibrahim means that you might show a little forbearance with her foibles."

Khalil nodded his head in agreement, with all the relief of a man who has reached a fire escape in the nick of time. Then he said, "That's right. My mother has a quick temper but should be shown the same respect as yours. If you'll be a little more understanding, you'll spare your nerves the discomfort of feuding with her."

Khadija huffed and said, "It would be much more accurate to say that she can't bear me or stand the sight of me. She's made me a nervous wreck. We never meet without her volunteering something, either directly or by insinuation, that makes my blood boil and poisons my nerves. Then I'm asked to be forbearing, as though I'm made of ice. . . . Isn't it enough that Abd al-Muni'm and Ahmad try my patience to the breaking point? Hear my prayer: Where can I find someone who will treat me fairly?"

With a smile Ibrahim said sarcastically, "Perhaps you'll find this equitable person in your father."

She shot back, "You're enjoying my bad luck. I understand everything. But our Lord is present."

In a strained voice, suggesting both resignation and defiance, Ibrahim answered, "Calm down so you'll be relaxed when you see your father."

How could she relax? The old lady had devised the most terrible vengeance. Shortly Khadija would be summoned before her father. Her blood ran cold at the thought of this encounter. Then Abd al-Muni'm and Ahmad's screams resounded through the closed door of their room. These were followed by Ahmad's sobs. Khadija, despite her plumpness, jumped up quickly and headed for their bedroom. Pushing the door open, she entered and screamed, "What's the meaning of this? Haven't I forbidden you to fight a thousand times? The one I'm after is whoever started this."

Once she had disappeared behind the door, Ibrahim said, "The poor dear seems to have a deep-rooted antagonism against tranquillity. Beginning first thing in the morning, she wades into a long series of skirmishes lasting the whole day. She doesn't quiet down until she goes to bed. Everything has to yield to her will and design—the servant, the food, the furniture, the chickens, Abd al-Muni'm, Ahmad, and me. Everything must adjust to her system. I feel sorry for her. I assure you that our residence could enjoy the most systematic order without any need for this obsessive behavior."

Smiling, Khalil said, "May our Lord come to her aid."

"And help me too!" Ibrahim added as he smilingly shook his head. Then he took his cigarette case out of the pocket of his black overcoat. He rose to offer it to his brother, who accepted a cigarette.

Ibrahim invited Aisha to have one as well, but she laughingly declined. Pointing to the door behind which Khadija had disappeared, she said, "Let's give the hour every possible chance of going smoothly."

Ibrahim resumed his seat and lit a cigarette. Gesturing toward the same door, he remarked, "A court of law. There's a trial being conducted in there now. But she'll treat the two defendants mercifully, even if that's against her better judgment."

Khadija returned, grumbling, "How can I enjoy any peace in this house? How and when?"

She sat down and sighed. Then, addressing Aisha, she said, "I looked out through the balcony peephole and saw that the mud left behind by yesterday's rain is still covering the road. So tell me, by your Lord, how my father's supposed to walk through it? Why this stubbornness?"

Aisha asked her, "What about the sky? What does it look like now?"

"Overcast! All the alleys will be lakes by nightfall, but is that enough to make your mother-in-law postpone, even for a day, the evil she's hatching? No, she went to the store despite the hardship walking there posed. And then she hounded the man until he promised to come. Anyone hearing her complain about me in the store under such adverse conditions would have thought I was a cold-blooded killer like those dreadful women in Alexandria: Rayya and Sakina."

They all laughed, seizing the opportunity she had provided to release their tension. Ibrahim asked, "Do you think you're less dangerous than the thieving sisters Rayya and Sakina?"

They heard someone knock on their door. When Khadija's servant opened it, the maid Suwaydan's face appeared. She glanced fearfully at Khadija and said, "My senior master has arrived." Then she speedily vanished.

Khadija's color drained from her face, and she said in a faint voice, "Don't leave us alone together."

She waited for Aisha to cast a searching look at her reflection in the mirror to see that her face was free of makeup. Then they left the apartment together.

Directly under a portrait of the late Mr. Shawkat, al-Sayyid Ahmad Abd al-Jawad sat on a couch in the center of a room decorated in the old style. Widow Shawkat, the mother of Khalil and Ibrahim, was sitting in a nearby armchair wearing a thick coat, which despite its bulk did not conceal her scrawniness or her bent back. Her face had grown thin, and her deep wrinkles were surrounded by folds of dry skin. Nothing about her remained the same except her gold teeth.

Al-Sayyid Ahmad was no stranger to this room or its antique furnishings, the age of which detracted in no way from the magnificence.

If the curtains had faded and the velvet of some of the chairs and couches had become bald or torn on the arms or backs, the Persian carpet had a lasting splendor and an increasing value. The room was fragrant with a delicate incense of which the old lady was enamored.

Leaning on her parasol, she said, "I told myself that if al-Sayyid Ahmad didn't come as he promised, he's not my son and I'm not his mother."

He smiled and said, "God forbid. I'm obedient to your command. I'm your son and Khadija's your daughter."

She made a face and said, "All of you are my children. Mrs. Amina is a fine daughter to me. You're a prince of a man. But Khadija . . ." She looked at him, and her eyes grew wide as she continued: "Khadija did not inherit a single quality from her excellent parents." Then, shaking her head, she added, "O Gracious One, be gracious to us."

Al-Sayyid Ahmad responded apologetically, "I'm shocked that she's made you so angry. The matter comes as an immense surprise to me. I won't stand for this at all. But won't you tell me what she's done?"

Frowning, the woman said, "This has been going on for a long time. We've kept everything from you out of respect for the pleas of her mother, all of whose attempts to reform Khadija have failed. But I won't say anything behind her back, al-Sayyid, sir, as I declared to you at the store."

At that moment the group arrived. Ibrahim entered first, followed by Khalil, Aisha, and finally Khadija. They shook hands with al-Sayyid Ahmad one by one until it was Khadija's turn. She leaned over with exemplary politeness to kiss her father's hand. The old lady could not restrain herself from saying in astonishment, "Lord, what is this charade of manners? Are you really Khadija? Don't let appearances deceive you, al-Sayyid Ahmad."

Khalil said to his mother critically, "Won't you give our father a chance to catch his breath? There's really no need for a tribunal."

The woman's voice grew louder as she replied, "Why are you here? What's brought all of you? Leave her with us, and the rest of you can go in peace."

Ibrahim said gently, "Think of God."

She shouted at him, "I'm acting more devoutly than you, you mule. If you were a real man, there would have been no reason for me to call in this fine gentleman. Why are you here? Shouldn't you be sound asleep as usual?"

Khadija was relieved at this opening. She hoped the quarrel would grow so intense that it would eclipse her case. But al-Sayyid Ahmad blocked the road for the anticipated battle between the old lady and her sons by saying in a loud voice, "What's this I've heard about you, Khadija? Is it true that you haven't been a polite and obedient daughter to your new mother? Asking God's forgiveness—she's a mother for all of us."

Khadija's hopes were disappointed, and she lowered her eyes. Her lips moved, but their whisper was indiscernible. She shook her head no.

The old lady waved her hand to get everyone's attention and began to speak: "This has been going on for a long time. I won't be able to recount all of it in one session. From her first day in this house she has opposed me for no reason whatsoever. She speaks to me with the sauciest tongue I've ever encountered in my whole life. I wouldn't like to repeat what I've heard over these five years or more. There have been many, many ugly remarks. She found fault with my management of the house and criticized my cooking. Can you imagine that, al-Sayyid, sir? She kept it up until she separated her living quarters from mine and thus split one home into two apartments. Even the maid Suwaydan was forbidden to enter Khadija's apartment, because Suwaydan is in my employ. Khadija hired a servant of her own. The roof! The roof terrace, al-Sayyid, sir, is very large, but she didn't think it big enough for both of us. I was forced to transfer my chickens to the courtyard. What else should I say, my son? This is a small sample, but we're not to blame. I told myself, 'What's done is done.' I bore it all and was patient, thinking that once she was independent of me the reasons for discord would be removed. But was my assumption correct? By your life, no!" She stopped talking, for she was overcome by a fit of coughing. She coughed so hard her veins swelled. Khadija prayed to God as she watched that He would carry off her mother-in-law before the indictment was finished. But the coughing died away. The old lady swallowed and recited the Muslim credo. Then, raising tearful eyes to al-Sayyid Ahmad, she asked in a voice not without a trace of huskiness, "Al-Sayyid Ahmad, do you have any aversion to calling me 'Mother'?"

Although Ibrahim and Khalil were smiling, their father-in-law put on a grave face as he answered, "God protect us, Mother."

"May God guard you, al-Sayyid Ahmad. Yet your daughter is averse to it. She calls me Auntie, although I've asked her repeatedly to say Mother. She retorts, 'Then what will I call the one at Palace Walk?' I tell her that I'm Mother and that her mother is also Mother. Then she tells me, 'I have only one mother, may our Lord preserve her for me.' Do you see, al-Sayyid, sir—me, the woman who received her with my own hands the moment she emerged from the unseen world."

Al-Sayyid Ahmad leveled an angry look at Khadija and asked her indignantly, "Is this true, Khadija? You must reply."

Khadija had virtually lost her ability to speak, for both her rage and her fear were extreme. In addition, she was anything but optimistic about the outcome of this discussion. Her instinct for self-defense prompted her to resort to humble entreaty. In a faint voice she said, "I'm unjustly accused. Everyone here knows I'm unjustly accused. By God, Papa, unjustly accused."

Al-Sayyid Ahmad was amazed by what he was hearing. Although from the beginning he had been aware of the influence of senility on Widow Shawkat and although the humorous atmosphere had not escaped his attention, since it was visible in the smiling faces of Ibrahim and Khalil, he was still determined to project a stern gravity in order to humor the grande dame and to intimidate Khadija. He was astonished by the disclosure of his daughter's obstinacy and irritability. He had never imagined that she was like this. Had her temper been so fierce when she lived in his home? Did Amina know more about this than he did? Would he eventually unmask a new image of his daughter, running counter to the one he had had of her, just as he had already found it necessary to revise his picture of Yasin?

"I want to know the truth. I want to know the truth about you. The person our mother has described is not the girl I know. Which of them is really you?"

The old lady joined the tips of her fingers together and then shook her hand up and down in a gesture asking him to be patient until she could finish what she was saying. Then she started off again: "I told her, 'I received you with my own hands when you were born.' She replied in a vicious tone I'd never heard before, 'In that case, it's a miracle I survived.'"

Ibrahim and Khalil laughed, and Aisha bowed her head to hide her smile. The matriarch told her sons, "Laugh, laugh! Laugh at your mother."

But al-Sayyid Ahmad was grim-faced, even though he too was

secretly amused. Was it possible that his daughters were fashioned after his pattern? Was this not worth relating to Ibrahim al-Far, Ali Abd al-Rahim, and Muhammad Iffat? He told Khadija roughly, "No, no. . . . I'll certainly find ways to hold you strictly accountable for all this."

Relieved, the old lady carried on: "What caused the row yesterday was that Ibrahim invited some of his friends to a luncheon. Among the dishes served was Circassian chicken. Afterwards Ibrahim, Khalil, Aisha, and Khadija passed the evening with me. There was reference to the luncheon and Ibrahim mentioned his guests' praise for the Circassian chicken. Mrs. Khadija was delighted. But she wasn't satisfied. She went so far as to assert that Circassian chicken was the favorite dish in her childhood home. I remarked with the best of intentions that it was Zaynab, Yasin's first wife, who had introduced Circassian chicken to your family and that Khadija must have learned to make it from her. I swear I meant no harm when I said that. I did not mean to injure anyone, may God watch over you, my dear sir. But she jumped up angrily and shouted in my face, 'Do you know more about our house than I do?' I replied, 'I knew your house years before you did.' She screamed, 'You don't really love us. You can't stand for anything praiseworthy to be attributed to us, even if it's only cooking Circassian chicken—the Circassian chicken that was eaten in our house before Zaynab was born. It's disgraceful for a woman your age to lie.' Yes, by God, this is what she hurled at me, al-Sayyid, sir, in front of everyone. So which of us is the liar—before your Lord at prayers?"

Al-Sayyid Ahmad said with furious indignation, "She accused you of lying to your face! O Lord of heavens and earth, this is not my daughter."

Khalil asked his mother disapprovingly, "Is that why you've summoned our father? Is it proper to disturb him and waste his time because of a childish quarrel over Circassian chicken? This is too much, Mother."

The old lady stared him in the eye. She scowled and shouted at him, "Hush! Get out of my sight! I'm not a liar. It's not right for anyone to accuse me of lying. I know what I'm saying. The truth, which no one needs to be ashamed of, is that Circassian chicken was not a dish known in the home of al-Sayyid Ahmad before Zaynab introduced it. There is nothing in that fact to demean or belittle anyone. But it's the truth. Here is al-Sayyid Ahmad. Let him say if I'm lying. The excellence of the casseroles in his home is proverbial and the dishes stuffed with rice are as good, but Circassian chicken was not served at his table before Zaynab arrived. Speak, al-Sayyid, sir. You alone are the judge."

Al-Sayyid Ahmad had been fighting back the temptation to laugh all the time the woman was speaking. But he said in a ferocious tone, "If only her offense were limited to lying and to making a false claim without her having added to it a breach of manners. . . . Were you tempted to act so badly by the thought that you were beyond the reach of my hand? Without any hesitation my hand will stretch as far as necessary. It's really sad when a father finds his daughter needs to be reprimanded and disciplined after she's fully grown and has taken her place among women as a wife and a mother." Waving his hand, he continued: "I'm angry at you. By God, it hurts me to see your face before me."

Influenced by her emotions and by a realistic assessment of her situation, Khadija suddenly burst into tears, for crying was the only means she had available for her defense. In a choked and quavering voice she sobbed, "I'm unjustly accused. By God, I'm innocent. The moment she sees my face, she flings harsh words at me. She never stops telling me, 'If it weren't for me, you would have remained a spinster your whole life.' I've never done her any harm. They can all testify to that."

Her melodramatic performance, half sincere and half counterfeit, was not without its effect. Khalil Shawkat frowned angrily. Ibrahim Shawkat bowed his head. Although al-Sayyid Ahmad's appearance underwent no change, his heart was moved by this reference to spinsterhood, just as it had been in the old days. The lady shot piercing glances at Khadija from beneath her white eyebrows, as if to tell her, "Play your part, crafty girl, but it won't work with me."

When Widow Shawkat sensed that the atmosphere was becoming sympathetic to the actress, she said defiantly, "Here's Aisha, your sister. I adjure you, Aisha, by your eyes and the holy Qur'an: Did you not witness what I heard and saw? Didn't your sister call me a liar to my face? Didn't I give a fair account of the Circassian chicken dispute, without any exaggeration or hyperbole? Speak, daughter, speak. Your sister now accuses me of injustice, after calling me a liar yesterday. Speak, so al-Sayyid Ahmad will learn who the unjust aggressor is."

Aisha was terrified at being suddenly dragged into the tumult of this case, which she had thought she could observe safely from the sidelines until the end. She felt danger encompassing her from every direction. She looked back and forth from her husband to his brother, as though begging for help. Ibrahim started to intervene, but al-Sayyid Ahmad spoke first. Addressing Aisha, he said, "Your mother is requesting your testimony, Aisha. You must speak."

Aisha was so upset that she turned quite pale. But the only movement of her lips came when she swallowed. She lowered her eyes to escape from her father's stare and kept silent.

Then Khalil protested, "I've never heard of a woman being called on to testify against her sister."

His mother shouted at him, "I've never heard before of sons ganging up against their mother the way you are." Then she turned to al-Sayyid Ahmad and said, "But her silence is enough to prove my point. Aisha's silence bears witness on my behalf, al-Sayyid, sir."

Aisha thought her torment was over at this point, but before she knew what was happening, Khadija, who was drying her tears, entreated Aisha, "Speak, Aisha: Did you hear me insult her?"

Aisha cursed her sister privately from the depths of her heart. Her golden head of hair began to twitch nervously.

Then the old lady cried out, "Now we're getting somewhere. She's the one asking you to testify. You no longer have an excuse, Shushu darling. My Lord, if I really were as unjust as Khadija claims, why haven't I been unjust to Aisha? Why do I get along so well with her? Why, my Lord, why?"

Ibrahim Shawkat rose and went to take a seat next to al-Sayyid Ahmad, telling him, "Father, I'm sorry we've troubled you in this manner and wasted your precious time. Let's set aside complaint and testimony and put the past behind us, so we can see what's truly important and beneficial. Your presence can only be a positive influence and a blessing. Let's impose a truce between my mother and my wife and have them promise to abide by it always."

Al-Sayyid Ahmad was pleased by this suggestion, but, shaking his head, he objected deftly, "No, I won't agree to oversee a truce, for it would have to be concluded between equals. Here one of the sides is our mother and the other our daughter, and a daughter does not have the status of a mother. First Khadija must apologize to her mother for all past incidents. Then her mother, if she is willing, can forgive Khadija. After that we'll talk about making peace."

The old lady beamed so wide that her wrinkles were pressed together, but she glanced cautiously toward Khadija. Then she looked back at al-Sayyid Ahmad without saying anything. He remarked, "It seems my proposal does not meet with your approval."

The old lady answered gratefully, "You always say the right thing. Blessings on your lips and life."

Al-Sayyid Ahmad motioned to Khadija, who stood up without any hesitation and approached him, feeling more forlorn than ever before. When she was directly in front of him, he told her resolutely, "Kiss your mother's hand and ask her, 'Forgive me, Mother.' "

"Oh!" She had never imagined, not even in a nightmare, that she might be put in this position, but her father, her adored father, was the one imposing it on her. Yes, the verdict had been handed down by a person whose verdicts she could never oppose. So this must be God's will. Khadija turned to the old lady and leaned over her. Then she took the hand that was raised to her—yes, by God, raised without any sign of protest—and kissed it, painfully conscious of her disgust and defeat. Then she mumbled, "Forgive me, Mother."

The old lady looked at her for a time, her face flushed with delight. Then she replied, "I forgive you, Khadija. I forgive you for your father's sake and in recognition of your repentance." A childish laugh escaped her. Then she said in an admonitory fashion, "There'll be no quarrel after today about Circassian chicken. Isn't it enough for your family that your casseroles and your dishes stuffed with rice are superior to any others in the world?"

Al-Sayyid Ahmad said joyfully, "Praise to God for this peace accord." Then, looking up at Khadija, he reminded her, "Mother always. She isn't Auntie. This is Mother exactly like the other one."

Then he continued in a low, sorrowful voice: "Where did you get this disposition, Khadija? No one who grew up in my house should be like this. Have you forgotten your mother and her mild, courteous character? Have you forgotten that any evil you cause tarnishes my honor? By God, I was astonished to hear what your mother had to say. It will continue to amaze me for a long time to come."

22

Following the departure of al-Sayyid Ahmad Abd al-Jawad, the group went back upstairs. Khadija led the procession, her face sullen and pale with angry resentment. The others knew that harmony was still nothing more than a remote possibility for their household. They were apprehensive about what was building up behind Khadija's silence. For this reason, Khalil and Aisha accompanied Khadija and Ibrahim to their apartment, although the racket from Na'ima, Uthman, and Muhammad clearly suggested that their parents would soon need to return home. After they had resumed their seats in the living room, Khalil took the pulse of the situation by saying to his brother, "Your final remarks were decisive and brought good results."

For the first time since the tribunal, Khadija spoke out, passionately: "It brought a truce—isn't that so? A truce that humiliated me more than ever before...."

Ibrahim said somewhat critically, "It's not humiliating to kiss my mother's hand or to ask her forgiveness."

His wife answered cavalierly, "She's your mother but my enemy. If Papa hadn't ordered me, I would never have called her Mother. Yes, she's only Mother on Papa's orders. Papa's orders alone!"

Ibrahim leaned against the back of the sofa and sighed dejectedly. Aisha was anxious, for she did not know what impression her failure to testify had made on her sister. Her anxiety was increased by Khadija's refusal to look at her. She decided to speak to prompt Khadija to reveal her true feelings. So she remarked gently, "There is no humiliation in the affair, since you parted friends. You mustn't remember anything but the happy ending."

Her torso rigid, Khadija glared angrily at Aisha. Then she said sharply, "Don't speak to me. You're the last person in the world who deserves to talk to me."

Aisha pretended to be astonished and, looking back and forth between Ibrahim and Khalil, asked, "Me? Why, God forbid?"

In a voice as cold and penetrating as a bullet, Khadija replied, "Because you betrayed me. Your silence testified against me. You chose to placate the other woman instead of helping your sister. This is treachery pure and simple."

"I don't understand you, Khadija. Everyone knows my silence worked to your advantage."

In as vicious a tone of voice or worse, Khadija retorted, "If you had truly had my best interests at heart, you would have testified for me, even if what you said wasn't exactly true. But you preferred the woman who cooks for you over your own sister. Don't speak! Not a word! We have a mother who will have something to say about this."

Shortly before noon the next day Khadija went to visit her mother, even though the roads were muddy, with pools of stagnant water in low-lying areas. She went to the oven room, and her mother rose to greet her warmly and happily. Umm Hanafi approached, jubilantly welcoming her. But Khadija returned their greetings with a only few terse words. Her mother gave her a searching, inquisitive look.

Without any preliminaries Khadija announced, "I've come to see what you think of Aisha, for I don't have the strength to put up with any more."

Amina's expression revealed her interest and her distress. Motioning with her head for Khadija to precede her out of the room, she said, "What's happened, may God requite us? Your father told me about the events at Sugar Street, but what role did Aisha play in them?"

Then, as they climbed the stairs, she continued: "Lord, Khadija, how many times have I asked you to be more understanding? Your mother-in-law is an old lady. You need to respect her age. The very fact that she went to the store alone in the weather we had yesterday is clear proof of her senility. But what can be done about it? How angry your father was! He couldn't believe you would ever say a spiteful word. But what did Aisha do to make you angry? She kept silent, didn't she? It wasn't possible for her to say anything."

They settled down side by side on a sofa in the sitting room where the coffee hour was held. Khadija admonished her, "Mother, please don't join forces with them. My Lord, why is it that I can't find anyone in this world to help me?"

The mother smiled reprovingly and remarked, "Don't say that. Don't even imagine that, my little daughter. Just tell me what you think Aisha did wrong."

Punching the air as though it were an enemy, Khadija answered, "The worst. She testified against me. So I was miserably defeated."

"What did she say?"

"She didn't say anything."

"Praise God."

"The catastrophe was a result of her silence."

Smiling fondly, Amina asked, "What could she have said?"

As though her mother's question was more than she could stomach, Khadija frowned and replied bitterly, "She could have sworn I never attacked the woman. Why not? If she had done that, it wouldn't have been more than a sister's duty. She could at least have said she didn't hear anything. The truth is, she favored that woman over me. She deserted me and let me fall prey to a malicious schemer. I'll never forget this about Aisha so long as I live."

Feeling hurt and apprehensive, her mother said, "Khadija, don't frighten me. Everything should have been forgotten by morning."

"Forgotten? I didn't sleep at all last night. I tossed and turned, and my head seemed to be on fire. Any disaster would have seemed insignificant, had it not come from Aisha. From my sister? She agreed to team up with Satan. Fine! Let her have what she wants. I used to have one mother-in-law. Now I have two. Aisha! Lord, how many times have I shielded her! If I were a traitor like her, I would have told my father about the streak of improper conduct running through her life. She wants to be thought of as a noble angel while I'm cast as a devil deserving to be pelted with stones. Certainly not! I'm a thousand times better than she is. My reputation is spotless." Her tone became increasingly strident as she added, "If it weren't for my father, no power on earth could have brought me to kiss my enemy's hand or to call her Mother."

Amina patted her daughter's shoulder gently as she said, "You're angry, always angry. Calm down. You'll stay here with me and we'll have lunch together. Then we can have a quiet chat."

"I'm in full control of my intellect. I know what I'm saying. I want to ask my father which is better: the wife who stays at home or the one who visits all the neighbors and sings to them while her daughter dances?"

Amina sighed and said mournfully, "There's no need to ask what your father thinks of this. But Aisha's a married woman, and the final word on her conduct is her husband's. If he allows her to visit the neighbors and knows that she sings when she's with her friends who love her and her voice, then what concern of ours is it? God takes care of everything, Khadija. Is this what you term 'improper conduct'? Does it really infuriate you that Na'ima dances? She's going on six, and dancing is a game for her. You're just angry, Khadija; may God forgive you."

Khadija said determinedly, "I mean every word I've said. If you approve of your daughter singing when she visits the neighbors and letting her daughter dance, do you also approve of her smoking—like men? Yes, you're astonished. I repeat in your hearing that Aisha smokes. She's become addicted and can't do without it. Her husband gives her a pack, telling her quite plainly, 'This is your pack, darling Shushu.' I've seen her, myself, take a puff on one and exhale the smoke through her mouth and nostrils. Her nose! Do you hear? She no longer attempts to hide it from me as she did at first. In fact, she suggested I try smoking, on the grounds that it helps calm agitated nerves. This is Aisha. What do you have to say about that? What would my father say? I wonder."

There was total silence. Amina appeared to be perplexed and at a loss. All the same, she decided to continue trying to calm her daughter. She said, "Smoking's a nasty habit even for men. Your father has never smoked. What can I say then about women smoking? But if it's her husband who tempted her and taught her how, what room is there for comment? What can be done about it, Khadija? She belongs to her husband, not to us. All we can do is give her some advice, whether or not it does any good."

Khadija began to gaze at her mother with a silence that betrayed hesitation. Finally she said, "Her husband pampers her so dreadfully he spoils her. He's made her his partner in all his depraved acts. Smoking isn't his only bad habit. He drinks liquor at home without any embarrassment. There's always a bottle in his house, as though it were one of the necessities of life. He'll get her hooked on drink just as he did with tobacco. Why not? The old lady knows her son's apartment's a tavern, but she doesn't care. He'll serve Aisha liquor. Indeed, I can state categorically that he has, for I smelled a strange fragrance on her breath once. When I questioned her, although she denied everything, she was nervous. I tell you, she surely has drunk alcohol and will become as addicted to it as she is to smoking."

The mother exclaimed gloomily, "Anything but this, O Lord! Have pity on yourself and on me: Fear God, Khadija."

"I am a devout person, God knows. I don't smoke and my mouth does not reek with suspicious odors. I don't allow liquor to come into my home. Don't you know that the other mule attempted to stock this sinful bottle? But I waylaid him and told him with the utmost candor, 'I won't remain in this apartment if there's a liquor bottle in it.' Faced by my resolve, he backed down. Now he leaves his bottle with his brother ... in the apartment of the lady who betrayed me yesterday. Whenever I shout insults at alcohol and those who drink it, he asks—may God slice out his tongue—'Where did you come by such fundamentalist Hanbalism? Your father's a wellspring of conviviality. His parties almost never lack a drink and a lute.' So you hear what they say about my father in the Shawkat household."

A look of sorrow and anguish was visible in Amina's eyes. She began to clench and release her fist with anxious agitation. Then she said in a plaintive, hurt tone, "Have mercy on us, Lord! We weren't meant for this. God, you're forgiving and compassionate. How men make women suffer! I won't keep still about it—that wouldn't be right. I'll take Aisha to task in no uncertain terms. But I can't believe what you've said of her. Your suspicions have tempted you to imagine groundless things about her. My daughter's pure and will remain pure, even if her husband turns into a demon. I'll speak to her quite bluntly. I'll even discuss it with Mr. Khalil himself, if that's necessary. He can drink as much as he wants until God grants him repentance, but I ask God to draw an invisible line between my daughter and Satan."

For the first time Khadija's soul felt a refreshing breeze. She observed her mother's concern with a satisfied eye, reassured that Aisha would soon experience the full impact of the loss her betrayal was destined to bring her. Khadija felt little remorse for having embellished the facts in her exaggerated portrayal of the situation or in its bitter characterization, which had led her to refer to her sister's apartment as a tavern. She knew that Ibrahim and Khalil rarely touched liquor and then only in moderation and that neither had ever been intoxicated, but she was upset and resentful. She repeated the remarks about her father being "a wellspring of conviviality" to her mother with an incredulous tone to make it clear that she rejected them, although long ago she had been forced to accept their accuracy. She had yielded to the testimony of Ibrahim, Khalil, and their aged mother, especially since they had made their comments not in a prejudiced or critical manner but when praising her father's generosity and according him a leading role among the witty people of his era. In the beginning, she had rejected that consensus with a fierce obstinacy. Then slowly, even if she did not admit it openly, doubt crept in. She found it extremely difficult to reconcile these new attributes with the somber and tyrannical person in whom she had believed all her life. All the same, this doubt did not in any respect lessen her regard and veneration, which may have increased, through the addition of wit and liberality to his qualities.

Khadija was not content with the victory she had won. Trying to goad her mother on, she said, "Aïsha didn't just betray me. She's betrayed you too." She fell silent to let her words penetrate deep into her mother. Then she went on: "She visits Yasin and Maryam in Palace of Desire Alley."

Staring at her daughter in alarm, Amina cried out, "What did you say?"

Feeling that she had scaled the peaks of victory, Khadija answered, "This is the sad truth. Yasin and Maryam have visited us more than once. They visited Aisha, and they visited me. I'll admit I was forced to receive them. Had it not been for my respect for Yasin, I wouldn't have been able to. But I did it guardedly. Yasin invited me to visit them at Palace of Desire. I don't need to say that I didn't go. They visited again, but that still did not shake my resolve. Finally Maryam asked, 'Why don't you visit us? We've been like sisters since childhood.' I offered various excuses, and she did her best to tempt me. She started to complain about Yasin's treatment, his sneaky behavior, and his neglect. Perhaps she hoped to arouse my sympathy, but I didn't open my heart to her—unlike Aisha, who receives her warmly, kissing her. Even worse, she exchanges visits with Maryam. She took Mr. Khalil with her once and another time Na'ima, Uthman, and Muhammad. She certainly seems happy to renew her friendship with Maryam. When I cautioned her about carrying it too far, she replied, 'Maryam's only sin was that we refused one day to make her the fiancée of our lamented brother. Is that fair?' I asked her, 'Have you forgotten the English soldier?' She replied, 'The only thing we should remember is that she's the wife of our oldest brother.' Have you ever heard anything like this, Mother?"

Amina yielded to her sorrow. She bowed her head and took refuge in silence. Khadija looked at her for a time. Then she resumed her denunciation: "That's Aisha, nothing added, nothing subtracted ... Aisha who testified against me yesterday, humiliating me in front of that prattling old woman."

Amina sighed deeply. She gazed at Khadija with tired eyes. Then she said in a faint voice, "Aisha's a child without any mind or substance. She'll always be like that, no matter how long she lives. What else can I say? I don't want to say more and I can't. Does the memory of Fahmy mean so little to her? I can't believe that. Why can't she be stingier with her affections when it comes to that woman, if only for my sake? But I won't let this pass. I'll tell her she's wronged me, that I'm angry and saddened, and then we'll see how she reacts."

Grasping a lock of her hair, Khadija said, "I'll chop this off if she reforms. She lives in a dream world all her own. God knows I'm not prejudiced against her. I've never had a fight with her since I got married, not a single óne. It's true I've often inveighed against her neglect of the children, her humiliating flattery of her mother-in-law, and other similar things I've related to you over the years. But my attacks have never gone beyond the limits of resolute advice and frank criticism. This is the first time she's upset me so badly that I'm publicly quarreling with her."

Although still looking vexed, her mother entreated her, "Let me handle this, Khadija. I don't want you ever to be estranged from her by a dispute. It's not right for your hearts to be alienated from each other when you live together in the same home. Don't forget that you're sisters ... and that you're her big sister. Your heart is not mean, praise God. It's filled with love for all your family. Whenever I have a problem, my one consolation is your affection. Despite her failings, Aisha is still your sister. Don't forget that."

Stung, Khadija cried out, "I'll forgive her everything except her testimony against me."

"She didn't testify against you. She was afraid of making you angry and afraid of angering her mother-in-law. So she kept silent. She hates to upset anyone, as you well know, even if her heedlessness frequently annoys people. She never meant to harm you. Don't expect too much from her. I'll come see you tomorrow and settle accounts with her. But I'll make peace between the two of you, and you'd better not object."

For the first time Khadija's eyes had an anxious, apprehensive look. She lowered them to keep her mother from noticing. She did not say anything for a moment. Then in a weak voice she asked, "You'll come tomorrow?"

"Yes, the situation requires my immediate attention."

As though to herself, Khadija remarked, "She'll accuse me of divulging her secrets."

"So!" Then, sensing her daughter's increasing anxiety and apprehension, Amina added, "In any case, I know what to say and what not to."

With relief Khadija concluded, "That's best, for it's unlikely she'll acknowledge that my intentions are good or that all I want is to help her improve."

23

"Oh!" he suddenly exclaimed with warmth and passion on seeing Aïda emerge from the gate of her mansion. As usual late each afternoon, he was standing on the sidewalk of al-Abbasiya Street watching her house from a distance. The most he had been hoping for was a glimpse of her on a balcony or at a window. He wore an elegant gray suit, as though wishing to keep pace with the good weather, which the last days of March had graciously and cheerfully provided. The more hurt and despondent he felt, the more dapper his attire became. He had not set eyes on Aïda since she had quarreled with him in the gazebo. But life would not have been possible without this afternoon pilgrimage to al-Abbasiya, where he circled the mansion from afar with unflagging zeal. He would give free rein to his dreams and satisfy himself temporarily with contemplation of the shrine and a review of his memories.

In the first days of their separation the pain had almost driven him crazy, leaving him prey to delirious paranoia. Had it lasted any longer, it would have done him in. He had escaped from that dangerous initial stage by virtue of the despair long embedded in his soul. Pain had crept back into its residence deep inside him, where it carried on its traffic without disturbing his other vital functions, as though it were an organic part of his body or an essential faculty of his spirit. His agony was like a severe illness that lingers on as a chronic malady after its worst symptoms subside. He was not consoled. How could he find any consolation for love? It was the most exalted thing life had ever revealed to him. Since he believed deeply in love's immortality, he realized he would have to bear it patiently, as if destined to live out the rest of his days with an incurable illness.

When he suddenly saw her leave the mansion, this moan escaped him. His eyes watched her graceful gait, which he had wanted to see for such a long time, and his spirit danced with a rapture of affectionate excitement. The beloved turned right and proceeded along Palaces Street. Revolt flared up in his spirit, sweeping away the sense of defeat his soul had nourished for nearly three months. His heart shocked him into a decision to cast his complaints at her feet regardless of the consequences. Without any hesitation he walked to Palaces Street. In the past he had spoken cautiously from fear of losing her. Now there was no further loss to fear. Moreover, the torment he had suffered during the last three months would hardly allow him to hesitate or retreat. Aïda soon noticed the approaching footsteps and turned to glance back when he was only a few steps behind her. But then she looked ahead again indifferently. He had not expected a gracious reception, but he reproached her, "Is this the way old friends greet each other?"

She responded by quickening her pace without even glancing at him. He lengthened his steps, deriving stubborn resolve from his pain. When he was almost beside her, he said, "Don't pretend you don't know me. That's unbearable. If you had any regard for fairness, there would be no need for this."

What he feared most was that she would ignore him until she reached her destination. But the melodious voice answered, "Please get away from me. Let me go in peace."

With humble determination he told her, "You will go on your way peacefully, but after we settle accounts."

In a voice that resounded clearly in the silence of the aristocratic street, which seemed almost deserted, she replied, "I don't know what accounts you're talking about and don't want to know. I wish you'd act like a gentleman."

With fervent passion he said, "I promise to conduct myself in a fashion exemplary even for a gentleman. I couldn't act otherwise, since you inspire me in everything I do."

Without ever looking his way she retorted, "I mean you should leave me in peace. That's what I want."

"I can't. I can't until you pronounce me innocent of the false charges for which you've punished me without listening to my defense."

"I'm punishing you?"

He paused for a fleeting instant to enjoy the magic of that moment, for she had agreed to debate with him and to slow her happy stride. Did she want to listen to him or was she deliberately giving herself more time to get rid of him before she reached her destination? In either case it was a dazzling fact that they were walking side by side along Palaces Street. The lofty trees there sheltered them and, from beyond the walls of the mansions, calm narcissus eyes and smiling jasmine mouths followed the couple's progress in a stillness profound enough to soothe his burning heart, if he could only have absorbed it.

He said, "You have punished me cruelly by disappearing for three whole months while I, although innocent, have suffered countless torments."

"Let's not rehash that."

Passionately and humbly he replied, "But we must. I'm determined to. I beg you in the name of the agony I've endured for so long that I lack the strength to suffer anymore."

She asked quietly, "How is that my fault?"

"I want to know whether you still consider me an adversary. One thing that's certain is that I could never harm you under any circumstances. If you would just consider my affection for you over the past years you would embrace my viewpoint without any hesitation. Let me tell you the whole story with total candor. After our conversation in the gazebo, Hasan Salim asked me to have a talk with him."

She interrupted him almost imploringly: "Let's drop this. It's over, finished."

This last sentence had the impact on him that laments at a funeral would make on a dead man if he could hear. Then, touched in a way that showed itself in his voice, where it was like a song dropping down an octave to an answering voice, he said, "Finished . . . I know it's finished, but I would like it to have a positive ending. I don't want you to leave thinking me a traitor or a slanderer. I'm innocent, and it's awful when you think ill of a person who harbors for you . . . harbors for you nothing but veneration and respect and whose every reference to you is coated with praise."

Leaning her head in the other direction, she cast him a look as if to ask teasingly, "When did you become so eloquent?" Then almost tenderly she said, "It seems there's been a misunderstanding. But that's all in the past."

Eagerly and hopefully he said, "It seems that you're still a little skeptical."

Giving in, she answered, "No, but I won't deny that I thought ill of you for a time. The truth only became clear afterwards."

His heart floated high over a cloud of happiness and swayed tipsily above it. He asked, "When did you learn that?"

"Quite a while ago."

He gazed at her with gratitude, so moved by love he felt like crying. Then he said, "You learned I'm innocent?"

"Yes."

Was Hasan Salim going to regain his good reputation? "How did you learn the truth?"

She said quickly and in a way that showed she wanted to end this interrogation, "I learned it. That's the important thing."

He did not insist, for fear of annoying her, but a thought crossed his mind. Sorrow clouded his heart, and he said plaintively, "Even so, you continued to hide yourself. You didn't bother to announce the pardon with a sign or a word, although you were able to express you anger most expertly. But your excuse is obvious and I accept it."

"What excuse is that?"

With a sorrowful voice he replied, "That you haven't ever known pain. I ask God most sincerely that you never will."

She said apologetically, "I thought you didn't care whether you were accused."

"May God forgive you. I cared more than you can imagine. It hurt me dreadfully to find the gap between us so vast. The problem wasn't merely your disinterest in the . . . affection I feel for you. It was also the unfair charges lodged against me. So consider your position and mine. But I'll tell you frankly that the unjust accusation was not responsible for my worst pains. . . ."

She smiled and asked, "So there wasn't just one type of pain?"

Encouraged by her smile as if he were a small child, he proceeded to pour out the story of his devotion. He said passionately, "No. Your accusation caused the least of my pains, and your disappearance the greatest. Each hour out of the past three months has witnessed some moment of pain. The way I've lived, I could easily have been considered insane. So I mean and know what I'm saying when I pray that God will not test you with pain. I've learned from my own experience. What a cruel time it's been! It's convinced me that if you're destined to disappear from my life, I might as well search for another existence. It was like a long, odious curse. Don't make fun of me. I'm always afraid you will. But pain's too exalted to be mocked. I don't picture a generous angel like you joking about the afflictions of other people. And of course you're the cause too. But what can a person do? It's been my fate to love you with all the force of my being."

The silence that followed was broken only by his irregular breathing. She was looking straight ahead, and he could not search her eyes. He was comforted by her silence, for it was easier to bear than a careless word. So he considered it a triumph.

"Imagine hearing her voice—soft and sweet—expressing the very same feelings. . . ."

He was crazy. Why had he released the floodwaters dammed up in his heart? He was like a vaulter who keeps trying to go just a foot higher only to find himself soaring high into the heavens. But what force could muzzle him after this?

"Don't remind me of things I hate to hear, for I've had my fill of that. I won't forget my head, for I carry it with me night and day, or my nose, for I see it repeatedly each day. But I've got something no one else comes close to possessing. My love for you is unequaled, and I'm proud of it. You should be too, even if you spurn it. I've felt this way ever since I saw you the first time in the garden. Haven't you been conscious of it? I haven't thought about confessing it before now, because I was afraid of spoiling our friendship and of being expelled from paradise. It was hideously difficult for me to consider risking my happiness. But now that I've been evicted, what do I have to fear?"

His secret flowed out of him like blood from a wound. He saw nothing in all of existence except her extraordinary person. The road, trees, mansions, and the few passersby vanished into a dense fog with only one gap through which his silent beloved could be seen with her slender build, halo of black hair, and a profile that openly revealed its grace while concealing its secrets. In the twilight shadows her face seemed a pure brown, but when they crossed a side street it was radiant and bright from the rays of the setting sun. He could have kept on talking until morning.

"Did I say I'd never considered confessing my love to you before? That's not quite true. The fact is, I started the day we met in the gazebo when Husayn was called to the telephone. I almost told you then, but before I could, you began attacking my head and nose." He laughed briefly before continuing: "I was like an orator who opens his mouth only to be showered with pebbles by the audience."

She was calm and silent. That was fitting. An angel from another world should not converse in a mortal tongue or take an interest in human affairs. Would it not have been nobler of him to guard his secret? Nobler? Pride vis-à-vis the beloved was blasphemy. For the assassin to be confronted with her victim was only proper.

"Do you remember your happy dream that left you in tears when you awoke? Dreams are quickly forgotten, but tears or rather the memory of them may become an immortal symbol."

Here she was saying, "I was only joking when I said those things, and I asked you then not to get angry."

This refreshing sensation deserved to be savored. It resembled the happy delight one feels after a throbbing toothache. The melodies latent within him echoed each other until a beautiful tune emerged. His beloved's features seemed the musical notation from which he was reading a heavenly composition.

"You'll find I'm content with hoping for nothing, because—as I told you—I love you."

With her natural grace she cast him a smiling look but withdrew it too quickly for him to decipher it. What kind of look had it been? Was she pleased, moved, affectionate, responsive, or politely sarcastic? Had she bestowed it on his face as a whole or directed it toward his head and nose?

Then her voice followed this look: "I can only thank you and apologize for unintentionally causing you pain. You're kind and generous."

His soul was ready to convey him to the warm embrace of happy dreams, but she added in a faint voice, "Now let me ask what follows from this."

Was he hearing the voice of his beloved or an echo of his own? This very sentence was soaring somewhere over Palace Walk, borne aloft by his sighs. Had the time come for him to find an answer for this question?

He asked anxiously, "Does something follow from love?"

"She's smiling," he thought. "I wonder what this smile means. But you want something more than a smile."

She answered, "The declaration is the beginning, not the end. I'd like to know what you want."

Still anxious, he said, "I want . . . I want you to give me permission to love you."

She could not hold back her laughter. She inquired, "Is this really what you want? But what will you do if I refuse?"

Sighing, he replied, "In that case, I'll love you anyway."

In a half-joking manner that upset him she asked, "What's the point of the permission then?"

How absurd it was when words betrayed a person and came out wrong. . . . What he feared most was falling back to earth as suddenly as he had risen from it. He heard her say, "You perplex me. It seems to me that you even perplex yourself."

He answered uneasily, "Me ... perplexed? Perhaps, but I love you. 'What follows from this?' I imagine occasionally that I aspire to things beyond the earth's capacities. But when I reflect a little, I'm unable to ascertain what my goal is. You tell me what this means. I want you to talk while I listen. Can you rescue me from my dilemma?"

She said with a smile, "I don't have anything to offer in this regard. You ought to be the speaker. I'll do the listening. Aren't you a philosopher?"

His face turning red, he commented dejectedly, "You're making fun of me."

She was quick to answer, "No. But I wasn't anticipating a conversation like this when I left my house. You caught me by surprise, telling me things I wasn't expecting to hear. In any case, I'm thankful and grateful. No one would be able to forget your tender and refined affection. It would be out of the question to make fun of them."

It was a captivating tune with sweet lyrics. Yet he did not know whether the beloved was being serious or frivolous. Were the portals of hope opening ... or closing with the gentleness of a breeze? When she had asked him what he wanted, he had not replied, because he had not known what he did want. Would it be wrong to say that he longed for communion, the communion of one spirit with another? Should he knock at the mysterious closed door with a hug or a kiss? Shouldn't that be the answer?

At the intersection where Palaces Street ended, Aïda stopped and said gently but decisively, "Here!"

He stopped walking too and gazed at her face with astonishment. " 'Here' meaning we must part here?" he wondered. "The sentence 'I love you' is not far-reaching enough to rule out questions."

With no deliberation or thought, he exclaimed, "No!" Then, as though he had suddenly seen the light, he cried out, "What's the point of love? Wasn't that what you were really asking? Here's an answer for you: that we don't part."

With a calm smile, she replied, "But we must part now."

He asked fervently, "Without any displeasure or ill feelings?"

"Absolutely not."

"Will you resume your visits to the gazebo?"

"If circumstances permit."

He anxiously reminded her, "Circumstances permitted it in the past."

"Things are different now."

He was deeply hurt by her response and said, "It seems you won't return."

As though to remind him of the necessity of parting, she said, "I'll visit the gazebo whenever circumstances allow it. Have a happy day."

She set off in the direction of School Street. He stood there gazing after her as though she were a dream vision. When a turn in the road was about to hide her, she looked back with a smile. Then she vanished from sight.

What had he said and heard? He would concentrate on all that shortly, after he came to. When would that be? He was walking all by himself. Alone? ... What of the pounding of his heart, the delirium of his spirit, and the echoes of that melody? All the same, a feeling of isolation shook his heart to its core. The captivating, enchanting fragrance of jasmine overwhelmed him, but what was its special ingredient? This fragrance and love were similar in their mysterious and captivating enchantment. Perhaps penetration of one's secret would lead to discovery of the other's. Yet he would not solve this puzzle until he finished reciting all the anthems of bewilderment.

24 ❧

Husayn Shaddad said, "Alas, this is our farewell meeting."

Kamal was peeved by this reference to leave-taking. He glanced quickly at Husayn to see if his face was actually as sorrowful as his words. All the same, Kamal had been aware of a valedictory atmosphere for more than a week, because the arrival of June usually signaled the departure of his friends for Ra's al-Barr and Alexandria. It was only a matter of days until the garden, the gazebo, and his friends would vanish from his horizons. The beloved had been pleased to disappear even before departure necessitated it. She had remained invisible even after reconciliation crowned their conversation on Palaces Street. Was the farewell meeting to conclude without a visit? Did his affection mean so little to her that she would begrudge him a fleeting vision before leaving for three months?

Kamal smilingly asked, "Why do you say, 'Alas'?"

Husayn Shaddad responded attentively, "I wish you would all go with me to Ra's al-Barr. My goodness! What a summer vacation that would be!"

It would be marvelous, no doubt about it. Kamal would be happy, if only because the beloved would not be able to continue hiding there. Isma'il Latif remarked to him, "May God come to your aid. How can you bear the summer heat here? Summer has barely begun, and yet see how hot it is today."

It was very hot, although the sun's rays were no longer shining directly on the garden or the desert beyond it. Even so, Kamal replied calmly, "There's nothing in life that can't be borne."

The next moment he was scoffing at his own words. He wondered how he could have responded that way and to what degree words could be considered a true expression of feelings. Around him he saw people who certainly looked happy. In their short-sleeved shirts and gray trousers, they seemed to be defying the heat. Only he was wearing a suit—a lightweight white one—and a fez, which he had placed on the table.

Isma'il Latif started praising the examination results: "One hundred percent success. Hasan Salim got his degree. Kamal Ahmad Abd al-Jawad, Husayn Shaddad, and Isma'il Latif all were promoted."

Kamal laughed and observed, "You could have skipped all but the final one, for the others were never in question."

Shrugging his shoulders scornfully, Isma'il retorted, "Each of us has attained the same goal—you with fatigue and exertion all year long, me after only one month's effort."

"That proves you're a scholar at heart."

Isma'il asked sarcastically, "Didn't you casually remark that George Bernard Shaw was the worst student of his day?"

Kamal laughingly replied, "Now I'm convinced that we have among us an equal to Shaw, if only in his failures."

Husayn Shaddad said, "I have news I need to disclose before we get carried away by our conversation."

When he found that this statement had not drawn much attention, he stood up suddenly and said in a theatrical tone, "Allow me to announce some fascinating and happy news." Glancing at Hasan Salim, he asked, "Isn't that so?" Then, looking back at Kamal and Isma'il, he continued: "Yesterday an engagement was arranged between Mr. Hasan Salim and my sister Aïda."

Confronted by this revelation, Kamal felt like a man who suddenly finds himself beneath a streetcar, after feeling completely satisfied about his safety and security. His heart pounded violently, as if an airplane were plunging downward in an air pocket. An inner scream of terror seemed trapped in his rib cage, unable to get out. He was amazed—especially when he thought about it later—that he was able to control his feelings and to flash Husayn Shaddad a congratulatory smile for his sister's good fortune. Perhaps Kamal was distracted from his calamity for the time being by the struggle within him between his soul and the stupor threatening it.

Isma'il Latif was the first to speak. He looked back and forth from Husayn Shaddad to Hasan Salim. The latter as usual projected a calm composure, although this time it seemed mixed with some embarrassment or discomfort. Isma'il cried out, "Really? What happy news, happy and sudden ... happy, sudden, and treacherous. But I'll postpone discussion of the treachery till later. At the moment I'm content to offer my sincere congratulations."

Isma'il rose and shook hands with Husayn and Hasan. Kamal got up immediately to offer his congratulations too. Despite the smile on his face, he was so startled by the speed of events and the bizarre things people were saying that he imagined he was in a strange dream. Rain was pouring down on his head. He was looking everywhere for shelter. As he shook hands with the two young men he said, "Really good news ... heartfelt congratulations."

When they had settled back in their places, Kamal could not keep himself from glancing stealthily at Hasan Salim, whom he found calm and composed. Kamal had been apprehensive, imagining that his friend would look conceited or gloating. Experiencing some fleeting relief, Kamal proceeded to rally all his strength to hide his bloody wound from their watchful eyes, in order to keep himself from becoming the target of mocking sarcasm.

"Be firm, my soul. I promise we'll return to all this later. We'll suffer together until we perish. We'll think through everything until we go insane. It will be a satisfying moment in the still of the night, with no eye to observe or ear to eavesdrop, when pain, delirium, and tears are unveiled ... far from any critic or scold. Then there's the old well. I'll remove the cover, scream down it to the resident demons, and confide my woes to the tears collected in the belly of the earth there from sad people everywhere. Don't capitulate. Beware, for the world seems as fiery red to you now as the pit of hell."

Adopting an accusatory tone, Isma'il said, "Not so fast! Both of you owe us an explanation. How did this come about without any advance warning? Or let's put that aside temporarily. How could you have celebrated the engagement without inviting us?"

Husayn Shaddad replied defensively, "There wasn't a party, not even a small one. The gathering was limited to immediate family members. Your time will come when we celebrate the marriage contract. Then you'll be among the hosts, not the guests."

"The wedding day! That could be the title of a funeral dirge. The heart will be conducted in solemn procession to its final resting place surrounded by flowers, as people pay their last respects with shrieking trills. In the name of love, the young woman raised in Paris will bow before the turbaned shaykh as he recites the opening prayer of the Qur'an. In the name of pride, Satan left paradise."

Smiling, Kamal said, "Your excuse is accepted, and your invitation welcomed."

Isma'il Latif objected loudly: "Eloquence like this belongs with the seminarians at al-Azhar Mosque. When some people see food on the horizon, they forget they have any cause for complaint and magnanimously begin singing the praises of their hosts, all for the sake of a hearty meal. You're a true writer or philosopher or some other type of beggar like that, but I'm not."

Then he continued his attack on Husayn Shaddad and Hasan Salim: "You two are a couple of rascals ... a long silence followed by the announcement of an engagement. Huh? Really, Mr. Hasan, you're the long-awaited successor for Tharwat Pasha, who did such a good job of suppressing information when he was Prime Minister."

Smiling apologetically, Hasan Salim said, "Husayn himself knew nothing of the matter until only a few days ago."

Isma'il asked, "Was this a unilateral engagement, like Great Britain's unilateral declaration of Egyptian independence on February 28, 1922?"

The conquered Egyptian nation as a whole had proudly rejected that declaration, but nominal sovereignty had been thrust upon it, with the inevitable consequences. Kamal laughed out loud.

Winking at Hasan Salim, Isma'il carelessly mangled and misattributed a quotation from the prophet Muhammad: " 'To accomplish'— I don't remember what—'rely on secrecy.' The caliph Umar ibn al-Khattab said that ... or the poet Umar ibn Abi Rabi'a, or Omar Effendi down at the department store. God only knows."

Kamal said suddenly, "It's customary for matters like these to come to fruition silently, although I must acknowledge that Mr. Hasan once referred to something of this kind in a conversation with me."

Isma'il gazed at him skeptically. Looking at Kamal with wide eyes, Hasan corrected him: "It was more like subtle hints."

Kamal asked himself in amazement how this statement had escaped from his mouth. It was a lie or at best a half-truth. How could he have wished to convince Hasan in this devious manner that he, Kamal, knew about the young man's intentions and had not been surprised or troubled by them? "What stupidity!"

Staring critically at Hasan, Isma'il told him, "But I didn't garner a single one of these subtle hints."

Hasan replied earnestly, "I assure you that if Kamal found anything in my remarks he considered a reference to a forthcoming engagement, he must have relied on his imagination, not my words."

Husayn Shaddad laughed loudly. He said to Hasan Salim, "Isma'il's your lifelong friend. He wants you to realize that even if you have gotten your degree three years ahead of him, that doesn't mean you should begrudge him your secrets or favor others with them instead."

Smiling as though to conceal his discomfort, Isma'il observed, "I don't question his friendship, but I'll keep after him so I'm not forgotten in a similar manner on his wedding day."

Smiling, Kamal said, "We're friends of both parties. If the bridegroom forgets us, surely the bride won't."

He spoke to prove to himself that he was still alive. But he was alive with pain, intense pain. Had he ever imagined his love would end in any other way? Certainly not ... yet belief in the inevitability of death does not diminish our anguish when it arrives. This was a ferocious, irrational, and merciless pain. He wished he could see it, so he might know where it was concealed or the microbe from which it had emerged. Between seizures of pain he was a victim of lethargy and listlessness.

"When will the ceremony take place?" Isma'il asked the question that was running through Kamal's mind, as though he had been delegated to represent Kamal's thoughts.

But Kamal would have to speak too. He commented, "Yes, it's very important for us to know, so we won't be taken by surprise again. When's the wedding?"

Husayn laughingly asked, "Why are you two in such a hurry? Let's give the bridegroom a chance to enjoy what's left of his bachelor days."

With his customary composure Hasan said, "First of all, I need to learn whether I'm to stay in Egypt or not."

Husayn Shaddad explained, "He's going to be appointed either to the attorney general's staff or to the diplomatic corps."

"Husayn seems delighted with this engagement," Kamal reflected. "I can assert that I hated him, if only momentarily, for having betrayed me. Has anyone double-crossed me? Everything seems such a confusion. But this evening I'll be alone...."

"Which would you prefer, Mr. Hasan?"

"Let him choose whatever he wants ... judicial service, diplomatic corps, the Sudan ... Syria if possible."

"Working as a prosecutor somewhere would be an insult. I'd prefer to be a diplomat."

"It would be good if your father understood that clearly, so he can concentrate on getting you into it." This sentence too jumped out of Kamal's mouth. No doubt it was on target. He would have to get control of his nerves. Otherwise he would find himself embroiled in a public dispute with Hasan. He would also have to keep Husayn Shaddad's feelings in mind, for these two now formed a single family. How cruel this stabbing pain was!

Isma'il shook his head sorrowfully and said, "These are your last days with us, Hasan. After a lifelong relationship, this comes as a sad end."

How stupid it was of Isma'il to think that sorrow could influence a heart grazing in the beloved's oasis.

"It really is a sad ending, Isma'il."

"Lie upon lie ..." Kamal thought, "like your congratulations to him. In this respect the merchant's son and the son of the superior court judge are equal."

He asked, "Does this mean you'll spend your whole life outside the country?"

"That's what I expect. We'll only see Egypt on rare occasions."

Isma'il marveled: "What a strange life! Have you thought about the difficulties it will pose for your children?"

"Alas, my heart! Is it right to toss around ideas like that? Does this wretch imagine that the beloved will get pregnant and endure cravings, that her belly will become distended and round, that she'll suffer through labor and give birth? Remember Aisha and Khadija in the final months of their pregnancies? This is blasphemy. Why don't you join an underground assassination society like the Black Hand? Murder's better than blasphemy and more beneficial. Then you'd find yourself in the defendant's dock one day. Presiding over the court would be Salim Bey Sabry, father of your friend the diplomat and father-in-law of your beloved, just as he presided this week over the trial of those accused of killing the supreme commander, Sir Lee Stack. The traitor!"

Husayn Shaddad laughingly asked, "Should nations cut off diplomatic relations so the children of diplomats may be raised in their own countries?"

"No, cut off their heads! Abd al-Hamid Inayat, al-Kharrat, Mahmud Rashid, Ali Ibrahim, Raghib Hasan, Shafiq Mansur, and Mahmud Isma'il sentenced to die on the gallows along with Kamal Ahmad Abd al-Jawad ... by the Egyptian judge Salim Bey Sabry and the English judge Mr. Kershaw. Assassination is the answer. Do you want to kill or be killed?"

Isma'il cautioned Husayn, "Your sister's departure will reinforce your father's determination to refuse your request to travel abroad."

Husayn Shaddad replied confidently, "My case is making steady progress toward a satisfactory solution."

Aïda and Husayn in Europe at the same time ... he was going to lose his true love and his best friend. "Your spirit will search for your beloved and not find her. Your intellect will search for your companion without finding him either. You'll live alone, exiled to the ancient district, like the echo of a yearning on the loose for generations. Ponder the pains lying in wait for you. It's time for you to harvest the fruit of the dreams planted in your gullible heart. Beseech God to make tears a cure for sorrows. If you can, string your body up with a hangman's ropes or put it at the front of a destructive force unleashed on the enemy. Tomorrow you'll find your spirit's empty —as empty as you once discovered al-Husayn's tomb to be. What a disappointment! Sincere patriots are hanged, while sons of traitors are made ambassadors."

As though to himself, Isma'il Latif remarked, "There'll be no one in Egypt except me and Kamal, and Kamal's not reliable, because his best friend—before, after, or besides Husayn—is the book."

Husayn said with confident conviction, "Travel won't end our friendship."

Despite his lethargy, Kamal's heart pounded. He commented, "My heart tells me that you won't be able to endure a permanent separation from your homeland."

"That's most likely. But you'll profit from my trip by the books I send you. We'll continue our conversations with letters and books."

Husayn was talking as though his voyage had become an established fact. Visits with this friend had been a captivating happiness for Kamal. When he was with Husayn, even silence was enjoyable. But there was some consolation. The departure of his beloved would teach him to minimize other calamities, no matter how great. Thus the death of his adored grandmother had seemed insignificant to his soul when it was scorched by the fire of his grief for Fahmy. But he had to keep in mind at all times that this was the farewell session. He had to fill his eyes with the roses and the other flowers that were tipsy with blooms and heedless of sorrow. There was a problem he had to solve: How could a mortal ascend high enough to live with the beloved or the beloved fall so far that she could coexist with a human being? If he could not find an answer, he would struggle ahead with shackled feet and a lump in his throat. Love was a load with two widely separated handles. It was designed to be carried by two people. How could he bear it alone?

The conversation raced along and branched off in different directions while Kamal followed it with his eyes, nods of his head, and words designed to demonstrate that the calamity had not polished him off yet. He had his hopes pinned on the fact that life's train keeps moving down the tracks, even though death's station certainly lies ahead somewhere.

"It's dusk. A time of dark stillness. You love it as you love the dawn. 'Aïda,' and 'pain' are two words with a single meaning. So you must love pain, even if from now on your rapture comes from defeat. The conversation keeps moving forward, and the friends laugh together and argue with each other as though none of them had ever experienced love. Husayn's laughter is full of healthy good spirits, Isma'il's of mischief and contention, and Hasan's of reserve and superiority. Husayn refuses to talk about anything but Ra's al-Barr. I promise to make a pilgrimage there one day. I'll ask what sand was trod by the beloved's feet, so I can prostrate myself to kiss it. The other two are singing the praises of San Stefano beach in Alexandria and talking about waves like mountains. Really? Imagine a body the waves cast onto the shore after the dreadful sea has sucked out its beauty and nobility. After all this, let us admit that weary vexation encompasses all living creatures. Possibly happiness lies beyond the gates of death."

The talk continued until it was time for them to go home. They shook hands with each other warmly. Kamal squeezed Husayn's hand, and Husayn squeezed his in return. Then, saying, "See you . . . in October," Kamal set off.

At a time like that any previous year he would have begun asking himself fretfully when his friends would return. Now his desires were not tied to anyone's returned. They would still be aflame whether or not October arrived and whether his friends returned or not. He would no longer be blaming the summer months for separating him from Aïda; an abyss much more profound than time had come between them. When time was the problem, he had been able to combat it with doses of patience and hope. Today he was fighting an unknown foe and a mysterious, supernatural force. He did not know a single word of the spells or charms used for it. He could only fall back on a wretched silence until God concluded what He had begun. Love seemed to be suspended over his head like destiny, and he was fastened to it with bonds of excruciating pain. It resembled a force of nature more than anything else in its inevitability and strength. He studied it sadly and respectfully.

The three friends said goodbye in front of the Shaddad family mansion. Hasan Salim went on down Palaces Street, while Kamal and Isma'il as usual headed for al-Husayniya together. There they would part, with Isma'il going to Ghamra and Kamal to the ancient district. As soon as the two of them were alone, Isma'il laughed hard and long.

When Kamal asked him what was so funny, he replied mischievously, "Haven't you figured out yet that you're one of the main reasons speeding up the announcement of this engagement?"

"Me?" This slipped out from Kamal, whose eyes were wide with astonishment.

Isma'il said scornfully, "Yes, you. Hasan wasn't comfortable about your friendship with her. I feel certain of this, even though he never breathed a word of it. As you know, he's really stuck-up. But I find out what I want to. I assure you he was unhappy about your friendship. Do you remember that flare-up between you two? It's obvious that he asked her to stop visiting Husayn's friends. It's equally apparent that she reminded him that he had no right to request that. So he took this major step to get the right."

The pounding of his heart almost drowned out his voice when Kamal said, "But I wasn't the only friend. Aïda was friends with all of us."

Isma'il replied sarcastically, "But she chose you to arouse his anxiety, perhaps because she sensed in your friendship a warmth she did not find with the others. In any case, she was not just reacting randomly to the situation. She decided long ago to win Hasan. Finally she's harvesting the fruit of her patience."

" 'Win Hasan'!" Kamal exclaimed to himself. " 'The fruit of her patience'! These phrases are like a fool's statement that the sun rises in the west."

With a sad heart, Kamal said, "How little you think of people! She's not at all the way you portray her."

Without grasping what his friend felt, Isma'il answered, "Perhaps it happened by chance. Hasan may have been imagining things. In any case, it all worked out to her benefit."

Kamal shouted angrily, " 'Her benefit'! What do you think? Glory to God, you speak as though her engagement to Hasan is a triumph for her, not for him."

Isma'il looked at him strangely and then said, "You don't seem to be convinced that men like Hasan are few and far between. He offers family, status, and a future. There are plenty of girls like Aïda ... more of them than you think. I wonder if you don't have a higher opinion of her than she deserves. In my opinion, Hasan's family agreed to let him marry her because of her father's immense fortune. She's a girl"—he hesitated before continuing—"whose beauty is not extraordinary at any rate."

"Either he's crazy or you are," Kamal thought. He was transfixed by a pain comparable to that he had felt on reading an offensive attack against the Islamic system of marriage. "God's curse on all unbelievers!"

With a calmness that masked his anguish, he asked, "Then why does she have so many admirers?"

Isma'il disdainfully stuck out his lower jaw while tilting up his chin. "Perhaps you count me among them," he said. "I don't deny that she's amusing and elegant. And her Western upbringing has provided her social graces that make her seem particularly charming and attractive. All the same, she's dark and thin. There's nothing especially seductive about her. Come with me to Ghamra and you'll see all types of beauty. They leave hers in the shade, whether taken as a whole or singly. There you'll see true loveliness ... fair complexions, swelling breasts, and plump hips. If you want beauty, this is it. There's nothing really desirable about Aïda."

"As if she were a female to be craved like Qamar or Maryam!" Kamal told himself. "Swelling breasts and plump hips? How can you describe a spirit using corporeal expressions? What stabbing pain!" It had been decreed that he should swallow the cup of anguish down to its dregs. Since lethal blows were falling in swift succession, death would be a mercy.

At al-Husayniya they parted, and each went his separate way.

25 ❧

Over the years his love for this street had never waned. Looking sadly at his surroundings, he mused, "If only my love for a woman were as constant as mine for this street, I'd escape many problems. What an excellent street . . . like a labyrinth!"

Every few meters it turned to the right or left. No matter where a person stood, he was always confronted by a curve, behind which an unknown world lay concealed. Narrowness gave the road an unassuming, familiar character, like that of a pet animal. A man sitting in a shop on the right could reach over and shake hands with his neighbor on the other side. Stretched between the tops of the stores, canvas awnings protected the street from the burning rays of the sun. Beneath them the humidity and diffused light created a dreamy atmosphere. Bunched together on shelves and benches were sacks of green henna, red cayenne, and black pepper—along with flasks of rose water and perfume, colored wrapping paper, and diminutive scales. Hanging from the rafters was a decorative fringe of candles of diverse sizes and colors. The fragrance of different perfumes and colognes filled the air like the aroma of a distant dream.

"The black wraps and veils, the gold nosepieces, the kohl-enhanced eyes, the heavy rumps—may He who bestows all blessings save me from them. To walk dreamily through these beautiful visions is one of my favorite sports, but I must acknowledge that it exhausts my heart and eye. If you start counting the women here, you'll never finish. What a blessed place it is that brings all of them together. The only way to protect yourself is to cry out from the depths of your heart, 'Yasin, you house wrecker!' A voice tells me that I should open a shop in al-Tarbi'a Alley and settle down. Your father's a merchant. He's his own boss. He spends much more on his amusements than you get from your salary. Open a store and put your trust in God, even if you have to sell the apartment in al-Ghuriya and the shop in al-Hamzawi. You arrive in the morning like a sultan. You're not bound to any schedule. There's no supervisor to terrify you. You sit behind the scales, and women come to you from every direction. 'Good morning, Mr. Yasin.' 'Stay healthy, Mr. Yasin.' I would have only myself to blame if I let a chaste woman pass without a greeting and a shameless one without a date. What a sweet idea this is, but what a cruel one for someone who will remain an officer of al-Nahhasin School to the end of his days. Love's a disease. Among its symptoms are constant hunger and a fickle heart. Have mercy, God, on one You created with the appetite of a caliph or sultan but gave the job of a school disciplinarian. My hopes have been destroyed. It's pointless to lie to myself. The day you brought her to Palace of Desire Alley you anticipated a happy, contented life. May God destroy boredom. It pervades the soul as totally as the bad taste sickness brings to the mouth. I pursued her passionately for a year but tired of her in a few weeks. What is misery if not this? Your home must have been the first one that ever overflowed with complaints during the honeymoon. Ask your heart what place Maryam has in it now and where the beauty is that drove you crazy. Let it reply with a laugh like a moan, 'We ate till we were full. Then we couldn't even stand the smell of food.' She's clever. It's hard to put something over on her. Nothing escapes her. She's a bitch and the daughter of one. Remember the virtues of your deceased family members. Was your mother any better than hers? The important thing is that, unlike Zaynab, Maryam's not easy to deceive. How hard her anger is to bear when she gets annoyed.... She's not willing to close her eyes, and you're not easily satisfied. It's absurd to think that your fiery cravings can ever be met by one woman or that your heart will settle down. Even so, you hoped to achieve a happy married life. How magnificent your father is and how vile you are.... You haven't been able to follow his example, even though that would have saved you. O Lord, what's this I see? Is it really a woman? How many hundred pounds do you suppose she weighs? My God, I've never seen a woman so tall and wide. How can you take possession of this fiefdom? I swear if a woman her size fell into my hands, I'd stretch her out naked in the center of the room and circle her ritually seven times, as if she were a shrine, before putting it in her."

"You!"

The voice from behind made his heart quiver. He quickly turned his eyes from the mammoth female and saw a young woman in a white coat. He could not help but exclaim, "Zanuba!"

They shook hands warmly and she laughed. He suggested they should keep walking to avoid attracting attention. So they strolled along side by side as the crowd swarmed around them. Thus they met again after a long separation. She had only rarely and infrequently crossed his mind after various considerations had distracted him. Yet he found her as beautiful as the day he left her, or possibly even more attractive. What was this new style of clothing she was wearing instead of the traditional black wrap? An invigorating wave of delight spread through him.

She asked, "How are you?"

"Great. And you?"

"Like this."

"Superb, praise God. You've changed the way you dress. I hardly recognized you at first. I still remember how you looked in your wrap when you walked."

"You haven't changed. You don't look older, but you've gained a little weight. That's the only thing."

"Now you're something else! You're a European girl!" He smiled cautiously before adding, "Except the hips come from al-Ghuriya."

"Watch your tongue!"

"You scare me. Have you repented or gotten married?"

"Nothing's beyond God's power."

"Your white coat belies a return to God. As for marriage, it's not farfetched to think a lack of sense would lead you to it someday."

"Watch out. I'm as good as married."

He laughed. As they turned into the Muski, he said, "Exactly like me."

"But you really are married. Isn't that so?"

"How did you learn that?" Then, reconsidering, he added, "Oh, I forgot that all our secrets eventually get to you."

He laughed again suggestively. Smiling mysteriously, she said, "You mean at the sultana's house?"

"Or my father's. Hasn't their affection continued?"

"Sort of."

"Everything with you is tentative now. Well, I'm sort of married. I mean I'm married and looking for a girlfriend."

She brushed a fly from her face, and the gold bracelets on her arm jingled. She said, "I'm a girlfriend who's looking for a marriage."

"A girlfriend? Who's the lucky son of a . . ."

She interrupted him, cautioning, "Don't insult people. He's an important man."

Eyeing her sarcastically, he said, "Important! Ha-ha, Zanuba, I wish I could ram my horn into you."

"Do you remember the last time we met?"

"Oh, my son Ridwan's six now. That must have been about seven years ago."

"A lifetime. . . ."

"While still alive, one should never despair of meeting again."

"Or of parting."

"You seem to have shrugged off loyalty with your black wrap."

She frowned at him and said, "Ox, who are you to talk about fidelity?"

He was pleased to see her become this familiar, for it encouraged his ambitions. He replied, "God only knows how delighted I am to see you again. I've thought of you frequently. But that's the way the world is."

"The world of women, huh?"

Pretending to be upset, he said, "The world of death, the world of troubles."

"You seem to bear your troubles well. Mules could certainly envy your health."

"If only the beautiful eye isn't envious. . . ."

"Are you afraid of the evil eye? You're as tall and broad as Abd al-Halim al-Masri."

He laughed conceitedly. After falling silent for a time, he asked in a new, serious tone, "Where were you going?"

"Why does a woman come to al-Tarbi'a Alley if not to shop? Or do you think everyone's like you with only one thought in life— sex?"

"Falsely accused, by God."

"You, innocent? When I caught sight of you, your eyes were assaulting a woman as big as a city gate."

"No. I was lost in thought and totally unaware of what I was looking at."

"You! My advice for anyone wishing to find you is to walk along al-Tarbi'a and look for the largest woman. I guarantee that he'll definitely find you stuck to her like a tick on a dog."

"Woman, your tongue gets more vicious every day."

"May God's holy name protect yours too."

"Never mind that. Let's stick to essentials. Where are you going now?"

"I'm shopping. Then I'll go home."

He fell silent for a moment, as if hesitating. Then he said, "What would you think about us spending some time together?"

She glanced at him with playful black eyes and replied, "I have a jealous man to consider."

Ignoring her objection, he continued: "A nice place where we can have a couple of drinks."

In a louder voice than before she answered, "I told you there's a jealous man in my life."

Paying no attention to that comment, he added, "The Tout-Va-Bien . . . what do you think? It's a charming place and respectable. I'll get this taxi."

A mumbled protest escaped her. Then she asked with a disapproving tone not matched by her facial expression, "By force?" She glanced at her wristwatch, and this new gesture almost made him laugh. In a voice that laid down the law, she said, "Just don't make me late. It's six now, and I must be home before eight."

As the taxi set off, Yasin wondered whether anyone had noticed them in al-Tarbi'a or the Muski. He shrugged his shoulders disdainfully and with the handle of his ivory fly whisk shoved back his fez, which was slanting down over his right eyebrow. What did he care? Maryam was alone in the world. She did not have a savage guardian like Muhammad Iffat, who had wrecked the first marriage Yasin had established. His own father was a suave man who realized that Yasin was no longer an inexperienced child to be punished in the courtyard of the old house.

They took seats opposite each other at a table in the garden of the Tout-Va-Bien. The bar was crowded with men and women. The player piano was belting out its monotonous pieces, and the aroma of grilled meat came with the evening breeze from a far corner. She was so ill at ease that he realized it was the first time she had ever patronized a public establishment. He felt a sharp delight. The next moment he was certain that he was in the grips of a genuine longing, not just a transient lust. Those bygone days with her seemed the happiest of his whole life.

He ordered a bottle of cognac and then some grilled meat. His cheeks were growing flushed, and his black hair, parted in the middle like his father's, was visible when he removed his fez. On noticing the resemblance, Zanuba smiled faintly. He naturally did not understand why. For the first time ever he was sitting with a woman in a tavern outside of the Wajh al-Birka entertainment district. It was also his first amorous adventure subsequent to his second marriage, with the exception of one indiscretion in Abd al-Khaliq Alley. And did he not normally drink good-quality cognac outside his house. He only got first-rate liquor when he purchased bottles to take home for what he termed licit, "medicinal" purposes.

He filled the two glasses with pride and relief. Then, raising his, he said, "To the health of Miss Zanuba Martell."

She answered with sweet arrogance, "I drink Dewar's scotch with the bey."

He grumbled, "I don't want to hear about him. May our Lord put him in the past tense."

"No way!"

"We'll see. Each glass we drink opens up new doors for us and smooths away difficulties."

They both sensed that the time was short and drank quickly. The glasses were filled and drained again and again. The cognac's fiery tongue began to trill in their stomachs, and the mercury of intoxication rose in the thermometer of their veins. The green leaves watching them from pots behind the wooden garden railing revealed glistening smiles. The piano's music fell on more indulgent ears. Faces both dreamy and feisty repeatedly exchanged fond and friendly looks. Waves of cool evening air flowed around them with silent music. Everything seemed pleasant and beautiful.

"Do you know what I felt like saying when I first saw you today —when you were gazing, as if possessed, at that woman?"

"Yes? ... But finish your glass first, so I can fill it."

Helping herself to a sliver of meat, she continued: "I almost shouted, 'You son of a bitch ...'"

Laughing fruitily, he asked, "Why didn't you, bitch's daughter?"

"Because I only curse men I love. You were little more than a stranger to me then."

"How about now?"

"A bastard for sixty generations."

"My goodness, an insult's even more intoxicating at times than alcohol. This blessed night will be in all the papers tomorrow."

"Why, God forbid? Do you intend to cause trouble?"

"Lord, be gracious to her, and to me."

Then she inquired with obvious interest, "Why haven't you told me about your new wife?"

Stroking his mustache, he answered, "The poor dear! Her mother died this year."

"May you have a long life. Was she rich?"

"She left a house, the one beside ours—I mean next to my father's. But she left it jointly to her new husband and my wife."

"Your wife must be a beauty, for you always get the best."

He replied cautiously, "She has a certain beauty, but it doesn't compare with yours."

"Shame on you."

"Have you ever known me to lie?"

"You! There are times when I even doubt that your name's Yasin."

"Then let's drink this round too."

"Are you getting me drunk so I'll believe you?"

"If I tell you I want you and long for you, would you doubt me then?"

"You probably talk like this to every woman you meet."

"Say rather that a hungry man desires all kinds of food yet retains a hankering for mallow greens."

"A man who really loves a woman will not hesitate to marry her."

He sighed and then said, "You're mistaken. I'd like to stand on this table and scream at the top of my lungs, 'Any of you men who's in love with a woman—don't marry her.' Yes, nothing kills love so effectively as marriage. Believe me. I've learned from my own experience. I married once and then a second time. I know how true this is."

"Perhaps you haven't yet found the woman who's right for you."

"Right? What kind of woman would that be? Which of my senses will guide me to her? Where is this woman who'll never be boring?"

She laughed lethargically and then commented, "It sounds as if you'd like to be a bull in a pasture full of cows. That's what you need."

Snapping his fingers appreciatively, he said, "God, God! Who used to call me that in the old days? It was my father, may he have a good evening. How I wish I could be like him. He acquired a wife whose obedience and moderation are exemplary and has been able to give free rein to his passions without encountering any problems. He's successful in his marriage and in his affairs. That's what I'd like."

"How old is he?"

"I think he's about fifty-five, but he's stronger than most young men."

"No one can hold out against time forever. May our Lord grant him good health."

"My father's the exception. He's the sweetheart of women other men crave. Don't you see him nowadays at your house?"

Laughing and tossing a bone to a cat meowing at her feet, she said, "I left that house some months ago. Now I have my own home. I'm the lady of the house."

"Really? I thought you were joking. Have you left the troupe as well?"

"Yes. You're speaking to a lady in every sense of the word."

He guffawed contentedly. Then he said, "So drink and let me drink. May our Lord be gracious to us."

He felt temptation inside and outside him. But which was the voice and which the echo? Even more marvelous was the life throbbing in material objects around them. The flowerpots whispered as they rocked back and forth. The pillars exchanged secrets. As the sky gazed down with starry, sleep-filled eyes at the earth, it spoke. He and his companion exchanged messages expressing their inmost feelings while a glow, both visible and invisible, confounded their hearts and dazzled their eyes. Something was at work in the world, tickling people until they were plunged into laughter. A look, word, gesture, anything was enough to induce all of them to laugh. Time fled as quickly as youth. The waiters carrying the fermented germ of exuberance distributed it to all the tables with grave faces. The tunes of the piano seemed to come from far away and were almost drowned out by the clattering wheels of the streetcar. On the sidewalk rowdy boys and men collecting cigarette butts created a commotion like the drone of flies, as night's legions set up camp in the district.

"You seem to be watching for the waiter to come ask, 'Are you too drunk to find your way home?' You're ignoring and avoiding that issue and an even more important one. If only Maryam would kneel before you and whisper, 'All I need is one room where I can busy myself obeying your every command. Fill the rest of the apartment with all the women you want.' If the headmaster at school would only pat you on the shoulder and say, 'How's your father, my son?' If only the government would carve out a new street in front of the store in al-Hamzawi and the residence in al-Ghuriya. If only Zanuba would tell you, 'Tomorrow I'm leaving my lover's house and then I'll be at your service.' If all this would happen, people would gather after the Friday prayer service and kiss each other with sincere affection. Tonight the best thing you can do is to sit on the sofa while Zanuba dances naked in front of you. Then you'll have a chance to monitor the beauty spot over her navel."

"How's the beloved beauty spot?" he asked as he smilingly gestured toward his own belly.

She laughed and replied, "It kisses your hand."

Glancing casually around the place, he said, "Do you see these men? Each is the debauched son of a fallen woman. All drunks are like this."

"We're honored. But my brain is flying off in every direction."

"I hope the part inhabited by your boyfriend soars away."

"Oh, if he knew what's become of us! He'll stab you one day with the tip of his mustache."

"Is he a Syrian with a colossal one?"

"Syrian?" Then she started singing in a loud voice the Syrian dialect word for salve: "*Barhum,* oh *barhum* . . ."

"Hush. Don't attract attention."

"Whose attention, blind man? Only a few people are left."

After rubbing his stomach and sighing, he observed, "Drink's a crazy thing."

"The crazy thing was your mother."

"You're talking louder than you should. Let's go."

"Where?"

"You know more than I do. Our feet will decide."

"Is a person successful when he lets his feet guide him?"

"That's safer at any rate than relying on a disordered brain."

"Think a little about . . ."

He interrupted her by rising tipsily and saying, "We need to act without any thought. Until tomorrow morning there's no point trying to think. Let's go."

26 ❧

"The houses have closed their eyes. The streets are vacant except for an occasional roving breeze or the light from a sleepy lamp. Free from any competition, silence has wandered everywhere, spreading its wings. What good are hotels? The desk clerks look askance at you, as if you've got a dizzying disease they don't want to catch. Yes, you can scoff at their hostility, but you still don't have a place to stay. Other lovers are tucked in bed. How long are you going to wander around? Here's a driver raising his head heavy with sleep. He's looking at you in a welcoming way. God's mercy on anyone who drags a woman around in the wee hours of the night looking for a place to stay."

"Where to?" Yasin asked.

The driver replied with a smile, "Anywhere you want."

Yasin told him, "I wasn't asking you."

The man replied, "At your service, in any case."

"Don't ask me," Zanuba said. "Ask yourself. Why didn't you think about that before you got drunk?"

Encouraged by seeing them stand beside his carriage, the coachman suggested, "The Nile! That's the best place. Shall I take you to the banks of the Nile?"

Yasin asked contentiously, "Are you a coachman or a sailor? What would we do by the Nile at this hour of the night?"

The driver said suggestively, "The light's dim, and no one's around."

"Ideal conditions for thieves."

Zanuba said fearfully, "Terrible! My ears, neck, and arms are weighted down with gold."

Shrugging his shoulders, the driver said, "There's nothing to fear. Every night I go there with fine people like you and we return in top condition."

Zanuba said sharply, "Don't mention the Nile. Talking about it makes my body shudder."

"May evil stay far from your body."

On taking his place in the carriage next to Zanuba, Yasin said, "Talk to me. What's her body to you?"

"Bey, I'm your servant."

"Everything's a mess tonight."

"May our Lord straighten it out. If you'd like a hotel, we'll go to one."

"We've quarreled with the clerks in three hotels. Three or four, Zanuba? Think of something else."

"There's always the Nile."

Zanuba said angrily, "The gold, fellow."

Putting his feet on the other seat, Yasin added, "Besides, there's no place to ..."

The driver answered, "There's always the carriage."

Zanuba shouted, "Are you trying to humiliate me?"

Twisting his mustache, Yasin said, "You're right. Absolutely. The carriage isn't the place. I'm not going to act like a foolish kid at this stage in my life. Listen...."

The man turned his ear, and Yasin yelled imperiously, "To Palace of Desire Alley."

"Clip-clop, clip-clop ... you're plunging into the darkness with no friend save the stars," Yasin reflected.

Anxiety loomed on the horizon only to sink back into a sea of forgetfulness, like an elusive memory. His willpower had dissolved in a glass of wine. Then his companion in merrymaking asked him with a drunken stammer where he was heading in Palace of Desire Alley.

He replied, "My house, which I inherited from my mother."

"The fates decreed that she lived for love there and left it in trust to love at her death," he thought. "It has greeted with yearning Umm Maryam and her daughter Maryam. Tonight it will open its arms to a lady from my past."

"What about your wife, drunkard?"

"She's sound asleep."

"Isn't there a reckoning for everything?"

"You're with a man whose heart doesn't know the meaning of fear. Pluck some pearls from the heavens and drape your forehead with them. Sing softly into my ear, 'Bring me my love tonight, Mother.'"

"Where am I going to spend the rest of it?"

"I'll take you anywhere you want."

"You couldn't carry a straw home."

"How about Paris on the Mediterranean?"

"If only I weren't afraid of him."

"Who is he?"

Throwing her head back, she answered despondently, "Who knows? I've forgotten."

Al-Gamaliya was scarcely visible in the darkness. Even the coffee-house had closed its doors. The carriage stopped at the entrance to Palace of Desire Alley. As Yasin stepped down, he belched. Supporting herself on his arm, Zanuba followed. They walked off together with a caution that did not keep them from swaying tipsily. Behind them they heard the cough of the driver and the squeaking shoes of the night watchman, who passed inquisitively by the carriage as it turned around.

She told him, "The ground's uneven. It's rough walking here."

He replied, "It'll be easy going in the house." Then he added, "Don't worry."

Although sporting a silly smile that was lost in the shadows, Zanuba tried in vain to remind him that his wife was in the apartment they were approaching. She almost stumbled twice climbing the stairs. When they reached the door of the apartment they were both panting. Alarm at the situation momentarily lent their scattered wits the impetus to collect the shreds of consciousness.

Yasin carefully turned the key in the lock, gently shoved the door open, and searched for Zanuba's ear in the darkness. Bending over, he whispered for her to remove her shoes. After taking his off, he stepped in front of her, put her hand on his shoulder, and headed for the parlor near the entrance. Opening that door, he slipped inside with her still behind him. They sighed with relief. Closing the door, he led her to the sofa, where they sat down together.

She said uneasily, "It's very dark, I don't like the dark."

Putting their shoes under the sofa, he replied, "You'll get used to it soon."

"My head's beginning to spin."

"Only now?"

Without paying any attention to her response, he rose suddenly and whispered with alarm, "I didn't shut the outside door." Putting up his hand to remove his fez, he cried out, "I forgot my fez too! Do you suppose I left it in the carriage or at Tout-Va-Bien?"

"To hell with your fez! Lock the door, fellow."

Once again he slipped into the hall and over to the outside door, which he shut with extreme care. On his way back a tempting idea struck him. He went to the console table, holding his hand out in front of him to keep from bumping into one of the chairs. Then he returned to the parlor holding a half-empty bottle of cognac.

Placing it in her lap, he said, "I've brought you the remedy for everything."

After feeling the bottle with her hand she exclaimed, "Liquor! . . . Enough's enough. Do you want us to spill over?"

"One sip to help us catch our breath after all this exertion."

He drank until he felt that he was capable of anything and that insanity was a desirable condition. Then the sea of inebriation began to rage. He rode high on a wave only to plunge down again. He spun round in an endless whirlpool. In the corners of the room there were protruding tongues, raving and ranting in the darkness. Boisterous laughter escaped from these throats with a clamor like the commotion of a market, followed by nothing less than singing. The bottle fell to the floor with a warning thump. But he had a lap to finish swimming, even if he had to do it in a sea of perspiration. The time might have been long or short. He was not keeping track. His eyes were closed and oblivious to the passing and graying of the darkness.

Thus he awakened to voices and movement like a happy dreamer just stretching out his hand to pluck a new treat. Opening his eyes, he saw light and shadow dancing together on the walls. He turned his neck and noticed Maryam at the door. She was holding a lamp, and its light clearly revealed scowling features and eyes flashing with anger. The couple sprawled across the sofa exchanged long, extraordinary looks with the woman standing at the door. Theirs were unsteady and confused, hers flaming with outrage. The silence was unbearable. Zanuba revealed her anxiety by opening her mouth to speak without being able to get any words out. Then she was suddenly overwhelmed by laughter for no apparent reason. She was so convulsed that she had to hide her face in her hands.

Yasin shouted at her with slurred diction, "That's enough laughter! This is a respectable home."

Maryam seemed to want to speak, but either her tongue would not cooperate or fury rendered her speechless. Without knowing what he was saying, Yasin told her, "I found this 'lady' in a severely intoxicated condition. So I brought her home to sober up."

Zanuba was not going to keep quiet about this. She protested, "He's the drunk, as you can see. And he brought me here by force."

Maryam made a motion as if she was seriously considering throwing the lamp at them. Yasin tensed his body and gave her a look that showed he was prepared. But she immediately had second thoughts, once she realized the serious implications of such an act. She placed the lamp on a table and clenched her teeth with rage. Then, her voice dry and trembling but coarsened by resentment and anger, she spoke for the first time: "In my house! . . . In my house? In my house, you criminal child of the devils."

Her voice reverberated like thunder as she poured curses upon him and called him the filthiest names. She screamed, raising her voice so loud that it could be heard through the walls. She summoned the tenants and neighbors, swearing to expose him and to awaken people to be witnesses against him.

Yasin tried in various ways to caution her to keep quiet. He waved his hand at her, stared at her, and scolded her loudly. When these methods failed, he rose excitedly. He went toward her with long steps to reach her as fast as he could without actually running, for he was afraid of losing his balance. He pounced on her and spread his hand over her mouth to keep her from talking. But she screeched in his face like a desperate cat and kicked him in the belly. He backed off unsteadily, his face clouded with resentment and pain. Then he fell flat on his face, like a building collapsing.

A resounding scream burst forth from Zanuba. Maryam ran and fell upon her, pulling the intruder's hair with her right hand while digging the nails of the other one into the woman's neck. She began to spit in Zanuba's face and then to curse and insult her. Yasin got up again at once, shaking his head violently, as if to expel his hangover. He went to the sofa and aimed a fierce blow at the back of his wife, who was lying on top of her rival. Maryam screeched and retreated. He pursued her. Blinded by anger, he rained punches on her until she got on the far side of the dining table. Then she took off one of her slippers and hurled it at him, striking him in the chest. He tried to catch her, pursuing her around the hall.

He shouted at her, "I never want to see you again." Then he pronounced the irreversible triple divorce formula: "You're divorced, divorced, divorced!"

There was a rapping on the door, and the woman who lived on the second floor could be heard crying, "Mrs. Maryam, Mrs. Maryam!"

Breathless, Yasin stopped running. Maryam opened the door and in a voice that filled the whole stairwell immediately said, "Come look in this room and tell me if you've ever seen anything like this before. A whore in my house, drunk and disorderly. Come and see!"

The neighbor said timidly, "Calm down, Mrs. Maryam. Come stay with me till morning."

Yasin cried out recklessly, "Go with her. You have no right to stay in my house."

Maryam screamed in his face, "Adulterer! Criminal! Bringing a whore to your wife's home!"

He pounded on the wall with his fist and shouted at her, "You're a whore! You and your mother!"

"You insult my mother when she's with God?"

"You're a whore. I know that for sure. Don't you remember the English soldiers? It's my fault for not paying attention to the warnings of decent people."

"I'm your spouse, the crown of your life. I'm better than your folks and your mother. Ask yourself what kind of man marries a woman he 'knows' is a whore—as you claim. What is he but a despicable pimp?" Gesturing toward the parlor, she suggested, "Marry that woman. She's the type that fits your filthy character."

"One more word and your blood will spill out where you're standing."

But screams and fiery invective kept leaping from her throat. Finally the neighbor got between them to be able to separate them if necessary. She began patting Maryam's shoulder and imploring her to leave the apartment until morning.

Yasin got even more upset and yelled at her, "Take your clothes and leave! Get out of my sight. You're not my wife. I don't know you. I'm going into this room now. You'll be sorry if I find you here when I come out again." He rushed into the parlor, slamming the door behind him so violently that the walls shook. Then he threw himself on the sofa and dried the sweat from his brow.

Zanuba whispered, "I'm frightened."

He replied gruffly, "Shut up. What are you afraid of?" In a loud voice he said, "I'm free! Free!"

As though to herself she remarked, "What could have happened to my mind to make me obey you and come here?"

"Hush! What's done is done. I'm not sorry about anything. . . . Phooey!"

Through the closed door several voices reached them, indicating that more than one of the neighbor women had gathered around the angry wife. Then Maryam's voice was audible, sobbing, "Have you ever heard of anything like this before? A prostitute off the street in a home? I woke up because they were making such a racket. They were laughing and singing. Yes, by God, they were singing shame-lessly. They were so drunk they were oblivious to everything. Tell me if this is a residence or a brothel."

Then a woman's voice protested, "Are you packing up your clothes and leaving home? This is your house, Mrs. Maryam. It's not right for you to leave. It's the other woman who should go."

Maryam cried out, "It's not my house anymore. That honorable gentleman has divorced me."

The other woman replied, "He wasn't in his right mind. Come with us now. Let's leave talk for the morning. In spite of everything, Yasin Effendi's a fine man and comes from a good family. God's curse on Satan. Come along, daughter. Don't grieve."

Maryam shouted, "No talking! No settling! May the sun never rise again on that criminal son of a crooked mother."

There were footsteps of people retreating. Finally only an indis-tinct buzz of voices could be heard. Then the door was closed with a loud bang. Yasin breathed deeply and stretched out on his back.

27

He opened his eyes to find the morning sunshine filling the room. He had the worst hangover of his entire life, although the preceding night had hardly been his first time to get drunk. Rotating his head mechanically, he noticed Zanuba snoring beside him. Then his memory recalled the events of the past night in one fell swoop. Zanuba was in Maryam's bed. And Maryam? . . . With the neighbors. And the scandal? . . . Broadcast everywhere. What a giant leap into the bottomless pit of destruction! What use was there for anger or regret now? What was done was done. Everything might change but not the previous day. Should he wake her up? Why should he? Let her sleep to her heart's content. Let her stay where she was, for she could not leave the house until dark.

He had to revive himself to meet his difficult day. He pulled the light cover from his body, slipped out of bed, and padded out of the bedroom. His hair was disheveled, his eyelids swollen, and his eyes red. He yawned in the hallway with a bovine sound. Looking at the open door of the parlor, he sighed deeply. He closed his eyes and moaned in response to his hangover. Then he headed for the bathroom. He really had a hard day in front of him. Maryam was at the neighbors, while the other woman occupied the bed. Day had overtaken him before he could conceal the traces of his crime. How crazy! He should have spirited her out before going to bed. How could he have been so negligent? What disaster had befallen him? When and how had he moved her from the parlor to the bedroom? He did not remember anything. He did not even recall how and when he had fallen asleep. The upshot was a colossal scandal with nothing to show for it. It had been a perfectly innocent evening but one now as filled with disgrace as his head was with distress and discomfort. But it was hardly amazing, for the apartment, a bequest from his mother, God forgive her, had long been inhabited by scandalous demons. The mother had passed on, but the son had remained to become the butt of the neighborhood gossip. By the following day the news would have reached Palace Walk.

"Forward, denizen of the abyss of debauchery. If this cold water you're using to wash your body could only cleanse your mind of its evil memories. . . . Who knows? Perhaps if you look out the window, you'll find a group of people watching at your doorway for the departure of the woman who expelled your wife and took her place. No, you won't allow her to leave today, no matter what. As for Maryam, you've divorced her. You divorced her without wanting to, when her mother's grave is still fresh. What will people say of you, liar?"

He felt a pressing need for a cup of coffee to revive his senses. On his way from bathroom to kitchen he noticed the console table in the front hall and remembered the bottle of cognac that had spilled in the parlor. He wondered for a moment if the rug was damaged but then remembered with ironic regret that the furniture was no longer his property. It would soon go to join the woman who owned it.

In a few minutes he was carrying a glass half filled with coffee to the bedroom, where he found Zanuba sitting up in bed as she stretched and yawned.

She turned toward him and said, "A good morning for both of us! We'll have breakfast at the police station, God willing."

He took a sip and looked at her over the rim of the glass. Then he said, "Pray to God the Omniscient Benefactor."

She waved her hands until the gold bracelets jangled. Then she blurted out, "You're responsible for everything that's happened."

He sat down on the bed near her outstretched legs. He answered uneasily, "A trial, huh? I told you to address God the Omniscient Benefactor."

She rubbed the small of his back with her heels as she moaned, "You've destroyed my home. God only knows what's waiting for me there."

As he crossed one leg over the other, his house shirt rode up to reveal a thigh that was firm and covered with a forest of coal-black hair. He asked, "Your boyfriend? . . . May God disappoint him! What's he compared with my wife, whom I've divorced? You're the one who's devastated my household. It's my home that's destroyed."

As though addressing herself, she said, "It's been a dark night. I haven't been able to tell my head from my feet, and the din is still ringing in my head. But it's my fault. I should never have listened to you."

He suspected she actually was pleased, her complaints notwithstanding, or that she was using them to get at him. Had he not known women in the Ezbekiya fleshpots who boasted of the number of bloody battles waged over them? But he did not get angry. Matters had reached such a desperate pass that he was spared the effort of trying to remedy them.

He could not help laughing as he observed, "It's the worst catastrophes that make you laugh. Laugh! You've wrecked my home and replaced my wife. Get up and pull yourself together. Prepare for a long stay ... till night falls. You won't leave the house until it's dark."

"What dreadful news! Imprisoned! Where's your wife?"

"I don't have a wife anymore."

"Where is she?"

"In divorce court, if my guess is correct."

"I'm afraid she'll attack me when I leave."

"You afraid? Lord have mercy on us! Last night, menacing though she was, you didn't lose a bit of your sly pluck, you niece of Zubayda."

She laughed for a long time. She seemed to be acknowledging the charge against her and to be proud of it too. Then she put out her hand to take the glass of coffee. After drinking a little, she returned the glass and asked, "Now what?"

"As you can see, I'm in the dark too. It hurts to be exposed in front of people the way I was last night."

Shrugging her shoulders disdainfully, she said, "Don't worry about it. There's not a man alive who hasn't more dirty linen than the earth has room to hide."

"Just the same, a scandal's a scandal. Think of the fight, the wailing, the divorce at dawn. Picture the neighbors coming with alarmed curiosity to my apartment. Their eyes took in everything."

She frowned and said, "She started it!"

He could not restrain his sardonic laughter. She persisted: "If she had been wise, she could have worked everything out. Even strangers in the street are considerate to boisterous drunks. She's the one who brought the divorce down on herself. What did you say to her? 'Whore and daughter of a whore'? Huh? And something else about English soldiers?"

He only remembered this now. Giving her a peeved look, he wondered how these phrases had taken root in her memory. He muttered uneasily, "I was angry. I didn't know what I was saying."

"Humbug!"

"Humbug to you!"

"English soldiers? Did you get her from one of their haunts like the Finish Bar?"

"God forbid. She's from a decent family, lifelong neighbors. It was just anger, a thousand curses on it."

"Without anger, secrets would never come to light."

"By your aunt's life, we have enough trouble as it is."

"Tell me about the English soldiers, as if there was anything I didn't know about them. . . ."

In a loud, defiant voice he replied, "I told you it was anger. That'll do."

She groaned sarcastically and then asked, "Are you defending her? Then go get her back."

"Curses on anyone shameless and cold-blooded enough to do that."

"Curses. . . ."

She got out of bed and went to the mirror. Picking up Maryam's comb, she began to fix her hair quickly as she asked, "What will I do if the man breaks up with me?"

"Tell him goodbye. My house is always open to you."

She turned toward him and said sadly, "You don't understand what you're saying. We were thinking seriously about marriage."

"Marriage! Haven't you dropped that idea after you saw what it's like last night?"

She answered shrewdly, "You don't understand. I'm tired of being a kept woman. All it brings is ruin. A woman like me who weds really values her marriage."

"Who's the idiot?" he asked himself. "In the troupe she was never anything more than a lute player. After thirty a prostitute's over the hill, and she'll be thirty soon. So marriage is her best bet. Is she aiming this talk at you? What a delightful devil! I won't deny I want her. I desire her in the strongest possible way. My scandal bears witness to that."

"Do you love him?"

As if angered, she replied, "If I loved him, you wouldn't find me imprisoned here now."

Although skeptical of her veracity, he longed for her. Yes, even if her heart was not sincere, she had clearly shown a weakness for him.

"I can't do without you, Zanuba. To get you, I've done crazy things, not caring about the consequences. You're mine, and I've been yours for a long time."

Silence reigned. She seemed to be waiting impatiently for more. When he did not continue, she asked, "Should I sever my ties with that man? I'm not a woman who can bounce back and forth between two lovers."

"Who is he?"

"A merchant from the Citadel region called Muhammad al-Qulali."

"Married?"

"And he's got children, but he has lots of money."

"He promised to marry you?"

"He's trying to talk me into it, but I've been hesitating. The circumstances and the fact that he's a husband and father suggest there could be problems."

He put up with her deceitfulness for the sake of her beautiful eyes. "Why don't we go back to the way we were. I'm not destitute, in any case."

"I don't care about your money, but I'm sick of living in sin."

"What's to be done?"

"That's what I'm asking."

"Explain."

"I've said more than enough."

What an unexpected attack! Yes, at first glance it seemed ludicrous, but he wanted her. So he was forced to play along. After a pause he said, "I won't try to hide my low opinion of marriage from you."

"I have a low opinion of living in sin."

"That wasn't how you talked yesterday."

"Then I had a husband within reach, but today ..."

"With a little flexibility, we can meet each other halfway. There's one thing you must never lose sight of: No matter how long I stay with you, I'll never let you go."

She cried out defiantly, "Your past adventures really bear that out!"

To hide the weakness of his position he replied earnestly, "A man doesn't learn without paying a price."

"Words no longer beguile me. Shame on you men!"

"And on you women too ... isn't that so?" he thought. "Have mercy, niece of Zubayda. You arrive here drunk after midnight, and in the morning you're tired of living in sin. Perhaps she told herself, 'If his second wife was a whore, why shouldn't I be the third one?' How low Yasin has fallen. Have you forgotten the trouble ready to pounce on you outside? Let those problems wait. Just don't lose Zan-

uba with an ugly remark the way you did Maryam. Maryam? I'm
atoning for my sin now, Fahmy."

He said calmly, "Our relationship must not end."

"It's up to you whether it continues or ends."

"We need to meet a lot and think a lot."

"As far as I'm concerned, I don't need to think anymore."

"So either I convince you of my opinion or you convince me of
the wisdom of yours."

"I'll never come around to yours."

She left the room and did not let him see her smile. He gazed after
her rounded back with a look of amazement. Yes, everything seemed
amazing. But where was Maryam? On her own, wherever she was.
He would not get any rest or peace. He would be questioned tomorrow at Palace Walk and the following day at the Islamic court. All
the same, their life during the last period had been one long wrangle.
She had even told him quite bluntly, "I hate you and I hate living
with you."

"I wasn't made to succeed in marriage. Was my grandfather's life
like this? I'm the one in the family who most resembles him, so they
say. Despite all this, that crazy woman wants to marry me."

28 ❧

The sun was about to set when al-Sayyid Ahmad Abd al-Jawad crossed the wooden gangplank to the houseboat. He rang the bell, and the door soon opened to reveal Zanuba in a white silk dress sheer enough to show off her body. On seeing him she cried out, "Welcome! Welcome! Tell me what you did yesterday. I imagine you came, rang the bell in vain, and stood there for a time before leaving." She laughed. "And you must have had some awful suspicions. So tell me what you did."

Despite the elegance of his appearance and the fragrance of his cologne, his face looked grim and his displeasure was visible in his staring eyes. "Where were you·yesterday?" he asked.

She went into the sitting room ahead of him, pausing in the center of the room near two windows that opened on the Nile. She took a chair between the windows, pretending to be calm, collected, and cheerful. Then she answered, "I went out yesterday, as you know, to do some shopping. On my way I ran into Yasmina the vocalist, and she invited me to her house. But she refused to let me leave and pestered me until I was forced to spend the night with her. I hadn't seen her since I moved to the houseboat. If you could have heard her criticize my disloyalty and ask me about the secret charm of this man who'd been able to make me forget my relatives and neighbors . . ."

Was she telling the truth or lying? Had he actually endured all those pains yesterday and today pointlessly? He knew the reason for every millieme he gained or lost. How could he have suffered those frightful torments for no reason at all? The world was a tricky place, but if this devil was telling the truth, he was prepared to kiss the ground at her feet. He had to determine whether it was true, even if that took the rest of his life. Had the time come for him to return to his senses? "Not so fast . . ." he admonished himself.

"When did you return to the houseboat?"

She lifted a leg and began to study her pink slipper decorated with a white rose and her toes tinted with henna. Then she said, "Why don't you sit down first and take off your fez so I can see the part in your hair. Sir, I came home a little before noon."

"Liar!" The word shot out like a bullet coated with rage and despair. Before she could open her mouth, he continued violently: "Liar! You didn't return before noon or after noon. I came here twice during the day and didn't find you."

She was speechless for a time. Then she said in a tone of indignant surrender, "The truth is that I got home just before sunset, about an hour ago. There was no reason for me to make up a story, but when I noticed the groundless look of displeasure in your eyes I wanted to dispel it. The fact is that this morning Yasmina insisted I go shopping with her. When she learned I had left my aunt's ensemble, she suggested I join hers, so I could substitute for her occasionally at a wedding. Naturally I didn't agree, because I knew without asking that you wouldn't be happy if I stayed out late with the troupe. What I'm trying to say is that I remained with her because I knew you wouldn't get here before nine. This is the story. So sit down and bless the Prophet."

"A trumped-up tale or the truth?" he wondered. "What if your friends saw you in this fix? The fates are certainly making fun of you. I'd forgive twice as much as this if I could win a little peace of mind. You're begging now. You never had to beg before. You've humiliated yourself for this lute player. She once had the job of waiting on you. She served you fruit at parties and departed in decorous silence. If I can't reassure myself, let the fires of hell flame up."

"Yasmina doesn't live in never-never land. I'll ask her if this story's true."

Waving her hand to show her disdain and disapproval, she answered, "Ask her anything you want."

He got control of his frayed and refractory nerves all of a sudden and said stubbornly, "I'll ask her this evening. I'm going to look for her. Now! I've satisfied all your requests. You must respect my rights completely."

She caught his contagious fury and responded sharply, "Not so fast! Don't insult me to my face. I've been very lenient with you until now, but everything has a limit. I'm a person made of flesh and blood. Open your eyes and pray to Fatima's father Muhammad."

He asked in astonishment, "Is this the tone you use to address me?"

"Yes, since that's how you're talking to me."

The grip of his hand on his stick tightened as he yelled, "I'm entitled to, since I'm the one who made you a lady and prepared a life for you that Zubayda herself would envy."

His statement provoked her, and like a raging lioness she snarled, "God made me a lady, not you. I only accepted a life like this after you pleaded with me fervently. Have you forgotten that? I'm not your captive or your slave. An interrogation and a police report—what do you think I am? Did you buy me with your money? If you don't like the way I live, then each of us can go his own way."

"O Lord of the heavens," he reflected, "is this how manicured nails turn into claws? If you still have any doubts about last night, then consider this impudent tone. You're suffering from tyranny like Nimrod's. Swallow the pain to the dregs. Drink the abuse till you've had your fill. So what's your response? Scream in her face, as loud as you can, 'Go back to the street where I found you!' Scream, yes, scream. What's stopping you? God's curse on the saboteur! The heart's treachery is far worse than a thousand other forms of treason. This is the romantic abasement you've heard about and mocked. How I'll hate myself for loving her!"

"Would you throw me out?" he asked.

In the same belligerent tone she said, "If your understanding of our relationship is that I'm to stay here as your prisoner while you make accusations against me whenever you please, then the best thing for both of us is to break it off."

She turned her face away from him. He studied her cheek and the side of her neck with an unnatural calm that was almost trancelike. "The ultimate happiness I ask of God is casting her aside without a second thought. She has humiliated and angered you, but could you bear to come here and find no trace of her?"

"I have little confidence in you, but I didn't think your ingratitude would reach this point."

"Do you want me to be a stone with no feelings or sense of honor?"

"If you only realized," he reflected, "that you're even less than that. . . ."

But he replied, "No, I want you to be a person who recognizes the rights arising from good deeds and companionship."

Changing from an angry tone to one of complaint, she said, "I've done more for you than you can imagine. I consented to leave my family and my profession to stay wherever you chose. I haven't even complained about it, to avoid troubling your peace of mind. I didn't wish to tell you in so many words that certain people want a better life for me than this, although I haven't paid any attention to them."

"Are there to be more problems, ones I haven't anticipated?" he asked himself.

"What do you mean?" he inquired indignantly.

She toyed with her gold bracelets, spinning them around her left arm. Then she said, "A respectable gentleman wishes to marry me. He won't take no for an answer."

"The heat and the humidity are stifling you," he thought, "and this shrew is opening her mouth to swallow you whole. How lucky that seaman is, trimming his sail outside the window. . . ."

"Who is he?"

"Someone you don't know. Call him any name you want."

He took a step back and sat down on a sofa flanked by two armchairs. Gripping the handle of his stick with both hands, he asked, "When did he see you? How did you learn of his intentions?"

"He saw me often when I lived with my aunt. Recently he's attempted to speak to me whenever he's run into me on the street, but I've ignored him. So he got one of my girlfriends to tell me. That's the whole story."

"How many stories you have!" he mused. "When I found you gone yesterday, a single pain devastated me. At the time I wasn't aware of all these other pains and troubles. Leave her if you can. Break with her. That's the way to find peace. Aren't people wrong to imagine death's the worst thing we face?"

"I want to know whether you wish to accept this proposal."

With a nervous flick of her wrist she stopped playing with her bracelets and stared at him haughtily. Then she asserted grandly, "I told you I ignored him. You should understand what that means."

"You mustn't go to bed tonight with such lethal thoughts," he counseled himself. "You don't need another night like the last one. Shield yourself from these fears."

"Tell me frankly whether any man has visited you on the houseboat."

"A man? What man do you have in mind? You're the only man who enters this houseboat."

"Zanuba, I can ferret it all out. Don't be secretive. Tell me everything, even trivial details. Then I'll forgive you, no matter what."

She protested angrily, "If you keep doubting my truthfulness, the best thing is for us to part."

"Remember the fly you saw die this morning in a spider's web?" he asked himself.

"Enough of that. Tell me if this man met you yesterday."

"I told you where I went."

In spite of himself he snorted, "Why do you torment me? I've never wanted anything so much as to make you happy."

She clapped her hands together, as though finding his suspicions hard to bear. Then she said, "Why won't you understand me? I've sacrificed everything I value for your sake."

What a beautiful song it was! The calamity was that it could easily have come from an empty heart, for a singer can dissolve into a sad and plaintive song while intoxicated with happy triumph.

"With God as your witness, tell me frankly who this man is."

"Why does it matter to you? I said you don't know him. He's a merchant from another district, but he used to frequent the coffeehouse of al-Sayyid Ali occasionally."

"His name?"

"Abd al-Tawwab Yasin. Do you know him?"

"I leased this houseboat to have a good time," he reminded himself. "Remember the happy hours? World, do you recall the Ahmad Abd al-Jawad whom nothing fazed? Zubayda, Jalila, Bahija . . . ask those ladies about him. No doubt he's some other man—not this anxious fellow with white ravaging the hair of his temples."

"The devil of unhappiness," he observed, "is the most energetic one."

"No, it's the devil of doubt, because he's able to create something from nothing."

He began to rap the floor with the tip of his stick. Then in a deep voice he said, "I don't want to live like a blind man. Certainly not! And nothing can make me violate my manly sense of honor. In brief, I can't tolerate your absence last night."

"We're back to that again!"

"And again and again and again. I'm not a child, and you're an adult too, a sensible woman. Today you've been telling me about that man. Has his promise of marriage really duped you?"

She answered proudly, "I know he's not deceiving me. His promise not to approach me till we're married is a proof of that."

"Does this marriage tempt you?"

She frowned disapprovingly and then said as if astonished, "Didn't you hear what I said? I'm amazed at how slow you are today. At any rate, you're not your normal self. Shake off this gloom you've needlessly courted and listen to me one last time: "I ignored the man and his wish—for your sake."

He wanted to learn how old this man was but did not know how to phrase the question. Youth and age were not matters he had paid attention to before. After some hesitation he said, "Perhaps he's a callow youth who says things without thinking about them."

"He's no child. He's in his thirties."

In other words, the man was a quarter century behind al-Sayyid Ahmad. In everything except age it is bad to be behind. Jealousy is a brazen assassin.

She continued: "I pretended not to know him, even though he promised me the kind of life I dream of."

"What a chip off the old block!" he told himself. "Zubayda could have learned a lot from you."

"Is that so?" he asked.

"Let me tell you bluntly that I can't stand this life any longer."

"Remember the fly and the spider," he reminded himself.

"Really?"

"Yes. I want a secure life and a legal one. Or do you think that's wrong?"

"You came to interrogate her," he reflected, "but where do you stand now? She's the one ready to throw you out. How come you're so forbearing? Reserve some self-respect for what's left of your life. Do you understand what she's hinting at? . . . How lovely the breaking waves are at sunset."

His silence was prolonged, and she calmly started up again: "This won't anger you, for you're a pious man in spite of everything. How can you obstruct a woman's desire to live according to the teachings of her religion? I don't want to be a mount for every rider. I'm not like my aunt. I have the heart of a Believer: I fear God. This has strengthened my resolve to abandon my sinful ways."

He listened to her last statement with astonishment and alarm. He started to scrutinize her with annoyance, which he hid behind a feeble smile. Then he replied, "You've never mentioned this to me before. Until yesterday we were getting along fine."

"I didn't know how to disclose my feelings to you."

"She's getting away from you with frightening and wicked speed. What a disappointment! I'm prepared to forget last night, ill-omened though it was. I'll forget my doubt and my pain . . . if she renounces this devilish scheme."

"We lived together happily and harmoniously. Does our relationship mean so little to you?"

"No, but I want to make it better. Isn't a godly life better than a sinful one?"

His lower lip tightened into a meaningless smile. Then he said in a faint voice, "For me the situation is quite different."

"How?"

"I'm married, my son's married, and my daughters are married. As you can see, the matter's extremely delicate." Then he added regretfully, "Weren't we blissfully happy?"

She answered testily, "I'm not telling you to divorce your wife and renounce your children. Many men have more than one wife."

He observed apprehensively, "Marriage for a man my a . . . in my situation is not an easy matter. It provokes a lot of comment."

She laughed sarcastically and said, "Everyone knows you have a mistress. That doesn't bother you. How come the possibility of gossip about a legal marriage worries you—if you want to marry me?"

Smiling with uneasy confusion, he said, "Only a few people know my secret. Besides, my family's totally in the dark about it."

She raised her penciled eyebrows in disbelief and said, "That's what you think. Only God knows for sure. What secret's secure from people's tongues?"

Before he could respond, she continued irately: "Or perhaps you don't think I'm good enough to have the honor of belonging to your family?"

"God forgive me," he thought, "the husband of Zanuba the lute player. . . ."

"I didn't mean that, Zanuba."

She said disdainfully, "You won't be able to hide your true feelings from me for long. I'll learn them tomorrow if not today. If marrying me would disgrace you, then goodbye."

"You came to get rid of the other man," he told himself, "but he's tossing you out. You've given up asking her where she was. She's offering you a choice between marriage and the door. What are you going to do? What's paralyzing you? It's your treacherous heart. Having your bones ripped from your flesh would be easier than leaving this lute player. Isn't it sad you're suffering an insane love like this only when you're getting on in years?"

He asked critically, "Is that what you think of me?"

"I don't think much of a person who treats me like spit."

Sadly and calmly he said, "You're dearer to me than my soul."

"Words! We've heard a lot of them."

"But it's the truth."

"It's time to learn that from your actions, not your words."

He looked down in distress and despair. He did not know how he could accept her proposal and yet did not have the strength to reject it, particularly since his desire for her had destroyed his mental concentration and shackled him. In a subdued voice he said, "Give me time to arrange my life...."

Hiding a sly smile, she said smugly, "If you really love me, you won't hesitate."

He quickly retorted, "It's not that. There are other matters...." He gestured as if to explain his words, although even he did not know precisely what they meant.

She smiled and said, "If that's how it is, I'll wait patiently."

He experienced the temporary relief of a collapsing boxer who hears the bell concluding a round other than the final one. A wish for consolation from his cares and reassurance after his anxiety pulsed through him. Holding his hand out to her, he said, "Come to me."

She drew herself back resolutely in the chair and said, "When God sanctions it."

29 ❧

He left the houseboat, made his way along the dark bank of the Nile, and headed down the deserted street toward the Zamalek Bridge. The gentle breeze cooled his hot brow and with a rustling whisper stirred the interlocking branches of the giant trees, which in the gloom resembled dunes or ebony clouds. Whenever he glanced up he found them hovering over him like phantoms of the worry troubling his breast. Did these lights pouring out of houseboat windows come from homes free of cares?

"But no anxiety's comparable to yours," he assured himself. "There's a difference between a man who dies and one who commits suicide. You've unquestionably agreed to commit suicide."

He continued walking, for he could think of no better way to release his nervous tension and to collect his thoughts before joining his friends. He would eventually closet himself with them and tell them everything. He would not take a step like this without consulting them, even though he could already guess what they would say. He would confess it all to them, no matter how painful, since he felt as overwhelming a desire to confide in them as a drowning man does to cry for help when seized by a violent wave.

He was well aware that he had agreed to marry Zanuba. He could hardly deny his abject craving for her but could not imagine that marriage would accommodate his desires. How could he break the "good" news to his wife and children or to other people? Although he wanted to keep walking for as long as possible and had no destination, he quickened his pace, took broad steps, and struck his stick against the ground as if in a great hurry to get somewhere.

She had rejected him and sent him away. These tricks were no novelty to a man of his worldly experience, but a weak person may knowingly fall into a snare. If the walking and the pure air revived him a little, he still remained befuddled and flustered. The flow of thoughts in his mind was so disordered that he could hardly bear it. He felt he would go crazy if a decisive solution, no matter how flawed, was not found.

In the shadows he had no hesitation or embarrassment about talking to himself. The canopy of branches shielded him from the sky, the fields stretching off to his right absorbed his ideas, and the waters of the Nile, flowing past him on the left, swallowed his feelings. But he had to avoid the light. He needed to be careful not to get caught by its bright ring, for fear of having to take off like a circus wagon trailed by boys and curiosity seekers. Then he could kiss his reputation, dignity, and honor goodbye. He had two personalities. One was reserved for friends and lovers; the other presented to his family and the world. It was this second visage that sustained his distinction and respectability, guaranteeing him a status beyond normal aspirations. But his caprice was conspiring against the respectable side of his character, threatening to destroy it forever.

He saw the bridge with its glowing lights ahead of him and wondered where he should go. Since he wanted more solitude and darkness, he did not cross over but continued straight ahead, taking the Giza road.

"Yasin!" he exclaimed. "The thought of your eldest son alarms you. Your forehead burns with shame. Why? He'll be the first to understand you and make allowances for you. Or do you think he'll rejoice at your misfortunes and make fun of you? You've scolded him and criticized him for a long time, but his foot's never slipped into a pit like yours. . . . Kamal! From now on you'll have to wear a mask to keep him from discerning your guilt. Khadija? Aisha? They'll have to hang their heads low in the Shawkat family. 'Zanuba's your father's wife!' A wedding applauded only by buffoons. . . . In your breast live sinful longings. Select some other stage for them than this world. Is there not a kingdom of darkness beyond the mortal realm where you can satisfy your base cravings in peace? Examine the spider's web tomorrow and see what's left of the fly. Listen to the croaking of the frogs and the chirping of the crickets. How happy these creatures are! Burrow underground if you want to be joyous and carefree. On the surface of the earth you can find happiness only as al-Sayyid Ahmad. Spend the next evening with members of your family, all of them—your wife, Kamal, Yasin, Khadija, and Aisha. Then tell them what you plan to do, if you're able. If you can do that, then and only then marry Zanuba.

"Haniya! Do you remember how you cast her out, even though you loved her? You've never loved a woman as much. It seems, alas, that we lose our senses when we become middle-aged. Drink tonight till they have to carry you out. How I long for a drink! It seems you haven't had one since the year of the prophet Muhammad's birth.

The bitter pains you've had to swallow this year could easily erase the happy benefits you've enjoyed throughout your lifetime."

He pounded the earth with his stick and stopped walking. Fed up with the gloom, the stillness, and the tree-lined road, he desired the consolation of his friends. He was not a man who could tolerate being alone for any length of time. He was a member of a group, a part of the whole. In his friends' company, his problems would be solved as usual. He turned to go back to the bridge, but then his being rebelled with anger and disgust. In a strange voice racked by protest, pain, and resentment he said, "She spends a whole night out ... in an unknown location, and then you agree to marry her."

He was afflicted with contempt for himself, like a sharp pain in his chest and heart. "With her friend Yasmina! How absurd! No ... she spent the night in the arms of a man she only left the next day after noon." She had stayed with that fellow knowing full well when al-Sayyid Ahmad visited the houseboat. So what did that mean? Clearly her infatuation with the other man had made her forget the time.

"Eternal damnation! Or have you slipped so low she doesn't care whether you're upset or not? Spellbound fool! After that, how could you have spoken ingratiatingly to her? How could you have left her with a promise of marriage? You're a disgrace in this world and the next. Worry has put so much pressure on you that you don't seem to have noticed the horn with which you're crowning the family. It will dishonor them for generations to come. What do you expect people to say about this horn on your handsome forehead?

"Anger, loathing, blood, and tears will not atone for your surrender and your weakness. How she must be laughing at you now as she lies on her back in the houseboat. Perhaps she hasn't yet washed away the sweat of that man, who'll soon be laughing at you too.... What's the point of getting up tomorrow if everyone's going to be making fun of you? Confess your weakness to your friends and hear their raucous laughter and comments. 'Attribute it to age and senility. Excuse it by saying he's experienced everything except the delight of sporting a cuckold's horns.' Zubayda will say, 'You refused to be my master and agreed to be my lute player's pimp.' Jalila will declare, 'You're not my brother; not even my sister.' I ask the forbidding road, gloomy darkness, and aged trees to bear witness that I'm racing through the shadows, crying like a child. May I not sleep tonight before I humiliate the tyrant.... She turned you away! Why? Because she's tired of a life of sin ... a sin from which she hadn't yet cleansed

her body? Say rather that she can no longer bear you. That's sufficient. How hideous the pain is! But I deserve it for having worshipped her. When a person's doing penance for an ungodly deed,
he may crush his head by beating it against a wall. Shaykh Mutawalli
Abd al-Samad thinks he knows many things, but how ignorant he
is. . . ."

Al-Sayyid Ahmad passed the Zamalek Bridge once more and took
the Imbaba road. He began to quicken his steps deliberately and stubbornly, for he was determined to wash away the ignominy staining
him. Whenever pain bore down on him, he renewed his efforts, striking the ground with his stick as though walking on three legs.

The houseboat came in sight. There was a light shining from the
window. His rage intensified, for he had regained his self-confidence
along with his feelings of manliness and honor. He felt composed
now that he had reached a decision. He went down the steps, crossed
the wooden gangplank, and banged on the door with the end of his
stick. He rapped violently until he heard a voice ask with alarm,
"Who's there?"

"Me!" he answered forcefully.

The door opened, revealing her astonished face. She stepped aside
to let him in as she mumbled, "Good news?"

He crossed into the sitting room. Once in the center, he whirled
around and stared at her. She approached with a questioning look
and stopped in front of him as she anxiously examined his scowling
face. Then she said, "Good news, God willing. Why have you come
back?"

With alarming restraint he answered, "Good news, praise God, as
you'll learn."

She did not speak but let her eyes ask the questions. So he continued: "I've come to tell you not to put any faith in what I said. The
whole matter was just a foolish joke."

Her torso slumped with disappointment. Her face expressed disbelief and resentment. Then she cried out, "'A foolish joke'! Don't you
know the difference between a silly prank and a binding word of
honor?"

His face ever more glowering, he cautioned her, "When addressing
me you'd better be polite. Women of your class earn their living in
my home as maids."

Staring him straight in the face, she screamed, "Have you returned
to favor me with this thought? Why haven't you ever said that be-

fore? Why did you make promises to me, attempt to gain my affection, and ingratiate yourself with me? Do you imagine talk like this will frighten me? I don't have time for foolish jokes."

He waved his hand angrily at her to make her keep still and yelled, "I've come to tell you that marrying a girl like you would be disgraceful and nothing but an anecdote for buffs of embarrassing jokes. They'll have fun with it. Since ideas like these fill your head, you're no longer fit to associate with me. It does me no good to frequent lunatics."

As she listened, sparks of anger flew from her eyes, but she disappointed his hopes and did not lose her temper. Perhaps the sight of his fury frightened her.

In a softer tone than before, she said, "I won't force you to marry me. I told you what I was thinking and left the decision up to you. Now you want to go back on your promise. Do whatever you want. But there's no reason to revile and insult me. Let each of us go his way in peace."

"Is this the most she'll do to hold on to you?" he asked himself. "Wouldn't it have been better if she'd dug her fingernails into you attempting to keep you? Recharge your anger from your pain."

"Each of us will go his own way, but first I want to tell you bluntly what I think of you. I don't deny it was my idea to pursue you— perhaps because the soul occasionally feels a desperate craving for filthy things. You left the people you were happily serving so I could lift you up to this style of life. It doesn't surprise me that I haven't found with you the kind of love and respect I won from them, for trash only appreciates trash. The time's come for me to cease stooping down to your level and to return to my proper environment."

Defeat was visible in her face, the defeat of a person afraid to release the fury pent up in her breast. In a trembling voice she muttered, "Goodbye. Go. Leave me in peace."

Struggling with his pains, he said bitterly, "I've lowered and demeaned myself."

At this point she lost control and shouted, "Enough! That'll do! Have mercy on this vile wretch, but beware of her. Remember how once you humbly kissed her hand. 'Lowered and demeaned,' huh? The truth is that you're getting old. I accepted you in spite of your age, and this is my reward. . . ."

He waved his stick and shouted furiously, "Shut up, bitch! Hush, vile creature! Collect your clothes and leave."

Raising her head jerkily, she shouted back, "Listen carefully to what I say. One more word from you, and I'll make such a row it'll resound throughout the houseboat, the road, and the riverfront until the entire police force arrives. Do you hear? I'm not some little morsel that's easily swallowed. I'm Zanuba!... May God repay me for my suffering. You go! This is my houseboat. The lease is in my name. Go peacefully before you're escorted out."

He tarried indecisively for a bit, looking scornfully and derisively at her. Eventually, in order to avoid a scandal, he abandoned the idea of attempting anything rough, spat on the floor, and departed with long, steady steps.

30 ❧

He went immediately to his friends and found Muhammad Iffat, Ali Abd al-Rahim, Ibrahim al-Far, and some of the others. As usual, he drank until intoxicated, but then he had some more. He laughed a lot and made the others roar with laughter. In the wee hours of the night he returned home and slept soundly. Once morning came, he antici- pated a quiet day free from thought. Whenever his imagination con- jured up a scene from the near or distant past he resolutely shut it out—except for the one scene he gladly recalled, the final vignette recording his victory over the woman and himself. He asserted, "It's all over, praise God. I'm really going to be careful during what's left of my life."

At first the day was quiet. He was able to reflect on his obvious triumph and to congratulate himself. Yet, as the day progressed, it started to seem dull or even dead. He could not think of any reason for this, unless it was a reaction to his nervous exhaustion of the last two days, in fact of the last months to a lesser degree. The truth was that his affair with Zanuba now appeared to have been a tragedy from start to finish. He had difficulty accepting this first defeat in his long string of romances, and it made a deep impression on his heart and imagination. He was enraged whenever his mind whispered that his youth had fled, for he was proud of his vigor, good looks, and vital- ity. He clung to the explanation he had provided the woman the previous evening—that she did not love him because trash can only appreciate trash. All day long he yearned for the reunion with his cronies. As the time neared, he grew impatient and rushed off to Muhammad Iffat's house in al-Gamaliya to visit with him before the others trooped in.

Al-Sayyid Ahmad proclaimed at once, "I'm finished with her."

Muhammad Iffat asked, "Zanuba?"

He nodded in the affirmative, and the other man asked smilingly, "So quickly?"

Laughing sarcastically, al-Sayyid Ahmad answered, "Would you believe she demanded I marry her? I got fed up."

Muhammad Iffat laughed scornfully and said, "Not even Zubayda herself would think of that. How amazing! Her excuse is that you pampered her beyond her wildest dreams. So she wanted even more."

Al-Sayyid Ahmad muttered derisively, "She's crazy."

Muhammad Iffat laughed again and said, "Perhaps love for you affected her brain?"

"What a jab," he thought. "Laugh to compensate for the pain."

"I told you she's crazy. That says it all."

"What did you do?"

"I told her bluntly that I was leaving, never to return. Then I left."

"How did she take it?"

"She cursed and threatened me. She said, 'Go to hell.' So I left the lunatic. It was a mistake from the very beginning."

Shaking his head with satisfaction, Muhammad Iffat replied, "Yes. We've all slept with her but never thought of having an affair with her."

"You've pounced and roamed with the lions only to be routed by a mouse," he told himself. "Hide your shame even from your closest friends and praise God that it's all over."

But in fact nothing really was over, for she lived on in his imagination. In the following days he realized that he could not think of her in the abstract. Her image was always linked to a deep pain, which spread and increased. It became clear to him that this pain was not caused merely by anger over outraged honor but by regret and longing. Apparently it was a tyrannical emotion that demanded nothing less than the destruction of the person experiencing it. All the same, he was fiercely proud of the victory he had recently won and indulged himself in the hope of eventually vanquishing his high-handed and traitorous emotions. For whatever reason, peace of mind had left him. He spent his time in thought, mulling over his sorrows, tormented by things he imagined and remembered. He occasionally felt so weak he considered telling Muhammad Iffat about the pains tormenting him. Indeed he went so far as to think once of asking for Zubayda's help. But these moments of weakness were like bouts of fever, and when he recovered from one he would shake his head with perplexed amazement.

His crisis lent a coarseness to his behavior, although he resisted as much as possible, relying on his forbearance and civility. His self-control was lessened only to a limited degree, and that change passed unnoticed except by friends and close acquaintances accustomed to his mildness, understanding, and tact. The members of his family were not aware of any shift, for his conduct with them remained much the same. What differed was the sentiment underlying his behavior. His feigned ferocity became so real that only he was aware of its intensity. Yet he did not escape his own cruelty. In fact, he may have been its primary target. He attacked himself, scolding and railing against his humiliation. Eventually he began to acknowledge his disgrace, wretchedness, and loss of youth.

He consoled himself by saying, "I won't make a move. I won't humiliate myself any further. Let my thoughts wander in all directions. Let my emotions be convulsed repeatedly. I'll stay right where I am, and only the compassionate and forgiving God will know the pain I'm suffering."

He would suddenly find himself wondering whether she was still on the houseboat or not. If still there, did she have enough of his money to make her independent of other men? Or was the other man meeting her there? He frequently asked himself questions like these, and each time the torture he experienced leached from his spirit to his flesh and bones, breaking him down bit by bit. The only time he felt at peace was when he recollected that final scene in the houseboat. He had left her with the impression, which he had almost shared, that he was repudiating and shunning her. But he could not help recalling scenes recording his humiliation and weakness, and others of unforgettable happiness. His imagination also created fresh scenes in which they met again, quarreled, settled accounts, scolded each other, and then were reconciled and reunited. . . . This was a dream he saw frequently in his inner world, which was teeming with countless varieties of sorrow and happiness. . . . But why should he not discover for himself what had become of the houseboat and its resident? After dark he could go there without being seen by anyone.

Concealing himself in the shadows like a thief, he set off. When he passed the houseboat he saw light filtering out from the shutters, but he did not know whether she or some new tenant was benefiting from this light. Yet his heart felt it was her light, not someone else's. Looking at the houseboat, he imagined that he could detect the mistress's spirit and that all he needed to do to see her face to face was to knock on the door. When it opened, there she would be, just as in the old days, both the happy and the miserable ones. But what would he do if a man's face confronted him? She really was close, but how remote. . . . He had been eternally forbidden use of this gangplank. Oh, had this situation appeared in any of his dreams? She had told him to leave. She had said it from her heart and then had proceeded on with her life as though she had never known him and was totally oblivious to his existence. Such a cruel person could not be expected to pay attention to a plea for mercy or forgiveness.

He went there repeatedly. It became a customary pastime for him to loiter in front of the houseboat after night fell and before he went to his friends' party. He did not seem to want to do anything in particular, except satisfy an insane but sterile curiosity.

He was about to go on his way one evening when the door opened and a figure he could not see clearly in the shadows emerged. His heart pounded with fear and hope. He crossed the road quickly and stood beside a tree, his eyes staring into the darkness. The figure crossed the wooden gangplank to the road and set off in the direction of the Zamalek Bridge. He could tell it was a woman. His heart told him it was Zanuba. He followed her at a distance, not knowing how the evening would end. Whether it was his former mistress or not, what did he have in mind? . . . Yet he continued on, concentrating his attention on the figure. When she neared the bridge and got in range of the lights, his hunch was confirmed. He was now certain that it was Zanuba. But she was cloaked in the traditional black wrap, which she had not worn during their affair. He was surprised by that and wondered what it implied. His suspicion was—and how many he had—that there was an incriminating reason for it. He saw her approach the stop for the Giza streetcar and wait there. He walked beside the fields until he passed the point opposite her and then crossed to her side, where he stood out of sight. When the streetcar came, she boarded it. He raced over and clambered up, taking a seat at the end of the bench nearest the steps, so that he could watch people get off. At every stop he looked out, no longer apprehensive about being discovered. Even if he were caught, she would have no way of knowing that he had been waiting for her in front of the houseboat and spying on her. She got off at al-Ataba al-Khadra. Climbing down, he saw her walk toward the Muski. Again he followed her at a distance, rejoicing in the darkness of the street. Had she resumed contact with her aunt? Or was she going to a new gentleman? But why would she go to his place when she had a houseboat for entertaining lovers?

When they reached the Husayn district, afraid of losing her in the crowd of women wearing wraps, he watched her even more closely. The point of this covert pursuit escaped him, but he was driven forward by a painful, futile, and even violent curiosity, impossible to

oppose. She walked past the front of the mosque and made her way
to Watawit Alley, where the pedestrians were fewer and the beggars
more persistent. She continued on as far as al-Gamaliya and turned
into Palace of Desire Alley. Although afraid Yasin would run into
him or see him from a window, al-Sayyid Ahmad trailed after her. If
he met his son he could claim he was going to visit Ghunaym Hamidu, a neighbor of Yasin's in Palace of Desire Alley and the owner
of an oil-pressing establishment. Before he knew what was happening
she had entered the first cul-de-sac, which had only one house—
Yasin's. His heart pounded and his feet felt heavy. He knew the
residents of the first two floors. The families that lived there could
have no conceivable link to Zanuba. He was so anxious and uneasy
that his eyes looked every which way. But he found himself going
into the cul-de-sac without worrying about the consequences. He
went close enough to the front door to hear her footsteps as she
climbed the stairs. Entering the stairwell, he raised his head to listen.
He heard her pass the first door and then the second. Then she was
knocking on Yasin's door. Breathing heavily, he remained nailed to
his spot. He turned his head, feeling weak and on the verge of collapse. He sighed deeply, pulled himself away, and retraced his steps.
He could not see the street, his mind was so crowded with jumbled
thoughts and ideas.

Yasin was the man! Did Zanuba know he was Yasin's father? He
tried to force peace into his heart as though pounding a thick stopper
into a narrow opening. He reminded himself that he had never mentioned any of his children in her presence. Besides, it was incredible
that Yasin should know about this secret. He remembered how Yasin
had come a few days before to tell him of the divorce from Maryam
with the troubled look of a person who knew he was at fault. But his
expression had also been innocent and sincere, untainted by any suspicion directed against his father. Of all the hypothetical conjectures
he might entertain, the one he could never accept was the thought
that Yasin would knowingly steal his mistress. Indeed, how would
Yasin know his father was having or had had an affair with any
woman? There was nothing for him to worry about in this regard.
Even if Zanuba knew he was related to Yasin or learned it one day,
she would never tell Yasin for fear of ending their relationship. He
continued walking along, postponing his visit with his friends. First
he needed to catch his breath and to restore calm to his soul. Although tired and exhausted, he walked in the direction of al-Ataba.

"You wanted to know and now you do. Shouldn't you have forgotten the whole matter and been patient? Praise God that circumstances didn't bring you face to face with Yasin in a scandalous way. Yasin's the man. When did she meet him? Where? How many times did she betray you with your son, without your being aware of it? These are questions for which you'll never attempt to find the answers. Assume the worst to allow your aching head to get some rest. Yasin's the man! He said he divorced Maryam because she was impolite. It would have made sense for him to offer an explanation like that when he divorced his first wife, Zaynab—if you hadn't learned the true cause when it all happened. You'll know the truth one day. But what do you care about truth? Are you still eager to chase after it? Your mind's devastated, and your heart's tormented. Is it possible you're jealous of Yasin? No, this isn't jealousy. To the contrary, it's almost a consolation. If it's inevitable that you're to be slain, then let your son be the assassin. Yasin's an extension of you. So part of you was defeated and part of you won. You're both the victim and the victor. Yasin has reversed the outcome of the battle. You were drinking a mixture of pain and defeat. Now triumph and solace have been added to the blend. You won't grieve about losing Zanuba anymore. You've been too confident. Promise not to omit time from your calculations in the future. If only you could pass this advice on to Yasin so he isn't caught off guard when his turn comes. You should be happy. There's no cause for remorse. You'll need to approach life with a new strategy, a new heart, and a new mind. Let Yasin carry the banner. You'll recover from your dizziness, and everything will proceed as though nothing had happened. But you won't be able to transform the events of the last few days into the usual series of anecdotes to be shared over drinks with your friends. These frightening times have taught you that many things need to be hidden away in your chest. Oh . . . how I long for a drink."

In the following days, al-Sayyid Ahmad proved that he was stronger than his misfortunes. His feet firmly on the ground, he looked to the future. The facts of Yasin's divorce reached him by way of Mr. Ali Abd al-Rahim, who had it from Ghunaym Hamidu and others, but these narrators did not know the identity of the woman whose escapade had provoked Maryam's divorce.

Al-Sayyid Ahmad smiled. He laughed a long time over everything. Then, on his way to Muhammad Iffat's house one evening, he felt such a horrible heaviness in his upper back and head that he gasped for breath. It was not an entirely new sensation. Of late he had frequently been afflicted by headaches, but none had been as severe as this. When he complained about his condition to Muhammad Iffat, the latter man ordered some iced lemonade for him. Al-Sayyid Ahmad stayed at the party to the end but awoke the next day in worse shape than before. He was worried enough to consider consulting a physician. The fact was that he never thought of seeing a doctor except in the most dire circumstances.

31 ~

Objects, like words, take on new meanings as circumstances change. The mansion of the Shaddad family was hardly lacking in grandeur for Kamal, but on that evening in December it appeared in a splendid new form suitable for a rite of passage. Lights had been strung over the structure until every segment was brightly illuminated. Each corner and wall wore a necklace of brilliant pearls. Electric lights of different colors sparkled over the surface from rooftop to ground and along the garden wall with its massive entrance. The flowers and fruit of the trees seemed transformed into red, green, and white lamps, and light flowed from all the windows of the house. Everything jubilantly proclaimed a wedding.

When Kamal first saw this as he approached, he felt transported to the kingdom of light. The sidewalk opposite the house was jammed with boys, and the entryway was strewn with golden sand. The gate was wide open, as was the door of the men's reception room, which had been prepared to receive the guests, its big chandelier aglow. The large upper balcony was filled with a resplendent group of young ladies in magnificent evening gowns. Shaddad Bey and men of the family stood at the entrance to the reception hall welcoming the arrivals. The porch was graced by a marvelous orchestra, and the music could be heard as far away as the desert.

Kamal quickly cast an all-inclusive glance around him, wondering whether Aïda was on the upper balcony with the girls who were looking down. Had she seen him enter with the other guests, his large head and celebrated nose introducing his lanky frame, formal attire, and the overcoat on his arm? He felt ill at ease and, unlike the others, did not go to the reception hall. Instead, he took "his" path, which he had followed to the rear garden so often in the past. Husayn Shaddad had suggested this idea to allow their group as much time together as possible in the beloved gazebo. Kamal seemed to be wading into a sea of light, for he found the door of the rear reception room open too. It was all lit up and crowded with guests, and the upper balcony was swarming with beautiful ladies. The gazebo was deserted except for Isma'il Latif, who wore an elegant black suit that lent his pugnacious appearance a charm Kamal had never observed before.

Isma'il Latif glanced at him and said, "Superb! But why did you bring an overcoat? . . . Husayn only stayed a quarter hour with me, but he'll return when he's finished with the receiving line. Hasan spent a few minutes with me. I doubt he'll be able to sit with us, as we had hoped. This is his day, and he has a lot to do. Husayn thought of inviting some of our acquaintances to the gazebo, but I stopped him. It's enough that he's asked them to share our table. We'll have a special room of our own. That's the most important news I have to give you tonight."

"There's more important news than that," Kamal told himself. "It will amaze me for a long time that I accepted this invitation. Why did you accept? To make it seem you didn't care? Or because you've fallen in love with terrifying adventures?"

"That's fine," Kamal said. "But why don't we go for at least a moment to the great hall to see the guests?"

Isma'il Latif replied scornfully, "You won't see what you want, even if we do. The pashas and beys have been given the front room for their exclusive use. If you go, you'll find yourself in the back room with young men from the family and their friends, and that's not what you want. I wish I could sneak us upstairs where the most glorious paragons of beauty are surging back and forth."

"Only one paragon interests me," Kamal thought. "The paragon for all others. I haven't laid eyes on her since I confessed my love. She discovered my secret and disappeared."

"I won't try to conceal my interest in seeing the important people. Husayn told me his father had invited many of the men I read about in the papers."

Isma'il laughed out loud and said, "Do you imagine you'll find some of them have four eyes or six feet? They're men like you and me, although older and not particularly good-looking. But I understand the secret behind your desire to see them. It's part and parcel of your excessive interest in politics."

"I really ought to drop all interests in the world," Kamal told himself. "She's no longer mine and I'm not hers. But my curiosity about famous people is derived from my love for greatness. You'd like to be great. Don't deny it. You have a promising aptitude for looking like Socrates and suffering like Beethoven, but you owe this aspiration to the woman who deprived you of light when she departed. By tomorrow you'll find no trace of her in Egypt. Delirium of pain, there's something intoxicating about you."

Kamal said longingly, "Husayn told me the reception would bring together men from all the different political parties."

"That's true. Yesterday Sa'd Zaghlul invited the Liberals and the Nationalists to a widely publicized tea party. Today Shaddad Bey invites them to his daughter's wedding. Of the Wafd Party politicians you admire I've seen Fath Allah Barakat and Hamad al-Basil. Tharwat, Isma'il Sidqy, and Abd al-Aziz Fahmy are also here. Shaddad Bey has lofty ambitions he's actively pursuing, and that's only right. The era of 'Our Effendi' the Khedive Abbas is over. People used to chant, 'God lives.... Abbas arrives.' The truth is that he's gone, never to return. So it's most judicious of Shaddad Bey to look to the future. To be on the safe side, all he has to do is to travel to Switzerland every few years to assure the Khedive formally but falsely of his loyalty. Then he returns to continue from success to success."

"Your heart abhors this type of judiciousness," Kamal thought. "Sa'd's recent tribulations demonstrate that the nation abounds with such 'judicious' men. Is Shaddad Bey really one of them? The beloved's father? Not so fast . . . the beloved herself has descended from the highest heavens to marry a human being. Let your heart crumble into so many scattered fragments you're unable to collect them."

"Do you think a celebration like this will be complete without singers?"

Isma'il replied sarcastically, "The Shaddad family's half Parisian. They have little respect for our wedding traditions. They wouldn't allow a woman entertainer to perform at one of their parties. And they don't recognize the worth of any of our male vocalists. Remember what Husayn said about this orchestra, which I'm seeing for the first time in my life? Every Sunday evening they play at Groppi's tearoom. After dinner they'll move into the hall to entertain the dignitaries. Forget about the music. You should realize that the high point of the evening's the dinner and the champagne."

"The musicians Jalila and Sabir . . . the weddings of Aisha and Khadija . . . what a different atmosphere!" Kamal thought. "How happy you were back then. . . . Tonight the orchestra will escort your dream to the grave. Remember what you saw through a hole in the door the night Aisha got married? I feel sorry for a goddess who grovels in the dirt. . . ."

"That doesn't matter," Kamal said. "What I really miss is not being able to see the big men up close. I'll regret that for a long time. There are two important things I'd be watching for. The first is to hear what they say about the political situation. After the coalition between the political parties, is there really any hope of having the constitution reinstated and of reviving parliamentary government? The second is to listen to the ordinary small talk of such festive occasions coming from the mouths of men like Tharwat Pasha. Wouldn't it be extraordinary to hear him gossip and crack jokes?"

Affecting disdain, although his scornful gestures betrayed his pride, Isma'il Latif said, "I've had many chances to sit with friends of my father's like Salim Bey and Shaddad Bey. I can assure you nothing there justifies this interest."

"Where's the difference then between the son of a superior court judge and the merchant's son? Why is it the fate of one to worship the beloved while the other marries her? Isn't this marriage a sign that these people are formed of a different clay than normal folks? But you don't know how your father talks to his friends and associates."

"In any case, Salim Bey isn't the kind of dignitary I had in mind."

Isma'il smiled at this last remark but did not comment on it.

The laughter from the men's reception hall was gleeful, that descending from the upper balcony fragrant with the enchanting perfume of femininity. The two types of laughter harmonized with each other like sounds from distant instruments heard at times in chords and then as a bouquet of different melodies. The tuneful laughter formed a rosy setting in which Kamal's sad and desolate heart stood out like a black funeral announcement in a floral arrangement.

Husayn Shaddad soon arrived, his tall, slender body sporting a frock coat. Beaming and radiant, he opened his arms wide, as did Kamal. Then they embraced each other warmly. He was followed by the handsome Hasan Salim, formally attired, his natural arrogance encased in a polite and refined exterior. Even so, he seemed short and insignificant standing next to Husayn. He shook hands heartily with Kamal, who congratulated him from the depths of his tongue if not his heart.

With his usual bluntness, which was often hard to distinguish from malicious wit, Isma'il said, "Kamal's really sad he's not getting to sit with Tharwat Pasha and his colleagues."

In an uncommonly jolly manner that brushed aside his customary reserve, Hasan Salim retorted, "He'll just have to wait until his 'forthcoming' books are published. Then he'll find he's one of them."

Husayn Shaddad protested, "Don't be stuffy. I'd like us to be completely at ease this evening and enjoy ourselves."

Even before Husayn sat down, Hasan excused himself and went off. That evening he flitted from place to place like a butterfly. Husayn stretched his legs out and said, "Tomorrow they leave for Brussels. They're getting to Europe before me, but I won't stay here long Soon I'll be able to amuse myself by traveling between Paris and Brussels."

"You'll be traveling between al-Nahhasin and al-Ghuriya," Kamal told himself, "without a lover or a friend. This is what you get for gazing at the heavens. You can look everywhere in the city helplessly, but your eyes will never recover from love's anguish. Fill your lungs with this air perfumed by her breath. Tomorrow you'll be pitying yourself."

"I imagine I'll join you there one day."

Husayn and Isma'il both asked, "How?"

"Let your lie be as enormous as your pain," Kamal advised himself.

"My father agreed to let me go there in a student group at my own expense once I've finished my studies."

Husayn cried delightedly, "If only this dream will come true. . . ."

Isma'il laughed and said, "I'm afraid I'll find myself alone in a few years."

The instruments of the orchestra joined together in a tumultuous movement that allowed each to demonstrate its agility and power. They seemed to be participating in a fierce race. The goal had come in sight of their eyes and ambitions. The music reached its climax, indicating that the end was near. Although Kamal was absorbed by his grief, his mind gravitated toward the fiery tunes, racing after them until his heart beat fast and he felt breathless. Soon he was overcome by tenderness and intoxicated by generosity. These sentiments turned his sorrow into tearful ecstasy. When the music ended, he sighed deeply, as its echoes reverberated melodiously in his spirit, making a powerful impression on him. He wondered whether inflamed emotions would not peak and then die away, like the music. If pieces of music—and everything else—had an end, why should not love have one? He recalled listless states he had experienced on rare occasions when he had seemed to recollect nothing about Aïda except her name.

"Do you remember those times?" he asked himself.

At such instants he had shaken his head in bewilderment and wondered whether everything really was over. But he had always imagined or thought of some idea or scene that had awakened him from his slumbers and cast him, bound in fetters, to drown in the sea of passion.

"If you experience one of these moments," Kamal thought, "try to cling to it with all your might. Don't let it slip away. Then you can hope for a cure. Yes, attempt to destroy the immortality of love."

Smiling, Husayn Shaddad said, "For good luck the party began with the recitation of a Qur'an sura."

"The Qur'an!" Kamal exclaimed to himself. "How charming! Even the beautiful Parisian could not get married without an Islamic clerk and the Qur'an. Her marriage will be associated in your mind with both the Qur'an and champagne."

"Tell us the schedule for the party."

Pointing toward the house, Husayn said, "The formalities will be concluded shortly. Dinner will be served in an hour. After the banquet, the party ends. Aïda will spend one last night in our house. Tomorrow morning she leaves for Alexandria, where she'll board the ship for Europe the following day."

"You'll be deprived of many sights that really ought to be recorded to provide sustenance for your insatiable pains," Kamal thought. "Like seeing her beautiful name inscribed on the certificate, her face waiting expectantly for the happy news, the smile with which she greets it, and then the couple meeting. . . . Even your pain needs nourishment."

"Will the marriage contract be drawn up by a Muslim notary?"

"Naturally," Husayn answered.

But Isma'il laughed loudly. "No, a priest," he said.

"What a silly question!" Kamal scolded himself. "Ask also whether they plan to spend the night together. Isn't it sad that a man of no significance like this marriage clerk should impede the progress of your life? But a lowly worm eats the corpses of the most exalted individuals. What will your funeral be like when the time comes? Will it be an overwhelming spectacle that fills the streets or a small gathering that soon disbands?"

Then silence spread through the house. There was light but no music. Kamal felt fearful and uncomfortable. "Now, somewhere, in one room or another, the wedding's taking place," he told himself.

A long resounding shriek of joy rang out. It revived old memories for him, for it was a trill of joy like all the other ones he had ever heard and totally un-Parisian. It was followed by a bunch of shriek-ing trills like sirens going off. At that time the mansion resembled any other home in Cairo. The shrieks made his heart race, and he felt out of breath. Hearing Isma'il congratulate the bride's brother, Kamal did so too. He wished he were alone but consoled himself with the thought that for days and nights to come he would be. He promised his pain limitless sustenance. The orchestra burst out playing a piece Kamal knew very well, "Your forgiveness, lordly beauty." He summoned his amazing powers of endurance and self-restraint, although every drop of his blood was tapping against the walls of his veins to announce it was all over. History itself had concluded. Life was at an end. Dreams worth more than life itself were terminated. He was faced with nothing less than a boulder studded with spikes.

Husayn Shaddad said reflectively, "A word and a trill, and one of us enters a whole new world. We'll all experience that someday."

Isma'il Latif said, "I'm going to postpone it as long as I can."

"All of us?" Kamal asked himself. "For me it's the sky or nothing."

"I'll never yield to that day," he said.

The other two did not appear interested in what he had said or at least seemed not to take it seriously. Isma'il continued: "I won't get married until I'm convinced that marriage is necessary and unavoidable."

A Nubian servant brought around glasses of fruit punch. He was trailed by another with a tray loaded with fancy containers of sweets. They were made of crystal and had four gilded legs. The dark blue glass was decorated with silver, and each box was tied with a green silk ribbon. On a crescent-shaped card attached to the knot were inscribed the initials of the couple's first names: A. H.

When Kamal received his box he felt relieved for perhaps the first time that day. The magnificent container guaranteed that his beloved was leaving behind her a memento that would be as long-lasting as his love. While he lived, this souvenir would remain a symbol of an unlikely past, a happy dream, a heavenly enchantment, and a spectacular disappointment. He was overcome by a sense of having been the victim of an atrocious assault. Conspiring against him had been fate, the law of heredity, the class system, Aïda, Hasan Salim, and a mysterious, hidden force he was reluctant to name. To his eyes he seemed a miserable wretch standing alone against these combined powers. His wound was bleeding and there was no one to bind it. The only response he could muster against this attack was a stifled rebellion he could not proclaim. In fact, circumstances obliged him to pretend to be delighted, as if congratulating those tyrannical forces for torturing him and eliminating him from the ranks of contented human beings. For all of them he harbored an undying rancor, but he postponed the question of pinpointing and directing it. Indeed, he felt that after this decisive trill he would not be so indulgent with life. He would no longer be satisfied with what was at hand. Events would not be met with magnanimous tolerance. His way would be arduous, rough, twisting, and crammed with hardships and problems, but he did not think of backing down in face of this assault and refused to consider a truce. He issued advance warnings and threats but left it up to destiny to choose a foe for him to tackle and his weapons.

Swallowing to clear his throat of the fruit punch, Husayn Shaddad said, "Don't claim to shun marriage. I believe—if you're allowed to travel as you say—that you'll find a wife who pleases you."

"As though you couldn't find anyone you'd like here," Kamal brooded. "Look for a new country, where the fair sex doesn't take offense at abnormally large heads and noses. Give me heaven or death."

Then, nodding his head as though in agreement, he said, "That's what I think."

Isma'il Latif asked sarcastically, "Do you know what it means to marry a European? In a word, you 'win' a woman from the lowest classes, one willing to submit to a man she secretly feels only fit for servitude."

"You've already experienced servitude," Kamal told himself, "in your own magnificent country, not in Europe, which you'll never see."

"You're exaggerating!" Husayn protested disapprovingly.

"See how the teachers from England treat us."

Husayn Shaddad responded with an enthusiasm that was almost pleading, "The Europeans in their countries don't act the way they do here."

Kamal asked himself, "Where can I find overwhelming power to annihilate oppression and oppressors? Lord of the universe, where's Your heavenly justice?"

Dinner was announced, and the three friends went to the reception hall and from there to a nearby room opening onto the rear parlor. A buffet dinner capable of serving at least ten was laid out there. They were joined by other young men, some relatives of the Shaddad family and others who were school friends. Even so, there were fewer than ten guests, a fact for which Kamal was deeply grateful to Husayn. They quickly set about eating with gusto and vigor, so the atmosphere became almost as lively as that of a race. They had to keep returning to the buffet to do justice to all the dishes spread out there, a small bouquet of roses separating one from another. Husayn signaled to the waiter to bring whiskey and bottles of soda.

Isma'il Latif called out, "I swear I expected only the best from this gesture even before I knew what it meant."

Husayn leaned over to entreat Kamal, "One glass, for my sake."

Kamal advised himself, "Drink," not from any desire, since he had no experience with it, but out of a wish to rebel. Yet his faith proved stronger than his grief or rebellion. He smilingly said, "As for that, no, thank you."

Raising a full glass, Isma'il said, "You've no excuse. Even a pious man permits himself to get drunk at weddings."

Kamal ate the tasty food calmly. He observed the eaters and drinkers from time to time or joined in their conversation and laughter.

"A man's happiness is proportionate to the number of wedding buffets he's enjoyed," Kamal told himself. "But is the pashas' buffet just like ours? We investigate them while devouring their food. Champagne! . . . This is an opportunity for you to taste champagne. The Shaddad family's champagne. . . . What did you say? 'Why doesn't Mr. Kamal touch alcohol?' Perhaps his belly's full and can't hold more. The truth is that I'm eating with unmatched appetite, uninfluenced by my sorrow or even encouraged by it. You ate like this at Fahmy's funeral. Keep Isma'il away from the food and drink or it will be exhausted. The deaths of the writer al-Manfaluti and of the musician Sayyid Darwish and Egypt's loss of the Sudan are events crowning our era with sorrow, but the coalition of political parties and this repast are happy news. We've eaten three turkeys, and one hasn't been touched yet. This fellow . . . O Lord, he's pointing at my nose. They're all convulsed with laughter. They're drunk. So don't get angry. Laugh along with them, merrily pretending you're not offended. But my heart is shaken by anger. If you're ever able to launch an attack on the world, do it. As for the effects of this splendid evening, it's preposterous to think you'll ever recover from them. . . . People are talking about Fuad al-Hamzawi, discussing his success and brilliance. Are you jealous? When you mention him, you'll gain their respect, even if only a little."

"He's been a diligent student since childhood," Kamal ventured.

"You know him?"

Husayn Shaddad answered for his friend, "Fuad's father's an employee in the store owned by Kamal's father."

"My heart feels comforted," Kamal reflected. "May God curse hearts."

Then he said, "His father's always been an honest and reliable man."

"What business is your father in?"

"The term 'merchant' was always surrounded by an aura of respect in my mind," Kamal reminded himself, "until the merchant's son was compared unfavorably with the son of the superior court judge."

"Wholesale groceries."

"Lying's a cheap dodge," Kamal told himself. "Watch them. Try to see what's going through their heads. But is there any man in this house as good-looking or vigorous as your father?"

After leaving the tables, most of the guests returned to their seats in the reception hall, although a good number went into the garden to stroll about. People felt relaxed but sluggish. When the guests started leaving, the family members went upstairs to congratulate the couple. The chamber orchestra soon joined them and played some ravishing selections in that happy setting. Kamal put on his overcoat and picked up his magnificent box of sweets. Then he left the Shaddad mansion arm in arm with Isma'il.

Casting his friend an inebriated glance, Isma'il said, "It's eleven. What do you think about walking down Palaces Street until I sober up a little?"

Kamal agreed willingly, because he felt this would provide a good opportunity for a scheme he had been plotting. They sauntered along together, over the same ground Kamal had previously covered with Aïda. Then he had confessed his love and revealed his pains. He would never forget the sight of this street with its elegant, silent mansions. It was lined by lofty trees that viewed the evening with the calm of a peaceful soul and the awe of a celestial imagination.

"Your heart will never stop pounding with desire, ardor, and pain," Kamal reflected, "no matter how often your feet tread on it or your imagination appeals to it. Your heart's like a tree that casts down its leaves and fruit when convulsed by a storm. Although your previous walk here was a failure, you'll always treasure the memory of a bygone dream, a disappointed hope, an illusory happiness, and a pulsing life filled with emotion. Even viewed in the most negative fashion, that was far better than the repose of nonexistence, the desolation of exile, or the extinction of emotion. What nourishment will you be able to find for your heart in the future unless it is places you observe with imagination's eye or names you listen for with passion's ears?"

He said, "I wonder what's happening upstairs now."

Isma'il answered, in a loud voice that disturbed the reigning silence, "The orchestra's playing Western music. The bride and groom are on the dais, smiling, and around them are the Shaddad and Salim families. I've seen a lot of gatherings like that."

"Aïda in a wedding gown!" Kamal exclaimed to himself.

"What a sight! Have you seen anything like that even in a dream?"

"How long will the party last?" he inquired.

"An hour at the most, to let the couple get some sleep, since they're leaving tomorrow morning for Alexandria."

"Words like daggers!" Kamal told himself. "Plunge any of them into your heart."

Isma'il asked, "But who's ever slept on their wedding night?" He laughed raucously. Then he belched and emitted a puff of breath reeking of alcohol. He frowned and grumbled with complaint. Then, as his face relaxed, he said, "May our Lord not condemn you to the sleep of lovers. My dear, they don't get any sleep at all. Don't let Hasan's reserve mislead you. He'll be leaping and bouncing like a stallion until the break of day. That's predestined. There's no way to escape it."

"Savor this new form of distilled pain," Kamal told himself. "It's the essence of pain, the pain of pains. Your consolation is that your pain's unique. No man before you has ever experienced it. Hell will seem easy for you by comparison if you're destined to be carried there by demons who dance you over its tongues of fire. Pain! It's not from losing your lover, because you never aspired to possess her. It's because she has descended from heaven and is wallowing in the mud, after living grandly over the clouds. It's because she's allowed her cheek to be kissed, her blood to be shed, and her body to be abused. How intense my regret and pain are. . . ."

"Is what they say about the first night true?"

Isma'il yelled, "By God, don't you know about these things?"

"How can people consecrate something filthy?" Kamal asked himself.

"Naturally I know, but I didn't until recently. There are things I'd like to hear about again."

Isma'il laughed. "At times you seem an idiot or a fool."

"Let me ask you if it would be easy for you to do that to a person you revere."

Isma'il belched again, bringing the accursed smell of liquor to Kamal's nostrils. He replied, "No one deserves to be revered."

"Your daughter, for example, if you had one."

"Not my daughter or my mother. Where did we come from? It's a law of nature."

"Us?" Kamal asked himself. "The truth's a dazzling light. So look away. Behind the curtain of sanctity, before which you've always prostrated yourself, they'll be cavorting like children. Why does everything seem so empty? Mother, Father, Aïda, the tomb of the Prophet's grandson al-Husayn, the merchant's profession, the aristocratic airs of Shaddad Bey.... How intense my pain is!"

"How filthy the law of nature is," he observed.

Isma'il belched for the third time. In a merry tone but without audible laughter he said, "The fact is that your heart's in pain. It's singing the same words as the new vocalist Umm Kalthoum: 'I'd give my life for her, whether she treasures my love or abandons it.' "

Alarmed, Kamal asked, "What do you mean?"

Trying to seem more intoxicated than he was, Isma'il replied, "I mean you love Aïda."

"My Lord!" How had his secret gotten out?

"You're drunk!"

"It's the truth, and everyone knows it."

Staring at his friend in the darkness, Kamal yelled, "What are you saying?"

"I'm saying that it's the truth and everyone knows it."

"Everyone? Who? Who spread this rumor about me?"

"Aïda!"

"Aïda?"

"Aïda ... she's the one who spilled your secret."

"Aïda? I don't believe it. You're drunk."

"Yes, I'm drunk, but it's the truth too. One of the good qualities of a drunk is that he doesn't lie." Isma'il laughed gently before continuing: "Does this make you angry? As you know, Aïda's a charming girl. For a long time she's secretly directed attention to your loving gaze, without your being aware of it—not to be sarcastic but because she's flirtatious and the attention of her admirers goes to her head. Hasan was the first to realize what was happening and pointed it out to me several times. Then he broke the secret to Husayn. In fact, I know that Madame Saniya, Aïda's mother, heard about the 'lovesick suitor,' as they called you. It's quite possible the servants overheard what was said about you by their employers, so that everyone learned the story of the lovesick suitor."

He felt weak. He imagined their feet were heartlessly trampling his honor. His lips were compressed with bitter grief. Were treasured secrets so easily squandered?

Isma'il continued: "Don't get upset. It was all an innocent joke on the part of people who like you. Even Aïda told your secret solely to boast of it."

"Her imagination deceived her!"

"Denying your love's as futile as denying the sun in broad daylight."

Surrendering sadly, Kamal fell silent. Suddenly he asked, "What did Husayn say?"

In a louder voice Isma'il responded, "Husayn? He's your loyal friend. He frequently expressed his unhappiness with his sister's innocent wiles and stressed your good qualities to her."

Kamal sighed with relief. If his hopes had been disappointed in love, friendship still was unaffected. But how could he ever enter the Shaddad mansion again?

In an earnest voice, as though encouraging his friend to face the situation courageously, Isma'il said, "Aïda was as good as engaged to Hasan for years before the engagement was announced. Besides, she's older than you are. You'll forget these feelings after a good sleep. Don't let it trouble or sadden you."

" 'You'll forget these feelings'!" Kamal exclaimed to himself. Then he asked with unconcealed interest, "Did she make fun of me when she mentioned this alleged infatuation?"

"Certainly not! I told you she enjoyed talking about her admirers."

"Your beloved was a cruel, mocking god," Kamal reflected. "It amused her to make fun of her devotees. Do you remember the day she joked about your head and nose? Like the laws of nature, she's cruel and powerful. After all that, how could she hurry jubilantly to her wedding night like any other girl? Your mother's natural modesty indicates that she at least is conscious of the offense involved in marriage."

They had gone a long way down the street. So they turned to retrace their steps silently, as though tired of their conversation and its sorrows. Soon Isma'il burst out singing poorly: "God's blessing on the girl who sells such treasures. . . ."

Kamal did not break his silence, and did not even seem to notice that his friend was singing. How embarrassed he was to have been a topic of conversation. . . . It appeared that the family, his friends, and the servants had all been winking at each other behind his back without his noticing. That was rude of them, and he did not deserve it. Was this how love and devotion were rewarded? How cruel his beloved was and how atrocious the pain. . . . When Nero sang as Rome burned, perhaps he was avenging a similar wrong.

"Be an invading general handsomely mounted on a charger, a leader borne aloft by the crowd, a metal statue on a column, a wizard who can appear in any form he wishes, an angel flying over the clouds, a monk secluded in the desert, a dangerous criminal causing honest citizens to quake, a clown captivating his merry audience, or a suicide upsetting the onlookers."

If Fuad al-Hamzawi learned the story, disguising his irony with his usual courtesy he would tell Kamal, "It's your fault, because you left us for those people. You scorned girls like Qamar and Narcissus, so enjoy being abandoned by the gods."

"My answer's that I wanted heaven or nothing at all," Kamal thought. "Let her marry as she pleases and go to Brussels or Paris. Let her grow old until her beauty fades. She'll never find a love like mine. Don't forget this road, for here you were intoxicated by enchanting dreams and later swallowed enough despair to make you choke. I'm no longer a resident of this planet. I'm a foreigner and must live like an exile."

When they passed the Shaddad mansion on their way back, they found that workmen were busy removing the decorations and strings of lights from the walls and trees. The large house, stripped of its wedding finery, was enveloped in darkness, except for a few rooms that still had light streaming from their balconies and windows. The party was over, and the crowd had dispersed. The scene seemed to announce that everything has an end. Here he was, going home with a box of candy like a child bribed not to cry by a few pieces of chocolate. The two young men walked along slowly until they reached the beginning of al-Husayniya. Then they shook hands and went their separate ways.

Kamal had not gone more than a few meters down al-Husayniya Street before he stopped. Then he turned and went back to al-Abbasiya Street, which seemed deserted and sound asleep. He walked quickly toward the Shaddad mansion. When he got within sight of it, he turned right, into the desert that surrounded the house, and went far enough through it to reach a place behind the back wall of the garden where he could observe the mansion from a distance. The enveloping curtains of darkness were so thick that a spy had nothing to worry about. For the first time that night he felt cold in this exposed and desolate spot. He fastened the overcoat around his tall, slender body. The shadowy house behind its high wall looked like a huge citadel. His eyes scouted around for the precious target until they came to rest on a closed window with light peeping out between the slats of the shutters. It was at the far right on the second floor. That was the bridal chamber, the only room awake on this side of the mansion. Yesterday it had been the bedroom of Aïda and Budur. Tonight it was decorated to host the strangest spectacle the fates provide. He stared at the window a long time, at first like a bird with clipped wings gazing at its nest atop a tree and then with deep sorrow, as though he could see with his own eyes the death lying in wait for him. What was going on behind that window? If only he could climb that tree in the garden and see. The rest of his life would be a small price he would willingly pay for a look through that window. Was it a trivial matter to see the beloved in the privacy of her bridal chamber? How were they situated? What happened when their eyes met? What were they chatting about? Where in the world had Aïda's pride hidden itself now? He was burning with desire to see this and to record the occurrence of each word, gesture, or hint provided by a facial expression. Indeed, he would have liked to pry into every thought, imaginary notion, feeling, and instinctual urge, everything even if frightening, disgusting, or painfully sad. Afterwards he would surrender his life without regret. He stayed put as time fled by. He did not budge, the light was not extinguished, and his imagination did not tire of its questions. What would he have done if he had been in Hasan Salim's place? He was too perplexed to answer. Lacking selfish goals, devotion had no place on a night like this. He had never aspired to have Aïda. Hasan Salim was obviously from a denomination in which devotion was not mandatory.

Kamal suffered torments in the desert while they exchanged kisses in the bridal chamber like any other human beings. There would be sweaty sighs and then swooning as blood trickled out. A nightgown would slip away to reveal a mortal body. Such was the world of human beings with its empty hopes and frivolous dreams.

"Weep to your heart's content over the abasement of the gods. Fill your soul with this tragedy. But what's to become of the astounding, dazzling feeling that's lit up your heart for the past four years? It wasn't imaginary or an echo of something imaginary, but life itself.

Even if the force of circumstances can overwhelm the body, what power's capable of taking on the spirit?"

Thus the beloved would remain his. Love would be his torment and refuge, just as bewilderment would be his diversion, until he stood before the Creator and asked about these complicated matters that perplexed him. If he could only see what was behind that window and discover the secrets of his existence. . . . The cold stung him at times, reminding him of his situation and of the reckless passage of time. But why should he hurry home? Did he really hope sleep would visit him that night?

32 ≈

The wheels of the carriage that stopped in front of Ahmad Abd al-Jawad's store were spattered with the mud of al-Nahhasin Street and with the water collected in its potholes. Mr. Muhammad Iffat, wearing a wool cloak, stepped down and went into the store. He laughingly commented, "We came in a carriage. It would have been safer to come by boat."

It had been pouring rain for a day and a half. The ground was soaked, and the alleys and cul-de-sacs were flooded. Although the rains had finally abated, the gloomy sky had not cleared yet. Clouds overshadowed the earth in a dark canopy that made the air murky enough to presage a pitch-black night.

Ahmad Abd al-Jawad welcomed his friend and invited him to sit down. Muhammad Iffat had scarcely settled himself in a chair by the corner of the desk when he disclosed the reason for this unexpected visit: "Don't be surprised that I've come in this weather even though we'll meet at our usual party in a few hours. I wanted to talk to you privately." He laughed as though to apologize for these strange words. Al-Sayyid Ahmad laughed too, but his laughter seemed almost more like a question.

Jamil al-Hamzawi, his head wrapped from chin to crown in a scarf, went to the door, where he called to the waiter at the Qala'un coffeehouse to bring some coffee. Then he returned to his chair, since the rain and cold had freed him from waiting on customers.

Al-Sayyid Ahmad sensed in his heart that there was an important reason for this visit, since it came at a time when only dire necessity could justify it. He was more anxious than usual because of the psychological crises he had suffered and the ill health he had experienced of late. All the same, he camouflaged his anxiety with a polite laugh and said, "Just before you arrived I was remembering last night and what al-Far looked like dancing. May God strike him down."

Smiling, Muhammad Iffat said, "We're all your pupils! With regard to this, let me tell you what Ali Abd al-Rahim's been saying about you. He claims the headache you've had for the past weeks results from a lack of women in your life during this time."

"A lack of women? Is there any cause for headaches besides women?"

The waiter appeared carrying a yellow tray with glasses of coffee and of water, placed it on the corner of the desk between the two friends, and then departed.

Muhammad Iffat drank some water and said, "It's pleasant to drink cold water in winter. What do you think? But why should I ask? You're one of winter's admirers and bathe every morning in cold water, even now in February. So tell me: Did you like the news of the nationalist conference held in the home of Muhammad Mahmud? We've lived to see Sa'd, Adli, and Tharwat all in a united front once more."

"Our Lord in His wisdom welcomes repentance."

"I don't trust those dogs."

"I don't either. But what can be done? King Fuad's made things worse. It's sad the struggle's no longer against the English."

They began to drink their coffee silently. This indicated, if anything, that the period for making polite conversation had ended. It was time for Muhammad Iffat to speak his mind. He sat up straight and asked al-Sayyid Ahmad earnestly, "What do you hear from Yasin?"

The anxious concern the question evoked was evident in the man's wide eyes. His heart began pounding at an alarming rate. He answered, "Good news! He visits from time to time. The most recent one was last Monday. Is there something new? A matter relating to Maryam? Her whereabouts are unknown. I learned recently that Bayumi the drinks vendor bought her share of her mother's house."

Trying to smile, Muhammad Iffat said, "The matter doesn't concern Maryam. Who knows? Perhaps he's forgotten her. I won't beat around the bush. It's a new marriage."

His heart was pounding again in a frightening way. He exclaimed, "A new marriage! But he's made absolutely no reference to it in his conversations with me."

Muhammad Iffat shook his head regretfully and said, "He's been married for a month or more. Ghunaym Hamidu told me just an hour ago. He assumed you knew all about it."

Al-Sayyid Ahmad's left hand began to fidget with his mustache nervously. Then, as though addressing himself, he said, "It's gone that far! How can I believe it? How could he have kept it from me?"

"The circumstances dictated secrecy. Listen to me. I wanted to tell you the truth before it came to you as an unpleasant surprise. But don't rail against it more than it deserves. And above all, you mustn't get angry. Anger's not something your health can withstand anymore. Remember how tired you've been and have pity on yourself."

Al-Sayyid Ahmad asked desperately, "Is there a scandal involved? That's what my heart senses. Tell me what you know, Mr. Muhammad."

Muhammad Iffat nodded his head sadly. Then in a low voice he said, "Be the brave Ahmad Abd al-Jawad we've always known.... Yasin's married Zanuba the lute player."

"Zanuba!"

They exchanged glances that showed their full grasp of the significance of this news. Ahmad's discomfort was obvious from his face, and his friend looked apprehensive. The question of the marriage itself no longer seemed so important. Al-Sayyid Ahmad asked breathlessly, "Do you suppose Zanuba knows he's my son?"

"I don't doubt it, but I'm almost certain she hasn't revealed your secret to him. Otherwise she would have had more difficulty getting him to fall into her trap. She's succeeded so admirably in this that she deserves our congratulations."

But Ahmad Abd al-Jawad asked again in the same breathless voice, "Or do you think he kept it from me because he knew what had happened?"

"Of course not. I don't believe that. If he had known this in advance he would never have married her. No doubt he's a reckless young man, but he's not depraved. If he kept it a secret from you, it's because he couldn't get up the courage to tell you he'd married a woman entertainer. What a burden headstrong sons are to their fathers.... The truth is that it upsets me terribly, but I hope you won't allow yourself to get angry. It's his fault. You're not responsible for what he's done. No one can blame you."

Ahmad Abd al-Jawad sighed audibly. Then he instructed his friend, "Tell me what Ghunaym Hamidu said about this."

Muhammad Iffat waved his hand disdainfully and replied, "He asked if al-Sayyid Ahmad had agreed. I told him, 'The man knows nothing about it.' He expressed his regrets and said, 'See how big a gap there is between the father and his son. May God come to his aid.'"

In a mournful voice Ahmad commented, "Is this the result of the way I've raised them? I'm bewildered, Mr. Muhammad. The disaster is that we lose effective control of them just when they most require our guidance for their welfare. They're old enough to take responsibility for themselves, but they mishandle their affairs and we're not able to straighten them out. We're men, but our sons aren't. What do you suppose has caused this? The ox! Why did he have to marry a woman within reach of every hand? Let's weep for ourselves. There's no power or might save God's."

Muhammad Iffat placed his hand sympathetically on his friend's shoulder. "We've done our duty," he said. "Beyond that each person's responsible for himself. It's impossible for anyone to think you're to blame."

Then al-Hamzawi's sad voice spoke up: "No fair person would blame you for something like this, al-Sayyid, sir. Although it seems to me there's still hope for reform. Give him some advice, al-Sayyid, sir."

"He'll stand before you like an obedient child. He'll certainly divorce her tomorrow or the next day. The best good deed is a quick one."

Al-Sayyid Ahmad asked plaintively, "What if she's pregnant?"

Al-Hamzawi's anxious voice said, "May God not decree or allow that."

Muhammad Iffat seemed to have more to say. He looked at his friend apprehensively and then remarked, "It's really sad that he sold his store in al-Hamzawi to refurnish his apartment."

Ahmad stared at him. He frowned in disgust and yelled resentfully, "As if I didn't exist! . . . He didn't even consult me about that."

Striking his hands together, he continued: "No doubt they robbed him blind. They came upon an easy prey . . . a mule without a groom, wearing a gentleman's clothes."

Muhammad Iffat said compassionately, "Childish behavior! He forgot his father and his son. But what's the use of getting angry?"

Ahmad Abd al-Jawad shouted, "It seems to me that regardless of the consequences I've got to deal with him firmly."

Muhammad Iffat stretched out his arms as though to ward off danger. Then he said imploringly, " 'When your son grows up, be a brother to him.' All that's required of you is some advice. Leave the rest to God and His decree." He lowered his eyes thoughtfully and seemed to hesitate for a few moments. Then he said, "There's something that concerns me as much at it does you . . . the question of our grandson Ridwan."

The two men exchanged a long look. Then Muhammad Iffat continued: "In a few months the boy will be seven. I'm afraid his father will ask for custody, and Ridwan will grow up in Zanuba's home.

This evil must be averted. I don't imagine you'd agree to it either. So convince Yasin to leave the boy with us, until God straightens things out."

It was contrary to the nature of Ahmad Abd al-Jawad to agree voluntarily to allow his grandson to remain with the mother's family beyond the period established by law for her custody, but he also did not wish to suggest that the boy become part of his own household, for fear of adding to Amina's burdens another one she could not be considered eager to assume, because of her age. So with sad resignation he answered, "I admit it wouldn't be right for Ridwan to be reared in Zanuba's home."

Sighing with relief, Muhammad Iffat said, "His grandmother loves him with all her heart. Even if unavoidable circumstances in the future forced him to be transferred to his mother's home, he would be in good hands, for his mother's married to a man in his forties or older, deprived by God of the blessing of offspring."

Ahmad Abd al-Jawad said hopefully, "But I'd prefer him to stay with you."

"Of course, of course. I was just speaking about remote possibilities, which I pray that God will never impose on us. Now all I have to say is to be gentle when you speak to Yasin so it'll be easier to convince him to leave Ridwan with me."

Then al-Hamzawi's conciliatory voice said, "Al-Sayyid Ahmad's the wisest man I know. He realizes Yasin's a man who, like other men, is free to act as he pleases and to dispose of his possessions. Al-Sayyid Ahmad knows these things. He simply needs to advise his son. The rest is up to God."

Ahmad Abd al-Jawad gave over the remainder of the day to sorrowful reflection. He told himself, "In a word, Yasin's a loss as a son. There's nothing more miserable than having a son who's a disappointment. Unfortunately, the direction he's heading is only too clear. No particular insight's required to discern it. Yes, he'll go from bad to worse and need all the grace God grants him."

Jamil al-Hamzawi asked him to postpone his talk with Yasin until the next day. He yielded to this request, more from despair than because he valued the advice.

He summoned Yasin to meet him the following afternoon. As was appropriate for an obedient son, Yasin hastened to comply with his father's request. The truth was that Yasin had not severed relations with his family. The old house was the only place he had not had the courage to visit, even though he felt homesick for it. Every time he met his father, Khadija, or Aisha he would ask them to convey his greetings to his stepmother. If he had not forgotten her anger with him or what he termed her obstinacy, he also refused to overlook the old days when she was the only mother he knew. He had not stopped visiting his sisters. Occasionally he met Kamal in Ahmad Abduh's coffeehouse. He would also invite his younger brother to his home, where Kamal encountered Maryam first and then Zanuba. Yasin visited his father at his store at least once a week. This call allowed him to observe another side of his father's personality, the one al-Sayyid Ahmad used to captivate people. A solid friendship and a deep affection flourished between the two men, encouraged both by the ties of blood and by Yasin's joy at discovering his father.

Even so, when Yasin examined his father's face that afternoon, its expression reminded him of the old look, which had so frequently terrified him. He did not ask what was bothering his father, for he was sure he would discover the secret sooner or later. No doubt he was encountering the tempest he had expected ever since acting so rashly.

Before he could speak, his father said, "I'm sad to find myself so humiliated. Why should I have to learn my son's news from third parties?"

Yasin bowed his head but did not breathe a word. His father was outraged by this deceitful veneer of humility, shouting, "Take off that mask. Don't play the hypocrite. Let me hear your voice. You know what I'm talking about."

In a scarcely audible whisper Yasin said, "I couldn't get up the courage to tell you."

"This happens when someone tries to conceal an offense or a scandal."

Yasin knew instinctively that he should not attempt any form of resistance. So he said with resignation, "Yes. . . ."

Aghast, al-Sayyid Ahmad asked, "If that's really what you think, then why did you do it?"

Yasin resorted to silence once more. His father imagined this failure to reply indicated: "I knew it was scandalous, but I gave in to love." He was reminded of his own disgraceful situation with the same woman.

"How shameful!" al-Sayyid Ahmad told himself. "You washed away your humiliation with an outburst of anger, but then you started pursuing her again. . . . And what a loss this ox is!"

"You embraced a scandal without any consideration of the consequences, which you let all the rest of us suffer."

Yasin cried out ingenuously, "All of you? God forbid."

Furious again, al-Sayyid Ahmad shouted, "Don't pretend to be stupid! Don't claim you're innocent. When you're trying to satisfy your lusts, you pay no attention to the damage you're doing to your father's reputation or that of your brother and sisters. You've forced a lute player on the family. She'll be one of us along with her children. I don't imagine I'm telling you anything new. But you ignore everything for the sake of lust. You've disgraced the family's honor. You yourself are collapsing stone by stone. In the end you'll find you're nothing but a ruin."

Yasin lowered his eyes and was silent for so long that his guilt and submission were obvious.

"This scandal will only cost you a certain amount of theatrics, so far as I can see," al-Sayyid Ahmad fumed to himself. "That's all it means to you, but tomorrow I'll be blessed with a grandson who has Zanuba for a mother and Zubayda as his great-aunt . . . a unique relationship linking the well-known merchant al-Sayyid Ahmad to Zubayda the notorious singer. Perhaps we're atoning for sins we're not even conscious of."

"I tremble when I think of your future. I told you that you're falling apart. Your collapse will become more and more evident. Tell me what you did with the store in al-Hamzawi?"

Yasin raised his melancholy eyes and hesitated momentarily. Then he said, "I was in urgent need of money." Looking down, he continued: "Had the circumstances been different, I would have borrowed what I needed from you, sir, but it was an embarrassing situation. . . ."

Al-Sayyid Ahmad replied furiously, "What a hypocrite you are! Aren't you ashamed of yourself? I bet you didn't see anything odd or reprehensible in what you did. I know you and understand you. So don't try to deceive me. I just have one thing to say to you, even though I know in advance it's pointless: You're ruining yourself, and your fate will be grim."

Yasin was silent once more and pretended to be distressed.

"The ox!" his father thought. "She's an attractive devil, but what forced you to marry her? I imagined she asked me to marry her because of my age. But she trapped this bull, even though he's young." He felt some relief and consolation at that. "Her premeditated plan was to get married at any cost, but she preferred another man. And this fool fell for it."

"Divorce her! Divorce her before she becomes a mother and we're disgraced for generations to come."

After hesitating for some time, Yasin mumbled, "It would be wrong for me to divorce her without any cause."

"You son of a bitch!" he exclaimed to himself. "You've presented me with an exquisite anecdote for tonight's party."

"You'll divorce her sooner or later. Do it before she bears a child, who'll be a problem for you and the rest of us."

Yasin sighed audibly, allowing that to serve as his response. His father began to examine him rather anxiously. Fahmy was dead. Kamal was an idiot or insane. Yasin was hopeless. "The sad thing is that he's the dearest to me of them all. Leave the matter to God. O Lord! What would have happened if my foot had slipped and I'd married her?"

"How much did you get for the shop?"

"Two hundred pounds."

"It was worth three hundred. It was an excellent location, ignoramus. Who bought it?"

"Ali Tulun . . . he sells sundries."

"Great! Congratulations! Was the whole sum squandered on the new furnishings?"

"I still have a hundred."

"You've done well," he said sarcastically. "So the bridegroom's not short of cash." Then he continued in a serious and mournful tone: "Yasin, listen to me. I'm your father. Watch out. Reform your conduct. You're a father yourself. Don't you think of your son and his future?"

Yasin protested vehemently, "The monthly support payment gets to him down to the last millieme."

"Is it just a matter of money? I'm talking about his future . . . and about the future of other children still unborn."

"Our Lord creates and provides sustenance," Yasin said with calm assurance.

His father yelled disapprovingly, "Our Lord creates and you fritter away your sustenance. Tell me. . . ." He sat up straight and then, focusing his eyes forcefully on his son, commented, "Ridwan's almost seven. What are you going to do with him? Are you going to take him and have him grow up under your wife's supervision?"

Yasin's plump face looked uneasy. He asked in turn, "What should I do, then? I haven't thought about it."

The man shook his head sadly and ironically. He said, "May God preserve you from the evil of thinking. Do you have any time to waste on it? Let me think for you. Allow me to tell you that Ridwan must stay in the custody of his maternal grandfather."

Yasin reflected for a moment. Then he expressed his agreement by lowering his head. He said obediently, "Whatever you think best, Father. No doubt that's in his best interest."

His father replied sarcastically, "It seems to be in your best interest too. That'll save you from troubling yourself with such trivial matters."

Yasin's only comment was a smile that implied: "I'm sure you're teasing me, but that's all right."

"I thought it would be hard to convince you to surrender custody."

"It's the confidence I place in your opinion that made it so easy to convince me."

With ironic astonishment al-Sayyid Ahmad asked, "Do you really place so much confidence in my opinion? Why don't you act on it in other matters?" Sighing sadly, he continued: "What's the point? . . . May our Lord guide you. The guilt's all yours. I'll speak to Muhammad Iffat tonight about retaining custody of Ridwan, with the understanding that you'll bear all the boy's expenses. Perhaps he'll agree."

Yasin rose then, said goodbye to his father, and headed for the shop door. He had only taken two steps when he heard his father's voice ask, "Don't you love your son like any other father?"

Stopping to look back, Yasin said reproachfully, "Is there any doubt of that, Father? He's the dearest thing in my life."

Al-Sayyid Ahmad raised his eyebrows. Shaking his head cryptically, he said, "Goodbye."

33 ✑

An hour before his departure for the Friday prayer service, Ahmad Abd al-Jawad summoned Kamal to his room. He never called a member of his family to see him unless the subject was important, and something was indeed troubling him. He was impatient to interrogate his son about a matter that had disturbed him. The previous evening some friends had directed his attention to an article in *al-Balagh* attributed to "the young writer Kamal Ahmad Abd al-Jawad." The men had not read any of the article except its title, "The Origin of Man," and the credit, but they took advantage of it to congratulate and tease al-Sayyid Ahmad, offering various comments. Concerned that such praise might attract the evil eye, he had seriously considered commissioning Shaykh Mutawalli Abd al-Samad to prepare a special talisman for the young man.

Muhammad Iffat had said, "Your son's name is printed in the same magazine with those of important authors. Take heart! Pray that God will prepare a career for him as dazzling as theirs."

Ali Abd al-Rahim had told him, "I heard from a reliable source that the late writer al-Manfaluti bought a country estate with the profits of his pen. So hope for the best."

Others had mentioned how writing had opened the way for many to find favor with the ruling elite, citing the authors Shawqi, Hafiz, and al-Manfaluti.

Ibrahim al-Far had used his turn to kid him: "Glory to the One who created a scholar from the loins of a fool."

Al-Sayyid Ahmad had cast one glance at the title and another at the reference to the "young writer" before placing the magazine on his cloak, which he had removed because of the June heat and a warm feeling derived from whiskey. He had postponed reading the article until he was alone—at home or in his store—and had continued to feel happy, boastful, and proud throughout the evening's festivities. In fact, for the first time he had begun to reconsider his hostility toward Kamal's choice of the Teachers College, telling himself it seemed "the boy" would amount to "something," in spite of that unfortunate choice. He started to fantasize about "the pen," gaining favor with the elite, and al-Manfaluti's country estate. Yes, who could say? Perhaps Kamal would not be just a teacher. He might really make a better life for himself than al-Sayyid Ahmad had dreamed possible.

The following morning, after prayers and breakfast, al-Sayyid Ahmad made himself comfortable on the sofa and opened the magazine with interest. He began to read it out loud to get the sense of it. But what did he find? He could read political articles and understand them without difficulty. But this essay made his head turn and agitated his heart. He read it aloud again carefully. He came across a reference to a scientist named Darwin and his work on some distant islands. This man had made tedious comparisons between various different animals until he was astonished to reach the strange conclusion that man was descended from animals; in fact, that he had evolved from a kind of ape. Al-Sayyid Ahmad read the offensive paragraph yet another time with increasing alarm. He was stunned by the sad reality that his son, his own flesh and blood, was asserting, without objection or discussion, that man was descended from animals. He was extremely upset and wondered in bewilderment whether boys were really taught such dangerous ideas in government schools. Then he sent for Kamal.

Kamal arrived, not having the least idea of what was on his father's mind. Since he had been summoned a few days before so his father could congratulate him on his promotion to the third year of the Teachers College, he did not suspect that this new invitation implied anything unpleasant. He had grown pale and emaciated of late. His family attributed this to the exceptional effort he put out before an examination. The real secret was hidden from them. It was the pain and torment he had suffered for the last five months as a prisoner of hellishly tyrannical emotion, which had almost killed him.

Al-Sayyid Ahmad gestured for him to sit down. Kamal sat at the end of the sofa, facing his father politely. He noticed that his mother was seated near the wardrobe, busy folding and mending clothes. Then his father threw the copy of *al-Balagh* down in the space between them on the sofa and said with feigned composure, "You've got an article in this magazine. Isn't that so?"

The cover caught Kamal's eye. His look of astonishment made it clear that he had certainly not been expecting this surprise. Where had his father acquired this new familiarity with literary journals? In a magazine called *al-Sabah*, Kamal had previously published some "reflections," or innocent philosophical speculations and emotional laments in both regular and rhymed prose. He was quite sure his father did not know about them. The only member of the family who did was Yasin. Kamal himself had read them to his brother. Yasin's comment had been: "This is the fruit of my early guidance. I'm the one who taught you about poetry and stories. It's beautiful, Professor. But this philosophy's really deep. Where'd you pick that up?" Yasin had teased him: "What pretty girl inspired this delicate complaint? Professor, one day you'll learn that nothing works with women except beating them with a shoe."

But now his father had read the most dangerous thing he had written—this essay that had stirred up the devil of a battle in his breast when he was thinking about it. His mind had almost been incinerated in that furnace. How had this happened? What explanation could there be unless some of his father's friends who were Wafd Party loyalists made a point of buying all the papers and journals affiliated with the party? Could he hope to escape safely from this predicament? He looked up from the magazine. In a tone that did not even begin to convey his inner turmoil, he answered, "Yes. I thought I'd write something to bolster what I was learning and to encourage myself to continue my studies. . . ."

With spurious calm, al-Sayyid Ahmad commented, "There's nothing wrong with that. Writing for the papers has been and still is a way to gain prestige and recognition from the elite. What's important is the topic a person writes about. What did you intend by this article? Read it and explain it to me. It's not clear what you were getting at."

What a disaster this was! The essay had not been intended for the general public and especially not for his father. "It's a long article, Papa. Didn't you read it, sir? I explain a scientific theory in it. . . ."

His father stared at him with an impatient, glinting look. "Is this what they claim is science nowadays?" al-Sayyid Ahmad asked himself. "God's curse on science and scientists."

"What do you say about this theory? I noticed some strange phrases that seem to imply that man is descended from animals, or something along those lines. Is this true?"

Kamal had recently struggled violently with his soul, his beliefs, and his Lord, exhausting his spirit and body. Today he had to contend with his father. In the first battle he had felt tortured and feverish, but this time he was even more frightened and alarmed. God might delay punishment, but his father's practice was to mete out retribution immediately.

"That's what the theory states."

Al-Sayyid Ahmad's voice rose as he asked in dismay, "And Adam, the father of mankind, whom God created from clay, blowing His spirit into him—what does this scientific theory say about him?"

Kamal had repeatedly asked himself this same question, finding it just as dismaying as his father did. The night he had worried about it, he had not been able to get any sleep. He had thrashed about in bed wondering about Adam, the Creator, and the Qur'an. If he had said it once he had said ten times: "Either the Qur'an is totally true, or it's not the Qur'an." Now he thought, "You're attacking me because you don't know how I've suffered. If I hadn't already grown accustomed to torture, I would have died that night."

In a faint voice he replied, "Darwin, the author of this theory, did not mention our master Adam. . . ."

The man yelled angrily, "Then Darwin's certainly an atheist trapped by Satan's snares. If man's origin was an ape or any other animal, Adam was not the father of mankind. This is nothing but blatant atheism. It's an outrageous attack on the exalted status of God. I know Coptic Christians and Jews in the Goldsmiths Bazaar. They believe in Adam. All religions believe in Adam. What sect does this Darwin belong to? He's an atheist, his words are blasphemous, and reporting his theory's a reckless act. Tell me: Is he one of your professors at the college?"

"How ridiculous this comment would seem if my heart were free to laugh," Kamal mused. "But it's crammed with the pains of disappointed love, doubt, and dying belief. The dreadful encounter of religion and science has scorched you. But how can an intelligent person set his mind against science?"

In a humble voice, Kamal said, "Darwin was an English scientist who lived a long time ago."

At this point, the mother's voice piped up shakily: "God's curse on all the English."

They turned to look at her briefly and found that she had put down her needle and the clothes in order to follow their conversation. They soon forgot her, and the father said, "Tell me: Do you study this theory in school?"

Kamal grabbed for this safety rope suddenly thrown to him. Hiding behind a lie, he said, "Yes."

"That's strange! Will you eventually teach this theory to your pupils?"

"Certainly not! I'll teach literature, and there's no connection between that and scientific theories."

Al-Sayyid Ahmad struck his hands together. At that moment he wished he had as much control over science as he did over his family. He yelled furiously, "Then why do they teach it to you? Is the goal to turn you into atheists?"

Kamal protested, "God forbid that it should have any influence on our religious beliefs."

His father studied him suspiciously and said, "But your essay spreads atheism."

Kamal replied gingerly, "I ask God's forgiveness. I'm explaining the theory so the reader will be familiar with it, not so he'll believe it. It's out of the question that an atheistic notion should influence the heart of a Believer."

"Couldn't you find some other subject besides this criminal theory to write about?"

Why had he written this article? He had hesitated a long time before sending it to the journal. He must have wanted to announce the demise of his religious beliefs. His faith had held firm over the past two years even when buffeted by gales coming from two of the great poets and skeptics of Islam: Abu al-Ala al-Ma'arri and Umar al-Khayyam. But then science's iron fist had destroyed it once and for all.

"At least I'm not an atheist," Kamal told himself. "I still believe in God. But religion? . . . Where's religion? . . . It's gone! I lost it, just as I lost the head of the holy martyr al-Husayn when I was told it's not in his tomb in Cairo . . . and I've lost Aïda and my self-confidence too."

Then in a sorrowful voice he said, "Maybe I made a mistake. My excuse is that I was studying the theory."

"That's no excuse. You must correct your error."

What a good man his father was—wanting to get Kamal to attack science in order to defend a legend. He really had suffered a lot, but he would not open his heart again to legends and superstitions now that he had cleansed it of them.

"I've experienced enough torment and deception," Kamal reflected. "From now on I won't be taken in by fantasies. Light's light. Our father Adam! He wasn't my father. Let my father be an ape, if that's what truth wants. It's better than being one of countless descendants of Adam. If I really were descended from a prophet like Adam, reality wouldn't have made such a fool of me."

"How can I correct my error?"

Al-Sayyid Ahmad said with equal measures of simplicity and

sharpness, "You can rely on a fact that's beyond doubt: God created Adam from dust, and Adam's the father of mankind. This fact is mentioned in the Qur'an. Just explain the erroneous aspects of the theory. That'll be easy for you. If it isn't, what's the use of your education?"

Here the mother's voice said, "What could be easier than showing the error of someone who contradicts the word of God the Merciful? Tell this English atheist that Adam was the father of mankind. Your grandfather was blessed by knowing the Book of God by heart. It's up to you to follow his example. I'm delighted that you wish to be a scholar like him."

Al-Sayyid Ahmad's displeasure was apparent in his expression. He scolded her, "What do you understand about the Book of God or scholarship? Spare us his grandfather and pay attention to what you're doing."

She said shyly, "Sir, I want him to be a scholar like his grandfather, illuminating the world with God's light."

Her husband shouted angrily, "And here he's begun to spread darkness."

The woman replied apprehensively, "God forbid, sir. Perhaps you didn't understand."

Al-Sayyid Ahmad glared at her harshly. He had relaxed his grip on them, and what had been the result? Here was Kamal disseminating the theory that man's origin was an ape. Amina was arguing with him and suggesting he did not understand. He yelled at his wife, "Let me speak! Don't interrupt me. Don't interfere in things you can't comprehend. Pay attention to your work. May God strike you down."

Turning to Kamal with a frowning face, he said, "Tell me: Will you do what I said?"

"You're living with a censor who's more relentless than any afflicting free thought elsewhere in the world," Kamal told himself. "But you love him as much as you fear him. Your heart will never allow you to harm him. Swallow the pain, for you've chosen a life of disputation."

"How can I answer this theory? If I limit my debate to citing Qur'an references, I won't be adding anything new. Everyone knows them as well as I do and believes them. To discuss it scientifically is a matter for specialists in that area."

"So why did you write about something outside your area?"

Taken at face value, this objection was valid. Unfortunately Kamal lacked the courage to tell his father that he believed in the theory as scientific truth and for this reason had felt he could rely on it to create a general philosophy for existence reaching far beyond science. Al-Sayyid Ahmad considered his silence an admission of error and so felt even more resentful and sad. To be misled on a topic like this was an extremely grave matter with serious consequences, but it was a field where al-Sayyid Ahmad could exercise no authority. He felt that his hands were as tied with this young freethinker as they had been previously with Yasin when he had escaped from paternal custody. Was he to share the experience of other fathers in these strange times? He had heard incredible things about the younger generation. Some schoolboys were smoking. Others openly questioned their teachers' integrity. Still others had rebelled against their fathers. His own prestige had not been diminished, but what had his long history of resolute and stern guidance achieved? Yasin was stumbling and practically doomed. Here was Kamal arguing, debating, and attempting to slip from his grasp.

"Listen carefully to me. I don't want to be harsh with you, for you're polite and obedient. On this subject, I can only offer you my advice. You should remember that no one who has neglected my advice has prospered." Then after a brief silence he continued: "Yasin's an example for you of what I'm saying, and I once advised your late brother not to throw himself to destruction. Had he lived, he would be a distinguished man today."

At this point the mother said in a voice like a moan, "The English killed him. When they're not killing people, they're spreading atheism."

Al-Sayyid Ahmad went on with his remarks: "If you find things in your lessons that contradict religion and are forced to memorize them to succeed in the examination, don't believe them. And it's equally important not to publish them in the papers. Otherwise you'll bear the responsibility. Let your stance with regard to English science be the same as yours toward their occupation of Egypt. Do not admit the legality of either, even when imposed on us by force."

The shy, gentle voice interposed once more: "From now on, dedicate your life to exposing the lies of this science and spreading the light of God."

Al-Sayyid Ahmad shouted at her, "I've said enough without any need for your views."

She returned to her work, while her husband stared at her in a threatening way until sure she would be quiet. Then he looked at Kamal and asked, "Understand?"

"Most certainly," Kamal answered in a voice that inspired confidence.

From that time on, if he wanted to write he would have to publish in *al-Siyasa*. Because of its political affiliation it would never fall into the hands of a Wafdist. And he secretly promised his mother he would consecrate his life to spreading God's light. Were not light and truth identical? Certainly! By freeing himself from religion he would be nearer to God than he was when he believed. For what was true religion except science? It was the key to the secrets of existence and to everything really exalted. If the prophets were sent back today, they would surely choose science as their divine message. Thus Kamal would awake from the dream of legends to confront the naked truth, leaving behind him this storm in which ignorance had fought to the death. It would be a dividing point between his past, dominated by legend, and his future, dedicated to light. In this manner the paths leading to God would open before him—paths of learning, benevolence, and beauty. He would say goodbye to the past with its deceitful dreams, false hopes, and profound pains.

34 ~

He carefully considered everything his eyes could soak up as he approached the Shaddad mansion. Once inside its grounds he redoubled the attention with which he scrutinized his surroundings. He understood that this visit would be his last chance to enjoy the house, its inhabitants, and the memories it held for him. What else could he think, since Husayn had finally won his father's approval to travel to France? With keen eyes and emotions he observed the side path leading to the garden and the window overlooking the path. He could almost see her elegant and graceful figure casting him a beautiful look, one as meaningless as the twinkling of a star. It was a tender greeting addressed to no one in particular—like the song of a bulbul so enthralled by its own happiness that it is oblivious to its audience. Next came the magnificent view of the garden, which stretched from the back of the house to the long wall bordering the desert. Scattered through it were trellises of jasmine, clumps of palms, and rosebushes. Finally there was the gazebo, where he had experienced the twin intoxications of love and friendship. He recalled the English proverb "Don't put all your eggs in one basket," and smiled sadly. Although he had memorized it long before, he had found it unconvincing then. Whether through carelessness, stupidity, or predestined decree, he had invested his whole heart in this one house, partly in love and partly in friendship. He had lost his love, and now his friend was packing for a trip abroad. In the future he would find himself without a lover or a friend.

What could console him for the loss of this view, which was imprinted in his breast and attached to his heart? It had become familiar and sympathetic, as a whole and in its individual parts—the mansion, the garden, and the desert. The names Aïda and Husayn Shaddad had been etched in his memory in similar fashion. How could he be deprived of this sight or content himself with glimpsing it from afar, like any other passerby? He was so infatuated with the house that once he had jokingly accused himself of idolatry.

Husayn Shaddad and Isma'il Latif were sitting opposite each other at the table, on which was placed the customary water pitcher with three glasses. As usual in summer, each wore a shirt with an open collar and white pants. They looked up at him with their contrasting faces. Husayn's was handsome and radiant. Isma'il's had sharp features and penetrating eyes. Kamal approached them in his white suit, holding his fez as the tassel swung to and fro. They shook hands, and he sat down with his back to the house ... a house that had previously turned its back on him.

Laughing naughtily, Isma'il immediately told Kamal, "It's up to us to find a new place to meet from now on."

Kamal smiled wanly. How happy Isma'il was with his sarcasm, which had never been racked by pain. He and Fuad al-Hamzawi were all Kamal had left. They were friends who would keep his heart company but never blend with it. He would rush to them to escape his loneliness. His only choice was to accept his destiny with good grace.

"We'll have to meet in the coffeehouses or streets, since Husayn's decided to leave us."

Husayn shook his head with the sorrow of a person who has won a coveted objective and is trying to humor friends by appearing sad about a separation that means little to him. He said, "I'll leave Egypt with regret in my heart over my separation from you. Friendship's a sacred emotion I cherish with all my heart. A friend's a partner who's a reflection of yourself. He echoes your sentiments and thoughts. It doesn't matter if we differ in many respects so long as our essential characteristics are the same. I'll never forget this friendship, and we'll keep writing each other until we meet again."

A pretty speech was the only consolation offered a wounded heart that was being forsaken ... as if Kamal had not suffered enough at the hands of Husayn's sister. "Is this how you abandon me, leaving me without any real friends?" Kamal wondered. "Tomorrow the forsaken friend will be slain by a mocking thirst for spiritual companionship."

He asked dejectedly, "When will we meet again? I haven't forgotten your keen desire to be a perpetual tourist. Who will guarantee your departure won't be permanent?"

Isma'il agreed. "My heart tells me the sparrow won't fly back into the cage."

Husayn laughed briefly but in a way that revealed his delight. He answered, "I wasn't able to win my father's consent to travel until I promised to continue my legal studies. But I don't know how long I'll be able to keep that promise. There's no great affection between me and the law. Besides, I imagine I won't have much patience with systematic instruction. I only want things I love. My heart's torn between various different forms of knowledge. No one college deals with all of them, as I've told you time and again. I wish to attend lectures on philosophy of art as well as others on poetry and fiction. I want to tour the museums and recital halls, fall in love, and have a good time. What college or faculty offers all these opportunities? Then there's another fact you both know. It's that I'd rather hear than read. I want someone else to do the explaining while I listen. Then I'll dash off—my senses at their most perceptive and my mind alert—to mountainsides, seashores, bars, cafés, and dance halls. You'll be receiving a series of reports from me on all these unique experiences."

Husayn seemed to be describing the paradise Kamal had ceased believing in. But Husayn's was a negative paradise, full of taking without any giving. Kamal had aspired to a more positive one. Once this rosy life embraced Husayn to her comely bosom, it was absurd to think he would ever long for his old home.

Isma'il expressed some of Kamal's concerns when he told Husayn, "You won't return. Farewell, Husayn! We have approximately the same dream. Leaving aside the philosophy of art, museums, poetry, mountain slopes, and so forth, we could be a single person. I remind you one final time that you'll never return to us."

Kamal cast Husayn a questioning glance, as if to see what he thought about Isma'il's words.

Their friend said, "No, I'll return frequently. Egypt will be on my extensive itinerary so I can see my family and friends." Then he told Kamal, "I'll be waiting for you to visit Europe with such anxious anticipation that I can almost feel it already."

Who could say? Perhaps Kamal's lie would turn out to be the truth. Maybe he would traverse those distant realms. No matter what happened, his heart told him that Husayn would return one day and that this profound friendship would not end. His heart sincerely believed this, just as it had believed love could not be plucked from the heart, roots and all . . . alas.

He entreated his friend, "Travel and do whatever you want, but come back to Egypt to reside here. Then you can leave for trips when you feel like it."

Isma'il added his support to this idea: "If you're really a decent fellow, you'll accept this obvious solution, which reconciles your wishes with ours."

Bowing his head as if convinced, Husayn said, "My travels will eventually lead me to this solution, I believe."

As Kamal listened to Husayn, he gazed at his friend, especially at the black eyes that resembled Aïda's and the gestures, which were both grand and gracious. Husayn's diaphanous spirit was almost a visible and tangible presence for Kamal. If this dear friend disappeared, what would remain of the blessing of friendship and the memory of love . . . that friendship through which Kamal had learned Platonic affection and relaxed happiness . . . and the love that had inspired in him feelings of heavenly joy and hellish torment?

Referring to each of them in turn, Husayn continued: "When I return to Egypt you'll be an accountant in the Ministry of Finance and you'll be a teacher. It's quite possible I'll find you're fathers. What an amazing idea!"

Isma'il asked laughingly, "Can you imagine us as government employees? Try to picture Kamal as a teacher!" Then he told Kamal, "You'll have to put on a lot of weight before you stand in front of your pupils. You'll find the next generation's a bunch of demons. Compared with them we were angels. Although a dedicated supporter of the Wafd Party, you'll find yourself forced by the government to punish students who strike in support of the Wafd."

Isma'il's observation forced Kamal away from the train of thought absorbing him. He found himself wondering how he could face pupils with his notorious head and nose. He felt resentful and bitter, imagining—on the basis of the behavior of odd-looking teachers he had known—that he would treat his pupils harshly in order to protect himself from their mischief. But he also wondered whether he would be able to be as strict with others as he was with himself.

He ventured, "I don't think I'll always be a teacher."

There was a dreamy look in Husayn's eyes as he said, "You'll go from teaching into journalism, I suspect. Isn't that so?"

Kamal found himself thinking about the future. He thought again of the all-inclusive book he had often dreamt of writing. But what was left of the original subject matter? He no longer considered the prophets to have been prophets. Heaven and hell did not exist. The study of man was merely a branch of animal science. He would have to search for a new topic. Speaking impulsively again, he said, "If I could, I'd start a magazine someday to promote modern thought."

Isma'il admonished him, "No, politics is what sells publications. If you want, you can devote a column on the back page to thought. There's room in this country for a new Wafdist satirical writer."

Husayn laughed out loud and said, "Our friend doesn't seem to be very positive about politics. His family's already made a big enough sacrifice for the nation. But thought's a wide-open field for him." Then he told Kamal, "What you mentioned is certainly possible for you.... Your rebellion against religion was a sudden leap I didn't expect."

This observation cheered Kamal, for it sanctioned his rebellion and his pride. Blushing, he said, "How beautiful it would be if man could devote his life to truth, goodness, and beauty."

Isma'il whistled three times, once for each of these qualities. Then he said sarcastically, "Listen and take note!"

But Husayn said seriously, "I'm like you, but I'm satisfied with knowledge and enjoyment."

Enthusiastically and sincerely Kamal replied, "The matter's more exalted than that. It's a struggle toward truth aiming at the good of mankind as a whole. In my opinion, life would be meaningless without that."

Isma'il struck his hands together in a way that reminded Kamal of his father and said, "Then life necessarily has no meaning. How you've worn yourself out and suffered to free yourself from religion.... I haven't tired myself like that, because religion never interested me. Do you suppose I'm a born philosopher? It's enough for me to live a life that doesn't need to be explained. I'm instinctively drawn to what you achieve only after a bitter struggle. God forgive me, you haven't achieved it yet, for you still—even after renouncing religion—believe in truth, goodness, and beauty. You wish to dedicate your life to them. Isn't this what religion requests? How can you claim to reject a principle when you believe in everything derived from it?"

"Pay no attention to this gentle mockery," Kamal advised himself. But why should the values he believed in always seem to be the object of ridicule? "Suppose you had to choose between Aïda and a righteous life. Which would you choose? ... But when I think of her, Aïda's always identified with what's most exemplary."

Feeling the silence had lasted too long, Husayn answered for Kamal: "The Believer derives his love for these values from religion, while the free man loves them for themselves."

"O Lord, when will I see you again?" Kamal asked himself.

Isma'il laughed in a manner that revealed his thoughts were shifting to a new direction. He asked Kamal, "Tell me: Don't you still pray? Do you intend to fast as usual during Ramadan?"

"My invocations for her were the most enjoyable parts of my prayers," Kamal mused. "My evenings in this mansion were the happiest moments of Ramadan for me."

"I no longer pray. I won't fast."

"Will you tell people you're not?"

Laughing, Kamal said, "No."

"You prefer to be a hypocrite?"

He answered resentfully, "There's no need to hurt people I love."

Isma'il asked sarcastically, "If you're this softhearted, how do you think you'll ever be able to confront society with unpopular views?"

"What about a satiric fable like the classic 'Kalila and Dimna'?" Kamal asked himself. This splendid thought drove away his resentment. "Lord, have I stumbled on an idea for a book I never thought of before?"

"Addressing readers is one thing; telling parents you're not fasting is something else."

Gesturing toward Kamal, Isma'il told Husayn, "Here's a philosopher who comes from a family deeply rooted in ignorance."

"You'll never be at a loss for companions to play and joke around with, but you'll never gain another friend for your spirit capable of conversing directly with it," Kamal told himself. "So be content with silence or with talking to yourself like a lunatic."

They were all quiet for a time. The garden was silent too, for there was no breeze. Only the roses, carnations, and violets seemed to be enjoying the heat. The sun had withdrawn its luminous gown from the garden, leaving only a hem trailing over the east wall.

Isma'il ended the silence by turning to Husayn Shaddad and asking, "Do you suppose you'll get a chance to visit Hasan Salim and Mrs. Aïda?"

"My God!" Kamal exclaimed to himself. "Is it just my heart pounding or has the end of the world begun in my breast?"

"After I'm settled in Paris, I'll definitely think of visiting Brussels." Smiling, he added, "We received a letter from Aïda last week. It seems she's having morning sickness. . . ."

"So pain and life are twins," Kamal thought. "I'm nothing but unadulterated pain in a man's clothes. Aïda has a swelling belly awash with fluids. . . . Is this one of life's tragedies or comedies? The most blessed event of our lives will be our extinction. I wish I knew the essence of this pain."

Isma'il Latif exclaimed, "Their children will be foreigners!"

"It's agreed that they'll be sent to Egypt when they're old enough."

"Will you find them one day in a class of your students?" Kamal asked himself. "You'll wonder where you've seen those eyes. Your pounding heart will reply that they've been living inside you for a long time. If her little boy makes fun of your head and nose, will you have the heart to punish him? Forgetfulness, are you a legend too?"

Husayn went on: "She wrote at great length of her new life and didn't conceal her delight with it. In fact, she only said she missed her family to be polite."

"She was created for a life like this in one of those dream countries," Kamal reflected. "That she should partake of human nature was one more example of irreverent toying by the fates with things you hold sacred. Do you suppose it didn't occur to her to refer to her former friends in her chatty letter, not even with one word? . . . But how do you know she still remembers them?"

They were silent again. The sunset colors gradually began to turn a calm brown. A predatory kite could be seen circling in the distant sky. The barking of a dog reached them. Isma'il got a drink from the pitcher. Husayn started to whistle, while Kamal stealthily watched him with a placid face and a broken heart.

"The heat this year's dreadful." Ismai'il said that and dried his lips with an embroidered silk handkerchief. Then he burped and put the handkerchief back in his pocket.

"Separation from loved ones is even more dreadful," Kamal reflected.

"When are you leaving for the beach?"

"At the end of June," Isma'il said with evident relief.

Husayn said, "We're going to Ra's al-Barr tomorrow. I'll stay there a week with my family. Then I'll go with my father to Alexandria, where I'll board the ship the thirtieth of June."

The history of an era would end, and perhaps a heart would die. Husayn gazed at Kamal for some time. Then he laughed and said, "We leave you with the country happily united in a coalition of political parties. Perhaps news of Egyptian independence will precede me to Paris."

Addressing Husayn but pointing at Kamal, Isma'il exclaimed, "Your friend's not too happy about the coalition. It rubs him the wrong way for Sa'd Zaghlul to hold hands with traitors. It's even harder on him that Sa'd's agreed to avoid conflict with the British by leaving the post of Prime Minister to his longtime foe Adli. So you'll find that his views are even more immoderate than those of his revered leader."

"The truce with former enemies and traitors is one more disappointment you have to swallow," Kamal told himself. "Is there anything in this world that has lived up to your hopes?"

But he laughed out loud and said, "This coalition wants to impose a deputy from the Liberal Party on our district."

The three of them roared with laughter. A frog hopped into sight and then quickly disappeared in the grass. A breeze stirred, announcing the approach of evening. The clamor and commotion of the world encircling them began to diminish. The gathering would soon break up. That fact alarmed Kamal and made him look around to fill his eyes with the sights. Here for the first time he had experienced love. Here the angelic voice had sung out, "Kamal." Here the devastating conversation about his head and nose had taken place. Here the beloved had leveled her accusations against him. Beneath this sky lay memories of emotions, feelings, and reactions. These could not be disturbed by any power weaker than one capable of bringing the desert to life and making it bloom. He soaked up all of this and took pains to remember the date, for events frequently seem not to have happened if the day, month, and year are not fixed.

"We appeal to the sun and moon for help in escaping from time's straight line when we wish to circle back and regain our lost memories, but nothing ever returns," brooded Kamal. "So break down and cry or dispel your worries with a smile."

Isma'il Latif stood up and said, "The time's come for us to leave."

Kamal allowed Isma'il to embrace their friend first. Then his turn came, and they hugged each other at length. Kamal planted a kiss on Husayn's cheek and received one in return. The fragrance of the Shaddad family filled his nostrils. It had a gentle, zesty bouquet rare for a human being, like a puff of air from a dream that had circled in a sky replete with delights and pains. Kamal inhaled this scent until he grew tipsy. He was silent while he attempted to gain control of his emotions. All the same, his voice trembled when he said, "Till we meet again, even if it's not for a while."

35 ❧

"There's no one here but the staff!"

"That's because the day's hardly over. The patrons usually arrive with the night. Does the emptiness of the place upset you?"

"Not at all. It encourages me to stay, especially since it's the first time."

"Bars here have the priceless advantage of being situated on a street frequented only by people in search of forbidden pleasures. No scolding critic will trouble your peace of mind. If someone you respect—like your father or guardian—stumbles upon you, he's more at fault than you are and more apt to pretend he doesn't know you, or even to flee if he can."

"The name of the street itself is scandalous."

"But that makes it safer than any other. If we go to a bar on Alfi, Imad al-Din, or even Muhammad Ali streets, we could be seen by a father, brother, uncle, or some other important person. But they don't come here to Wajh al-Birka, hopefully."

"That makes sense, but I'm still uncomfortable."

"Be patient. The first step's always difficult, but alcohol's the key to joy. I promise you'll find the world a sweeter and more charming place by the time we depart."

"Tell me about the different kinds of drinks. What should I start with?"

"Cognac's strong. If it's mixed with beer, a person drinking it's as good as gone. Whiskey has an acceptable taste and produces excellent effects. Raisin liqueur . . ."

"That should be the most enjoyable! Haven't you heard Salih sing 'He poured me raisin liqueur'?"

"For a long time I've told you the only thing wrong with you is that you live in a fantasy world. Raisin liqueur's the worst drink of all, no matter what Salih says. It tastes like anise and upsets my digestion. Don't interrupt."

"Sorry!"

"Then there's beer, but that's a hot-weather drink, and, praise God, it's September. There's wine too, but its effect is like a slap from a bitch."

"So . . . so . . . it's whiskey."

"Bravo! For a long time I've had great hopes for you. Perhaps you'll soon agree you have an even greater aptitude for fun than for truth, goodness, beauty, nationalism, humanitarianism, and all the other fancy items over which you've pointlessly exhausted your heart." He called the waiter and ordered two whiskeys.

"The wisest thing would be for me to stop after one glass."

"That might be wise, but we didn't come here in search of wisdom. You'll learn for yourself that delirium's more pleasant than wisdom and that there's more to life than books and thought. Remember this day and don't forget who's to thank for it."

"I don't want to pass out. I'm afraid of that."

"Be your own physician."

"For me the important thing is to find the courage to walk down that alley with no hesitation and to enter one of those houses when I need to. . . ."

"Drink till you feel unconcerned about going in one."

"Fine. I hope I won't live to regret what I've done."

"Regret? I asked you repeatedly, but you excused yourself on religious grounds. Then you proclaimed you'd stopped believing in religion. So I renewed my invitation but was amazed to find you refusing in the name of morality. I must admit you finally bowed to logic."

Yes, at last he had . . . after a long period of anxiety and apprehension, when he was torn between the ascetic skepticism of Abu al-Ala al-Ma'arri and the more hedonistic version of Umar al-Khayyam. He was naturally inclined toward the former doctrine, although it preached a stern and sober life, because of its compatibility with the traditions in which he had been raised. But before he had known what was happening, he had found his soul longing for annihilation. A mysterious voice had whispered in his ear, "There's no religion, no Aïda, and no hope. So let death come." At that juncture, al-Khayyam had appealed to him, using this friend as an intermediary, and Kamal had accepted their invitation. All the same, he had retained his lofty principles by broadening the range of meaning for "goodness" to include all the joys of life. He had told himself, "Belief in truth, beauty, and humanity is merely the highest form of goodness. For this reason, the great philosopher Ibn Sina concluded each day of deep thought with drinks and beautiful women. In any case, only a life like this offers an alternative to death."

"I agreed, but I haven't abandoned my principles."

"Well, I'm sure you haven't abandoned your fantasies. You've lived with them so long they seem truer to you than reality itself. There's nothing wrong with reading or even writing, if you can find readers. But make writing a way of obtaining fame and fortune. Don't take it too seriously. You were intensely religious. Now you're intensely agnostic. But you've always been intensely concerned, as though you were responsible for all mankind. Life's not nearly that complicated. Get a government position you like, one providing an acceptable standard of living, and enjoy the pleasures of life with a heart free from cares. Be strong and assertive when you need to, and you'll find your honor protected, your success ensured. If this life's compatible with religion, then be proud of that and enjoy it. If it's not, then religion's at fault."

"Life's too profound and vast to be reduced to one activity, not excluding happiness," Kamal told himself. "Pleasure's my recreation, but ascending rugged mountains is still my objective. Aïda's gone. So I must create a new Aïda exemplifying everything she meant to me. Otherwise you should abandon life with no regrets."

"Don't you ever give any thought to values that transcend human life?"

"Ha! I've been distracted from all that by life itself, or more precisely by my life. No one in my family's an atheist, and no one's overly devout. I'm that way too."

"A friend's as necessary a part of life as time for relaxation," Kamal advised himself. "He's odd-looking too and linked to your memories of Aïda. So his place in your heart's guaranteed. He knows his way around these lively alleys. A tyrant if you defy him, he's at home with pleasures and avoids serious issues. He has no time for spiritual concerns. Your intellectual and spiritual companion has vanished overseas. Fuad al-Hamzawi's bright but has no taste for philosophy. He's self-centered even in the appreciation of beauty. From literature, he desires eloquence to use in drafting legal briefs. Who can ever replace Husayn for me?"

The waiter arrived and placed on the table two tall glasses with polygonal bases. Opening a bottle of soda, he poured some into the glasses, transforming their golden liquid into platinum encrusted with pearls. Then he set out plates of salad, cheese, olives, and bologna before leaving. Kamal looked back and forth from his glass to the smiling Isma'il, who said, "Do as I do. Start with a big swig. To your health!"

Kamal was content to take a sip and savor it. Then he waited expectantly, but his mind did not take flight as he had anticipated. So he took a big drink and picked up a piece of cheese to dispel the strange taste spreading through his mouth.

"Don't rush me!"

"Haste is from the devil. The important thing's for you to be ready for what you want when you leave here."

What did he want? Was it one of those women who inspired disgust and aversion when he was sober? Would alcohol sweeten the bitter sacrifice of his dignity? He had once fought off instinct by appealing to religion and to Aïda. Now instinct was free to express itself. But there was another incentive for this adventure. He wanted to investigate woman, the mysterious species that included Aïda herself. Perhaps this investigation would provide some consolation for sleepless nights when tears were shed secretly. It might give some compensation for bloody torment curable only by despair or by a loss of consciousness. He could now say he had emerged from the confining cell of resignation to take a first step along the road to freedom, even if this road was paved with inebriation and bordered by passions and other reprehensible things. He drank again and waited. Then he smiled. His insides celebrated the birth of a new sensation, one exuding warmth and sensuality. Kamal responded with abandon, as though reacting to a beautiful melody.

Isma'il, who was watching him closely, smiled and said, "If only Husayn were here to witness this."

"Where is Husayn?" Kamal wondered silently. "Where?"

"I'll write him about it myself. Have you answered his last letter?"

"Yes. I sent him a note as brief as his."

Husayn wrote long letters only to Kamal. They were so extensive that every thought was recorded. This great happiness was exclusively Kamal's, but he was obliged to keep it secret, for he did not want to arouse his coach's envy.

"His letter to me was brief too, except for the kind of discussion you know we enjoy but you don't."

"Thought!" Then Isma'il laughed. "What need does he have for it? He'll inherit a fortune big enough to fill an ocean. So why's he infatuated with such gibberish? Is it an affectation or conceit or both?"

"It's Husayn's turn to come in for a pounding," Kamal reflected. "I wonder what you say about me behind my back."

"Contrary to what you think, there's no conflict between thought and wealth. Philosophy flourished in ancient Greece when some gentlemen were able to devote themselves to learning because they weren't preoccupied by earning a living."

"Your health, Aristotle."

He drained the rest of his glass and waited expectantly. He wondered whether he had ever experienced a state like this before. A discharge of psychic heat raced off through his veins. As it progressed, it swept away the crannies where grief's residue had collected. The sorrow sealing his soul's vessel dissolved. Out flew singing birds of gaiety. One was the echo of a moving tune, another the memory of a promising hope, and yet another the shadow of a fleeting delight. Alcohol was the elixir of happiness.

"What would you think of ordering two more drinks?"

"May your life last longer than mine. . . ." Isma'il laughed out loud and summoned the waiter with the flick of a finger. Then he said with relief, "You're quick to recognize a good thing."

"I have my Lord to thank for that."

The waiter brought two more drinks and fresh appetizers. Customers started to flock in, some in fezzes, some in hats, and others in turbans. The waiter welcomed them by wiping off the tabletops with a towel. Since night had fallen and the lamps had been lit, the mirrors on the walls flashed with reflections of Dewar's and Johnnie Walker bottles. Outside in the street laughter reverberated like the call to prayer, but this summons was to debauchery. Smiling glances of tolerant disapproval were directed at the table occupied by the two adolescent friends. A shrimp seller from Upper Egypt entered the bar. He was followed by a woman with two gold teeth who was selling peanuts, a man offering to shine the customers' shoes, and a kabob vendor who was also a pimp, as the greetings he received from the men demonstrated. Finally there was an Indian palm reader. Soon nothing was heard except "To your health" and scattered laughter.

In a mirror adjacent to his head, Kamal saw his own flushed face and his gleaming, smiling eyes. Behind his reflection, he saw that of an elderly man, who raised his drink and rinsed his mouth with a rabbitlike twitch before swallowing. In an audible voice, this gentleman told a companion, "Rinsing my mouth with whiskey's a habit I acquired from my grandfather, who died drunk."

Turning away from the mirror, Kamal told Isma'il, "We're a very conservative family. I'm the first to taste alcohol."

Isma'il shrugged his shoulders scornfully and said, "How can you offer opinions about something you've never observed? Were you there to see what your father did in his youth? My father has a glass with lunch and another with dinner, but he's stopped drinking outside the house . . . or that's what he tells my mother."

The elixir of the god of happiness stealthily gained entry into the kingdom of the spirit. This strange transformation happened in moments. Unaided, mankind could not have achieved it in countless generations. All in all, it provided a dazzling new meaning for the word "enchantment." Amazingly Kamal did not find it a totally new sensation. His spirit had experienced this briefly once before; but when, how, and where? It was an inner music performed by the spirit. Normal music was like the apple's peel, while this music was the tasty fruit. What could be the secret of this golden liquid that accomplished such a miracle in only a few moments? Perhaps it cleansed life's stream of foam and sediment, allowing the restrained current to burst forth with the absolute freedom and unsullied intoxication life had enjoyed at the very beginning. When liberated from the body's noose, society's shackles, past memories, and fears for the future, this natural feeling of life's forward thrust becomes a clear, pure music, distilled from and exciting emotion.

"I've felt something like this pass through my spirit before," Kamal told himself. "But when, how, and where? Oh, what a memory . . . it was love! The day she called out, 'Kamal,' that intoxicated you before you knew what intoxication was. Admit your long history with inebriation. You've been rowdy for ages, traveling passion's drunken path, which is strewn with flowers and sweet herbs. That was before the transparent drops of dew were trampled into the mud. Alcohol's the spirit of love once love's inner lining of pain is stripped away. So love and grow intoxicated or get drunk and experience love."

"In spite of everything you've said and reiterated, life's beautiful."

"Ha-ha. You're the one who's been doing the saying and reiterating."

The warrior planted a sincere kiss on the cheek of his foe. Then peace settled over the earth. Perched on a leafy bough, the bulbul warbled. Lovers throughout the inhabited world were ecstatic. Stopping at Paris on the way, desires flew from Cairo to Brussels, where they were received with affection and songs. The sage dipped the point of his pen in his heart's ink and recorded a divine revelation. Then the seasoned man retreated into old age, although a tearful memory inspired a hidden springtime in his breast. Like the black cloth covering of the Kaaba in Mecca, the strands of black hair on her forehead sheltered a shrine toward which drunkards in the taverns of love directed their prayers.

"Give me a book, a drink, and a beautiful woman. Then throw me in the sea."

"Ha-ha. The book will spoil the effect of the drink, the beautiful woman, and the sea."

"We don't agree on the meaning of pleasure. You think it's fun and games. To me it's something extremely serious. This captivating intoxication is the secret of life and its ultimate goal. Alcohol's only the precursor and the symbol for it. In a similar fashion, a bird like the kite was the forerunner of the airplane and observation of fish was a first step in the invention of the submarine. Thus wine's a necessary scout for human happiness. The question boils down to this: How can we turn life into a perpetual state of intoxication without resort to alcohol? We won't find the answer through debate, productivity, fighting, or exertion. All those are means to an end, not ends in themselves. Happiness will never be realized until we free ourselves from the exploitation of any means whatsoever. Then we can live a purely intellectual and spiritual life untainted by anything. This is the happiness for which alcohol provides us a representation. Every action could be a way of obtaining this. If it's not, it serves no end."

"May God devastate your home."

"Why?"

"I hoped I'd find you a charming, witty conversationalist when drunk. But you're like a sick man whose malady only becomes more severe with drink. I wonder what you'd talk about if you had a third drink?"

"I won't have another. I'm happy now and feel capable of soliciting any woman I like."

"Shouldn't you wait a little?"

"Not a single minute."

Kamal walked along bravely and resolutely, arm in arm with his friend. They fell in with the flow of men going their way and ran into another stream coming from the opposite direction, for the curving street was too narrow for its pedestrian traffic. The men swiveled their heads from right to left at prostitutes who stood or sat on either side. From faces veiled by brilliant makeup, eyes glanced around with a seductive look of welcome. At every instant a man would break ranks to approach one of the women. She would follow him inside, the alluring look in her eyes replaced by a serious, businesslike expression. Lamps mounted above the doors of the brothels and the coffeehouses gave off a brilliant light in which accumulated the clouds of smoke rising from incense burners and water pipes. Voices were blended and intermingled in a tumultuous swirl around which eddied laughter, shouts, the squeaking of doors and windows, piano and accordion music, rollicking handclaps, a policeman's bark, braying, grunts, coughs of hashish addicts and screams of drunkards, anonymous calls for help, raps of a stick, and singing by individuals and groups. Above all this, the sky, which seemed close to the roofs of the shabby buildings, stared down at the earth with unblinking eyes. Every beautiful woman there was available and would generously reveal her beauty and secrets in exchange for only ten piasters. Who could believe this without seeing it?

Kamal commented to Isma'il, "Harun al-Rashid struts through his harem."

Laughing, Isma'il asked, "Commander of the Faithful, hasn't one of the maidens found favor with you?"

"She was standing in that empty doorway. Where do you suppose she went?"

"She's with a customer inside, Commander of the Faithful. Will Your Majesty wait while one of his subjects accomplishes his objective?"

"How about you? Haven't you found what you're looking for?"

"I'm a habitué of the street and its inhabitants, but I won't tend to my interests until I've delivered you to your girlfriend. What did you like about her? There are many prettier."

She had a brown complexion, and makeup did not conceal her color. The sound of her voice was slightly reminiscent of that immortal music of Aïda. After all, an eye might even see some resemblance between the skin coloring of a man being strangled and the pure blue surface of the sky.

"Do you know her?"

"Here she's called Rose. Her real name is Ayusha."

"Ayusha-Rose!" Kamal exclaimed to himself. "If only a person could change his essence as easily as he changes his name. There's something of this Ayusha-Rose combination about Aïda herself, and about religion, Abd al-Hamid Bey Shaddad, and vast dreams. Alas! But wine's raising you to the throne of the gods. So watch these contradictions drown pathetically in waves of uproarious jests."

He felt an elbow nudge him in the side as Isma'il said, "Your turn."

Kamal looked toward the doorway and saw a man leave the house hurriedly. Then the woman returned to her post where he had first seen her. He advanced toward her with firm steps, and she received him with a smile. He went inside, trailed by her. She was singing, "Let down the curtain around us." Finding the narrow stairway, he started climbing it with a pounding heart. At the top was a hallway leading into a parlor. Her voice caught up with him, saying now, "Go right," then, "Go left," and finally, "The door that's partway open."

It was a small room decorated with wallpaper, containing a bed, a dressing table, a clothes rack, a wooden chair, a basin, and a pitcher. Confused, Kamal stood in the center of the room as he examined it. She proceeded to close the door and the window, through which the rattling of a tambourine, whistling, and clapping could be heard. Her face seemed so grave and even glowering and stern that he wondered ironically what she had in mind for him. She confronted him and looked him up and down. When her eyes reached his head and nose, he felt apprehensive. Wishing to quell his anxiety, he moved toward her and put out his arms. But she brusquely gestured for him to stay back and said, "Wait." So he stood stock-still where he was.

Determined to overcome all obstacles, he said with an innocent smile, "My name's Kamal."

Staring at him in astonishment, she replied, "We're honored."

"Call to me. Say, 'Kamal.' "

All the more amazed, she answered, "Why should I call you when you're staring me in the face like a calamity?"

"I take refuge in God!" he exclaimed to himself. Was she making fun of him?

Even more resolved to rescue the situation, he said, "You told me to wait. What am I waiting for?"

"You're right to ask that," she said. Then she removed her dress with a theatrical gesture and leaped onto the bed, which creaked from her weight. She stretched out on her back and began to caress her belly with hennaed fingers. His eyes opened wide with disapproval. He had not been expecting this acrobatic performance and sensed they were on different sides of a mountain. What a distance there was between the valley of pleasure and that of work. In one moment everything he had built up in his imagination over the past few days was demolished. There was a bitter taste of resentment in his mouth, but his curiosity was still intense. So he overcame his dismay and ran his eyes down the naked body until they reached their target. For a moment it seemed he could not believe his eyes. With uneasy aversion he looked more closely, but in the end experienced something close to alarm. Was this what women really looked like or had he picked a poor example? But even if he had chosen poorly, would that affect the essential characteristics?

"We claim to love the truth," he told himself. "People have been terribly unfair about your head and nose."

His soul instructed him to flee, and he was on the verge of obeying. But he suddenly wondered why the man before him had not fled and what Isma'il would say if Kamal returned right away. No, he would not flee. He would proceed with the ordeal.

"Why are you standing there like a statue?"

"This voice shook your heart," he reminded himself. "Our ears don't mislead us, but our ignorance may. You'll have a good time laughing at yourself later, but you're a winner not a deserter. Suppose life is a tragedy; still, it's a duty to play your role in it."

"Are you going to stand like that till dawn?"

In a curiously calm voice he answered, "Let's turn out the lights."

Sitting up in bed, she said coarsely and cautiously, "On condition that I see you first in the light."

He asked disapprovingly, "Why?"

"So I can be sure you're healthy."

He stripped for this medical examination. The sight seemed ludicrous to him in the extreme. Then it was pitch-black.

When he returned to the street, he took with him a dreary heart filled with sorrow. He imagined that he and everyone else were suffering from a painful decline and that their salvation was remote. He saw Isma'il coming toward him. His friend, who looked satisfied, tired, and sarcastic, asked, "How's philosophy?"

Kamal took his arm and walked off with him, asking earnestly, "Are all women alike?"

The young man cast a questioning glance at him. After Kamal had revealed his doubts and fears in a concise fashion to Isma'il, the latter smilingly said, "In general the essential traits are the same, even if some of the accidental ones differ. You're so laughable, you deserve pity. Should I assume from your state of mind that you'll not be returning here again?"

"To the contrary, I'll come back here more often than you think. Let's have another drink." Then he continued as though to himself: "Beauty . . . beauty! What is beauty?"

At that moment his soul yearned for purification, isolation, and meditation. He longed to remember the tormented life he had lived in the shadow of his beloved. He seemed to believe that truth would always be cruel. Should he adopt the avoidance of truth as his creed? He walked along the road to the bar, so lost in thought that he scarcely paid any attention to Isma'il's chatter. If truth was cruel, lies were ugly.

"The problem's not that the truth is harsh but that liberation from ignorance is as painful as being born. Run after truth until you're breathless. Accept the pain involved in re-creating yourself afresh. These ideas will take a life to comprehend, a hard one interspersed with drunken moments."

36 ❧

Kamal had come to the alley by himself this evening. Inebriated, he was singing under his breath as he made his way boldly through the boisterous tide of humanity. Finding Rose's door vacant, he did not hesitate as he would have when first getting to know the alley. Instead, he headed straight for the house and entered without knocking. He climbed the stairs to the hallway and once there glanced at the closed door, where light was visible through the keyhole. He went to the waiting room, which fortunately was empty. He sat down in a wooden chair and stretched his legs out with satisfaction. A few minutes later he heard the door creak open and prepared to stand up. The other man's movements as he left the bedroom and headed for the stairs were revealed by his footsteps. Kamal tarried a few moments before rising to go into the hall. Through the open door of her room he saw Rose, who was remaking the bed. When she noticed him, she smiled and called for him to sit back down a minute. He retraced his steps, smiling with the confidence of a regular customer. He soon heard someone come up the stairs, and that upset him. He hated to have to wait with other clients, but the new arrival headed for Rose's room.

Kamal heard the woman tell this man gently, "I have a customer. Go to the parlor and wait." Then she raised her voice to summon Kamal: "Please come in."

He rose without any hesitation and ran into the new arrival in the hall. He found himself face to face with Yasin. Their stunned eyes met. Kamal immediately looked down, seething with shame, confusion, and discomfort. He was about to run off as fast as he could, but Yasin forestalled that with a laugh so loud it reverberated strangely against the hall ceiling. The youth looked up at his brother, whose arms were opened wide as he yelled delightedly, "A thousand magnificent evenings! A thousand days of imperial splendor!" He roared with laughter as the dazed Kamal stared at him. When life started to flow through the youth again, he emerged from his stupor and a quizzical smile appeared on his lips. He regained his composure but did not lose his embarrassment.

In an oratorical tone, Yasin burst out, "This is a happy night: Thursday, October 28, 1926, a truly joyous evening. We'll have to celebrate it every year, for on this night two brothers discovered each other and it was demonstrated that the baby of the family's grown up. He's bearing aloft the banner of our glorious traditions in the world of pleasures."

Rose walked up and asked Yasin, "Your friend?"

Laughing, Yasin replied, "No, my brother. The son of my father and ... No, my father's son. That says it all. So you see, you're the darling of the whole family, you nobody."

She murmured, "Swell." Then she told Kamal, "Etiquette dictates that you yield your turn to your older brother, kid."

Yasin roared his mighty laugh and said, " 'Etiquette dictates'! Who taught you the manners of sex? Can you imagine a brother waiting outside the door? Ha-ha ..."

Giving him a warning look, she said, "If you laugh in that alarming way, drunkard, the police will hear. But you're excused, since your kid brother's always tipsy when he gets here."

Yasin looked at Kamal with astonished admiration. "You've learned that too!" he exclaimed. "My Lord, we really are blood brothers, in every way. Bring your mouth up close so I can smell it. But what's the use? A drunk can't detect the smell of liquor on anyone else's breath. Tell me now: What's your opinion of this wisdom you've gained from life instead of from books?" Then he pointed toward Rose and exclaimed, "One visit to this hussy's equivalent to reading ten banned books. So, you get drunk, Kamal.... A thousand bright days! We've been friends from the beginning. I'm the one who tau ..."

"God, God! Am I going to have to wait till daybreak?"

Yasin gave Kamal a shove and said, "You go with her, and I'll wait."

But Kamal fell back, shaking his head in vehement rejection. Then he spoke for the first time: "No way! Not ... not tonight." Putting his hand in his pocket, he took out ten piasters, which he gave to the woman.

Yasin cried out admiringly, "Long live gallantry! But I won't let you go off alone...." Giving Rose's shoulder a goodbye pat, he took Kamal's arm, and they left the building together.

Yasin was saying, "We must celebrate this evening. So let's spend some time in a bar. I usually do my drinking on Muhammad Ali Street with a group of civil servants and some others, but it's not an appropriate place for you, and besides, it's far. Let's choose some-where nearby, so we can get home in good time. Since my latest marriage, I'm as eager as you to return home early. Where did you get drunk tonight, hero?"

Kamal stammered with embarrassment, "The Finish."

"Great! Let's go there. Take advantage of this moment and make the most of it. Tomorrow when you're a teacher, visiting this district with its brothels and taverns will be difficult for you." Then, laugh-ing, he continued: "Imagine one of your pupils running into you here. . . . Even so, the field of pleasure's wide open, and you'll soon advance in it to ever more beautiful experiences."

They continued on to the Finish Bar in silence. Fortunately the bond between Yasin and Kamal had not been affected by Yasin's exodus from the old house, and there was no artificial reserve be-tween them. It was typical of Yasin to overlook his prerogatives as the eldest brother. What Kamal knew from firsthand observation of his brother's conduct as well as from other people's comments gave him every reason to believe that Yasin was addicted to women and easily influenced by passion. Even so, meeting his brother at Rose's was a violent shock, for his imagination had never pictured Yasin intoxicated or loitering down this alley. As time passed, Kamal began to recover gradually from the shock, and his alarm began to give way to confidence and even relief. When the brothers reached the Finish, they found it packed. So Yasin suggested they take a table outside, choosing one toward the edge of the sidewalk at the corner of the street, to be as far as possible from other people. Smiling, they sat down opposite each other.

Yasin asked, "How much have you had to drink?"

Kamal answered hesitantly, "Two glasses."

"No doubt our unexpected meeting destroyed their effect. Let's start all over. I only have a few, seven or eight. . . ."

"You don't say! Is that a few?"

"Skip the naïve astonishment, because you're not naïve anymore."

"By the way, two months ago I didn't even know what it tasted like."

Yasin observed disapprovingly, "It seems I've given you more credit than you deserve."

They laughed together, and Yasin ordered a couple of drinks. Then he renewed his questioning: "When did you meet Rose?"

"I was introduced to Rose and whiskey the same night."

"What other experiences have you had with women?"

"None."

Yasin bowed his head slightly and looked at Kamal from beneath eyebrows contracted in a smiling frown as if to protest: "Come on now!" Then he said, "Don't play the fool. I had many opportunities to observe your flirtations with the daughter of Abu Sari', who grills snacks. At times it was a glance, then a gesture. Remember? Pimp, these matters can't be hidden from an expert. No doubt you were content to play with her, so you wouldn't find yourself obliged to make Abu Sari' your father-in-law—unlike my former mother-in-law, who got involved in a marriage with Bayumi the drinks seller. Yes? Now he's a man of property and your next-door neighbor. I wonder where Maryam's hiding. No one's heard anything about her. Her father was a good man. Don't you remember Mr. Muhammad Ridwan? See what's become of his household. But it's all a question of manners. Any woman who neglects them will find herself despised."

Kamal could not help laughing as he asked, "What about men? Can they neglect their manners without getting in trouble?"

Yasin laughed in his forceful way and replied, "Men and women are two different things, smart aleck. Tell me, how's your mother? Is that good woman still angry at me, even after I've divorced Maryam?"

"I think she's forgotten the whole affair. She has a fine heart, as you know."

Yasin endorsed his brother's words and then shook his head sadly. The waiter brought the drinks and the appetizers. Yasin immediately raised his glass and said, "To the health of al-Sayyid Ahmad's family."

Kamal raised his too and drank half, hoping to regain his lost mirth. His mouth full of black bread and cheese, Yasin commented, "I imagined that, like our late brother, you resembled your mother in temperament. I thought you'd be a straight arrow, but you, but we . . ."

Kamal cast his brother a questioning look. Yasin smilingly continued: "But we're both created from our father's mold."

"Our father! He's so serious it's hardly possible to live with him."

Yasin roared with laughter. He hesitated a little before saying, "You don't know your father. I didn't either, but then an entirely different man was disclosed to me, an extraordinary one." He stopped speaking.

With great curiosity and interest Kamal asked, "What do you know that I don't?"

"I know he's a princely wit with a deep appreciation of music. Don't stare at me like an idiot. Don't think I'm drunk. Your father's a master of jests, music, and love."

"My father?"

"I learned that for the first time in the home of the singer Zubayda."

"Zubayda! What are you saying? ... Ha-ha ..."

But since Yasin's expression was anything but joking, Kamal stopped laughing even before his face could regain its serious look. His mouth closed gradually, until his lips were pressed together. He gazed silently at his brother's face as Yasin related in exhaustive detail what he had seen and heard of their father.

Was Yasin fabricating lies about his father? How could that be? What motive would justify it? No, he was only telling what he knew. So this was what Kamal's father was like.

"My Lord!" Kamal exclaimed to himself. "The seriousness, dignity, and gravity—what are they? If you hear tomorrow that the earth's flat or that mankind really did spring from Adam, don't be surprised or alarmed."

Finally Kamal asked, "Does my mother know about this?"

Yasin laughingly replied, "She's no doubt aware of the drinking at least."

"I wonder what effect that's had on her," Kamal brooded. "She becomes alarmed for no reason at all. Is my mother like me in presenting a happy front while feeling wretched inside?"

As though marshaling excuses he did not believe in, Kamal observed, "People love to exaggerate. Don't believe everything they say. Besides, his health shows he's a temperate man."

Gesturing for the waiter to bring another round, Yasin said admiringly, "He's a marvel! His body's a miracle. His spirit's another. Everything about him's miraculous, even his glib tongue." They both laughed. Then Yasin continued: "Imagine, in spite of all this, he rules his family with the firm hand you know and maintains his dignity as you can plainly see. How come I'm such a failure?"

"Consider these wonders," Kamal advised himself. "You're drinking with Yasin. Your father's a shameless old man. What's genuine and what's not? Is there any relationship between reality and what's in our heads? What value does history have? What connection is

there between the beloved Aïda and the pregnant Aïda? I myself—
who am I? Why did you suffer this savage pain from which you've
yet to recover? Laugh till you're exhausted."

"What would happen if he saw us sitting here?"

Yasin snapped his fingers and exclaimed, "I take refuge in God!"

"Is Zubayda really beautiful?"

Yasin whistled and wriggled his eyebrows.

"Surely it's unfair that our father gets to enjoy such a sumptuous
treat while all we can find are skinny girls."

"Wait your turn. You're still a beginner."

"Hasn't your relationship with him changed since you discovered
his secret?"

"Anything but that!"

There was a dreamy look in Kamal's eyes as he said, "If only he
had bestowed some of his charm on us...."

"If only...."

"We couldn't be much worse off than we are."

"What's so bad about loving women and drinking?..."

"How can you reconcile his conduct with his deep faith?"

"Am I an atheist? Are you? Were those caliphs who indulged their
carnal appetites pagans? God's merciful and forgiving."

Kamal asked himself, "What would my father say? I really wish I
could discuss these issues with him. Anything's possible, but I can't
believe he's a hypocrite. No, he's not that. The only new dimension
of his character revealed is love."

Kamal's final swallow left him in a jesting mood. He commented,
"It's too bad he didn't go into acting."

Yasin laughed loudly and replied, "If he'd known the opportunities
life offers actors to enjoy women and wine, he would have dedicated
his life to this art."

"Is al-Sayyid Ahmad Abd al-Jawad really the butt of this joke?"
Kamal wondered. "But is he any more exalted than Adam? And even
so, you learned the truth of man's origin by accident. Chance occurrences have played a most significant role in your life. If I had not
met Yasin by accident in the alley, the veil of ignorance would not
have been lifted from my eyes. If Yasin, ignorant though he is, had
not gotten me interested in reading, today I'd be in the Medical
School, as my father hoped. If I'd enrolled in a different secondary
school, like al-Sa'idiya, I wouldn't have met Aïda. In that case, I
would be a different person now. I'd see existence in some other

fashion. People like to fault Darwin for his reliance on chance in the explanation of the mechanics of his system. . . ."

Yasin observed sagely, "Time will teach you what you haven't learned yet." Of himself he said sarcastically, "It's taught me to get my enjoyment early in the evening, so I don't awaken my wife's doubts." Then he added, "She's the most forceful of my three wives. I imagine I'll never get rid of her."

Pointing toward the alley, Kamal asked with considerable interest, "What takes you there, now that you're on your third marriage?"

Yasin repeated a famous phrase from the song Kamal had first heard at Aisha's wedding: "Because . . . because . . . because . . ." Then, smiling uneasily, he continued: "Zanuba told me once, 'You've never been married. You've always considered marriage a love affair. It's time for you to start taking it seriously.' Isn't it strange that a woman entertainer should say such things? But she seems more dedicated to married life than either of my two previous spouses. She's determined to remain my wife until I die. But I can't resist women. I fall in love quickly and get bored quickly. For this reason, I repair to alleys like this one to satisfy my desires immediately without any need to get involved in a long affair. If it weren't for boredom, I wouldn't look for women in Massage Alley."

With ever-increasing interest, Kamal asked, "Aren't these women like any others?"

"Certainly not. A prostitute's a woman without a heart. For her, love's a commodity."

His eyes sparkling with hope, Kamal asked, "What do you think distinguishes one woman from another?"

Yasin nodded his head proudly because of the status conferred on him by Kamal's questions. With the confident tone of an expert, he responded, "A woman's place within the ranks of females is determined by her moral and emotional qualities, without consideration of family or class. I think more highly of Zanuba, for example, than I did of Zaynab, because Zanuba's more emotional, more sincere, and more dedicated to our marriage. But in the end, you'll find they're all the same. Even if you had an affair with the Queen of Sheba herself, you'd inevitably find she became boring to look at and like a song you're tired of hearing."

The gleam in Kamal's eyes disappeared. Had Aïda become boring to look at and an overly familiar song? "That's really hard to believe," he told himself. "But you are reality's victim. It's even hard to gloat at her misfortune. Learning that time could turn the beloved, whom the soul still misses, into an overly familiar sight and a tired song might drive a person crazy. In fact, if you had a choice, wouldn't you rather regret her loss than come to find her boring? Of course, at times I sigh for boredom because my desire's so strong, just as Yasin longs for desire because he's bored. Raise your head to the Lord of the heavens and ask Him for a happy solution."

"Haven't you ever been in love?"

"So what do you think I'm currently drowning in?"

"I mean genuine love, not passing lust."

Yasin finished his third drink, wiped his mouth with the back of his hand, twisted his mustache, and then said, "Don't hold it against me if love's concentrated for me in certain locations, like the mouth, the hand, and so forth."

"Yasin's handsome," Kamal observed to himself. "She would never have made fun of his head or nose. But his words make him seem truly pitiable. How can a man be a real man without love? But what's the use of it, since all it has brought you is pain?"

Gesturing for Kamal to empty his glass, Yasin continued: "Don't believe what they say about love in novels. Love's an emotion that lasts a few days or at best a few weeks."

"I've stopped believing in immortality, but is it possible to forget love?" Kamal asked himself. "I'm no longer the way I was. I'm escaping from love's hellish suffering. Life occasionally distracts me. But then I slip back. Once I directed my attention toward death. Today I look to life, although a hopeless one. It's amazing that you rebel against the idea of forgetting her. You almost seem to be blaming yourself for something. Or are you afraid you'll discover the most exalted thing you ever reverenced was just a fantasy? Are you refusing to let oblivion carry off this splendid manifestation of life for fear you'll wake up to find yourself of no more significance than if you'd never been born? Don't you remember why you spread your hands out in prayer to ask God to rescue you from torment and grant you forgetfulness?"

"But true love exists. We read about its effects in the papers, not just in novels."

Yasin smiled sarcastically and said, "Afflicted though I am by the love of women, I won't admit that 'true' love exists. The tragedies we read about in newspapers are actually accounts of youthful inexperience. Have you heard of the ancient Arab poet called 'Layla's

Fool' because love for her drove him crazy? There are probably others like him in your stories, but he, Majnun, never married Layla. Show me one person who went insane because he loved his wife too much. Alas! Husbands are rational men, very rational, even when it goes against the grain. But a wife's madness commences with her wedding day, because nothing less than devouring her husband will satisfy her. It seems to me that crazy people become lovers because they're crazy. Lovers don't go insane just because they're in love. You'll observe these lunatics talking about a woman as though she were an angel. A woman's nothing more than a woman. She's a tasty dish of which you quickly get your fill. Let those crazy lovers share a bed with her so they can see what she looks like when she wakes up or smell her sweat or other odors. After that are they going to talk about angels? A woman's charm is a matter of cosmetics and other seductive devices. Once you fall into her trap, you see her for the human being she really is. The secret forces holding marriages together aren't beauty or charm but children, the dowry's balance demanded in exchange for a divorce, and the support payments."

"It would only be fitting if he'd change his opinion on seeing Aïda," Kamal told himself. "But you better rethink this question of love. You once considered it an angelic inspiration, but now you deny the existence of angels. So search for it within man's essence. Insert it into the list of theoretical and practical realities you wish to confront boldly. In this way you'll learn the secret of your tragedy and strip the veil away from Aïda's hidden essence. You won't discover her to be an angel, but the door of enchantment will swing open for you. How wretched it makes me to think of things like pregnancy and its craving, Aïda as an overly familiar sight, and body odors."

With distress that Yasin did not notice, Kamal said, "Man's a filthy creature. Couldn't he have been created better and cleaner?"

Although not looking at anything in particular, Yasin reared his head back and said with curious joy, "God ... God, my soul's so shimmering it's turning into a song. My limbs are turning into musical instruments. The world's sweet and full of creatures dear to my heart. The weather's delightful. Reality's a figment of our imaginations, and what's imaginary's real. Trouble is nothing but a legend. God, God, what a beautiful thing alcohol is, Kamal. May God grant it a long existence, perpetuate it for us, and grant us the health and strength to drink it to the end of our days. May God destroy the home of anyone who tampers with it or fabricates lies about it. Relish this beautiful intoxication. Reflect on it. Close your eyes. Does any other pleasure compare with this? God ... God ... God!"

Lowering his head to look at Kamal, he continued: "What did you say, my son? 'Man's a filthy creature'? Were you offended by my comments about women? I wasn't saying that to arouse disgust for them. The fact is that I love them. I love them with all their faults. But I wanted to demonstrate that the angelic woman does not exist. In fact, if she did, I doubt I'd love her. Like your father, I love full hips. An angel with a heavy bottom wouldn't be able to fly. Take care to understand me and don't misinterpret my words, by the life of our father, al-Sayyid Ahmad."

Kamal quickly grew as tipsy as his brother and said, "Once alcohol's circulating through the body, the world certainly seems adorable."

"God bless your mouth! Now even the usual refrain of beggars in the street sounds enchanting to the ear."

"And our sorrows seem to belong to other men."

"But their women seem our own."

"It all amounts to the same thing, my father's son."

"God, God, I don't want to sober up."

"One vile aspect of life is that we can't stay drunk as long as we'd like."

"Please understand that I don't see drunkenness as just an amusement but as the heavenly goal of life on a par with knowledge and our highest ideals."

"In that case I'm a great philosopher."

"You will be, when you believe what I've said; not before."

"May God grant you a long life, Father, for you've begotten philosophers just like you."

"Why should a man be miserable when all he needs is a drink and a woman, since there are plenty of bottles and women too?"

"Why? ... Why?"

"I'll tell you the answer once I've drunk one more."

"No," Yasin said in a voice that betrayed a fleeting sobriety. Then he cautioned Kamal again, "Don't overdo it. I'm your drinking partner tonight, so I'm responsible for you. What time is it?" He took out his watch and exclaimed, "Twelve-thirty! Hero, we're in trouble. We're both late. You have our father to worry about, and I've got Zanuba. Let's go."

In no time at all they had left the bar and boarded a carriage that rushed off with them toward al-Ataba, circling the fence around the Ezbekiya Garden on a road buried in darkness. Every now and then they saw a pedestrian hurry or stagger by. Whenever the carriage passed an intersection, the fresh breeze carried to them the sound of people singing. Above the buildings and the lofty trees of the Garden, vigilant stars glittered.

Yasin laughingly said, "Tonight I'll be able to swear quite confidently that I've done nothing reprehensible."

Kamal said rather anxiously, "I hope I get home before my father."

"Nothing's more wretched than fear. Long live the revolution!"

"Yes, long live the revolution!"

"Down with the tyrannical wife!"

"Down with the tyrannical father!"

Kamal knocked gently on the door until it opened to reveal the shadowy figure of Umm Hanafi. When she recognized him, she whispered, "My master's on the stairs."

Before entering, he waited to be sure his father had reached the top floor, but then a voice called down the stairs sharply, "Who knocked?"

Kamal's heart pounded. He felt obliged to step forward and reply, "Me, Papa."

By the light of the lamp that Kamal's mother was holding at the top of the stairs, his father's form was visible on the first-floor landing. Al-Sayyid Ahmad looked down over the railing and asked with astonishment, "Kamal? What's kept you outside the house till this hour?"

"The same thing that kept you," Kamal commented to himself.

He answered apprehensively, "I went to the theater to see a play that's required reading for us this year."

His father shouted angrily, "When did people start studying in theaters? Isn't it enough to read and memorize it? What disgusting nonsense! Why didn't you ask my permission?"

Kamal stopped a few steps below his father and replied apologetically, "I didn't expect it to end so late."

The man said angrily, "Find some other way to study and skip the foolish excuses." Grumbling to himself, he resumed his climb up the stairs. Some of these muttered complaints reached Kamal: "Studying in the theaters till all hours ... one A.M. ... just children ... curses on your author and the author of the play."

Kamal ascended to the top story and went into the sitting room, where he took the lamp from a table. Entering his bedroom with a sullen face, he deposited the lamp on his desk and stood there, resting his hands on the desk, while he asked when his father had last insulted him. He could not remember precisely but was sure his years at the Teachers College had passed without a comparable incident. For this reason the curses made a painful impact on him, even though they had not been directed at him. He turned away from his desk, removed his fez, and started to undress. Then he suddenly felt dizzy and nauseous. He fled to the bathroom, where he vomited everything with bitter violence. When he returned to his room he felt exhausted and disgusted with himself, for the pain in his chest was less intense and profound than that in his spirit. He took off his clothes, extinguished the lamp, and stretched out on the bed, exhaling with nervous annoyance.

In a few minutes he heard the door open softly. Then his mother's voice reached him, asking sympathetically, "Asleep?"

Adopting a natural and contented tone to discourage her, so he could confront his ordeal alone, he said, "Yes. . . ."

Her figure approached the bed and stopped near his head. Then she said apologetically, "Don't let it worry you. I know your father better than anyone."

"Of course! . . . I understand."

As though expressing her own reservations, she said, "He knows how serious and upright you are. That's why he couldn't believe you'd stayed out this late."

Kamal was sufficiently enraged to ask, "If staying out late merits so much disapproval, why does he do it so persistently?"

The darkness prevented him from seeing the expression of astonished disapproval on her face, but her nasal laugh showed that she did not take his question seriously. She replied, "All men stay out at night. You'll be a man soon. But right now, you're a student."

He interrupted her as if he wanted to end the conversation: "I understand. Naturally. I didn't mean anything by what I said. Why did you bother to come? Go in peace."

She said tenderly, "I was afraid you were upset. I'll leave you now, but promise you'll sleep soundly and not worry about it. Recite the Qur'an sura about God's absolute and eternal nature until you fall asleep" (Sura 112).

He sensed her move away. Then he heard the door close as she said, "Good night." He exhaled deeply again and began to stroke his chest and belly as he stared into the darkness. Life had a bitter taste. What had become of the enchanting intoxication of alcohol? What was this stifling depression that had taken its place? It resembled nothing so much as the disappointment supplanting his heavenly dreams of love. But if it had not been for his father, the enchantment would have lasted. Kamal feared the man's despotic power more than anything else. He dreaded and loved it at the same time. Why should that be? Al-Sayyid Ahmad was just a man. Except for the geniality

other people attributed to him, there was nothing so special about
him. Why did Kamal fear him and feel intimidated by this fear? It
was all in Kamal's head, like the other fantasies that had afflicted him.
But what use was logic in combating emotions?

His hands had pounded on the gate of Abdin Palace during a great
demonstration in which people had defiantly challenged the king:
"Sa'd or revolution!" Then the king had backed down, but Sa'd Zaghlul had resigned from the cabinet. Faced by his father, though, Kamal
was reduced to nothing. The meaning and significance of everything
had changed: God, Adam, al-Husayn, love, Aïda herself, immortality.

"Did you say 'immortality'? Yes . . . as it applies to love and to
Fahmy, that martyred brother who is annihilation's guest forever.
Remember the experiment you attempted when you were twelve in
hopes of discovering his unknown fate? What a sad memory! You
grabbed a sparrow from its nest and strangled it. Covering it with a
shroud, you dug a small grave in the courtyard near the old well and
buried the victim. Days or weeks later you dug up the grave and
took out the corpse. What did you see and smell? You went weeping
to your mother to ask her what became of the dead . . . all the dead
and especially Fahmy. The only way she could silence you was by
bursting into tears herself. So what's left of Fahmy after seven years?
What will remain of love? What else does the revered father have to
show us?"

As his eyes grew accustomed to the dark, he could make out the
shapes of the desk, the clothes rack, the chair, and the wardrobe. The
silence itself receded enough to grant indistinct sounds a hearing. He
was troubled by feverish insomnia as the taste of life seemed to grow
increasingly bitter. He wondered whether Yasin was sound asleep.
How had Zanuba received her husband? Had Husayn retired to his
Parisian bed? On which side was Aïda sleeping now? Was her belly
round and swollen? What were they doing on the far side of the
world where the sun was perched in the center of the sky? What of
those luminous planets—were the creatures inhabiting them free of
human misery? Could Kamal's faint moan be heard in that infinite
orchestra of existence?

"Father! Let me tell you what's on my mind. I'm not angry about
what I've learned of your character, because I like the newly discovered side better than the familiar one. I admire your charm, grace,
impudence, rowdiness, and adventuresome spirit. That's your gentle
side, the one all your acquaintances love. If it shows anything, it
reveals your vitality and your enthusiasm for life and people. But I'd

like to ask why you choose to show us this frightening and gruff mask? Don't appeal to the principles of child rearing, for you know less about that than anyone. The clearest proof is what you do and don't see of Yasin's conduct and mine. What have you done besides hurt and punish us with an ignorance your good intentions do nothing to excuse? Don't be upset, for I still love and admire you. I'll always feel that way, sincerely. But my soul can't help blaming you for all the pain you've inflicted on me. We've never known you as a friend the way outsiders do. We've known you as a tyrannical dictator, a petulant despot.

"The saying 'An intelligent enemy's better than an ignorant friend' might well have been coined for you. For this reason, I hate ignorance more than any other evil in life. It spoils everything, even the sacred bond of fatherhood. A father with half your ignorance and half your love would be far better for your children. I vow that if I'm ever a father I'll be more a friend to my children than a disciplinarian. All the same, I still love and admire you, even after the godlike qualities my enchanted eyes once associated with you have faded away. Yes, your power lingers on only as a legend. You're not a superior court judge like Salim Bey, rich like Shaddad Bey, a leader like Sa'd Zaghlul, a crafty politician like Tharwat, or a nobleman like Adli, but you're a beloved friend, and that suffices. It's no small accomplishment. If you just wouldn't begrudge us your friendship.

"But you're not the only one whose image has changed. God Himself's no longer the god I used to worship. I'm sifting His essential attributes to rid them of tyranny, despotism, dictatorship, compulsion, and similar human traits. I don't know at what point I ought to limit my thought or whether it's right to limit it at all. In fact, my soul tells me I'll never stop and that debate, no matter how painful, is better than resignation and slumber. This may interest you less than learning that I've decided to limit your tyranny, which envelops me like this all-embracing darkness and torments me like this cursed sleeplessness. I won't drink alcohol again, because it has betrayed me, alas. If alcohol's a deceitful illusion too, then what's left for man? I tell you I've decided to limit your despotism—not by defying you or rebelling, for you're too dear for that—but by fleeing. Yes, I'll surely leave your house as soon as I'm able to support myself. There's plenty of room in the districts of Cairo for all the victims of oppression.

"Do you know what other consequences there were to loving you despite your tyranny? I loved another tyrant who was unfair to me for a long time, both to my face and behind my back. She oppressed me without ever loving me. In spite of all that, I worshipped her from the depths of my heart and still do. You're as responsible for my love and torment as anyone else. I wonder if there's any truth to this idea. I'm not satisfied with it or overly enthusiastic about it. Whatever the reality of love may be, there's no doubt that it's attributable to causes more directly linked to the soul. Let's allow this to ride until we can study it later. In any case, Father, you're the one who made it easy for me to accept oppression through your continual tyranny.

"And you, Mother, don't stare at me with disapproval or ask me what I've done wrong when I've harmed no one. Ignorance is your crime, ignorance ... ignorance ... ignorance. My father's the manifestation of ignorant harshness and you of ignorant tenderness. As long as I live, I'll remain the victim of these two opposites. It's your ignorance, too, that filled my spirit with legends. You're my link to the Stone Age. How miserable I am now as I try to liberate myself from your influence. And I'll be just as miserable in the future when I free myself from my father.

"It would have been far better if you had spared me such exhausting effort. For this reason, I propose—with the darkness of this room as my witness—that the family be abolished, for it's nothing but a pit in which brackish water collects, and that fatherhood and motherhood cease. Indeed, grant me a nation with no history and a life without a past. Let's look in the mirror now. What will we see? This enormous nose and huge head.... You mercilessly gave me your nose, Father, without consulting me and thus treated me unjustly even before I was born. On your face it has an august majesty, but its shape and size look ludicrous on a narrow one like mine, where it stands out like an English soldier at a gathering of Sufi mystics. Even stranger than that's my head, because it's of a different type than either yours or my mother's. What distant grandfather bequeathed it to me? I'll continue to hold both of you responsible until I learn its true origin.

"Just before we go to sleep we ought to say, 'Farewell,' because we may never wake up. I love life, despite what it's done to me, just as I love you, Father. There are things about life worth loving, and its page is covered with question marks that evoke our wildest affection. But what's useful in life is to no avail in love. And what's most useful in love is still of little importance.

"I probably won't drink again. Say, 'Farewell, alcohol.' But not so fast! Remember the night you left Ayusha's house fully determined never to go near a woman again as long as you lived? Then afterwards you became her favorite customer. It seems to me that all mankind is moaning from hangovers and nausea. So pray they'll have a speedy recovery.

38 ❧

After Kamal left his older brother alone in the carriage, Yasin's zeal dwindled. Although intoxicated, he seemed pensive. It was past 1 A.M., late enough to inspire doubts. If Zanuba was not awake and angrily awaiting him, she would wake when he entered. In either case, the night would not end in an entirely peaceful manner.

He left the carriage at the corner of Palace of Desire Alley and made his way through the profound darkness. Shrugging his shoulders, he whispered to himself, "Yasin's not accountable to any woman." He repeated that statement as he mounted the steps, guiding himself in the darkness by the railing. But this reiteration did not appear totally assured. He opened the door, entered, and made his way to the bedroom by the light from a lamp in the hall. Looking at the bed, he found his wife asleep and shut the bedroom door to keep out the faint light from the hall. He began to undress quietly and cautiously, feeling increasingly confident that she was sound asleep. He sketched a plan in his mind to allow him to slip into bed without making any noise.

"Light the lamp so I can shadow my eyes with the sight of you."

He turned his head toward the bed and smiled with resignation. Finally, with feigned astonishment, he asked, "You're awake? I thought you were asleep and didn't want to disturb you."

"How kind of you! What time is it?"

"Not later than midnight. I left the gathering around eleven and walked straight home."

"Your meeting must have been out of town then, maybe as far as Banha."

"Why? Am I late?"

"Wait a moment till the crowing cock provides your answer."

"Perhaps he hasn't fallen asleep yet."

Stripped to his shirt and underpants, he sat on the sofa to remove his shoes and socks. He saw her shadowy form sit up as the bed creaked. Then he heard her say sharply, "Light the lamp."

"There's no need for that. I've finished undressing."

"I want to settle accounts with you in the light."

"Settling accounts in the dark is more fun."

She snorted angrily and got out of bed. From his nearby seat he put out his arms, grabbed her flank, and pulled her over to the sofa. Sitting her down beside him, he remarked, "Don't make a row."

She escaped from his grip and replied, "What's happened to our agreement? I let you get drunk in bars as often as you want on condition that you return home early. I accepted that against my better judgment, because if you did your drinking at home, you'd save a lot of money that's just wasted. Yet you come home shortly before dawn—in flagrant disregard of our agreement."

"What hope does a man have of fooling a woman who's grown up playing the lute in a troupe of musicians?" Yasin asked himself. "If she can ever prove you've been unfaithful to her, will her response be limited to a quarrel or ... what? Think it over carefully and don't forget that her loss would not be a laughing matter. I love her best of all my wives. She knows exactly how to help me and takes our marriage seriously. If I just didn't get bored...."

"I was with my usual group and stayed with them until I set out for home. I have a witness you know. Can you guess who he is?" He laughed out loud.

But she answered coldly, "Don't change the topic."

Still laughing, he said, "My companion tonight was my brother Kamal."

Contrary to his expectations, she was not surprised. Her patience exhausted, she asked, "And who's testifying for the girl?"

"Don't be difficult. My innocence is as obvious as the sun." Then he grumbled, "By God, it makes me sad that you're suspicious of my behavior. I've had more than my fill of playing around. All I want now is a quiet life. The bar's simply an innocent pastime. There's nothing objectionable about that. A man has got to see people...."

In a passionate voice she replied, "Shame on you! You know I'm not a child. Putting something over on me is a difficult feat. It would be better for both of us if there were no room for suspicion."

"A sermon or a threat?" Yasin asked himself. "Why can't I have a model life like my father's? The man does what he wants and finds stability, love, and obedience when he returns home. I wasn't able to realize this dream with Zaynab or Maryam, and it seems unlikely I will with Zanuba either. This beautiful lute player must find nothing to regret while she's in my care."

He declared firmly, "If I'd wanted to violate God's laws any further, I wouldn't have married you."

She yelled sharply, "But you'd been married twice before, and marriage didn't prevent you from doing forbidden things then."

He exhaled a puff of breath reeking of alcohol and said, "You're in a different situation from my other wives, dummy. My first wife was chosen by my father, who imposed her on me. My second wouldn't let me touch her unless I married her. So I did. But no one imposed you on me. You didn't lock me out before we got married. Marrying you brought no promise of any novelty I hadn't experienced before. So, dummy, why did I marry you, unless marriage itself—in other words, a settled, stable life—was my goal? By God, if you had a speck of sense, you'd never doubt me."

"Not even when you return at dawn?"

"Not even if I come home in the morning."

She cried out sharply, "Stop! If that's all you have to say, then a most cordial goodbye."

Frowning nervously, he snapped back, "A thousand goodbyes!"

"I'm leaving. God's earth is vast, and God will provide me a living."

With deliberate scorn he commented, "Do what you like."

In a threatening voice she countered, "I'll leave, but you'll find I'm a thorn that's not easily removed."

Still trying to sound scornful, he said, "Nonsense! Ridding myself of you would be like taking off a pair of shoes."

Changing her tune from defiant challenge to complaint, she yelled, "Should I jump out the window so we'll both feel better?"

He shrugged his shoulders. Then, standing up, he said in a lighter tone, "There's a better solution. That's for you to jump in bed. Let's go to sleep and send the devil packing."

He went to the bed and stretched out, sighing as if he'd been wanting to lie down for a long time. She commented to herself, "Anyone living with you is destined to have trouble."

"I'm destined to have trouble too," Yasin complained to himself. "Your sex is responsible. There's not a single one of you who can keep me from wanting others. You're all powerless to conquer boredom. But I won't voluntarily resume a bachelor's life, and I can't sell a store every year for a new marriage. So let Zanuba stay as long as she doesn't try to control me. A crazy man needs a clever wife ... clever like Zanuba."

"Are you going to stay on the sofa till morning?"

"I won't close my eyes. Leave me alone and enjoy your sleep."

"Some things are so necessary they're inevitable," he reflected.

Stretching out his arms, he took hold of her shoulder. Then he drew her to him as he murmured, "Your bed!"

She resisted a little before yielding. As she climbed in bed she said plaintively, "When will I be granted the peace of mind other women enjoy?"

"Relax. You must have complete confidence in me. I deserve your trust. A man like me isn't happy unless he goes out at night. You won't find any happiness by making me unhappy and giving me a headache. All you need to do is to believe that my evening was spent innocently. Trust me. You won't regret it. I'm not a coward or a liar. Didn't I bring you to this house one night when my wife was here? Would a coward or a liar do that? I've played around enough. You're all I've got left in life."

She sighed audibly as though wishing to say, "If only you were telling the truth. . . ."

He stretched his hand out playfully and remarked, "My goodness! That sigh broke my heart. May God strike me dead."

Responding to the touch of his hand ever so gradually she said prayerfully, "If only our Lord would guide you."

"Who'd believe a lute player would make a wish like that?" Yasin asked himself.

"Don't ever quarrel with me. Quarreling drains our energy."

"The cure is working," he congratulated himself. "But it won't in all situations. If I'd had Ayusha tonight, it wouldn't have been so easy."

"Don't you see that your suspicions were misplaced?"

39 &

When Yasin entered the store and approached the desk, al-Sayyid Ahmad Abd al-Jawad was absorbed in his work. An examination of his son's face revealed immediately that Yasin had come to ask for help. There was a distracted, glazed look in the eyes of the young man, who smiled politely and leaned down to kiss his father's hand but seemed to perform these ceremonies unconsciously as his mind strayed God only knew where. When al-Sayyid Ahmad gestured for him to have a seat, he moved the chair close to his father's desk before sitting down. He looked at his father, lowered his eyes, and smiled palely. Al-Sayyid Ahmad wondered what had motivated this visit. Concerned about his son's silence, he asked curiously, "Good news? What's come over you? You're not your normal self."

Yasin looked at him for a long time as if appealing for sympathy. Then, lowering his eyes, he said, "They're going to transfer me to the farthest reaches of Upper Egypt."

"The Ministry?"

"Yes."

"Why?"

Shaking his head in protest, Yasin answered, "I asked the headmaster, and he mentioned things with no bearing on my work. It's unfair."

The father asked suspiciously, "What things? Explain."

"Vile slander. . . ." After some hesitation he added, "About my wife. . . ."

Al-Sayyid Ahmad's interest was heightened. He asked his son apprehensively, "What did they say?"

Yasin's discomfort was visible in his face as he replied, "Some fools said I'd married . . . a professional entertainer."

Al-Sayyid Ahmad looked around his store anxiously. He saw Jamil al-Hamzawi waiting on customers—a man standing on one side and a woman seated on the other. They were only a few feet away. Suppressing his rage, the father responded in a low voice not without a tremor of anger, "Perhaps they are fools, but I warned you about this. You do anything you want, never considering how scandalous it is, but then the consequences always catch up with you. What can I say? You're a school official, and your reputation ought to be beyond reproach. I've told you this time and again. There's no power or might save God's. It seems I must neglect all my other responsibilities in the world to care for you."

With apparent bewilderment Yasin observed, "But she's my legal wife. How can a man be blamed for obeying religious law? And why is it the Ministry's business?"

Restraining his fury, al-Sayyid Ahmad replied, "The Ministry must be solicitous of the reputations of its employees."

"Shouldn't you leave talk about reputations to someone else?" Yasin asked silently.

"But this is an unfair and unjust way to treat a married man."

Waving his hand angrily, the father retorted, "Do you want me to set the policies for the Ministry of Education?"

Yasin entreated him dejectedly, "Certainly not, but I hope you'll be able to stop the transfer by using your influence."

Preoccupied by his own thoughts, al-Sayyid Ahmad began to twist his mustache as he stared blankly at Yasin, who tried to gain his father's sympathy and apologized for upsetting him. Yasin asserted that, except for God, he relied exclusively on his father. He did not leave the store until his father promised to try to block the transfer.

That same evening al-Sayyid Ahmad went to al-Guindy's coffeehouse in Opera Square to see Yasin's headmaster, who immediately invited al-Sayyid Ahmad to join him and said, "I was expecting you. Yasin's gone too far. I regret the trouble he gives you."

Taking a seat opposite the headmaster, on a balcony overlooking the square, al-Sayyid Ahmad said, "In any case, Yasin's as much your son as mine."

"Of course, but this matter's out of my hands altogether. It's between him and the Ministry."

Although there was a smile on his face, al-Sayyid Ahmad protested, "Isn't it a bit odd to punish a civil servant for marrying a musician? Isn't that a private matter? And marriage is a legal bond. No one should denigrate it."

The headmaster frowned thoughtfully but inquisitively, as though not understanding his friend's words. Then he said, "The only mention of the marriage has been incidental and at the last minute. Don't you know the whole story? I thought you knew everything."

The man's spirits sank. He asked anxiously, "Is there some other offense?"

The headmaster leaned toward him a little and said sorrowfully, "The problem is, al-Sayyid Ahmad, that Yasin had a fight in Massage Alley with a whore. A police report was filed, and a copy reached the Ministry."

The man was stunned. His pupils opened wide, and his face became pale. The headmaster shook his head sadly and commented, "That's the truth. I did my utmost to lighten the punishment and successfully scuttled the idea of handing him over to a disciplinary panel. They agreed to transfer him to Upper Egypt."

Al-Sayyid Ahmad sighed and muttered, "The dog!"

Gazing at him sympathetically, the headmaster said, "I'm very sorry, al-Sayyid Ahmad. But this kind of conduct is not appropriate for a civil servant. I don't deny that he's a fine young man and diligent in his work. In fact, I'll tell you frankly that I like him, not merely because he's your son but because of his personality. Yet people say the strangest things about him. . . . He's got to reform and change his ways or he'll destroy his future."

Al-Sayyid Ahmad was silent for a long time, his anger obvious from his face. Then, as though addressing himself, he exclaimed, "A fight with a whore! Let him go to hell, then."

But he did not abandon his son. Without delay he met with acquaintances who were in parliament or distinguished in other ways and asked them to intercede to stop the transfer. Muhammad Iffat was his chief assistant in this campaign. A barrage of mediating efforts was aimed at top men in the Ministry of Education. Eventually it succeeded and the transfer was rescinded. But the Ministry insisted on assigning Yasin to a job within its secretariat. Then the head of the Ministry's records office—the new husband of Yasin's first wife —announced his readiness to accept Yasin in his department, on the recommendation of his father-in-law, Muhammad Iffat, and that was agreed to. Thus early in the winter of 1926 Yasin was transferred to the records department, but he did not emerge from the scandal scotfree. An entry was made in his file that he was unfit to work in a school, and he was passed over for promotion to the seventh grade in the civil service, although he had more than ten years' service in the eighth rank immediately below it.

By arranging this assignment to his son-in-law's department, Muhammad Iffat had meant to ensure that Yasin was well treated, but the young man was uncomfortable with working for Zaynab's husband. One day he told Kamal, "She's probably delighted by what's happened and thinks it justifies her father's refusal to return her to me. I know how women think. No doubt she's rejoicing over my misfortune. It's too bad that the only decent position I could find was working for this goat. He's so old he has nothing to offer a woman. It's absurd to think he could fill the void I left. So let the stupid woman gloat. I'm rejoicing at her loss too."

Zanuba never learned the secret behind the transfer. The most she could find out was that her husband had been assigned to a better position in the Ministry. Similarly al-Sayyid Ahmad skirted the real scandal in his discussions with Yasin. When the original transfer was rescinded, the father refrained from saying anything more than "The ending won't always be so happy. You've made a lot of trouble for me and embarrassed me. From now on I won't intervene in your affairs. Do what you like, and may our Lord protect me from you."

Al-Sayyid Ahmad could not stop thinking about Yasin. One day he summoned his son to the store and remarked, "It's time you thought seriously about your life and returned to honorable ways. Free yourself from the life of an outcast you're currently enjoying. There's still plenty of time for us to start all over. I can prepare a suitable life for you. So listen and obey me." Then he presented his proposals to Yasin: "Divorce your wife and return home. I'll marry you off again in a suitable fashion, so you can begin an honorable life."

Yasin blushed and said in a faint voice, "I appreciate your sincere desire to improve my life. I'll do my part to try to reform without troubling anyone else."

His father yelled angrily, "A new promise as meaningless as those of the English! It's plain that you won't be satisfied till you end up in prison. Yes, the next time you scream for help it will be from behind bars. I keep telling you to divorce that woman and return home."

Yasin sighed loudly to make sure his father heard and responded, "She's pregnant, Father. I don't want to add another sin to my list of offenses."

"God preserve us!" Al-Sayyid Ahmad exclaimed to himself. "Your new grandchild is being formed in Zanuba's belly. Could you possibly have imagined all the problems this young man had in store for you the moment you received him as an infant—on a day you thought one of the happiest of your life?"

"Pregnant?"

"Yes."

"And you're afraid of adding another sin to your list?" Then before his son could answer he exploded, "Why didn't your conscience trouble you when you were mistreating good women from fine families? By the truth of God's Book, you're a curse."

When Yasin left the store, his father looked after him with eyes filled with pity and scorn. He could not help taking some pride in the young man's appearance, inherited from him, but not in Yasin's character, inherited from the mother. He suddenly remembered how once he had almost fallen into this abyss, courtesy of the same Zanuba. But he also recalled restraining himself just in time. Had it really been self-restraint? He felt vexed and anxious. He cursed Yasin and then cursed Yasin again.

40 ❧

When the twentieth of December arrived, he sensed the day was unlike any other, at least for him. On this date he had entered the world and that fact was recorded on his birth certificate, so that no one would be able to fib about it. Clad in an overcoat, he was pacing back and forth in his room. Glancing at his desk, he saw his diary, which was open to a blank page with the date of his birth at the top. He was thinking about what to write for his birthday. He kept moving to stay warm in the biting cold. As he could see through the windowpane, the sky was concealed behind gloomy clouds. The intermittent rain made him pensive and dreamy.

A birthday had to be celebrated, even if the birthday boy was the only one at the party. The old house had no tradition of commemorating birthdays. His mother herself did not know this was a day she should not forget. Of the births of her children all she retained were vague memories of the seasons when they had occurred and of the pain accompanying them. The most she could say of his birth was: "It was in winter and the delivery was difficult. My labor pains and screams lasted two days."

Formerly, when he had thought of his birth, his heart had been filled with pity for his mother. When he had witnessed Na'ima's birth, these feelings had intensified, as his heart pounded painfully with sympathy for Aisha. Today he thought of his birth in a new way, for his mind had drunk so avidly from the fountains of materialist philosophy that in two months he had grasped ideas mankind had taken a century to develop. He wondered about his delivery and whether part or all of its difficulty was attributable to neglect or ignorance. He asked this as though interrogating a suspect who stood before him. He thought about difficult deliveries, the damage they might cause the brain or nervous system, and the profound effect such injuries could have on the life, destiny, and happiness of the newborn. Might not his exaggerated interest in love be the result of shocks to the top or side of his large head in the hidden reaches of the womb nineteen years before? Why not consider his idealism—which had misled him for so long with ignorant fantasies and induced him to shed countless tears on torment's bloody altar—a sad consequence of the clumsiness of an ignorant midwife?

He thought about the prenatal period, including the time before conception, the uncharted territory from which life sprang, the mechanical and chemical equation to which a living creature could be reduced, the scornful rejection this creature accorded his actual origin from the start as he claimed descent from the stars at which he gazed. Kamal had learned that his origin was not nearly so remote. It was something called sperm. Nineteen years and nine months before, he had been nothing but a drop of sperm ejected because of an innocent desire for pleasure, a pressing need for solace, a bout of excitement inspired by an intoxication extinguishing common sense, or even a feeling of obligation toward a wife who was confined to the house. To which of these did he owe his conception? Perhaps duty had caused him to come into the world, for he was haunted by a concern for doing his duty. He had not allowed himself certain pleasures until they presented themselves as a philosophy he ought follow and a view he should adopt. Even then, he had engaged in a painful struggle with himself first. His approach to life was hardly one of carefree abandon.

Sperm penetrated a living creature, found the ovum in the Fallopian tube, and fertilized it. Then they slid together into the womb, where they changed into a fetus, which developed flesh and bones. This creature then emerged into the light, causing pain it could not appreciate. It started crying even before its features could be seen clearly. The development of its instincts gave rise in time to so many beliefs and ideas that it was crammed with them. It fell in love and as a result claimed to partake of the divine. Then it was badly shaken, its beliefs were destroyed, and its thoughts were turned upside down. Its heart was broken, and it was reduced to a humbler status than its initial one.

In this manner nineteen years had passed ... what a long period! Youth fled with the speed of lightning. What consolation was left, besides enjoying life hour by hour and even minute by minute until a crow's call heralded the end?

The age of innocence was over. He had reached a stage of life in which he dated things by love: B.L. and A.L. Today he was conscious of many desires, but the identity of his beloved was unknown. The closest he could come to identifying his beloved was through attribution to it of some divine names, like truth, the joy of life, and the light of knowledge. It seemed his journey would be long. His lover appeared to have boarded the train of Auguste Comte and passed by the station of theology, where the password was "Yes, Mother." This train was now traversing the realm of metaphysics, where the password was "Certainly not, Mother." In the distance, visible through a telescope, was the mountain of reality on which was inscribed its password: "Open your eyes and be courageous."

He stopped in front of the desk and fixed his eyes on the diary, wondering whether to sit down and allow his pen to record whatever it chose for his birthday or to postpone that until his ideas had crystallized. Hearing the drone of falling rain, he glanced at the panes of the window overlooking Palace Walk. He noticed pearly drops clinging to the surface of the glass, which was misty from the humidity in the air. A pearl soon slid to the bottom, tracing on the surface a bright line with a curving path like a shooting star's.

Kamal went to the window and looked up at the raindrops pouring from the heavy clouds. The heavens were united with the earth by these glittering threads. The minarets and domes of the district seemed oblivious to the rain, and the horizon behind them resembled a silver frame. The entire scene was washed with a white blended with the brown of teak, a combination suitable for exalted dreams. The cries of children rose from the street. Kamal glanced down and saw the earth streaming with water and mud. Carts were moving with difficulty, their wheels spattering everything in reach. The shops had withdrawn their outdoor displays, and pedestrians sought refuge in shops and coffeehouses or under balconies.

This view of the sky struck a responsive chord in Kamal's mind. What could be more appropriate than drawing inspiration from it as he contemplated his situation at the beginning of another year of his life? Since Husayn Shaddad had left his homeland, Kamal no longer had a companion with whom he could discuss his spiritual secrets. He had to mull them over by himself if he felt a need for discussion. Since his soul mate had left him, Kamal had been forced to make his own soul his companion.

He asked his spirit, "Do you believe in the existence of God?"

When his spirit's turn came, it asked, "Why don't you jump from star to star and planet to planet as you do from one step to another on the stairs?"

It also inquired about the chosen elite among the self-proclaimed descendants of the heavens who had elevated the earth to a central place in existence, making even the angels bow down to Adam's clay. Then their brother Copernicus had returned earth to the status originally granted it by existence as nothing more than the sun's small servant. He was followed by his brother Darwin, who exposed the secrets of man, this bogus prince, announcing for all to hear that man's true ancestor was the ape held captive in a cage in the zoo, where man invited his friends to gawk at it during holiday excursions.

"In the beginning, the universe was one large nebula. Then stars spread out from this center as if spattered into space by the rotating wheel of a bicycle. Through the eternal interplay of gravitational fields, these stars gave birth to planets. The earth itself was flung out like a molten ball trailed by the moon, which teased the earth by frowning at it with one side of its face and smiling with the other. When the earth's fire cooled, its features assumed their permanent shape as mountains, plateaus, plains, and rock formations. Then life crept forth. Crawling on all fours, earth's son arrived, questioning anyone he encountered about high ideals.

"I won't hide my impatience with legends. In the immense raging wave, I discovered a three-sided rock, which from now on I'll call the rock of knowledge, philosophy, and idealism. Don't say that philosophy, like religion, has a mythical character. It rests on solid, scientific foundations and advances systematically toward its objectives. Art is an elevated form of entertainment and enhances life, but my aspirations stretch beyond art. What I want is to draw inspiration only from the truth. Compared with truth, art seems an effeminate pursuit. To attain my goal, you'll find I'm prepared to sacrifice everything except life itself. My qualifications for this important role include a large head, an enormous nose, disappointment in love, and expectations of ill health. Be careful not to mock youthful dreams, for that's a symptom of senility. People affected by this disease term their sarcasm 'wisdom.' There's nothing to prevent a sensible person from admiring Sa'd Zaghlul as much as Copernicus, the chemist Ostwald, or the physicist Mach; for an effort to link Egypt with the advance of human progress is noble and humane. Patriotism's a virtue, if it's not tainted by xenophobia. Of course, hating England is a form of self-defense. That kind of nationalism is nothing more than a local manifestation of a concern for human rights.

"You ask if I believe in love. My response is that love is still in my heart. I must acknowledge this truth of human nature. Although the roots of love were tangled up with those of religion and of other legends, the collapse of the sacred temples did not shake the pillars of love or diminish its importance. Its status remained unchanged even when its ceremonial niche was invaded by study and analysis.

Examination of its biological, psychological, and sociological components has not harmed it. None of these investigations can make the heart pound any less fiercely when a special memory or image comes to mind."

"Do you still believe in love's immortality?"

"Immortality's just a myth. Presumably love will be forgotten, like everything else in the world."

"A year has passed since Aïda's wedding; why do you still hesitate to pronounce her name?"

"I've made some progress on the path to forgetfulness. I've traversed stretches of insanity, stupor, intense pain, and then less frequent discomfort. Now a whole day may pass without my thinking of her, except when I wake up or go to bed, and then once or twice during the day. When I remember her, that affects me in different ways. A mild longing is revived, a sorrow flees by like a cloud, or a regret stings but doesn't burn me. At times my soul will suddenly erupt like a volcano, as the earth turns under my feet. In any case, I've come to believe that I'll continue my life, even without Aïda."

"What do you rely on in your search for forgetfulness?"

"I depend on the study and analysis of love, as previously mentioned, and on minimizing my individual pains through speculations that embrace all of existence so that by comparison man's world seems a trivial speck. I also refresh my soul with alcohol and sex. I seek consolation with philosophers who specialize in it—like Spinoza, who thinks that time is unreal, that passions linked to an event in the past or future make no sense, and that we're capable of overcoming them, if we can form a clear and distinct idea of them."

"Did it make you happy to discover love can be forgotten?"

"It did, because that promised me release from captivity, but the experience also saddened me by introducing me to death prematurely. In no matter what context, I'll despise bondage and love absolute freedom as long as I live."

"It's a happy person who has never thought of suicide or longed for death. It's a happy person who has the torch of enthusiasm blazing in his heart. A person's immortal when working or preparing seriously for work. A person's truly alive when he responds to Umar al-Khayyam's invitation to take up a book, a drink, and a sweetheart. A soul full of fervent hopes forgets or is oblivious to marriage in the same way that a glass full of whiskey has no room for soda water. What more can you want if your infatuation with drink continues happily and your encounters with women are not blocked by disgust or aversion. If you long occasionally for purity and asceticism, that could be a holdover from your previous piety."

The rain kept pouring down. Thunder roared, and there was a gleam of lightning. The street was deserted and all its cries silenced. Wishing to look at the courtyard, he left the bedroom and went to the window of the sitting room. Gazing out the peephole, he saw that water was washing away the loose dirt on the surface, eroding it, and then rushing off toward the old well. Water was also flowing out of the well on the other side and flooding a depression between the oven room and the storeroom. In that declivity, where a residue of wheat, barley, and fenugreek seed, accidentally dropped by Umm Hanafi, had collected, a growth like green silk brocade would sprout. For some days it would thrive, until trampled by their feet. In his childhood, that area had served as the setting for his maneuvers and his dreams. That wellspring of memories still supplied his heart with a yearning and a delight shaded by sorrow like a diaphanous cloud veiling the face of the moon.

Turning away from the window to go back to his room, he became aware of the presence of other people in the sitting room. They were the last remnants of the old coffee hour. His mother sat on the sofa with her legs tucked beneath her and her arms spread over the brazier. She had no one to keep her company save Umm Hanafi, who sat cross-legged on a sheepskin opposite her mistress. He thought of the gathering in its brightest days and of the beautiful memories it had left behind. The brazier was the only survivor not to have undergone changes the viewer wished to reject.

Ahmad Abd al-Jawad walked slowly along the bank of the Nile on his way to Muhammad Iffat's houseboat. The night was calm, the sky clear, the stars twinkling, and the weather cool. When he reached the gangplank and started across it, he glanced from force of habit at the distant houseboat he had once called Zanuba's. A year had passed since those painful events, and all that was left of them in his heart was resentful embarrassment. One other consequence had been his boycott of parties comparable to his previous ban following Fahmy's death. He had avoided them scrupulously for a year, before becoming exasperated. After a change of heart, he was now seeking out the forbidden bacchanal.

The next moment he was joining the beloved gathering and seeing his three male friends and the two women. The men he had seen as recently as the previous night, but he had not set eyes on the women for about a year and a half—or, to be precise, not since the night Zanuba had been introduced to his life. The party had yet to begin, for the liquor bottles were full and decorum was still being observed. Jalila, who occupied the main sofa, was toying with her gold bracelets as if wanting to make them jingle. Zubayda, who stood beneath the hanging lamp, was examining her appearance in a small mirror she held in her hand. Her back was to the table crowded with whiskey bottles and plates of appetizers.

Bareheaded, the three men, who had removed their cloaks, were scattered around the room. Ahmad Abd al-Jawad shook hands with them and then warmly clasped the hands of the women.

Jalila greeted him, "Welcome, dear brother."

Zubayda cast him a censorious smile as she said, "Welcome to a person who would deserve nothing but goodbye from us, except for common courtesy."

The man removed his cloak and fez and looked around for a vacant place. Zubayda had taken a seat next to Jalila. He hesitated a little before going to their sofa and sitting there. His vacillation did not escape the eyes of Ali Abd al-Rahim, who said, "You almost seem a novice at this."

Jalila tried to encourage al-Sayyid Ahmad by telling Ali Abd al-Rahim, "Leave him alone. There's never been any reserve between us."

Zubayda was quick to laugh and say scornfully, "I'm the one with the most right to say that. Isn't he my in-law?"

Al-Sayyid Ahmad understood her allusion and wondered anxiously how much she knew of the whole affair. But he replied tenderly, "It's my honor, sultana."

Gazing at him suspiciously, Zubayda asked, "Are you really pleased with what's happened?"

He answered suavely, "Only because you're her aunt."

Waving her hand in disapproval, she said, "My heart will never forgive her."

Before al-Sayyid Ahmad could ask why, Ali Abd al-Rahim, who was rubbing his hands together, yelled, "Save the conversation till we've filled our heads." After rising and going to the table, he opened a bottle and poured drinks, which he presented to them, one at a time, with a solicitude that revealed his customary satisfaction with tending bar. Then he waited until everyone was ready before saying, "To the health of our lovers, our brothers, and music. May we never lack these three things."

Smiling, they raised their glasses to their lips. Ahmad Abd al-Jawad looked over the rim of his at the faces of his companions, these friends with whom he had shared affection and loyalty for almost forty years. They almost seemed slivers of his heart. He could not keep his feelings of sincere fraternal affection from agitating his breast. As his eyes turned to Zubayda, he resumed his conversation with her, asking, "Why won't your heart forgive her?"

She cast him a glance that made him feel she welcomed this chance to talk and replied, "Because she's a traitor with no respect for promises. She betrayed me more than a year ago. She left my house without asking permission and disappeared."

Was it possible she really did not know where Zanuba had been during that time? Since he did not care to offer the least comment on her words, she finally asked him, "Didn't you hear about that?"

"I did eventually."

"I've taken care of her since she was a child and have looked after her as though I were her mother. See how I've been rewarded! To hell with her genes!"

Pretending to object, Ali Abd al-Rahim teased her, "Don't insult her family. You're part of it."

But Zubayda replied seriously, "She doesn't have any of my genes."

Al-Sayyid Ahmad inquired, "Who do you suppose her father was?"

"Her father!" This comment emerged from Ibrahim al-Far in a tone that suggested a string of sarcastic remarks was to follow, but Muhammad Iffat headed him off by interjecting, "Remember you're talking about Yasin's wife."

The mirthful look left al-Far's face, and he retreated into an uneasy silence. Then Zubayda spoke up again: "I'm not joking about her. She envied me for a long time. Even when she was in my custody she wanted to rival me. I spoiled her and pretended not to see her defects." Then she laughed and continued: "She wanted to be a soloist, a vocalist." Looking around at her friends, she observed sarcastically, "But she failed and got married."

Ali Abd al-Rahim asked incredulously, "In your opinion, does marriage constitute failure?"

She squinted an eye at him and raised the eyebrow of the other one and then answered, "Yes, fellow. A performer never leaves her troupe unless she's a failure."

Then Jalila sang, "You're the wine, my love. You've cheered us up."

Al-Sayyid Ahmad grinned broadly and greeted the song with a gentle sigh that revealed his delight. But Ali Abd al-Rahim rose once more, saying, "A moment of silence until we finish off this round." He filled the glasses again, redistributed them, and returned to his seat with his own drink.

Grasping his glass, al-Sayyid Ahmad glanced at Zubayda, who turned toward him and smilingly raised her drink as if to say, "To your health." He imitated her and they both drank at the same time. She was gazing at him with a merry look. A year had passed since he had felt like looking for a woman. The harsh experience he had endured seemed to have deadened his enthusiasm, but pride or ill health could also have been responsible. Even so, the combined influence of alcoholic intoxication and this affectionate look stirred his heart. He savored the sweetness of this welcome, which followed a bitter rejection. He considered this a friendly greeting from the entire sex he had been so fond of all his life. It bound up his wounded dignity, which had fallen victim to betrayal and age. Zubayda's eloquent smile seemed to say, "Your day's not finished yet." He kept looking and smiling at her.

Muhammad Iffat brought the lute and placed it between the two women. Jalila picked it up and began to play. Once she was confident of their attention, she sang, "Beloved, I promise you ..."

As usual when he heard Jalila or Zubayda sing, Ahmad Abd al-Jawad pretended to be moved by the music. He nodded his head appreciatively, as if wishing to induce ecstasy by acting it out. The truth was that all he had left from the world of song was a set of memories. The great performers he had admired, like al-Hamuli, Uthman, al-Manilawi, and Abd al-Hayy, had passed away—just as his youthful era of conquests had vanished. He would have to accustom himself to taking pleasure in what was at hand and in triggering a feeling of ecstasy by going through the motions. His love of song and infatuation with music had led him to visit the theater of Munira al-Mahdiya, but he had not liked the combination of theater and music. Besides, he chafed at sitting in a theater like a school auditorium. At Muhammad Iffat's house he had also listened to records of the new singer Umm Kalthoum but only with a cautious and suspicious ear. He did not enjoy her singing, even though it was said that Sa'd Zaghlul had praised the beauty of her voice.

Yet his appearance gave no hint of his feelings as he gazed at Jalila with happy delight and sang the words of the refrain, "I hold you responsible," with the others in his pleasing voice.

Then al-Far cried out with regret, "Where, oh where is the tambourine? Where is it so we can hear the son of Abd al-Jawad?"

"Ask rather: Where's the Ahmad Abd al-Jawad who used to play the tambourine?" he said to himself. "Oh ... why has time changed us?"

Jalila ended her song in an atmosphere of receptive approval. But with a grateful smile she said apologetically, "I'm tired."

Zubayda heaped her with praise. The two performers frequently complimented each other either from politeness or from a desire to keep the peace. Everyone realized that as a performer Jalila's star was rapidly setting. One of the most recent indications of that was the desertion of her tambourine player, Fino, to another troupe. This eclipse was only natural, given the withering away of all the qualities on which her past glory had rested: her charm, beauty, and voice. For that reason, Zubayda no longer felt particularly envious of her and was capable of flattering her former rival good-humoredly, especially since Zubayda had reached the pinnacle of her career, one that could only be followed by a decline.

The friends often wondered whether Jalila had prepared properly for this dangerous stage of her life. It was Ahmad Abd al-Jawad's opinion that she had not. He accused some of her lovers of squandering much of her fortune but at the same time proclaimed that she was a woman who knew how to get money one way or another. Ali Abd al-Rahim supported him, saying, "She profits from the beauty of the women in her troupe, and ever so gradually her home's turning into a different kind of house."

Their consensus was less sanguine about Zubayda's future, for despite the freedom with which she helped herself to her lovers' wealth, she spent liberally and was fond of the showy possessions that dissipate money quickly. Moreover, she was addicted to alcohol and narcotics, cocaine in particular.

Muhammad Iffat told Zubayda, "Allow me to express my admiration for the sweet looks you are directing to one of us."

Jalila laughed and said softly, "His infatuation's revealed by his eyes. . . ."

Ibrahim al-Far asked with sham disapproval, "Do you think you're in a charitable institution for the blind?"

With feigned regret Ahmad Abd al-Jawad replied, "If you continue to speak so bluntly, you'll never fulfill your ambition to be pimps."

Zubayda told Muhammad Iffat, "The only reason I'm looking at him, God forgive me, is out of envy at his youth. Look at his black head of hair among your white ones and tell me if you'd think he's a day over forty?"

"I'd give him about a century more."

Ahmad Abd al-Jawad retorted, "From your surplus years."

Jalila sang the opening of the song "The envious eye has a log in it, sweetheart."

Zubayda commented, "He doesn't need to fear my envy, for my eye would never harm him."

Shaking his head suggestively, Muhammad Iffat replied, "Your eyes are the cause of all the trouble."

Ahmad Abd al-Jawad told Zubayda, "Why are you talking about my youth? Haven't you heard what the doctor said?"

As though she could not believe it, she said, "Muhammad Iffat told me, but what's this pressure you're supposed to have?"

"He wrapped a strange sack around my arm and began to pump it up. Then he told me, 'You've got pressure.' "

"Where did this pressure come from?"

Al-Sayyid Ahmad laughingly answered, "I imagine that pump induced it."

Clapping his hands together, Ibrahim al-Far said, "Perhaps it's a contagious disease, because within a month of our friend's attack each of us had a doctor's examination too, and the diagnosis in each case was the same: pressure."

Ali Abd al-Rahim observed, "I'll tell you the secret behind it. This is one of the side effects of the revolution. The proof is that no one ever heard of it before then."

Jalila asked al-Sayyid Ahmad, "What are the symptoms of this pressure?"

"A bitch of a headache and difficulty breathing when I walk."

Smiling somewhat anxiously, Zubayda murmured, "Who doesn't have those symptoms, if only occasionally? Do you think I've got pressure too?"

Ahmad Abd al-Jawad asked, "Above or below your waist?"

They all laughed, including Zubayda herself, and then Jalila said, "Since you're experienced with pressure, why don't you examine her. Perhaps you can discover what ails her."

Ahmad Abd al-Jawad replied, "If she'll bring the sack, I'll supply the pump."

They laughed again. Then Muhammad Iffat protested, "Pressure, pressure, pressure ... all we ever hear nowadays is the doctor giving us orders as though we were his slaves: Don't drink alcoholic beverages. Don't eat red meat. Beware of eggs."

Ahmad Abd al-Jawad asked scornfully, "What's a man like me to do? I eat only red meat and eggs and drink nothing but alcohol."

Zubayda replied immediately, "Eat and drink in good health. A man should be his own physician, letting our Lord have the last word."

During the time he had been forced to stay in bed he had followed his doctor's orders. When he had been able to get around again, he had forgotten this medical advice completely.

Jalila spoke up again: "I don't believe in doctors, but I'll admit they have an excuse for what they say and do. They make their living from illnesses just as we performers make our living from joyous occasions like weddings. They couldn't get by without their sack, pump, orders, and prohibitions any more than we could survive without the tambourine, lute, and songs."

With enthusiastic relief, al-Sayyid Ahmad said, "You're right. Illness and health, like life and death, arise solely from God's command. Anyone who trusts in God will have no cause for sorrow."

Laughing, Ibrahim al-Far said, "Feast your eyes on this man, folks. He drinks with his mouth, lusts with his eye, and preaches with his tongue."

Between guffaws, Ahmad Abd al-Jawad retorted, "There's nothing wrong with that, so long as I do my preaching in a brothel."

Examining Ahmad Abd al-Jawad and shaking his head with wonder, Muhammad Iffat commented, "I wish Kamal were here to profit from your sermon along with us."

Ali Abd al-Rahim asked, "By the way, is he still of the opinion that man's descended from an ape?"

Striking her hand against her breast, Jalila exclaimed, "How dreadful!"

"An ape?" Zubayda asked with astonishment. Then, as though reconsidering, she said, "Perhaps he was referring to his father, not a forefather."

Al-Sayyid Ahmad cautioned her, "He also showed that women are descended from a lioness."

Bursting into laughter, she replied, "I'd certainly like to see the child of a monkey and a lioness."

Ibrahim al-Far commented, "When Kamal grows up and leaves his family circle he'll observe that normal people are descended from Adam and Eve."

Ahmad Abd al-Jawad shot back, "Or I'll bring him here one day. That will convince him man's descended from dogs."

Ali Abd al-Rahim went back to the table to fill their glasses again and asked Zubayda, "Since you know al-Sayyid Ahmad more intimately than any of us, can you say which animal family you'd place him in?"

She reflected a little as she watched Ali Abd al-Rahim's hands pour the whiskey. Then, with a smile, she replied, "The ass!"

Jalila asked, "Is this a compliment or an insult?"

Ahmad Abd al-Jawad answered, "Only her belly knows for sure."

They drank some more in the best of humors. Zubayda picked up the lute and sang, "Let down the curtain around us."

The body of Ahmad Abd al-Jawad began to sway to the music in an overwhelming intoxication. He raised his glass, which was empty except for a film of whiskey at the bottom, and looked through that at the woman, as though wishing to observe her with a golden spyglass. Whatever private resentment there might have been between them had vanished. It was clear that the bond between Ahmad and

Zubayda had been reestablished. They all sang the chorus with Zubayda, Ahmad's voice growing loud with delight and ecstasy. The song concluded to their jubilant applause.

Muhammad Iffat immediately asked Jalila, "Speaking of the song 'His passion's revealed by his eyes,' what do you think of Umm Kalthoum?"

Jalila answered, "Her voice, with God as my witness, is beautiful, but all too often she's as shrill as a child."

"Some people say she'll be the next Munira al-Mahdiya. Others say her voice is even more marvelous than Munira's."

Jalila cried out, "Nonsense! How does this shrillness compare with Munira's magnificently husky voice?"

Zubayda remarked disdainfully, "There's something about her voice that reminds one of a Qur'an reciter—as though she was an entertainer in a shaykh's turban."

Ahmad Abd al-Jawad said, "I don't care for her, but a lot of people are wild about her. The truth is that the vocal era ended with the death of Abduh al-Hamuli."

Muhammad Iffat teased his friend, "You're a reactionary. You always try to cling to the past." Winking, he continued: "Don't you insist on ruling your home by fiat and force, even in the age of democracy and parliament?"

Al-Sayyid Ahmad replied scornfully, "Democracy's for the people, not the family."

Ali Abd al-Rahim said seriously, "Do you think you can rule the young people of today in the old-fashioned way? These youngsters are used to demonstrating in the streets and confronting the soldiers."

Ibrahim al-Far said, "I don't know what you're talking about, but I agree with Ahmad. We each have sons—God help us."

Muhammad Iffat said playfully, "Both of you are strong advocates of democracy, but you're tyrants at home."

Ahmad Abd al-Jawad protested, "Do you really want me to assemble Kamal, his mother, and Yasin to let them vote before I deal with a problem?"

Zubayda burst into laughter. She reminded him, "Please don't forget Zanuba!"

Ibrahim al-Far said, "If the revolution's the cause for the problems our children are causing us, may God forgive Sa'd Zaghlul."

The drinking, chatting, singing, and joking continued. The din became louder, and their voices blended together. The night advanced, oblivious to the world. He would look at her and find her watching him, or she would be the one to glance at him and catch him watching her. He told himself, "In this world there's only one true pleasure." He wanted to express this thought but did not, either because his enthusiasm for sharing it weakened or because he did not feel he could say it. But why should he feel weak?

Once again he asked himself whether this was to be an hour's enjoyment or a long affair. His soul pined for entertainment and consolation, but there was a ringing in his ears, as though the waves of the Nile were whispering to him. He was almost halfway through his sixth decade. "Ask scholars how a lifetime can pass like this. We know it's happening, but at the same time we don't."

"What's silenced you? May God spare us evil."

"Me? A little rest . . ."

"Yes, how sweet it is to rest," he told himself. "A long sleep from which you'll rise in good health. How delightful it is to be healthy. . . . But they're always after you, not leaving you a single moment to enjoy peace. This look is fascinating, but the whispering of the waves is growing louder. How can you hear the singing?"

"Certainly not. We won't leave until we give him a proper wedding procession. What do you think? A procession . . . a procession!"

"Rise, my camel."

"Me? A little rest."

"The procession . . . the procession, like the first time at the house in al-Ghuriya."

"That was long ago."

"We'll revive it. The procession . . . the procession."

"They're merciless. That time's vanished. It's hidden by dark shadows. How thick the darkness is! How my ears are ringing! What an overpowering forgetfulness!"

"Look!"

"What's wrong with him?"

"A little water. Open the window."

"O Gracious One, O Lord . . ."

"It's all right . . . all right. Wet this handkerchief in cold water."

42 ❧

During the week after the father's "accident," he was visited every day by the doctor, but his condition was critical enough that no one else was allowed to call on him. Even his children had to tiptoe into the room for a glimpse of his sleeping face. They would carefully note his look of resigned exhaustion before retreating with gloomy expressions and sinking hearts. They glanced with interest at one another but shrank from the sad reinforcement this exchange provided.

The physician said the seizure was a result of high blood pressure. He cupped the patient, filling a basin with blood, which Khadija, trembling all over, described as black. Amina emerged from the room now and again, looking like an aimless phantom. Kamal seemed to be in a daze, as though asking himself how such earthshaking events could occur in the twinkling of an eye and how this colossus of a man could have succumbed. Whenever he stole a look at his mother's ghostly form, Khadija's tearful eyes, or Aisha's pale face, he wondered again what all this meant. He found himself unconsciously led to imagine the end his heart dreaded. He pictured a world without his father, and this vision chilled his breast and alarmed his heart. He asked himself apprehensively how his mother could possibly survive. She already appeared as good as dead, and nothing had happened yet. Then he thought of Fahmy and wondered whether their father would be forgotten as easily as their late brother. The world seemed lost in gloom.

Yasin learned of the incident the day after it occurred and came to the house for the first time since he had left to marry Maryam. He went directly to his father's room and silently looked at al-Sayyid Ahmad for a long time. Then he retreated to the sitting room in a state of shock. He found Amina there, and they shook hands after their long separation. He was deeply touched, and his eyes filled with tears as he held her hand.

Al-Sayyid Ahmad remained in bed. At first he could not speak or move. The cupping put some life into him, and he was then able to get out a word or a brief phrase to make his wishes known. But at that time, he became conscious of his pain, which he expressed in assorted moans and groans. Once the intensity of his physical pain diminished, he became restless with this compulsory bed rest, which deprived him of the blessings of motion and cleanliness. He was obliged to eat, drink, and do things that disgusted him all in one place—his bed. His sleep was interrupted, but his annoyance was continual. The first thing he wanted to know was how he had been conveyed to the house when unconscious.

Amina replied that his friends—Muhammad Iffat, Ali Abd al-Rahim, and Ibrahim al-Far—had brought him home in a carriage and had gently taken him up to bed. Then they had found a doctor for him, even though it was very late.

After that, he asked if he had had visitors, and the woman told him they had come regularly, although the physician had forbidden them to see him for the time being.

In a weak voice he repeated, "The matter's in God's hands, both first and last," and "We ask God for a good outcome." But the truth was that he did not despair and did not feel his end was near. His confidence in the life he loved was no weaker, despite his pains and fears. Hope came back with the return of consciousness. He favored no one with last words of advice, made no disposition of his effects, said farewell to no one, and did not reveal any secrets of his business or fortune to those involved. To the contrary, he summoned Jamil al-Hamzawi and asked him to arrange some commercial transactions he himself would not have known how to conduct. He sent Kamal to the tailor to collect and pay for some new clothes he had ordered. His only mention of death was in these phrases he repeated as if to mask fate's cruelty.

At the end of the first week the doctor explained that the invalid had successfully survived the critical stage and would regain his health completely and feel as energetic as ever, with a little patience. The physician repeated the previous warning about high blood pressure, and al-Sayyid Ahmad promised to obey. He also vowed secretly to abstain from licentious behavior, for its disastrous consequences were now clear to him and had convinced him that his health was not a joking matter anymore. He consoled himself by saying, "A healthy life with a little self-denial's better at any rate than being sick." Thus the crisis was successfully overcome. The family members caught their breath, their hearts full of gratitude.

By the end of the second week, al-Sayyid Ahmad was permitted to receive visitors. That was a happy day, and his family were the first to celebrate it. His children with their spouses called on him and conversed with him for the first time since he had been confined to bed. The man looked from face to face, from Yasin to Khadija, Aisha, Ibrahim Shawkat, and Khalil Shawkat. With his customary charm, which did not desert him even in such circumstances, he asked about their children: Ridwan, Abd al-Muni'm, Ahmad, Na'ima, Uthman, and Muhammad. They said they had not brought the children for fear of disturbing him and prayed he would have a long life and be totally restored to good health. They told him of their sorrow over his suffering and their delight at his recovery. Khadija's voice trembled when she spoke, and the tear Aisha left on his hand when she kissed it required no explanation. Yasin suavely said that he had felt ill when his father did and had recovered with him when God had granted a cure. The father's pale face was radiant with joy, and he spoke to them at length about God's decrees, mercy, and grace, explaining that it was the Believer's duty to meet his fate with patience and confidence and to trust only in God.

On leaving his bedroom, they went to Kamal's room so the sitting room would be free to serve as a corridor for the anticipated throngs of visitors.

Yasin approached Amina then and clasped her hand in his as he said, "I haven't spoken to you of my feelings during the last two weeks because Papa's illness left me no mind with which to think. Now that God has restored him to health, I want to apologize for returning to this house without first asking your permission. The truth is that you received me with the same affection as in the happy bygone days, but now it's my duty to present my formal apology to you."

Amina blushed as she replied emotionally, "What's done is done, Yasin! This is your home. You're most welcome to stay here whenever you want."

Yasin said firmly, "I don't like to rake up the past, but I swear by my father's head and the life of my son Ridwan that my heart never harbored any grudge against the members of this family. I love you all as much as I do myself. Perhaps Satan prompted me to err. That could happen to anyone. But my heart was never corrupted."

Amina placed her hand on his broad shoulder and said sincerely, "You've always been one of my children. I don't deny I got angry once, but the anger's gone, praise God. All that's left is the previous love. This is your home, Yasin. Welcome home!"

Yasin sat down forcefully. When Amina left the room, he proclaimed to the others, "What a fine woman! May God never forgive a person who wrongs her. God's curse on Satan, who once tempted me into something that hurt her feelings."

Casting him an eloquent look, Khadija remarked, "Scarcely a year goes by without Satan tempting you into a new disaster. You're just a toy in his hands."

The glance he directed at her seemed to plead for mercy from her tongue. Then Aisha said in his defense, "That's all ancient history."

Khadija asked sarcastically, "Why didn't you bring madame your wife to 'entertain' us on this blessed occasion?"

Attempting to sound proud, Yasin answered, "My wife no longer entertains at parties. Today she's a lady in every sense of the word."

In an earnest voice without a trace of sarcasm, Khadija asked, "How can you do such things, Yasin? May our Lord grant you repentance and guide you."

As though to apologize for his wife's bluntness, Ibrahim Shawkat said, "Don't be offended, Mr. Yasin ... but what am I to do? She's your sister."

Smiling, Yasin replied, "May God assist you, Mr. Ibrahim."

Aisha sighed and said, "Now that God has come to Papa's aid, I'll tell you frankly that I'll never forget, as long as I live, the way he looked in bed the first time I saw him there. May our Lord not condemn anyone to ill health."

Khadija commented sincerely and ardently, "This life wouldn't be worth a fingernail clipping without him."

Yasin responded passionately, "He's our shelter in every adversity, a man like no other...."

"And what about me?" Kamal asked himself. "Do you remember how you stood in the corner of the room overwhelmed by despair? My heart was shattered by the sight of my mother beside herself with grief. We're familiar with the concept of death, but when its shadow looms on the horizon, the earth spins under us. There will be new attacks of pain each time, no matter how many loved ones you lose. You'll die too, leaving your hopes behind you. But life's desirable, even if you suffer from love."

The ringing of a carriage bell could be heard from the street. Aisha ran to the window to look out the peephole. She turned back to say proudly, "Important visitors!"

There was a steady stream of visitors representing the many friends with whom the father's life was filled—civil servants, attorneys, dignitaries, and merchants. All but a few had been to the house before, although some had come only as guests at the banquets al-Sayyid Ahmad hosted on special occasions. There were also some faces frequently seen in the Goldsmiths Bazaar and on New Street. These men were his friends too, but not in the same class as Muhammad Iffat and his cronies.

The visitors did not stay long, as was appropriate for a sick call, but al-Sayyid Ahmad's children found plenty to satisfy their vanity and pride in the distinguished appearance of these guests and in all the carriages with their beautiful horses.

Aisha, who was still watching the street, said, "Here are his pals."

They could hear the voices of Muhammad Iffat, Ali Abd al-Rahim, and Ibrahim al-Far as the men laughed and raised their voices with thanks and praise for God. Yasin said, "There are no other friends left in the world like these."

Ibrahim and Khalil Shawkat agreed with him. Then Kamal observed with a sorrow that passed unnoticed, "It's rare for life to allow friends to stay together for as long as these men."

Yasin marveled, "A day hasn't gone by without their visiting the house. During his crisis, there were tears in their eyes whenever they left."

Ibrahim Shawkat said, "Don't be amazed by that, for they've spent more time with him than you have."

At this point Khadija went to the kitchen to offer her assistance, since the flow of visitors was continuing unabated. Jamil al-Hamzawi came after closing the store. He was followed by Ghunaym Hamidu, who owned an oil press in al-Gamaliya, and Muhammad Ajami, who sold couscous in al-Salihiya. Then, pointing to the street from the window, Aisha cried out, "Shaykh Mutawalli Abd al-Samad! I wonder if he'll be able to climb to the top floor."

Leaning on his stick, the shaykh began to cross the courtyard, clearing his throat from time to time to warn anyone in his way that he was coming. Yasin responded, "He can climb to the top of a minaret." Then, seeing Khalil Shawkat try to figure up the shaykh's age with his fingers, Yasin continued: "Between eighty and ninety! But don't inquire about his health."

Kamal asked, "Did he never marry during this long life?"

Yasin answered, "It's said that he was a husband and a father but that his wife and children passed on to the mercy of God."

Aisha cried out again, not having budged from her post at the window, "Look! This foreigner! I wonder who he could be."

The man crossed the courtyard, casting a cautious, inquisitive glance around. He wore a round straw hat, and visible beneath the rim was a pockmarked, curved nose and a bushy mustache. Ibrahim said, "Perhaps he's a goldsmith from the Goldsmiths Bazaar."

Yasin muttered anxiously, "But he looks Greek. Where do you suppose I've seen that face before?"

A blind youth arrived wearing dark glasses. He was being dragged along by a man in traditional attire with a shawl wrapped around his head, sporting a long black overcoat beneath which could be seen the tail of a striped gown. Yasin recognized them immediately and was utterly astonished. The blind youth was Abduh, who played the zither-like qanun in Zubayda's troupe. The other man, called al-Humayuni, was the proprietor of a famous coffeehouse in Wajh al-Birka and a gangster, ruffian, pimp, and so on.

Khalil was heard to say, "The blind man's a qanun player for the vocalist Zubayda."

With feigned astonishment Yasin asked, "How does he know Papa?"

Ibrahim Shawkat smiled as he replied, "Your father's a music lover from way back. It's hardly strange that all the musicians know him."

Aisha kept her head turned toward the street to hide her smile. Yasin and Kamal observed Ibrahim's smile and understood what it implied. Finally Suwaydan, the Shawkat family's ancient maid, tottered into view. Pointing to her, Khalil murmured, "Our mother's emissary has come to ask after al-Sayyid Ahmad's health."

The widow of the late Mr. Shawkat had visited al-Sayyid Ahmad once but was unable to repeat that effort because of the pains of rheumatism that had recently been conspiring with old age to cripple her.

Khadija soon returned from the kitchen with a complaint that was actually a boast: "We need a man from the coffeehouse just to serve all the coffee."

Al-Sayyid Ahmad was sitting up in bed, leaning against a pillow that had been folded back, with the covers drawn up to his neck. His visitors sat on the sofa or the chairs arranged in a circle around the bed. He seemed cheerful, in spite of his weakness, for nothing could make him as happy as having his friends gather around him and compete in flattering him and assuring him of their affection. Although the ailment had harmed him, he could not deny the favor it had done him by allowing him to see his brothers' alarm at his suffering and their grief at his absence from their parties, which had seemed desolate during his seclusion. He appeared to want to elicit all the affection he could from them, for he began to recount the pains he had endured as well as the tedium. He allowed himself considerable license to exaggerate and embellish.

Sighing, he said, "During the first days of my illness I was convinced that I was finished. I started reciting our Muslim credo and the Qur'an sura about God's absoluteness [Sura 112], but when I wasn't occupied with those I thought of you a lot, and the idea of leaving you troubled me greatly."

More than one voice was raised to say, "The world wouldn't be the same without you, al-Sayyid Ahmad."

Ali Abd al-Rahim said emotionally, "This illness of yours has made an impression on me that will never be erased."

Muhammad Iffat ventured in a faint voice, "Do you remember that night? My Lord, our hair turned white then."

Ghunaym Hamidu leaned toward the bed a little to say, "You've been saved by the One who rescued us that night the English made us fill in the trench under the city gate at Bab al-Futuh."

"Those happy days ..." al-Sayyid Ahmad reflected. "Days of health and romance, when Fahmy was so outstanding and showed such promise...."

"Praise to God, Mr. Hamidu," he replied.

Shaykh Mutawalli Abd al-Samad said, "I want to know how much you paid the doctor, who wasn't entitled to anything. You don't need to reply, but I implore you to feed the friends of God who live near the mosque of al-Husayn."

Muhammad Iffat interrupted him to inquire, "What about you, Shaykh Mutawalli? Aren't you one of them? Explain this to me."

Terminating each phrase by a blow to the floor with his stick, the shaykh continued: "Feed the saints of al-Husayn with me at the head of them, whether or not Muhammad Iffat approves. He ought to feed them too in your honor, starting with me. And you ought to perform the pilgrimage to Mecca this year, since it is your religious duty. How grand it would be if you took me with you, so that God would multiply your reward...."

"What a fine man you are, Shaykh Mutawalli, and how dear to me," al-Sayyid Ahmad thought. "You're one of the landmarks of the age."

"Shaykh Mutawalli, I promise to take you with me to the Hijaz and Mecca, if the Compassionate God permits."

At that point, the foreigner, whose fine white hair was visible since he had removed his hat, said, "A little too much agitation. . . . Agitation's the cause of everything. Give it up and you'll be strong as a bomb."

"Manuli's sold you alcohol for thirty-five years—a purveyor of happiness and an agent for the cemetery," al-Sayyid Ahmad mused privately.

"It's the fault of your goods, Manuli."

The foreigner looked at the faces of his other customers and said, "No one's ever said that alcohol's bad for your health. That's nonsense. Is sickness caused by gaiety, laughter, and comfort?"

Training a nearly sightless eye on the foreigner, Shaykh Mutawalli Abd al-Samad cried out, "Now I've recognized you, source of calamities. When I heard your voice the first time I wondered where I'd heard this devil before."

The couscous vendor, Muhammad Ajami, asked Mr. Manuli with a wink in the direction of Shaykh Mutawalli, "Wasn't Shaykh Mutawalli one of your customers once, Manuli?"

The smiling foreigner replied, "His mouth's so full of food, where would he find room for wine, dear friend?"

Gripping the handle of his stick, Abd al-Samad shouted, "Manners, Manuli!"

Then Ajami shouted at him, "Do you deny, Shaykh Mutawalli, you were a big consumer of hashish before age made it hard for you to breathe?"

The shaykh waved his hand in protest, saying, "Hashish is not forbidden by Islam. Have you ever tried performing the dawn prayer under the influence? . . . God is most great. . . . *Allahu Akbar!*"

Noticing that al-Humayuni was silent, Ahmad Abd al-Jawad turned to him with a smile and to be polite said, "How are you, sir? By God, it's been a long time!"

In a voice like an ox's, al-Humayuni responded, "By God, a long time. Ages, by God. It's your fault, al-Sayyid Ahmad. You're the one who left us, but when Mr. Ali Abd al-Rahim told me, 'Your adversary's confined to bed,' I remembered the days of our youthful passions as though they had never ceased. I told myself, 'It would be disloyal not to visit the dear man myself—such a virile, sociable, jolly man.' If it were not for fear of creating problems for you, I would have brought Fatuma, Tamalli, Dawlat, and Nahawand. The girls are all eager to see you. My goodness, Mr. Ahmad. You're dear to us whether you honor us with a visit every evening or avoid us for years." Looking at the others with his sharp eyes, he continued: "You've all forsaken us. Blessings on Mr. Ali. May our Lord protect

Saniya al-Qulali, who keeps him coming to us. Anyone who loses track of his past goes astray. We provide the sincerest form of fellowship. What's drawn you away from us? If it were repentance, we'd forgive you. But it's not time for repentance yet. May God keep that far in the future by granting you a long life and many happy times."

Pointing to himself, Ahmad Abd al-Jawad remarked, "If you look at me, you can see I'm finished with all that."

The pimp replied enthusiastically, "Don't say that, master of men. A temporary indisposition that will depart, never to return. . . . I won't leave till you announce you'll return to Wajh al-Birka, even if only once, when God restores you to health."

Muhammad Iffat said, "Times have changed, Master Humayuni. Where's the Wajh al-Birka that we used to know? Look for it in history books. What remains is a playground for today's youngsters. How can we walk among them when our sons are there?"

Ibrahim al-Far said, "Don't forget that we can't trick our Lord when it comes to age or health. As Mr. Ahmad said, we're finished. We're all forced to visit a doctor, who says, 'You have this. You have that. Don't drink. Don't eat. Don't breathe.' And he has many other disgusting prescriptions for us. Haven't you heard of the pressure disease, Master Humayuni?"

Glancing at him, the pimp replied, "Treat a disease with drunkenness, laughter, and sport. If you find any trace of it after that, give it to me."

Manuli shouted, "By your life, that's what I told him."

Muhammad Ajami, as though completing his companion's thought, said, "And don't forget drugs, sir."

Shaykh Mutawalli Abd al-Samad shook his head in astonishment. He asked anxiously, "Tell me where I am, good people: in the home of Abd al-Jawad's son or in an opium den or a tavern? Listen and advise me."

Giving Shaykh Mutawalli a suspicious look, al-Humayuni asked, "Who's your friend?"

"A blessed saint."

The pimp said sarcastically, "If you're a saint, tell my fortune."

Mutawalli Abd al-Samad exclaimed, "Prison or the gallows!"

Al-Humayuni could not keep from laughing out loud. Then he remarked, "He truly is a saint, for this is the end I expect." Then he told the shaykh, "But watch your tongue, or your prophecy may fall upon you."

Bringing his head close to al-Sayyid Ahmad's face, Ali Abd al-

Rahim said, "Rise, my dear. The world's not worth the skin of an onion without you. What's happened to us, Ahmad? Don't you think we'll have to take ill health more seriously after this? Our fathers married new wives when they were over seventy. What's changed?"

With enough force that a drizzle of saliva flew from his mouth, Mutawalli Abd al-Samad exclaimed, "Your fathers were Believers. They were pure. They did not get drunk and fornicate. There's the answer for you."

Ahmad Abd al-Jawad told his friend, "The doctor told me that if I ignore my pressure, the result will be paralysis, and then only God can help me. That's what happened to our friend al-Wadini, may God honor him with a suitable end. I ask God, if it's my time, to grant me death. Confinement to bed for years without being able to move. . . . O God, have mercy on us."

At this point Ajami, Hamidu, and Manuli excused themselves and left, praying that al-Sayyid Ahmad would have a long and healthy life. Muhammad Iffat leaned over al-Sayyid Ahmad and whispered to him, "Jalila sends you her greetings. She would have liked to see you for herself."

The ears of Abduh, the qanun player, overheard that. He snapped his fingers and said, "And I'm the sultana's representative to you. She was ready to dress up in men's clothes to come visit you herself but felt apprehensive about the unforeseen consequences that might have. She sent me to tell you. . . ." After clearing his throat a couple of times he sang in a low voice:

> "Godspeed, my messenger to him.
> Kiss the sweet fellow on his lips
> And tell him, 'Your infatuated slave's
> At your service.'"

Al-Humayuni smiled and revealed his gold dentures. He commented, "An excellent remedy. Try this and pay no attention to the friend of God who predicts the gallows."

"Zubayda?" al-Sayyid Ahmad asked himself. "I don't desire anything. The world of illness is a despicable one. If the worst had happened, I would have died drunk. Doesn't this mean I've got to turn over a new leaf?"

Ibrahim al-Far told him in a low voice, "We all vowed we wouldn't taste alcohol while you're stuck in bed."

"I free you from that oath, and ask forgiveness for what you've already missed."

Smiling, Ali Abd al-Rahim said enticingly, "If only it were possible to celebrate your recovery here this evening."

Addressing his appeal to all the men present, Mutawalli Abd al-Samad said, "I call you to repentance and pilgrimage."

Al-Humayuni retorted angrily, "You're acting like a soldier in an opium den."

At a prearranged signal from al-Far, the heads of Muhammad Iffat, Ali Abd al-Rahim, and Ibrahim al-Far drew close to that of al-Sayyid Ahmad, and the three began to sing softly:

> *"Since you're not man enough for wine*
> *Why do you get drunk?"*

For this, they appropriated the tune of

> *Since you're not man enough for passion*
> *Why do you fall in love?*

Then Shaykh Abd al-Samad started reciting verses from the Qur'an sura called "Repentance" (Sura 9). Ahmad Abd al-Jawad laughed so hard that tears came to his eyes.

Time passed without anyone noticing, until Shaykh Mutawalli Abd al-Samad began to look alarmed. He said, "I want you to understand that I'm going to be the last to leave. I wish to speak privately with Abd al-Jawad's son."

43 ～

Ahmad Abd al-Jawad was able to leave the house after two more weeks. The first thing he did was to take Yasin and Kamal on a visit to the tomb and mosque of al-Husayn to perform their prayers and give thanks to God.

At the time, news of the death of the politician Ali Fahmy Kamil was in the papers. After pondering this event at length, on the way out of the house al-Sayyid Ahmad told his sons, "He dropped dead after addressing a great gathering. I'm walking on my own two legs after a stay in bed when I almost saw death face to face. Who can know the mysteries the future holds? Truly our lives are in God's hands."

He had to wait patiently for days and even weeks to regain his lost weight, but despite that fact, his dignified appearance and good looks seemed not to have been affected. He walked ahead, followed by Yasin and Kamal. This weekly parade had been abandoned after Fahmy's death. On the way from Palace Walk to the mosque, the two young men observed the prestige their father enjoyed throughout the district. Every merchant with a shop on the street greeted him with open arms and shook hands while applauding his recovery.

Yasin and Kamal responded to these warm demonstrations of mutual affection with joyful pride and smiles that lasted the whole way. All the same, Yasin asked himself innocently why he did not enjoy the same standing as his father, since they were equal both in their dignified and handsome exterior and in their shortcomings. Kamal, although momentarily touched, reexamined his perceptions of his father's remarkable prestige in a new light. In the past, to his small eyes his father's status had seemed the epitome of distinction and greatness. Now he saw it as nothing special, at least not in comparison with his own high ideals. It was merely the prestige enjoyed by a good-hearted, affable, and chivalrous man. True greatness was something totally unlike that, for its thunder shook sluggish hearts and drove sleep from dozing eyes. It was capable of arousing hatred not love, anger rather than satisfaction, and enmity instead of affection. Before it rebuilt, it forced disclosure and destruction. But was it not happiness for a man to be blessed with such love and respect? Yes ... and the proof was that at times the greatness of important figures was measured by the amount of love and tranquillity they sacrificed for lofty goals. In any case, his father was a happy man who was to be congratulated on that.

"See how handsome he is," Kamal told himself. "And how charming Yasin is too! What a strange sight I make between the two of them—like a distorted, trick photograph at a carnival. Claim to your heart's content that good looks are the domain of women not men, but that will never erase from your memory that alarming scene at the gazebo. My father's recovered from his high blood pressure. When will I recover from love? Love's an illness, even though it resembles cancer in having kept its secrets from medical science. In his last letter Husayn Shaddad says, 'Paris is the capital of beauty and love.' Is it also the capital of suffering? My dear friend is growing as stingy with his letters as if they were drops of his precious blood. I want a world where hearts are not deceived and do not deceive others."

At the corner of Khan Ja'far, they could see the great mosque. He heard his father say, "O Husayn!" in a heartfelt way, which combined the charm of a greeting with the fervor of a plea for help. Then al-Sayyid Ahmad quickened his steps. Looking into the mosque with an enigmatic smile, Kamal trailed after him and Yasin. Did he suspect for a moment that Kamal was only accompanying him on this blessed visit to please him or that his son no longer shared any of his religious beliefs? To Kamal, this mosque was now nothing more than one of the many symbols of the disappointment his heart had suffered. In the old days when he had stood beneath its minaret, his heart had pounded, tears had come to his eyes, and his breast had throbbed with ardor, belief, and hope. As he approached it today, all he saw was a vast collection of stone, steel, wood, and paint covering a great tract of land for no clear reason.

"Although forced by obedience to my father's authority, respect for the other people present, and fear of what they might do," Kamal reflected, "to play the role of a Believer until the visit to the shrine's concluded, I find my hypocritical conduct an affront to honor and truth. I want a world where men live free from fear and coercion."

They removed their shoes and entered one after the other. The father headed for the prayer niche and invited his sons to perform a prayer in front of it as a way of saluting the mosque. He raised his hands to his head to begin the prayer ritual, and they followed his example. As usual, the father lost himself in his prayers, and his eyelids drooped as he yielded his will to God's. Yasin too forgot everything except that he was in the presence of God the Merciful and Forgiving. Kamal began to move his lips without reciting anything. He bowed, straightened up, knelt, and prostrated himself as if performing insipid athletic exercises.

He told himself, "The most ancient remaining human structures, on the face of the earth or carved inside it, are temples. Even today, no area is free of them. When will man grow up and depend on himself? That loud voice coming from the far corner of the mosque reminds people of the end. When has there ever been an end to time? How beautiful it would be to see man wrestle with his illusions and vanquish them. But when will the struggle cease and the fighter announce that he's happy and that the world looks so different that it might have been created the day before? These two men are my father and brother. Why shouldn't all men be my fathers and brothers? How could this heart I carry within me let itself torment me in so many different ways? How frequently throughout the day I'm confronted by people I don't like. . . . Why should the friend I love have departed to the ends of the earth?"

When they finished praying, the father said, "Let's rest here a little before circling the tomb."

They sat there silently, their legs folded beneath them, until the father said gently, "We haven't been here together since that day."

Yasin replied emotionally, "Let's recite the 'Fatiha' for Fahmy's spirit."

They recited the opening prayer of the Qur'an, and then the father asked Yasin somewhat suspiciously, "I wonder whether wordly affairs have not kept you from visiting al-Husayn."

Yasin, who had not set foot in the mosque all those years except a handful of times, answered, "I don't let a week go by without visiting my master al-Husayn."

The father turned toward Kamal and cast him a glance as if to ask, "And you?"

Feeling embarrassed, Kamal replied, "Me too!"

The father said humbly, "He's our loved one and our intercessor with his grandfather Muhammad on a day when no mother or father can be of any assistance."

He had recovered from his illness this time, but only after it had taught him a lesson he would not forget. He had found its violence convincing and feared a recurrence. His intention to repent was sin-

cere. He had always believed he would repent, no matter how long
he waited. He was now certain that postponing it after this sickness
would be stupidity and a blasphemous rejection of God's blessings.
Whenever he happened to think of forbidden amusements, he consoled himself with the innocent pleasures awaiting him in life, like
friendship, music, and jests. Therefore he entreated God to preserve
him from the whispered temptations of Satan and to strengthen his
resolve to repent. He proceeded to recite some of the Qur'an's sim-
pler, shorter suras that he knew by heart.

When he rose, his sons did too. Then they went to the sepulcher,
where they were greeted by the sweet fragrance pervading the place
and a murmur of whispered recitations. They walked around the
tomb with the throngs of visitors. Kamal's eyes looked up at the great
green turban and then rested for a time on the wooden door, which
he had kissed so often. He compared the present with the past and
his former state of mind with his current one. He remembered how
revelation of this tomb's secret had been the first tragedy in his life
and then how the succession of tragedies following it had carried off
love, belief, and friendship. Despite all that, he was still standing on
his own two feet as he gazed worshipfully at truth, so heedless of the
jabs of pain that even his bitterness caused him to smile. He had no
regrets over his rejection of the blind happiness illuminating the faces
of the men circumambulating the tomb. How could he buy happiness
at the price of light when he had vowed to live with his eyes open?
He preferred to be anxious and alive rather than comfortable and
sleepy. He chose wakeful insomnia over restful sleep.

When they had finished walking around the sepulcher, the father
invited them to rest for a while in the shelter of the shrine. They
went to a corner and sat down next to each other. Some acquaintances noticed al-Sayyid Ahmad and approached to shake hands and
congratulate him on his recovery. Some stayed to sit with them. Most
of them knew Yasin either from his father's store or from al-Nahhasin
School, but hardly anyone knew Kamal. Some of them noticed how
thin the boy was and one jokingly asked al-Sayyid Ahmad, "What's
wrong with this son of yours? He's skinny as a ramrod."

As if returning the man's compliment with an even nicer one, al-
Sayyid Ahmad shot back, "No, you're the ram!"

Yasin smiled. Kamal did too, for this was the first chance he had
had to observe his father's secret personality of which he had heard
so much. His father was obviously a man who would not miss a
chance for a little joke even when he was beside the tomb of al-

Husayn in a sacred place devoted to praise of God and repentance. Yasin was inspired to reflect on his father's future, wondering whether al-Sayyid Ahmad would return to his previous joys even after this serious illness.

Yasin told himself, "Knowing this is extremely important to me."

44 ❧

Umm Hanafi was sitting cross-legged on a mat in the sitting room while Aisha's daughter Na'ima and Khadija's sons Abd al-Muni'm and Ahmad sat on the sofa opposite her. The two windows overlooking the courtyard of the house were open because of the hot, humid August weather, but scarcely a breeze stirred and the large lamp suspended from the ceiling cast a steady light throughout the room. The bedrooms opening off the sitting room seemed dark and silent. Umm Hanafi's head was bowed, and her arms were folded across her chest. She would look up at the children on the sofa for a moment and then lower her eyes again. She said nothing but her lips never stopped moving.

Abd al-Muni'm asked, "How long will Uncle Kamal stay on the roof?"

Umm Hanafi muttered, "It's hot down here. Why didn't you stay up there with him?"

"It's dark, and Na'ima's afraid of bugs."

Ahmad asked angrily, "How long are we going to remain here? This is the second week. I'm counting every day. I want to go back to Papa and Mama."

Umm Hanafi said hopefully, "God willing, you'll all return and be in the best possible shape. Pray to God, for He answers the requests of pure young children."

Abd al-Muni'm said, "We pray before we go to sleep and when we wake up, just the way you instructed us."

The woman said, "Pray to God all the time. Pray to Him now. He's the only one who can remove our distress."

Abd al-Muni'm spread out his hands in prayer and looked at Ahmad to invite him to join in. The vexed look still on his face, Ahmad complied. Then they repeated together, as they had grown accustomed to during the last few days, "O Lord, cure Uncle Khalil and our cousins Uthman and Muhammad so we can return home with minds at ease."

The impact this made on Na'ima was apparent in her face. Her features had a sad look and her blue eyes were filled with tears. She cried out, "Papa, Uthman, and Muhammad—how are they? I want to see Mama. I want to see all of them."

Abd al-Muni'm turned toward her to say in a consoling voice, "Don't cry, Na'ima. I've told you repeatedly not to cry. My uncle's fine. Uthman's fine. Muhammad's fine. We'll return home soon. Grandmother said so. Uncle Kamal said so too not very long ago."

Na'ima, who was sobbing, said, "I hear this every day. But they don't let us return. I want to see Papa, Uthman, and Muhammad. I want Mama."

Ahmad grumbled, "I want Papa and Mama too."

Abd al-Muni'm said, "We'll go back when they're well."

Na'ima cried out anxiously, "Let's go back now. I want to go home. Why are they keeping us away?"

Abd al-Muni'm replied, "They're afraid we'll catch the disease."

Na'ima answered stubbornly, "Mama's there. Aunt Khadija's there. Uncle Ibrahim's there. Grandmother's there. Why won't they catch it?"

"Because they're adults!"

"If adults can't catch diseases, why is Papa sick?"

Umm Hanafi sighed and said tenderly, "Is something upsetting you? This is your house too. And here are Masters Abd al-Muni'm and Ahmad to play with you. And your Uncle Kamal loves you more than all the world. You'll soon return to Mama, Papa, Uthman, and Muhammad. Don't cry, little lady. Pray for Papa and your brothers to get well."

Ahmad complained, "Two weeks! I've counted the days on my fingers. Besides, our apartment's on the third floor, and the disease is on the second. Why can't we return to our apartment and take Na'ima with us?"

Umm Hanafi put a finger to her lips as though to caution them and said, "Your uncle Kamal will get angry if he hears what you said. He buys you chocolates and melon seeds. How can you say you don't want to stay with him? You're not babies anymore. Master Abd al-Muni'm, you'll be starting primary school in a month. And you will too, dear Na'ima."

Backing down a little, Ahmad said, "At least let us go outside to play in the street."

Abd al-Muni'm seconded that suggestion: "That makes sense, Umm Hanafi. Why don't we go out and play in the street?"

Umm Hanafi replied firmly, "You have the courtyard, which is as big as the universe. And you also have the roof terrace. What more do you want than that? When Mr. Kamal was young, he only played in the house. When I finish my work, I'll tell you stories. Wouldn't you like that?"

Ahmad protested, "Yesterday you told us you'd finished all your stories."

Drying her eyes, Na'ima said, "Aunt Khadija knows more stories. If Mama was here we could sing together."

Umm Hanafi said ingratiatingly, "I keep begging you to sing for us and you refuse."

"I can't sing here. I can't sing when Uthman and Muhammad are sick."

Sighing, the woman said, "I'll fix supper for you, and then we'll go to bed. How about some cheese, watermelon, and cantaloupe?"

Kamal was sitting in a chair on the open side of the roof, next to the arbor of jasmine and hyacinth beans. He was scarcely visible in the darkness except for his loose-fitting white house shirt. His legs stretched out languidly, he looked at the sky studded with stars. He was lost in thought, and the silence encompassing him was broken only by an occasional voice from the street or a cluck from the chicken house. The family's affliction during the last two weeks had left its imprint on his face. During this time the normal household routine had been disrupted, and his mother had disappeared except for rare moments. The atmosphere of the house was transformed by the complaints of the three young prisoners who had roamed its expanses asking for Papa and Mama until Kamal had run out of stratagems for cajoling and amusing them.

Over on Sugar Street, Aisha no longer sang or laughed in the way that had once caused so much talk. She stayed up nights with her beloved family of invalids—her husband and her sons. Kamal had yearned for Aisha to return to her old home when he was young. Now he was extremely apprehensive that she would be forced to return, her wing broken and her heart shattered.

His mother had whispered to him, "Don't visit Sugar Street, and if you do, don't stay long." He did go there occasionally and would leave with his hands smelling strangely of disinfectants and his heart overwhelmed by anxiety.

The most amazing thing was that typhoid germs, like other ones, were incredibly tiny and invisible to the naked eye but capable of stopping the flow of a life, deciding the destiny of men, and breaking up a family. Poor Muhammad had been the first to fall ill. Uthman had been next. Finally and unexpectedly, the father had succumbed.

The maid Suwaydan had come to tell Kamal that his mother would spend the night at Sugar Street. Quoting his mother without comment, she had added that there was no cause for concern. If that was so, why was his mother staying over? Why did his breast feel such forebodings? Despite all this, it was always possible that the gloom might disperse in the twinkling of an eye. Khalil Shawkat and his two darling sons might recover. Aisha's face might sparkle and shine. Could he forget how the household had suffered through a similar ordeal only eight months before? And now his father was up and about, his health totally restored. His muscles had regained their strength and his eyes their attractive sparkle. He had returned to his friends and loved ones like a bird to the leafy tree. So who could deny that it was possible for everything to change in the twinkling of an eye?

"You're here alone!"

Kamal recognized the voice. Turning toward the door of the roof, he rose and stretched out his hand to the newcomer, saying, "How are you, brother? Have a seat."

Kamal got a chair for Yasin, who was breathing heavily after climbing up the stairs. Filling his chest with the scent of jasmine, he sat down and said, "The children have gone to sleep and Umm Hanafi has too."

Resuming his seat, Kamal asked, "What time is it? The poor kids won't rest and won't let anyone else rest either."

"It's eleven. The air here's a lot better than on the street."

"Where have you been?"

"Back and forth between Palace of Desire and Sugar Street. By the way, your mother's not coming home tonight."

"Suwaydan told me that. What's new? I've been extremely apprehensive."

Sighing, Yasin said, "We're all anxious. Our Lord is gracious. Our father's there too."

"At this hour!"

"I left him there." After a pause he continued: "I was at Sugar Street until eight this evening. Then a messenger came from Palace of Desire Alley to say that my wife's labor had begun. I went immediately to Umm Ali, the midwife, and took her to my house, where I found my wife was being cared for by some neighbors. I stayed there an hour but could not bear the moaning and screaming for long. I went back to Sugar Street again and found Father sitting with Ibrahim Shawkat."

"What does this mean? Tell me what you think."

In a low voice Yasin said, "Their condition's extremely grave."

"Grave?"

"Yes. I came here to try to calm my nerves. Couldn't Zanuba have picked some other night to have a baby? I'm exhausted from going back and forth between Palace of Desire and Sugar Street, between the doctor and the midwife. Their condition's critical. When Widow Shawkat looked at her son's face she cried out, 'Protect us, Lord. You should have taken me first.' Your mother was very alarmed, but the old lady paid no attention to her and said in a hoarse voice, 'This is what members of the Shawkat family look like when they die. I saw his father and his uncle die, and his grandfather before them.' There's nothing left of Khalil but a shadow, and the children are the same way. There's no power or might save with God."

Kamal swallowed and said, "Perhaps these suspicions are unfounded."

"Perhaps. . . . Kamal, you're not a child anymore. You ought to know at least what I do. The doctor said the situation's critical."

"For all of them?"

"All! Khalil, Uthman, and Muhammad. O Lord! How wretched your luck is, Aisha. . . ."

In the darkness he imagined Aisha's laughing family as he had seen them in the past. They were joyful, happy individuals who pursued life as though it were an innocent entertainment.

"When will Aisha be able to laugh again?" Kamal wondered. "Fahmy was snatched away. The English or typhoid, it's all the same . . . like any other cause. Belief in God makes death seem a bewildering but wise decree, when actually it's nothing but a cruel joke."

"That's the most atrocious thing I've ever heard."

"That it is, but what can anyone do? What has Aisha done to deserve this? O God, forgiveness and mercy. . . ."

"Is there any sublime philosophy that can justify mass slaughter?" Kamal asked himself. "Death follows the rules for jokes precisely. Yet how can we laugh when we're the butt of the joke. Perhaps I'd be able to meet it with a smile if I could always confront it with contemplation, understanding, and impartiality. That would be a victory over both life and death. But what would any of this mean to Aisha?"

"My head's spinning, brother."

In the sagest voice Kamal had ever heard him use, Yasin remarked,

"This is the way the world is. You must come to know it as it really is." Then he rose suddenly and said, "I've got to go now."

Kamal implored him, "Stay with me a little longer."

But Yasin answered apologetically, "It's eleven. I must go to Palace of Desire Alley to reassure myself about Zanuba. Then I'll return to Sugar Street to be with them. I won't sleep an hour tonight, it seems. And by God I know what's awaiting us tomorrow."

Kamal stood up and said with alarm, "You talk as though it was all over. I'm going to Sugar Street right away."

"No, you must stay with the children until morning. Try to get some sleep. Otherwise I'll regret speaking so frankly to you."

Yasin left the roof of the house and Kamal accompanied him downstairs to the door. When they passed the top floor, where the children were sleeping, Kamal said sorrowfully, "What poor kids! Na'ima's wept bitterly during the past few days, as though her heart sensed what would happen...."

Yasin replied frankly, "The children will soon forget. Pray for the grown-ups."

As they went into the courtyard, they could hear a voice from the street crying out, "Special edition of *al-Muqattam!*"

Kamal murmured inquisitively, "A special edition for the paper?"

In a sad voice, Yasin said, "Oh! I know what it's about. When I was on my way here, I heard people spreading the news. Sa'd Zaghlul has died."

Kamal cried out from the depths of his heart, "Sa'd?"

Yasin stopped walking and turned toward his brother to say, "Don't take it so hard. We have enough problems of our own."

Kamal stared into the darkness without speaking or moving. He seemed oblivious to Khalil, Uthman, Muhammad, and Aisha, to everything except the death of Sa'd Zaghlul.

Yasin walked on and remarked, "He died after receiving his full share of life and greatness. What more would you wish for him than that? May God be merciful to him."

Still stunned, Kamal followed him silently. He did not know how he would have received this news in circumstances that were not so grim. When disasters come at the same time, they compete with each other. Thus Kamal's grandmother had died soon after Fahmy had been slain, at a time when no one had tears to spare for her. So Sa'd was dead. The hero of the exile, the revolution, the liberation, and the constitution had died. Why should he not mourn for Sa'd Zaghlul, when the best qualities of his personality came from Sa'd's guidance and leadership?

Yasin stopped once more to open the door. Then he held out his hand to Kamal. After shaking hands with him, Kamal remembered something that had slipped his mind for too long. Embarrassed that he had forgotten, he told Yasin, "I pray to God that you'll find your wife has given birth safely."

Starting to leave, Yasin replied, "God willing. And I hope you sleep soundly."

Acknowledgments

I want to thank Mary Ann Carroll
for being the first reader,
Jacqueline Kennedy Onassis
for her sensitive editing,
Riyad N. Delshad for assistance
with some obscure vocabulary and expressions,
and Sarah and Franya Hutchins
for their patience.
Although others have contributed
to this translation, I am happy
to bear responsibility for it.

—William Maynard Hutchins

About the Author

NAGUIB MAHFOUZ was born in Cairo in 1911 and began writing when he was seventeen. A student of philosophy and an avid reader, he has been influenced by many Western writers, including Flaubert, Balzac, Zola, Camus, Tolstoy, Dostoevsky, and above all, Proust. He has more than thirty novels to his credit, ranging from his earliest historical romances to his most recent experimental novels. In 1988, Mr. Mahfouz was awarded the Nobel Prize for Literature. He lives in the Cairo suburb of Agouza with his wife and two daughters.

About the Translators

WILLIAM MAYNARD HUTCHINS is an associate professor in the Philosophy and Religion Department of Appalachian State University in North Carolina. He is the editor and principal translator of *Egyptian Tales and Short Stories of the 1970s and 1980s* and other works.

LORNE AND OLIVE KENNY live in Toronto. Together they have published a number of translations from the Arabic. Olive Kenny is the translator of *Wedding Song* by Naguib Mahfouz.

Modern Arabic Writing
from the American University in Cairo Press

Ibrahim Abdel Meguid *The Other Place* • *No One Sleeps in Alexandria*
Yahya Taher Abdullah *The Mountain of Green Tea*
Leila Abouzeid *The Last Chapter*
Salwa Bakr *The Wiles of Men*
Hoda Barakat *The Tiller of Waters*
Mourid Barghouti *I Saw Ramallah*
Mohamed El-Bisatie *Houses Behind the Trees* • *A Last Glass of Tea*
Fathy Ghanem *The Man Who Lost His Shadow*
Tawfiq al-Hakim *The Prison of Life*
Taha Hussein *A Man of Letters* • *The Sufferers* • *The Days*
Sonallah Ibrahim *Cairo: From Edge to Edge* • *Zaat* • *The Committee*
Yusuf Idris *City of Love and Ashes*
Denys Johnson-Davies *Under the Naked Sky: Short Stories from the Arab World*
Said al-Kafrawi *The Hill of Gypsies*
Edwar al-Kharrat *Rama and the Dragon*
Naguib Mahfouz *Adrift on the Nile*
Akhenaten, Dweller in Truth • *Arabian Nights and Days*
Autumn Quail • *The Beggar*
The Beginning and the End • *The Cairo Trilogy:*
Palace Walk • *Palace of Desire* • *Sugar Street*
Children of the Alley • *The Day the Leader Was Killed*
Echoes of an Autobiography • *The Harafish*
The Journey of Ibn Fattouma • *Midaq Alley* • *Miramar*
Naguib Mahfouz at Sidi Gaber • *Respected Sir* • *The Search*
The Thief and the Dogs • *The Time and the Place*
Wedding Song • *Voices from the Other World*
Ahlam Mosteghanemi *Memory in the Flesh*
Buthaina Al Nasiri *Final Night*
Abd al-Hakim Qasim *Rites of Assent*
Somaya Ramadan *Leaves of Narcissus*
Lenin El-Ramly *In Plain Arabic*
Rafik Schami *Damascus Nights*
Miral al-Tahawy *The Tent* • *Blue Aubergine*
Bahaa Taher *Love in Exile*
Fuad al-Takarli *The Long Way Back*
Latifa al-Zayyat *The Open Door*